S0-AHP-096

# LOVE IS JUST A WORD

*Books by Johannes Mario Simmel*

LOVE IS JUST A WORD

IT CAN'T ALWAYS BE CAVIAR

*Translated from the German by Rosemarie Mays*

# LOVE IS JUST A WORD

*by*

Johannes Mario Simmel

*McGraw-Hill Book Company New York Toronto*

Excerpt from the song "Love Is Just a Word" © 1961 United Artists Music Co., Inc., New York, N.Y. Used by permission.

LOVE IS JUST A WORD



Library of Congress Catalog Card Number: 69-12265

FIRST EDITION 57384

# Prologue

The first word wiped out by the snow was *never*. The second word that vanished was *always*.

These words were written on a sheet of paper that had slipped under a splinter jutting from the floor of the tower room. Therefore the paper was able to fight the draft that knifed its way through the narrow windows slitting the masonry. Crystals of snow powdered the bloodstained floor. The boards of the floor were old. The blood that colored them was young, moist, and still warm. The boards were as antique as the black beams or the roughly hewn and shapeless bricks, or the crumbling spiral staircase that was also bespattered with blood. Yet older than all of them was the tower itself, which was centuries, yes, many centuries old. This tower had been standing there to greet the arrival of Christianity many, many centuries ago.

The words *forgotten* and, elsewhere on the sheet of paper, *with all my heart* were now swamped by the snow, the snow that also obliterated the name at the end of the letter. The nervous strokes of the handwriting suggested that the signature belonged to a woman, and that she had rushed it onto the paper in panic, as if in a fierce fever. It must have been scrawled in great haste, in deep fear, in wild desperation. But now it lay entombed by the snow that drifted upon it so hushed and so gentle.

The tower had been a ruin sixteen hundred years ago. Since then it had been renovated eleven times by Hessian bandit knights, Hessian counts, and finally by His Most Gracious Highness Wilhelm IX. In 1804 it had been reconstructed in accordance with the express wishes of this noble lord and in line with the traditions of its structure. The tower was to stand as an observation post and as a memorial to the past. Since then, however, the walls had again deteriorated to a state of near-ruin. A plaque stood at the foot of the crumbling tower. It carried a warning to travelers:

DANGER OF COLLAPSE. ENTRY FORBIDDEN.

If you were willing to ignore this order, however, you would enjoy a magnificent view of the whole countryside through the slender windows of the tower rooms. You would see many things: the river Nidda as it meandered down the valley, its banks overgrown with weeds, twining its way along ripe meadows and pastures; sprawling countryside rich in shrubs and alders; the Great Feldberg, its wide ridges darkened with forest; the Winterstein with its triple humps; the blue ranges of the Vogelsberg and the massif of the Hohenrodskopf, whose mighty three-cornered flanks, green with meadow, stand in the sunlight contrasted majestically to the vast night-black ocean of trees. Close by you would see small villages, castles, farmsteads, dark and light-brown speckled cows, as well as trains that trickled away into the far-off haze, trailing with them their melancholy whistle. When the weather was fine, you would catch a glimpse of such places as Bad Vilbel, Königstein, Dornholzenhausen, Oberursel—all these and hundreds of other communities, the largest of which was Frankfurt-am-Main.

It was night. Although it had been a bright day, darkness now blindfolded the land. It was impossible to see more than a few yards ahead, since a colossal snowfall had been descending for three hours from the glowering clouds.

On this particular night it was snowing so densely that the very air seemed molded by the snow. It was almost as if there was no air left at all, only a stifling weightlessness, a tangible and oppressive pall tumbling from an infinity of skies, an endless surge of millions and millions of flakes illuminating the gloom and making the darkness pale. Streets and paths were already blocked, and the brittle branches of the trees moaned and crackled under the white weight. Yet it had been snowing for only three hours. If it kept on like this for two more days, the old folks in the district could safely say that this was the worst snowstorm in living memory. A traveler standing at one of the narrow tower windows wouldn't have been able to see more than a few yards because of the terrible drifts. Yet for all that, in good weather these same windows afforded a superb view over the highest treetops of the Taunus, far, far off into the distant countryside.

It was an ideal location for a tower of this kind. This certainly was the opinion of the Roman commander-in-chief in 10 B.C., when he had a line of fortifications erected as a defense against the Germans. Barely a hundred years later, another Roman emperor and commander-in-chief must have thought the same when he ordered his legions to start building the Limes for the protection of the province. These particular fortifications coiled their way across mountain and gorge, past prehistoric cairns and fens, through woods and fields, and made up a five-hundred-fifty-mile-long fortified border intended to guard the provinces of Obergermanien and Ratian. The emperors Trajan, Hadrian, and Antoninus Pius had continued the immense project of constructing military installations between the Rhine and the Danube. They started off with ramparts and palisaded ditches, and proceeded to build more than a thousand watchtowers and over a hundred forts. The remains of this vast structure could still be seen—these huge works that had been erected by powerless men against powerless men, by order of tyrants and butchers of men.

A pair of brown fur-lined shoes swayed to and fro above the

sheet of paper. They dangled quite loosely in the air. Gently, ever so gently, they drifted back and forth, back and forth. Sometimes they touched each other. Sometimes they didn't.

. . . *il nostro concerto* . . . Snow inches high smothered these words. These also: *Porto Azzuro*. Snowflakes drifted down upon the moist bloodstains on the floorboards, turning them rose-red, rosy, bright red. Making them white. Beneath the snow, more and more bloodstains vanished; more and more words disappeared. Snow blotted out the blood, melted the ink, obliterated the message. The snowflakes moved slowly, slowly. And so did the shoes, the stout winter shoes hanging there.

The shoes drifted over the letter like the needles of a compass. Their tips swung from north to north-northeast. Then east. The motion of the shoes slackened with the wind. They swung back. North-northeast. North.

*I swear to you* . . .

The words blurred and were gone. The oath was silenced.

The shoes of the hanged man hovered over these words: *in the sight of my eyes*. Two minutes later the words were no more.

North. North-northeast. East.

Snowflakes also settled firmly on the shoes and on the clothes. The dead man was hanging from a black beam, an old piece of rope around his neck. There was a lot of dilapidated furniture in the tower room: things like broken chairs, rotting wood, some old rusting tools. There was light overhead, but it was the light that goes with fog-dark, dark light. And silence almost. Almost. (Not that the snow made sound. It fell in silence, with the noiseless strength of all beings that wield great power yet know they can use it at will, as they please.) No. You would have heard no sound, had it not been for the tiny mice. Hungry and freezing, they rustled restlessly under the pages of an old newspaper, where they had sought refuge from the bitterness of that night.

The newspaper wasn't near the dead man. It lay in a corner

of the room, and was therefore sheltered from the snow. It was open, and its title read:

HERALD FOR THE EMPIRE OF JUSTICE
NEWSPAPER OF BROTHERLY LOVE FOR EVERYONE
AIMED AT THE MORAL AND SOCIAL BETTERMENT OF MANKIND
PUBLISHER:
THE ANGEL OF THE LORD, FRANKFURT-AM-MAIN

The mice rustled.

Frozen to death, crushed together and black, spiders hung locked in their shattered webs.

*. . . the fishing boat with its sails of red blood,*
*blood-red in the sunset . . .*

Stifled.

*that wine we sipped in the harbor of Marciana Marina*

Smothered.

*. . . our bay, those green waves in which*
*we lay embraced . . .*

Silenced. Gone.

The boyish face of the hanged man was smeared with blood and bruised with wounds. The blood was frozen to a crust in the icy cold. Snowflakes tumbled gently upon the wounds, onto the cropped brown hair, into his open, brown eyes. Open, brown eyes with pupils huge and bulging. Yet the flakes melted as they landed there, as they touched the skin and hair and eyeballs. For the dead man was still warm. He had not been dead long.

Those staring, unseeing eyes gazed upon the endless, aimless odyssey of the shoes. For the whole body was making that voyage.

East. East-northeast. North.

And back again.

North. North-northeast. East.

The hanged man had slender hands. They were bloody. Their knuckles had burst open. He was wearing a thick turtleneck sweater and gray sports trousers. They too were bloodstained and were ripped in several places. The snow that had settled on the sweater, the shoes, and the trousers had not melted, however, for the clothing was cold. As cold as the hanged man's body would be very soon. Cold enough to hold and keep the falling flakes.

. . . *our first meeting* . . .

East. North-northeast. North.

. . . *our first kiss* . . .

North. North-northeast. East.

And then they melted, they vanished, all these tender words, under the tender pressure of the snow that banished them all, all. . . .

The dead man, who was about twenty years old, had the body of a youth, tall, slim, and well-built. It was really hard to tell if he had looked good when he was alive, about a couple of hours before. For now he looked hideous. His tongue, blue, swollen and gruesome, bulged from a twisted mouth that had been perhaps sensitive and even sensuous not so long ago. And the crystals of snow that now fell upon it melted, since his tongue was still warm.

The man who was hanging here now had probably known the history of the Limes. He had probably known that this observation tower had been built once by Roman soldiers whose chiefs, dizzy with victory and drunk with power, had driven people from the happy south and warmth of their homes into this dark, icy north. Before the Christmas holidays the dead man's class had started rereading Tacitus, who knew how to document the early history of towers and castles. (Tacitus, Cornelius, the greatest of all Roman historians, born about A.D. 55, died about the year 116. Was praetor, then consul, later governor of the province of Asia. Wrote the *Germania*—the first ethnology of Germany—the *Historiae* and the *Annals.* Tacitus was linked to Sallust in style, composition, and fundamentally pessimistic attitude, and attempted to explain the deeds of the conquerors from a psychological point of view.)

The dead man had known all this. Yes, the man who was hanging there in the deepening dusk, a rope around his neck, slowly growing more cold and stiff, had translated the following words of Cornelius Tacitus only a few weeks before his death. The translation had been done as part of his preparation for his final examination: "Thus Germanicus surrendered four legions to the Caecina, an auxiliary force consisting of five thousand men, and thereupon gathered together hordes of Germans living on this side of the Rhine. He himself took with him the same number of legions and twice the number of allies. Upon the ruins of the fortifications constructed by his father Drusus, he built new installations, ramparts, lake-dwellings, watchtowers, and a fort. . . ."

The corpse kept swaying.

*. . . you my soul, you my breath . . .*

There was no word that the flakes did not obliterate. The tiny, freezing mice rustled beneath the old newspaper. From outside somewhere came a sharp roar, as if a bomb had exploded. Another bough had cracked again under the white deluge. And the snow continued to fall, growing more violent from minute to minute, mute and ceaseless. The snow had come upon the land like a heavy sickness, a paralysis, a burden as heavy as the plague, a disease that could not be escaped or resisted. This snow was something you had to submit to, as to death itself.

*Oliver, my beloved Oliver . . .*

The letter had begun with this line, which now disappeared with the rest. Over it the shoes drifted and swayed. The mice squeaked lamentations. Time ticked away on a watch around the dead man's bloodstained wrist. It was 9:34 P.M. The body swung back again. Now the snow reached the last words that remained uncovered. The flakes were in no hurry to destroy them, but rather crept upon them gently, cautiously, tenderly. Yet the snow finally shattered them. The last words perished. They said *love of my life.*

At precisely this moment—9:35 P.M. on January 7, 1962

—a gruff, chilled voice echoed from various loudspeakers throughout the drafty, ice-cold departure halls in Frankfurt's main railway station: "Attention, please, on track fourteen! Announcing the departure of the Paris express to Vienna via Karlsruhe, Stuttgart, Munich, Salzburg, and Linz. Please step back from the train and close the doors. We wish you a happy journey."

The last doors of the D train were slammed shut. Slowly the diesel locomotive started to crawl forward. Wheels began to roll, quicker and quicker; axles pounded. The long train slipped into the dismal blizzard, which swallowed it up a few seconds later.

The Paris express had three sleeping cars, the third of which was the last on the train. In a single first-class compartment of this car stood a big, heavy man, fifty-eight years old. Staring at the second hand of an old-fashioned golden repeater watch that lay on the mahogany top of a closed corner washstand, he counted his pulsebeats. Eighty-six to the minute.

The thick-set man twisted his small, round mouth into a wry smile, the woeful grin of a dying man who knows only too well that he won't live to see the next day, yet who intends to pass away alone and with dignity. He gave a deep groan, and anxiously inspected the state of his tongue in the mirror that stood over the washstand. The man examined his tongue as if some black, diseased fungus was growing on it. (It happened to be pink and perfectly healthy.) Moaning once more, he removed from an old-fashioned suitcase that lay on the bed a silver box in which there were bottles of medicine, phials of pills, little cartons of all descriptions, as well as a clinical thermometer. The box bore the initials *A.L.*

The stout man had a healthy, rosy complexion, blond hair that grew far too long and was turning gray, and a big bushy mustache that was still completely blond. He grew this mustache after the style of Albert Schweitzer, whom he revered. Carefully, very carefully, he made his choice from the box. Albert (Albert!) Lazarus gulped down two pills, two red, longish capsules, and washed them down with water he had poured into a plastic flask out of a soda-water bottle. He always carried bottles of soda water with him. He mistrusted all water whose origins he couldn't check, all strange glasses and toilets. (To his anguish, he couldn't do anything about the toilets.)

Sighing continually and wearily, he removed his old-fashioned suit with meticulous care. He had had it made so that it would fit loosely around his large body and still leave room for pleats, in much the same way as the man from Lambaréné preferred to wear *his* clothes. As a matter of fact, Albert Lazarus had such reverence for the philanthropist in distant Africa that he not only aped Schweitzer in his way of speaking and dressing, but also went as far as to indulge in the same kinds of scholarly and resolute—and consequently irrational—activities.

"Your name?" He had been asked this officially on many occasions.

"*Albert* Lazarus." He had always given this emphatic answer.

His real name was actually *Paul* Robert Wilhelm Albert Lazarus. This fact had been registered in the birth-registry office in Leipzig, but fortunately for him the truth lay far away and for some time now inaccessible. He had hidden this fact carefully from people, and throughout his life had chosen Albert as his first name. Albert Lazarus also played the organ, a little one that fitted into his apartment. And, of course, he revered Bach. . . .

Very carefully he placed his suit on a coathanger and continued to undress. He wore a self-tying cravat, the knot of which was already shiny and pinned with a real pearl. His shirt had a stiff collar and stiff cuffs with the embroidered initials *A.L.* He wore long woolen underpants. He put all these items of clothing into safekeeping with infinite care—all of them except his hand-knitted knee-length stockings. The skin on his plump body was as pink and smooth as that of his face. Pink and smooth like a baby's.

Now he put on a white nightgown that could be closed round the neck with two rose-red cords. The nightgown reached all the way down to his feet, had a delicately embroidered rose-red hem, and at the breast appeared once more the initials *A.L.* From the suitcase the man removed a candy box and a large black folder. With a groan he hoisted up the piece of luggage —which was certainly not heavy—onto the aluminum shelf above the window. He left a toilet case inside. Albert Lazarus had most emphatically no intention of using the washbasin in the compartment. Who knows who might have used it before him? Who could possibly count the germs that were undoubtedly swarming in the porcelain bowl and around the toothbrush glass? The stout man felt positively nauseated at the very thought of it. He never, never washed himself in sleeping cars.

Now he checked carefully to see if there was any draft coming through the chinks in the windows, adjusted for safety's sake the black plastic curtain drawn over the window pane, and turned the knob of the central heating system from ½ to *Full,* even though there was dry heat in the compartment. Opening the candy box, he peeped inside. Suddenly his eyes sparkled, and he popped a brandy cherry into his mouth. He then hung the golden repeater watch on the brass hook, green with age, that protruded from a round velvet patch on the mahogany wall beside his pillow. In the last forty years many a watch had undoubtedly hung there. The sleeping car harmonized beautifully with the man who was using it: it was an antique, as he was. The former was to be dumped on the scrapheap in two years' time. So was the latter. For Albert Lazarus was being retired two years from now.

Albert Lazarus had been a reader with a large Frankfurt publishing house for thirty-one years, and for the past twelve years he had held the position of editor. He had never married. He had no children. In fact he didn't like children. He had no ambition, he was good-natured, he was shy, and he was firmly convinced that he was mortally ill. The truth of the matter is that he was perfectly healthy, apart from a trifling liver complaint acquired from consuming huge and unreasonable quantities of varied medicines unprescribed and even forbidden by the doctor. His eating habits were even more unreasonable. Albert Lazarus was in fact a man with no real needs. Money intrigued him as little as did women or his career. He was consumed with one vice, and one vice alone: sweets! In the mornings he ate pudding for breakfast, in the evenings he drank hot chocolate. When he was at work in the publishing house, he religiously visited a local pastry shop every single lunchtime, where, year after year, day after day, he gobbled three different kinds of cake—colossal, creamy, poisonously colored slabs of it. And he never forgot the whipped cream.

His boss knew all Albert's weaknesses. He knew, for example, that his editor was the grossest hypochondriac in the city of Frankfurt as well as an incorruptible critic of submitted manuscripts. For the last three decades Albert Lazarus had discovered and fostered new talent, and had rendered greater service to the publishing house than any of the other employees.

The admirer of the renowned humanitarian and physician placed the candy box on the red carpet next to the bed, switched off the ceiling light, turned on the reading lamp above his bed, loosened up the tightly drawn blankets, and crawled under them with a groan. He reached for the folder lying at his feet. Before opening it, he selected another piece of chocolate, ingrained with gruesomely green nuts, from the candy box and placed it in his mouth, muttering: "Poison. This is absolute poison for me." He gulped it back, pressed his hand against his heart, but couldn't feel even a twinge of pain. This seemed to irritate him, for he pulled an angry face. And angrily he opened the folder which contained a thick manuscript. On the page beneath the cover of the folder these words were written:

*Whoever reads this book:*
*My name is Oliver Mansfeld. I am 21 years old and son of Walter Mansfeld.*

The stout man dropped the manuscript.

Oliver Mansfeld?

A piece of nougat. (I won't live to see next Christmas anyway. We're all in God's hands.)

Son of Walter Mansfeld . . .

Albert Lazarus didn't know anything about Oliver Mansfeld. So far the young man hadn't stood out in the literary field, or in any other field for that matter. His father Walter, however, was known to almost every adult in the Federal Republic as being the creator of one of the biggest scandals of the postwar period.

A piece of candy.

Lazarus sucked away completely absorbed. The train was now speeding along, its axles pounding furiously. Hmm. So this scoundrel's son has written a novel, has he? Well, well. Lazarus checked the cover leaf of the folder. It showed that the manuscript had arrived at the publishing house on the twentieth of December 1961, and had naturally remained unnoticed over Christmas and New Year—doubtless due to the sloppiness of that Meyer woman. I'll have a word with her when I get back. It wasn't until yesterday morning that the Meyer female—with whom Albert would have a word when he got back—had slipped the manuscript into his hands, saying: "Maybe you could have a look at this during your trip, Mr. Lazarus."

The Frankfurt publishing house had branches in Vienna, Berlin, and Zurich. Lazarus was to attend a business conference in Vienna on Monday the eighth of January 1962. The journey to his destination would take about twelve hours. That's why he had taken the manuscript along. He liked to read at night.

Let's see, now (another brandy cherry, perhaps?) . . . let's see what this young fellow has to say.

*I would like to become a writer. This manuscript represents my first attempt. No one knows better than I do the faults contained in this book, which has no closing chapter for reasons that won't need explaining to the reader. The submitted manuscript is a novel in which living persons appear under assumed names—but in which the names have not yet been changed.*

Lazarus began to ponder.

This young fellow is either very naïve or extremely cunning. Sensation-seeking, perhaps? Revenge on Papa? Stimulate the reader's interest? Lazarus was well acquainted with most of the tricks that authors could get up. Yet, for all that, here we've got something a bit different, for a change.

*It is my opinion that in his first book, every author draws on exclusively personal experiences which have made a deep impression on him.*

Poison. Pure poison for me. Lazarus stuck a piece of chocolate in his mouth. The chocolate was armed dangerously with splinters of nut.

*My book is also written in this way—or perhaps I should rather call it my diary, for in its present form it seems to be just that. Neither the names of the participants, nor the scenes of the action, nor the action itself have been altered. What stands on the following pages is the truth . . .*

Fair enough. Now a tiny morsel of nut slipped into his hollow tooth. Which had to be expected.

*. . . the truth as I experienced it.*

What do you know already about the truth, little boy?

*One doesn't submit a diary very readily, especially if it contains such highly personal and intimate details as this one does. One is even more reluctant to see it circulated in print. Yet this is what I want, and I submit my manuscript with the express approval of that woman for whom it was written. This woman and I love each other. My novel is the story of this love . . .*

Thank God I've managed to remove the splinter with my tongue. Why should I bother to drag myself along to the dentist, when I won't even live to see next spring? But no more nuts. A little bit of marzipan, perhaps.

*. . . and we are totally indifferent as to what other people think. If we had a say in the matter, neither her name nor mine would have to be altered. One hour from now we are taking this manuscript to the post office and mailing it to your publishing house, for we have made a resolution which now allows me to*

*tell the truth to the whole world, without any fear and with no shame at all.*

With his free left hand, Lazarus caressed the wide, drooping left half of his mustache, dropping a small piece of chocolate on the bedspread as he did so. He grunted. Without any fear and with no shame at all. What did I tell you. Now at last we know what it is. Pornography.

This young fellow has looked all around him, and has come to the conclusion that this is the century of pornography. By that we mean refined pornography, of course, the kind that's produced by the more exclusive publishing houses. By one such as ours, for example. Except that we haven't published any pornography as yet.

The fact that we haven't yet published pornography is due to me, not my publisher. To date I've found nothing suitable. My publisher: a go-ahead type of man: "Smut. That's what modern literature is. Smut." That's how he speaks. "For example, look at *Lady Chatterley* or *Lolita!* If you publish things like that, you can afford to put out all kinds of fancy stuff. And non-fiction books too! They always catch on. But fiction? Now I ask you, Lazarus. Why do I really keep you on my payroll, eh? I'll tell you why. So that you can sit here year in, year out on your fat behind, wanting to palm me off on your fancy writers—isn't that why?" That's how my boss talks. A modern man. Me? I'm from the old school. I believe that we could still make a go of it without pornography. Hemingway's to blame for it all. It was he who started it. But in his case they printed only the first and last letters of the worst words—and in between? Dot . . . dot . . . dot. Nowadays they print the whole word!

On the other hand: He has always been good to me, my publisher. I've spent my life with him. I'm leaving him two years from now—that's to say, well—probably even earlier. Due to circumstances. I don't want to give him reason to complain about a dead man. It would actually be an act of real friendship to provide him with a real juicy piece of goods before I kick the bucket.

So let's hope, then, that this young fellow's style is the

chopped-up crap they call "inner monologue" nowadays—ugh! And yes! Please, please make the grammar atrocious—and please give us lousy punctuation. Or better still, none at all! Then we can promote him as a German James Joyce. Or Henry Miller's sidekick.

But let's hope he hasn't written the smut abstractly. We've got loads of idiots who do just that. (That's why I haven't come across anything suitable yet.) So then. There sits the German housewife, then, and if she doesn't have an intellectual teenage daughter who's "with it," who can explain things to her, she has to despair of knowing anything at all about anatomy and must ask herself as she wrings her hands: "What's really the matter here? What on earth is she doing with him? How many people are taking part in it?" And believe me, she won't find that strange vocabulary in any dictionary.

But maybe we'll have some luck this time.

Albert Lazarus checked the thickness of the manuscript.

743 pages.

19 marks 80.

We won't be able to produce it for less. But if the young fellow is reasonable, talks sense, and expresses himself lucidly, and moreover if he exposes that racketeer father of his—well then, we'll print a cool ten thousand as a first edition!

"If."

Maybe another piece of nougat?

*Many a character in the story of our love is repulsive, or is at least depicted as being so. They will therefore have their characters besmirched and their feelings wounded . . .*

There we have it. Nothing again. I knew it, I knew it.

*. . . above all my father and Fräulein Stahlmann, and I admit that it would give me the greatest satisfaction to unmask them directly before the world in all their perversions and depravities, and to portray them as they really are.*

A ray of hope. The young fellow seems to be really näive. Näiveté can be sold very simply and naturally: But näiveté *plus* pornography! Mmm. . . .

Quiet, quiet!

Read on.

We've been disappointed far too often in the past. You see, these youngsters are naïve and coarse and they just can't write. We've seen it all before.

*Yet supposing we retain the names Mansfeld and Stahlmann and change only the names of all other persons and scenes, we wouldn't gain anything. I've heard it said that every man possesses so-called individual rights . . .*

So, young fellow, you've already heard that, have you?

*. . . and can take precautions against it, to be used in recognizable form as a character in a novel, even if this character is depicted in a positive and thoroughly amiable light.*

I just can't eat any more sweets or I'll be sick. But then, I'm dying anyway. Cancer of the liver. Only the doctors won't come out in the open and tell me. So—another brandy cherry. This really is a strange young fellow. Certainly no idiot. And if others print *The Key* and *The Pillow,* why can't we one day?

*That's the dilemma I find myself in. I beg you gentlemen, who are experts in the field, to examine my manuscript taking these points of view into consideration, and to advise me legally if you find my manuscript of interest to you. I will be most willingly prepared to revise the book in any way recommended by you. I thank you in advance for taking the trouble to read my manuscript. Oliver Mansfeld.*

Nougat's the best of the lot, thought Lazarus. He turned over a page of the book. On the page stood these words:

LOVE IS ONLY A WORD

NOVEL

Albert Lazarus gradually felt a mild burning sensation in his stomach. What did I tell you, he thought with smug satisfaction; I'm feeling ill now. With that he started to read.

He read until about three in the morning, then wound up the alarm of the golden repeater watch, which he had set at seven-thirty, and brushed his teeth with mineral water. Finally he pulled the glossy fabric curtain a little bit to the side and looked out into the night. By this time the train was on the section between Munich and Rosenheim. It was not snowing here. Lazarus could see solitary lights flitting hurriedly by, and heard the soughing of the night storm as it drove against the carriages of the Paris Express. He had skimmed through almost half the manuscript—a "preliminary reading" it was called in the trade jargon—and suddenly had become sad and puzzled.

Once more in bed, he analyzed his condition. It wasn't the manuscript that made him so confused (he had completely forgotten his publisher and his publisher's opinions on what constituted subjects ripe for publication). No. As a matter of fact, this novel was very much a "firstborn," in need of polishing in many places, if not unusable. Moreover, it was written in a language that had at first irritated and repelled the reader so much that again and again he had been tempted to throw the folder onto the table—yet continued again and again to read on.

Lazarus decided that there were two reasons for this. To begin with, as an aging eccentric who didn't like children, he had not expected to know the slightest thing about the world this book dealt with. He believed himself to be a Gulliver who had been catapulted unexpectedly, unprepared, violently into a kingdom of dwarfs. And secondly—well—now certainly, to tell the truth (Lazarus rolled on his bed with a mild attack of heartburn), secondly, this was the first love story he had read for years. On and on he thought about what he had read. At last, the fifty-eight-year-old man fell into a deep sleep and had a tangled, confused dream from which the shrill cry of his repeater watch awoke him at exactly 7:30 A.M.

In Vienna it was very cold, but dry.

Albert Lazarus spent the day in conferences. He settled his business all right, but he was so confused and obviously preoccupied with thoughts other than those of business that his colleagues were more than once annoyed by this man who was usually a model of propriety and concentration. Yet out of politeness they kept silent.

As soon as he entered the compartment of the sleeping car, which left Vienna with the Paris express at a quarter after ten,

Lazarus again went to bed and finished reading the manuscript. This time he didn't eat any candy. Around four in the morning, he put down the folder and stared into nothingness for a long time, this fat man sitting upright in a ridiculous nightgown. He fell asleep like this, without having wound the clock or brushed his teeth. An hour before the train reached Frankfurt, the conductor woke him and brought him tea. He found the traveler lying in his rumpled bed in a particularly grouchy mood.

In Hesse it was snowing relentlessly, and the tracks were partly covered. While the gentleman was sleeping, there had been a few delays due to the snow, according to the conductor. Sipping his hot tea, Lazarus listened dumbly to the man in the brown uniform, who, after asking permission, pulled up the black blind in front of the window. Bleary-eyed, Lazarus looked out upon a white desert.

"They say it's even worse up in north Germany."

"So?"

"Most of the train connections are completely interrupted, and the telephone lines destroyed. The Frankfurt airport and other airfields have suspended their services."

"So?"

"They say the Autobahn from Frankfurt to Kassel hasn't been cleared yet, and that it's out of order. We're being delayed."

"So?"

"I don't want to disturb you, sir."

"Then don't do it," said Lazarus. For a quarter of a century such an impolite remark had not passed the narrow, round lips of this stout man who, despite all his robustness, suffered from an almost unhealthy bashfulness.

The conductor, insulted, disappeared.

Albert Lazarus felt sick this morning. On this morning, January 9, 1962, one hour before the train reached Frankfurt, Albert Lazarus, who went to a specialist every week and to another one every six weeks and who called all specialists charlatans—since all they ever did was confirm time and time again what he didn't want to hear, namely that he was perfectly healthy—Albert Lazarus displayed all the symptoms of a man who is on the brink of a major illness and who cannot locate the dull, painful source of his discomfort, since the disease is in its early stages.

Picking up his box of medicine, Lazarus swallowed some pills and counted a few drops into a teaspoon. Cursing his housekeeper for having omitted to put his slippers in his suitcase, he put on his socks in front of a wall mirror, shaved with an electric razor, and dressed. Meanwhile his discomfort continued to grow. His head ached. He felt cold. Again he dressed in his old-fashioned suit, and although this compartment was also overheated, slipped into the sleeves of his lined winter coat, wound a scarf around his neck, and put on an ancient slouch hat (Schweitzer!) before sitting down near the window. He stared into the insanity of the snowdrifts, which drowned the whole countryside in their boundless, relentless white chaos. The flakes melted only on the warm windowpanes.

After a while Lazarus felt faint. Looking down, he noticed that he was still sitting there in his socks.

"That miserable Martha!" he thought as he bent down laboriously, because of his stoutness, and slipped on a pair of outdated laced boots.

"I've probably caught a cold," he thought, "because I walked around the compartment yesterday and today without any slippers on."

This "miserable Martha" was an elderly spinster who had been taking care of Albert Lazarus' small household for the past seventeen years. He didn't smoke. He didn't drink. There had never been any women in his life. And even with Miss Martha—who was now fifty-two—there had never been anything approaching a real human relationship despite the seventeen years they had known each other. Occasionally during a fit of rage (which always happened when one of his specialists had just confirmed to him his excellent state of health) the aging man fired the aging girl for ridiculous reasons—always after the fifteenth of the month, however. Since, by contract, the working relationship could not be terminated until the fifteenth of each month, Miss Martha quite promptly and coldly refused to quit each time she was dismissed, whereupon Lazarus used to let the matter rest. This weird game, which they had been playing with each other for seventeen years, was actually the only bond that lay between them, the only bridge across the abyss of their lonely lives.

"I'll wait a few more days," pondered Lazarus as he laced his boots, "and if it turns out to be the flu, I'll definitely throw her out this time. In a few days it'll be the fifteenth. . . ."

He straightened up and resumed his vigil at the window.

What was it really all about? He was really too clever not to know why he felt so miserable, beat, weak, and sick. The source of his condition was emotional, not physical. The manuscript which he had read in two nights—was it good or was it bad? Lazarus couldn't tell. This had never happened to him before. The accuracy of his judgment had always been admired by his colleagues. But now, for the first time, he was at a loss. He was absolutely certain of only one thing: the story he had read was not invented. No, it had been experienced. And the love which this book spoke of was probably as real as the manuscript itself. Yet if it *was* true, then the young man, who had here exposed the most intimate events in a most flagrant way, was in danger. In great danger. In danger of his life.

Lazarus suddenly noticed that he felt scared—scared for Oliver Mansfeld and the woman he loved. They were both in danger, and they needed help! By whom? And how? Who could possibly know what their intentions were, or what they planned to do? Nervously, Lazarus stroked his mighty mustache.

He, and he alone, knew about it. Only he: an aging, sluggish bookworm who had never loved, and who had never met a woman who could ever love him. Only he: a bashful, woebegone character with no friends, a man whom other men laughed at and whom women had always found ridiculous.

Only he: an old-fashioned, dull, stout man who ate too much candy and who wouldn't be missed when he died. No one would even shed a tear if he were to die. And yet this was the only man who knew about a love threatened by disaster, grief, and a violent end.

With a sudden flash of insight, Albert Lazarus realized that this was why he felt sick, faint, and miserable. Because I am scared, scared for a twenty-one-year-old whom I don't even know, and for an unknown woman whose secrets I know completely—all of them—scared that something terrible will happen before I can act and maybe prevent a catastrophe from happening.

What can I possibly do? Me, an insignificant man with no power, no money, and no strength? All my life I've been unable to do anything to help anybody. Never. Nobody. But now I must do something, and immediately. No one can relieve me of this obligation. I must act.

Act—but how? Do—but what? I don't know. I just don't know. But if these pages are telling the truth—he lifted up the black folder which had slipped to the floor and stared at it—if all this is true, and it certainly is true (this is about the only thing I've learned in the past thirty years: to distinguish so-called art, which is always full of lies, from the truth, which has never anything to do with so-called art), then I must warn this young man immediately, I must call him to come to me. At top speed. Or else it will be too late. . . .

Once more he opened the manuscript. He remembered that the title page bore an address. There it was:

*All rights reserved by:*
*Oliver Mansfeld*
*c/o Professor Florian*
*Friedheim im Taunus*
*Tel: 3 43 21*

I'll ring him up, thought Lazarus, as soon as I reach the office. He now began to feel himself transported, like a man with a mild fever, as he skimmed once more through the manuscript. He did so somewhat absentmindedly, as if his thoughts were wandering wild and bewildered. For the manuscript spoke to him with the vocabulary of passion, and told him strange things about so much that Albert Lazarus had never experienced in fifty-eight uneventful years. It told him about the boundless despair of love, about jealousy, hate, ecstasy, and hope. "Yes, I'll call up immediately," thought Lazarus. Then it occurred to him that the conductor had mentioned something about interrupted telephone connections. Albert Lazarus held the manuscript on his knees and shuddered.

After a one-and-a-half-hour delay the Paris express at last reached Frankfurt-am-Main. In the railway station the stout man, who was carrying a small suitcase, bought a noon paper. When his eyes fell on the headline, he stood still. He put the suitcase down on the wet, dirty floor as people bustled and hurried past him. Silently his lips moved, and his ruddy face lost its color. The headline read:

SON OF MILLIONAIRE RACKETEER MANSFELD MURDERED

Lazarus stood motionless. Only his hands trembled as they held the newspaper that was still wet with printer's ink. Below the headline, in thick type three columns wide and then one column wide, he read:

*Frankfurt, January 9 (from our own correspondent). Drenched in blood, and with injuries indicating a violent struggle, twenty-two-year-old student Oliver Mansfeld was discovered hanged early today in the gable room of a ruined observation tower near the village of Friedheim im Taunus. All the accompanying circumstances support the view that Oliver Mansfeld was the victim of a crime.*

*The student Mansfeld—despite his age he was only in the ninth class at the Professor Florian boarding school—had been reported missing on Sunday evening. Since Monday noon the local police and the military have been combing the thick wooded area around the boarding school, where Mansfeld had been seen for the last time on Sunday afternoon. The continuously heavy snowfall made the search extremely difficult.*

*About noon members of the military found the dead man's car, completely snowed in, in a forest clearing about two kilometers away from the school building. The seats, the steering wheel, the floor, and the instrument panel, as well as the outside and inside of the left door, were completely covered with blood.*

Too late. He had come too late.

With slumped shoulders, his mouth open and his eyes staring, Albert Lazarus stood there, a fat old man whose limp gray-blond hair spilled from under the brim of his hat and fell disheveled over his ears. Mechanically he fumbled at his mustache, in which some chocolate was still sticking. He was unaware that people were bumping into him. He heard and saw nothing. Too late. Too late. If only this Meyer female hadn't neglected the manuscript, and had given it to him before the holidays. . . .

Or would it have happened in any case? Was there nothing in life that one could prevent? Lazarus was freezing. He had a splitting headache. One of Oscar Wilde's sayings came to mind: "We always recognize the truth only when we can do absolutely nothing about it."

He sneezed, then with great difficulty forced himself to continue reading.

*Since all telephone connections between Frankfurt and the Taunus were disrupted, the local police then requested by telegraph the help of the Frankfurt police headquarters. A homicide squad under the direction of Chief Criminal Commissioner Hardenberg was rushed by helicopter to the place where the body was found. They landed near the school on a tennis court that had been shoveled free of snow. Since the boarding school has a card file of the blood groups of all the students, the police physicians were easily able to determine that the blood found on the car was identical with Oliver Mansfeld's blood group. Officials of the Identification Bureau have obtained clues which at the moment are still being kept secret.*

*Even after dark the search for the missing man was . . .*

"Can't you park yourself somewhere else?"

Lazarus, violently jolted by a man carrying a rucksack and a pair of skis over his shoulder, reeled to the side. Mumbling an apology, he tugged his old hat and walked with his suitcase toward a flower shop near the exit. Although there was a violent draft there, Lazarus was not aware of it.

*. . . not suspended. Using hand searchlights and torches, and traveling on skis, over 70 men continued the activity, which met with success today at 2:35* A.M. *Oliver Mansfeld's corpse, which, frozen stiff and snowed in, was discovered in the snow-filled observation room of an old tower about two kilometers away from the school building, was in such a condition that the doctor from the Homicide Squad was able to establish the following after a brief preliminary examination.*

1. *Death must have occurred in the afternoon, or at the latest in the early hours of Sunday evening.*

2. *All the signs indicate that Oliver Mansfeld was beaten, severly injured and then, probably while still unconscious, he was hanged. Chief Commissioner Hardenberg told our reporter, who had also arrived by helicopter at the place the body was found, that it was assumed to be murder. This assumption was made after officials of the Identification Bureau had found certain clues and objects in the tower room, the nature of which is being kept secret for the time being.*

In the center of the page, set in three columns and surrounded by black lines, the following text appeared:

THE POLICE REQUEST ASSISTANCE

*Did anyone see Oliver Mansfeld (22 years old, 1.78 metres tall, tanned and very narrow face, brown eyes, thick brown hair cut short) after Sunday, January 7, at 3:30* P.M. *at the Rhein-Main Airport, on the Autobahn, or any other place? When last seen, the dead man was dressed in a camel-hair-colored duffle coat, a thick blue turtleneck sweater, gray sports trousers, and stout, brown, fur-lined winter shoes.*

*Did anyone see a white Jaguar 500, with black pigskin upholstery, after 3:30* P.M. *on January 7? The car in question is a blacktop convertible, which was probably open. In all prob-*

*ability Oliver Mansfeld was sitting at the wheel, with a foreign-looking eleven-year-old youngster beside him. The car has the police registration number L 43131-Z.*

*Can anyone supply details of a telephone conversation Oliver Mansfeld held in the Blue Bar of the Rhein-Main Airport on January 7, 1962, between 3:30 and 3:45* P.M., *from a telephone that stands on the bar counter? Indications suggest that the party on the other end of the line was a woman. Did Oliver Mansfeld mention her name or her Christian name? Numerous customers were in the bar at the time.*

*Every police station is taking any relevant information, which will be dealt with confidentially upon request. Administrative Department 1 of Frankfurt Police Headquarters, telephone 23 65 31, is especially interested in any relevant information.*

Albert Lazarus let the paper slip from his hands and stared out into the snow that swirled along the square in front of the railway station. He meditated for a long time like a man who is scrupulously pondering the pros and cons of a weighty decision. For he knew that something quite monstrous could depend on what he was now about to do—something monstrous for those actors of the drama who were still alive. At length he dragged his steps to the long row of telephone booths which stood in the hall, stepped into one of them, and dialed the number specified by the paper.

He heard the phone ringing twice, then a man's monotonous voice announced: "Police Headquarters. Administrative Department 1. Police Inspector Wilms speaking."

"This is . . ." Lazarus had to clear his throat. His voice was completely hoarse, and his throat felt choked. "This is Albert Lazarus." He gave his profession and the name of the publishing house he worked for. "I've just come back from a trip and I've just read about Oliver Mansfeld's death."

The voice at the other end of the line showed more interest: "Yes? And?"

"Before Christmas my publishing house received the typewritten manuscript of a novel. The sender and the author is a certain Oliver Mansfeld."

"How do you know?"

"It says so on the manuscript."

"It might not be true."

"It is true, Inspector. I read the manuscript on the trip. The events of the novel take place in the Taunus, in the boarding school of a certain Professor Florian. The boarding school isn't far from Friedheim."

The other voice sounded breathless now: "Does this author give the right names?"

"Quite specifically in all cases, as he explains in a foreword. The action begins in September 1960, and Mansfeld proceeds to relate what has happened since then—up until immediately before Christmas 1961. Although the manuscript is unfinished, I believe just the same—"

"The police headquarters is only five minutes away from the station. May I ask you to come here immediately, Mr. Lazarus?"

"That's exactly what I was about to do."

"Don't go to the old building on the Friedrich-Ebert. Come into the new building on the Mainz main road. We're on the third floor, to the left. Homicide department. I'll be expecting you."

"I'll come immediately."

"Many thanks."

Albert Lazarus hung up and stepped out of the booth. He went to the exit and walked out into the snowstorm, which almost blinded him. A minute later the snow had frozen to small particles of ice in his walrus mustache, his long hair, and his bushy, gray-blond eyebrows.

At the edge of the street, cars were desperately trying to free themselves from the gigantic snowdrifts, but in vain. Tires raged round and round senselessly. There was a strong smell of scorched rubber. A radio patrol car rushed past with its siren howling and its headlights blazing.

When Albert Lazarus, the unknown man with the crucial evidence in his hands, crossed Poststrasse in order to turn down Ottostrasse, he walked right into a large, angry crowd of passengers who had just left a streetcar that stood frozen in its tracks. At once dizzy and excited, sweating and freezing, Lazarus jostled his way through the throng of men and women, who swore at him.

He didn't hear their curses. As though protecting it, he lifted the small suitcase in front of his broad chest and held it there with both hands. He carried it like this through the white inferno of the snowstorm, with infinite care and with the unsure steps of an old invalid (which he was not); he, Albert Lazarus, in whose insignificant, unimportant life nothing important or meaningful had ever happened—until this hour.

And so we lose sight of him behind the whirling wheels and billowing shawls of the flakes, this man unknown among the anonymous, this solitary figure alone among millions, this stooped, fifty-eight-year-old man carrying in an old-fashioned suitcase a manuscript of 743 typewritten pages as if it were a precious treasure. This manuscript is now meant to help solve a crime, to unravel a puzzle, and for all that tells the story of a love that has no end and never will have, a love that had its beginning more than fifteen months earlier, on a beautiful autumn afternoon on the fourth of September in the year one thousand nine hundred and sixty.

# The Manuscript

# Chapter One

[ 1 ]

If you couldn't cry about it, you would most certainly have to laugh over it. Every time I return to Germany, it's the same story. It's been like that for seven years. People have gradually got used to the idea that my goddam father is in their files, and is to be arrested immediately. He—not I.

To think how often I've rushed back and forth between Luxembourg and Germany these past seven years! But no, there's nothing anyone can do about it, it's always the same story, just as it is right now on this fourth day of September 1960. It's always like this, it always was like this, and it always will be like this. Until grass grows over the whole business and they allow my father into the country again. It's insane that such a mess will blow over legally one day, and that no one will then be able to get near him in his beautiful car! So what? Even homicide falls under the statute of limitations after five years. Fine laws we've got.

Like I've just said: it's the same as always. Only this time we don't have to circle over the airfield as we usually do. Two planes are landing before ours. Teddy keeps flying in left loops. His name is Teddy Behnke. He's my father's pilot. During the war he flew bombers. Now he flies a Cessna and a Beech Bonanza. My dear old dad has got himself two planes, since he's no longer allowed into Germany. Cute little things. Still, it would make you puke. On both sides of the fuselage of the Bonanza my father has had smeared on in huge letters: *MANSFELD*. Red on a silver background.

That's typical of him. A typical *nouveau riche*. Compared to him, Teddy is high English aristocracy. Yet Teddy can't do anything but play golf and tennis and fly. So Teddy has to fly. During the war he did it for the precious Fatherland, and now he does it for a dirty racketeer. It must be really bad, when you can't do anything but fly. I don't think Teddy likes working for my father. He always has the same poker face and doesn't show anything, but sometimes you can feel it anyway.

We land, and he lets the buggy taxi in front of the airport building.

"If you don't mind, Mr. Oliver, I'd like very much to fly back immediately."

"You mean you won't go with me to the passport office and let yourself be grilled?"

"I didn't say that, Mr. Oliver."

"But you were thinking it. Do you suppose for a minute that *I* would go in there at all if I didn't have to?"

He looks at me, puts on that old poker face, and doesn't make a sound.

"Such is life," I say, lifting up my big brown traveling bag and clambering out of the plane. He leaps toward me and babbles pretty inarticulately: "I still have to get my safety check."

"Happy landing, old chap," I say. I've still kept this English expression in my mind from my last boarding school. Let's hope he disappears soon. I'm curious to find out what they've got up their sleeves in the Taunus. We all have something. Nothing to worry about. It'll blow over. Nothing serious.

"I hope you're not angry with me for not going with you and waiting until you leave?"

"Not at all. Give my regards to my mother."

"Certainly, Mr. Oliver. I'll pay a visit to the gracious lady tomorrow in the sanatorium, I promise you."

"Take her flowers," and I give Teddy some money. "Red roses. Tell her I said that I'll pull up my socks. I'm not going to be thrown out of school again this time. Something like that always reassures her." Again he doesn't answer, so I ask: "What's the matter, old boy?"

"It's all very embarrassing for me, Mr. Oliver."

"Ah, Teddy my boy! Do you think it's all wine and roses for me? At least you're not his son! You can always give your notice! You've got it made. That son-of-a-bitch!"

"You shouldn't speak about your father that way."

"Father! You're breaking me up! For all I care, my old man can go and drop dead," I reply. "And dear Aunt Lizzy into the bargain. It would be a day of rejoicing for me. Well then," I say, giving Teddy my hand, "keep it in mind!"

He answers softly: "God protect you."

"Who?"

"God." (Teddy's the religious type.)

"And what is He to do?"

"He's to protect you."

"Ah," I say, "that He will. And He'll protect you too. And also the Bonanza. And the Cessna! He's supposed to protect everything generally. After all, He even protects a pig like my old man. That's why you've got every right to demand His protection. So long, Teddy."

"Goodbye, Mr. Oliver," he says, then limps over the concrete ground to a door over which stand the words AIR WEATHER CONTROL. He caught a bit of flak in his knee right at the end, in forty-five, when everything was going to the dogs. That's why he's got a limp. And that's probably why he's very religious. This Teddy's a fine fellow. I wonder what he thinks about our family. I can just imagine. Probably the same as I do.

I pick up my satchel and make for the passport-examination room. There's a lot of activity today. There always is on Sundays. A lot of big planes. On the opposite side, in front of the restaurant, people are sitting out in the open drinking coffee and watching the Boeings and Caravelles taking off and landing. It's a beautiful day too. Blue sky, quite warm. With all these silver streaks in the air, it's an Indian summer. It smells of potato fires in the fields. Outside, on the airfield grass, a flock of sheep is grazing.

"Your passport, please."

I hand over my passport to the official behind the high counter. He opens it and immediately pulls that certain face that they all pull. Always. Many of them also give a whistle when they read my name. Or they hum a little. But they always pull the same face.

Moreover, this is a new official, one I've never seen before. I've also never seen the one who's leaning on the barrier in front of me, so that I won't escape, for Christ's sake.

I'm wearing flannel trousers, a white shirt without a tie, and a blazer. No cufflinks. Sneakers. I always dress this way when I come to Germany. The undressing goes faster then.

"Your name!"

I'm tempted to say that my name's written right there in the passport you're holding in your hand, so why do you ask? But I don't say it, for I already know from past experience that there's no point to it. You say it, then you allow yourself half an hour of waiting in the transit room while they're pretending they're telephoning, and everything takes five times as long. Nevertheless: I said it several times, seven years ago. I was fourteen then and didn't know any better. Meanwhile I've smartened up.

With a courteous smile I reply: "I am called Oliver Mansfeld. But I'm the son, not the father."

The man behind the counter hears nothing at all, makes no sound, bends down and looks for something.

"To the left, in the upper compartment," I say.

"What's there?"

"The criminal search files," I say. "If it's still the last issue, then it's page 134, below, last line but one. There he is."

"Who?"

"My fatherly creator."

In a matter-of-fact way he actually takes the search file out of the compartment I pointed out to him and obediently turns over the pages to page 134, licking a finger as he does so. Then he travels down the whole page with it, although I told him that my father is right at the bottom, and there he finds him at last and reads what there is to be read, silently moving his lips.

The other one, who has placed himself in front of me, asks meanwhile:

"Where have you come from?"

I have learned a lot in the past seven years, so I do not say: You know that as well as I do. The control tower called you and told you I was coming, when we were still circling. I answer softly and politely: "From Luxembourg. As usual."

"What do you mean by that—as usual?"

"That means that I always come from Luxembourg."

"His family lives there," says the one behind the barrier as he closes the search file.

"It says so here."

After that everything proceeds as always, perhaps a bit more detailed this time, because at the moment they both have nothing else to do.

"Where are you going now?"

"Up to the Taunus. Boarding school begins tomorrow."

"What class are you going into?"

"The senior."

"At twenty-one?"

"Yes."

"Then you've been kept back three times?" Smart boy, eh? Always polite, always friendly.

"Yes indeed. I'm a very bad student. I just don't take to mathematics and physics. I'm an idiot. But my father insists that I graduate." That he insists on it, true. That I'm an idiot, not true. In fact I do take to mathematics and physics. I've kept myself back three times just to show the old man. I succeeded. He has fumed for weeks on end. For me these were the happiest weeks in the past seven years. I also intend to flunk the final school examination. And how! It's time I made a few beautiful hours for myself again.

"That's all your luggage?"

"Yes."

"What's in it then?"

"Books. Records. Toilet case."

"And everything else?"

"I left in Frankfurt. At a friend's place. He's already sent my things up to school in the meantime."

There is a piercing whistle outside that gets louder and louder. It dwindles, and we hear a whining noise. Then it becomes silent. A turboprop has landed, and I can see it through the open door.

"Lufthansa, London," says the man behind the counter. Thank God, for now he'll get some work to do and cut out the bullshit. He makes a sign to his colleague.

"I'm coming," I say.

"Where to?" asks the colleague.

"So what were you about to say?" I ask his colleague.

"I must ask you to follow me to the customs."

"Would you imagine?" I say, "I would never have guessed."

"Now don't you get fresh with me, young man, okay?"

That's what you get for letting yourself go. It's always advisable to keep your mouth shut. In the meantime they've rolled a gangway alongside the Lufthansa plane, the cabin door stands open, and the first passengers are stepping out into the open. They are a young man about my age, a younger girl, and a man with his arm around a woman's shoulder. They are all laughing. They are being photographed. They are all in one group. A happy family. That actually does exist.

My old man's a shit.

Stop.

Enough.

Don't think about it.

All we need now is for me to start whining.

In the beginning I used to do that sometimes, out here in the passport office, when I saw a happy family like this one. Father, mother, children. Yes, I really cried.

[ 2 ]

Have you ever been examined by the customs? So meticulously, I mean, in one of these compartments? It has happened to me at least fifty times. At least! Let me tell you what it's like and how you should conduct yourself. You never know!

As for your conduct: Friendship, friendship! Not one mean word. Not one angry look. Do everything the customs official says. Speak only when you are asked to. For heaven's sake don't protest. Something like that merely succeeds in putting the fellow in a bad mood. And you, what do you get out of it? Zero.

The wooden compartments are no bigger than a toilet. Two men just about fit in. In every box there's a stool, a table, and a hook on the wall. The cells stand lined up one beside the other, a bit in the background. They stand in the shadow of the general customs clearing shed, which you're all acquainted with, in the shadow of this long sheet-metal chute where you open your bags. Behind this, you see, lie the cells, which are discreetly hidden. The male passengers are inspected by male customs officials, the female by women customs officials. Even they exist. Sometimes it's very amusing. Because the cells *do* have only wooden walls, like bathing cabins. So you hear every word, from left and right.

"Take off your bra. Panties too, please."

"What's that? A truss? I'm sorry, you'll have to open it."

On this particular Sunday, of course, I'm the only one who's being frisked. It's quite quiet in the wooden cell where it takes place. The customs official is wearing a green uniform and is very stout. First of all he rummages through my traveling bag. He pulls every single record out of its wrapper and looks inside the jacket. Ray Coniff. Louis Armstrong. Ella Fitzgerald. Oscar Peterson. Then the books. *Mila 18. La Noia. The Rise and Fall of the Third Reich. The Last of the Just Men.* Martin Buber and Camus. Leon Trotsky: *My Life.* The stout man skims through every book in such a way that everything between the pages simply must fall out. Nothing falls out. You see, there's nothing inside them. When he reaches Trotsky he speaks for the first time: "Do you read this?"

Humbly: "Oh yes, Inspector. For heaven's sake, surely it isn't forbidden?" No answer. That's the right procedure.

Nevertheless he skims twice through Trotsky. (Because naturally, of all the books I have with me, I'd quite calculatingly hide a secret message in this autobiography, wouldn't I?) Trotsky turns out to be unfruitful.

After the books comes the toilet case. Toothpaste tube open, toothpaste tube closed. Soap case opened, soap case closed. Electric razor: He needs two minutes for that. That's a long time, and since I know that it will take much longer, and since I cannot lose my patience under any circumstances, I look out of the small window. Every cell has a small window like this in the door. Strictly speaking, it must be closed by means of a curtain. But this one is not completely pulled together.

The luggage of the Lufthansa passengers is being unloaded now on the customs chute. A lot of people are waiting there in front of three customs officials. They are very quickly dispatched. There's the married couple again with the two children. Since they're all still laughing so cheerfully, I prefer to look elsewhere. There's a hallway leading into a dark hanger. At the entrance I see a notice board: ENTRY FORBIDDEN. Behind the notice board, in the half-dark, a couple are standing. They are kissing. Gangbusters!

He has put his arms around her shoulders, and she has put hers around his waist. They are standing there just like that.

The kiss doesn't stop at all. He looks terrific. Black hair. Black eyes. Tall. Slender. Gray suit. Pointed shoes. Small mustache. Probably an Italian. She is smaller than he, maybe as big as I am. She is wearing beige-colored pants, flat beige-colored shoes, a beige-colored sweater, and a scarf worn loose around the neck. I think to myself: Beige is her color, and she knows it. This dame is built. Man! Like a racing yacht. Although she's no longer young. Certainly over thirty.

Well, at last! *Le baiser fantastique* has ended. They are looking at each other. That means: She can see his eyes, but he certainly can't see hers, for half her face is hidden behind a gigantic pair of sunglasses. She probably has her reasons. If this gentleman is her husband, then my old man's an honest Joe!

It's a pity she's wearing glasses, for I'd like to see her eyes. As it is, I can see only a fairly narrow face with very white skin, a black dot on the left cheekbone, full red lips, a dainty nose, a high forehead, and bluish-black hair that tumbles onto the nape of her neck in a soft billow.

Now she's speaking with the fellow. She's got very beautiful teeth. He says something and she twists her mouth as if she were on the verge of tears. Then she keeps kissing him quickly, quite quickly, on the mouth, on the cheeks, on the eyelids. If only they knew that someone was watching them! After all, they've hidden themselves quite well at the entrance to the hangar. The girl must be crazy about him, the way she's carrying on. It gets you all worked up just looking at it.

"Empty your pockets, please. Lay everything on the table."

Fatty is finished with the traveling bag. Now the performance gets under way with the wallet, the pencil case, the cigarette package, the handkerchief. He actually takes out all the matches and all the cigarettes and shakes the handkerchief. Once more I look out of the window. They're both in a clinch again. What a woman. . . .

"Undress, please."

"Certainly." It goes quite quickly, for I certainly know what to wear when I come to Germany. In half a minute I'm standing in my socks and underpants in front of the fat man, who cheerfully begins to fleece my clothes. He turns the lining of all the pockets inside out, fingers the material of the blazer, and examines the cuffs of the flannel trousers. Maybe there's an H-bomb inside.

"You can sit down."

"Thank you, I prefer to stand." You see, she's kissing him again.

"I suppose you consider this an unnecessary annoyance, Mr. Mansfeld."

"Forget it!" She's stroking his black hair now, and holding his head with both hands.

"I'm only doing my duty, believe me."

Now she's kissing him on the hand. Once. Twice. Three times. Then she presses his hand to her cheek. This guy's got it good. She's going wild! If only I could see her eyes.

"I'm only a minor official. If it says make a thorough search, then I have to make a thorough search. Duty is duty. I've got nothing at all against you personally."

It's really disgusting—I mean that I persist in looking at them. Turning round, I say to Fatty: "And I've got nothing against you, Mr. . . ."

"Koppenhofer."

"I've really got nothing against you, Mr. Koppenhofer. I know you've got to do your duty. I've been thoroughly searched here so often that I'm surprised I've never seen you before."

"I've only been working here three weeks. They transferred me from Munich."

"That's why!" I pull off my socks and give them to him. "You know, of course, that it's all because of my father." He looks embarrassed and nods. Fatty's a nice fellow. He stands there looking into my socks, still embarrassed. "I don't look on all this as a deliberate annoyance. Not as something directed against me personally. My father's the one that should be annoyed. He should be suffering at the thought of his son always being frisked like a criminal when he returns to his own country. It's no use trying to explain to the people here that they're proceeding on a false assumption. My father doesn't go through any pain because of it. In fact my father doesn't give a damn. He doesn't give a damn about anybody. Above all, about me."

Mr. Koppenhofer looks at me disconcertedly.

I ask him: "Underpants too?"

He shakes his head, looking embarrassed.

"If I may just once, very quickly . . ."

As I am standing, he pulls down my pants quickly from behind and in front and examines what there is to examine.

"You can put your clothes on again."

"Thank you, Mr. Koppenhofer," I say, taking my socks. Why shouldn't I be friendly toward him now? It's not his fault. After all, our brethren in the passport office can't help it. They've got their orders.

I say: "Passport officials are only doing their job. As I've already explained to you: My *father* is the one that should be pestered, not me. That would only be fair and just. But you're all under the wrong assumption. You see, you all think my father loves me."

"You're saying pretty terrible things, Mr. Mansfeld."

"I'm only telling the truth. Do you think my old man's stupid enough to hand over to me or any of his underlings any material that would be of interest to you? If he was as stupid at that, you would have been able to put him under lock and key a long time ago."

What's the matter with me? Why do I talk so much nonsense? On and on and on!

"You also frisk his men each time they pass through. They're as used to it as I am. So far, have you found one single document, one single memorandum on one trifling scrap of paper in the last seven years? Nothing! The filthy schemes my old man hatches up in Luxembourg are never put down on paper! His henchmen have got them tucked away in their heads when they return. Unfortunately you can't say to them: 'Please remove your head now, sir!' "

"You're annoyed with me after all."

"No, I swear." I'm dressed now and I'm putting all my things back into my pockets. They don't amount to much. I never put much in my pockets when I come to Germany. I get held up too long if I do.

They're both still there. Now they're holding hands and gazing at each other in silence. He's probably catching a flight soon. Obviously he is—just look at the way he's dressed.

While I was being frisked, I heard voices continually speaking over the loudspeaker. You all know the kind of thing: "Attention, please! Air France announces the departure of her Clipper 345 for Rome via Munich, Zurich. Passengers will go on board through gangway three. We wish you a pleasant flight." "Attention, please! Will passengers Wright, Tomkinson, and Harris, booked with Pan American World Airways to New York, please come to the desk."

And so on. Then, while I'm putting my cigarettes away, I hear it. "Mrs. Verena Lord, Mrs. Verena Lord! Please come to the Information Desk. We have a telephone call for you."

Through the small window I can see how the lady with the huge sunglasses is startled. Terrified, she stares at the man who is holding her in his arms. She says something. He says something. She shakes her head. That beautiful blue-black hair swishes to and fro.

"Mrs. Verena Lord . . . Mrs. Verena Lord. . . . You are wanted on the telephone. . . . Please come to the Information Desk!"

Now he's talking to her imploringly. With his hands too. Certainly an Italian. She stamps one of her feet.

The stout customs official opens the door.

"Well, good luck, Mr. Mansfeld! You can go. And please. No hard feelings."

"Yes, yes," I say, giving him my hand. But I'm not looking at him any more. I see only the woman with the dark glasses. Carrying my traveling bag, I walk past her and the fellow. Just then she turns round and we bump into each other.

"I'm so sorry," I say.

She looks at me absentmindedly, then runs away through the hall. The fellow follows her hesitantly. Is he afraid? Apparently so. I would be too. Afraid that the lady might be wanted on the telephone by her husband.

How come there's a smell of lily of the valley?

Ah, yes. The scent of her perfume. That's Diorissimo. I know it. In the last boarding school I was bounced from, I knew a little gal who loved the stuff. I sometimes gave it to her. Not that I'm stingy. Certainly not. But it costs a fortune, and the aroma is as fleeting, it vanishes as quickly, just as quickly as—as I was expelled on account of that same little gal.

Diorissimo.

Verena Lord.

By the way, I too have to go to the Information Desk. I'll inquire how I get to Friedheim. Over the Autobahn, that I know. But then?

"Porter!"

"Yes, sir?"

"Would you be good enough to fetch my car out of the garage? It's a white Jaguar."

"Did you garage it with us when you left?"

"Yes."

"Do you have the papers?"

I gave them to him.

"Do you have any luggage?"

"No. The ignition key is in the car."

"I'll drive it directly in front of the main entrance."

"Okay."

As I make my way to the Information Desk, I overtake the slow, black-haired Mr. Handsome. He's worried, you can see that.

Diorissimo. I keep on smelling it. Long legs. Blue-black hair. Verena Lord. All at once I feel as if someone had given me a kidney punch.

Hold on. Just a minute. Verena Lord . . .

Verena Lord?

## [ 3 ]

"Please excuse this surprise attack."

Ten minutes have gone by.

Just as I'm throwing my smooth, brown traveling bag behind the seat of the Jaguar, I hear a voice that is smoky and deep, almost husky. I turn around, and she's standing in front of me. And there again is the aroma of lily of the valley.

"Madame?"

But I've got a tight grip on the car, for something like this only happens in novels, right?

Mrs. Verena Lord is standing there wringing her hands as if she were washing them with a piece of invisible soap. Her face is scarlet and she seems at a loss for what to do next.

So I ask her: "Can I help you?"

What a dumb question! Would she have spoken to me otherwise? If the lady keeps looking at me this way, I'll need a cognac. A double. And I can't even see her eyes. Still, what I do see is more than enough.

"Yes," she says with that throaty voice that must drive every normal man crazy, "I believe you can help me . . . that's to say, if you want to . . . I mean . . . Oh God, this is embarrassing. . . ." And again she looks as if she wants to cry—like a short time ago, for example, when she was embracing her man in the dark entrance to the customs shed.

However, the fellow is walking toward us now, slowly, even though he's noticed that the lady doesn't know how to deal with her problem. I bet he would give an Alfa Romeo not to have to talk to me. But he has to, for the lady looks quite helpless.

At last Mr. Handsome is standing there, right in front of me.

He speaks fluently, though with an Italian accent: "Signor, the lady finds herself in a desperate hurry. Weren't the three of us in the Information Office a short time ago . . ."

"Yes," I say.

". . . and I was standing beside you, while the lady was making a phone call?"

Her eyes are clinging to me. Why are my hands getting moist? This is idiotic. Or is it? After all, I've had my share of birds. But something like this . . . no, never anything quite like this! Her cheeks are pale now, and her breasts are heaving rapidly. He talks on like a guidebook or like someone who's explaining to you how to play poker.

"While I was standing near you—*scusi,* signor—I couldn't help overhearing the girl behind the counter explaining to you how to get to Friedheim."

"Yes, that's where I have to go."

"The lady also has to go there." Say, this fellow really is good-looking. If only I could look like that, just once. For two days. Or even one. If I could look just half as good! Man, I'd be taken to the hospital with exhaustion.

The lady and this fellow are really well matched; they look terrific together. It often seems to be like this with people who aren't supposed to get together and in fact never will get together.

But he was kissing her. I don't give a shit. Yet it's funny. When I think of it I'm eaten up with blind, raging jealousy.

Then I look at his olive-colored, gentleman's hands until he clasps them behind his back and, it's funny, right at that moment I stop feeling jealous.

So what?

I had a piece of ass once, she was forty-one, who cried hysterically when I was bounced out of boarding school and told her I couldn't see her any more for that reason. But now, on the other hand, Verena Lord. *Verena Lord!*

The fellow says: "The lady has to get to Friedheim at top speed, but she doesn't have a car."

"How did she get here?"

She grasps his arm and says, like someone about to faint: "Please sir, stop—this is madness."

Sir. Sir! Of course she has to call him "Sir" if he's her lover. She can't possibly throw herself round his neck right in front of me.

Have you ever had that feeling: when everything, but *everything* about a certain woman pleases you? When she can say and do anything she wants, and she sends you half-crazy with longing and desire? And you don't even know the woman? That happened to me once in a D train. But her man was with her, and they got off at Karlsruhe. I couldn't sleep for a couple of nights after that. Now it's happening to me a second time.

And with Verena Lord. It *would* happen with her. If only she knew! Naturally she must come to know about it soon. It'll be almost impossible to keep it a secret. Of all the women in the world. Verena Lord. Would you believe it?

What beautiful hands she has! On the middle finger of her right hand she is wearing a platinum-set emerald surrounded by diamonds, and on the wrist a bracelet with diamonds and emeralds. The stone and the bracelet make quite a display, indeed they do! I'm an expert on jewelry, of course. My old man, the pig, buys loads of them. Capital investment. Leading experts from Amsterdam advise him when he buys them. I've listened in on their conversations several times. So I know what's what. No one can put one over on me when it comes to jewels. The lady is wearing a real beauty there on her finger. At least five carats. And if that bracelet didn't cost at least a hundred fifty thousand marks between friends, then I didn't get bored to death from reading Karl Marx and the Marquis de Sade.

The fellow puts his arm round the lady. (Why does she wear all this armor with pants and sweater? Is she perhaps one of *those?* Often the most beautiful ones are. No. Nonsense. This lady doesn't come from that world. She comes from a world . . . from a world where one is so free, so safe, so unconcerned about others, that one can wear expensive jewelry even with pants and sweater. Today I know what world Verena came from before she was Mrs. Lord. I didn't know at that time.)

The fellow with his arm round the lady's shoulder smiles happily and freely and says to her: "One moment, please, yes? You musn't lose your nerve now." And to me: "The lady came here in my car. She accompanied me. I'm flying to Rome. Naturally she could take a taxi. Or even my car. But that's not the problem."

"Then what is it?"

"The fact is that the lady has to get to Friedheim very quickly. As quickly as possible. When I saw that you have a Jaguar, it occurred to me that I might ask you to take the lady with you. What can the car do?"

"Well, I can get one sixty-five out of it."

"Would you take the Signora with you?"

"With pleasure."

"Wonderful." Now he brings his hairy hands again from behind his back, rubs them, and whispers something into her ear. I can make out only the end of the sentence: ". . . he'll be out of Frankfurt, you will be easily up in Friedheim by then."

He whispers the familiar form of address to her, but he doesn't whisper it low enough. Who might that be who will only have left Frankfurt by the time we're up in Friedheim?

I don't know why, but I'm suddenly feeling quite sentimental. Is this *my* love? Of course not! So I say boldly: "If the lady would like to be home before her lord and master . . ."

She turns more pale, stares at me, and murmurs: "Her lord and master?"

"Or maybe it's your little brother. How am I to know for sure?" I always say things like this when I'm feeling sentimental. Why is that?

"Look here," she begins, "I don't know you. It was very kind of you to want to take me with you. But under the circumstances, I certainly won't—"

The fellow gives her a slight nudge. She stops talking. The

gentleman and I are of one mind. I say: "Of course. I understand perfectly. I've hurt your feelings. Please accept my humble apologies, Mrs. Lord."

"You know my name?"

"Not only your name."

"What do you mean?"

"Later. First, let's get started."

"I'm not getting in unless you explain to me what you mean."

"You must go with him," says Mr. Mustachio, "you must."

"I think so too," I say.

"How do I know you're not blackmailing me?" she whispers.

"You don't." At this point I'm playing the big shot. This is slowly turning into a French boulevard comedy.

The guy steps forward, grasps my blazer, and hisses: "I'm warning you. If you plan to take advantage of this situation, God help you! I'll find you wherever you are, and then . . ."

"Don't," I say.

"Don't what?"

"Let go of my jacket. I don't like that."

But I'm misjudging him. He doesn't let go, but only smiles behind his little mustache, and his eyes turn sinister when he says:

"I don't care if you like it or not, Mr. Mansfeld."

*"Mansfeld?"* she says.

I feel quite small again.

"Mansfeld?" she repeats.

"He mentioned his name at the Information Desk, Signora. His father is the well-known . . . Mansfeld."

"Mansfeld?" Again. That son-of-a-bitch, my father!

"You can trust Mr. Mansfeld," says Mr. Handsome, "he's a gentleman. With a daddy like that you can't help being a gentleman."

That piece of scum, my father! There are a lot of ways of being humiliated. The worst way is when you have to tell yourself it isn't even your own fault—someone else has cooked your goose for you. But that makes no difference. I have to keep my mouth shut. And so I only say: "Four minutes have passed already."

Tenderly, Mr. Handsome kisses the lady's hand, gazes at her with those moist boudoir eyes and says: "Mr. Mansfeld is right. We've already lost four minutes." And to me: "I thank you."

"But it's my pleasure to take the lady to Friedheim," I say as I walk round the Jaguar.

He bows—not too deeply—and says: "Farewell, Signora. And thank you for coming with me."

Her voice is so choked that I can barely understand her (I hope she doesn't start splashing my car with tears!): "Have a good flight. Come back safe and sound."

"Certainly," he says as he opens the door on her side and pushes her gently (ever so gently) into the car and onto the seat next to me. *"Avanti, avanti, carina."*

Suddenly I notice that the hand which is holding the doorknob, the olive-colored, hairy hand, is trembling.

Would you believe it?

Even His Lordship is human.

And since that story about my father, I must be a little punch-drunk . . .

Don't think about it. At least I've got one consolation now: other people's nerves show too. But I've just learned something new: if you feel pretty miserable, you've got to put on a tough-guy act.

I've been feeling miserable now for seven years.

Okay, tough guy, I say to myself. Go ahead, tough guy. The Lady Verena is sitting next to you. Start the motor, tough guy, and put your foot down.

Make it howl.

## [ 4 ]

Foot down. Shift gear. When the Jaguar leaps forward, the lady is thrown back in her seat, and we lean into the curve from the parking lot. I've got to keep my wits about me here. There are loads of cops around.

I glance into the rear-view mirror and say: "Your friend is waving goodbye."

No answer.

She doesn't move.

I couldn't hear what he whispered in her ear at the last moment, but she didn't seem too pleased about it. She sits there as though she has just died while she was biting her lower lip.

And what a lip!

I don't think I've ever seen a more beautiful woman. Never.

I said *woman*. Not *girl*.

Intentionally.

I think I have to clarify something, since I don't know if you're aware of it. It's a funny business with us boys and girls, with us Teens and Tweens.

To the girls, the boys are too goofy, and to the boys, the girls are likewise. Girls especially can't stand boys of the same age. (And rightly so.) So they look for older ones. Around thirty-five, they have a great time nowadays. They don't know what to do with the sixteen-year-olds! It's more than they can handle, with all the offers they get. Of course, it's understandable. Those guys have money, and they know the score. A girl is safe with them. I remember when I was eighteen. Man, the things I did! Only the fifteen-year-olds would put up with it. I was like a bull in a china shop. It wasn't until I got to know the forty-one-year-old—the one I mentioned before—that I learned what it was all about.

You see, nowadays girls seem to have an instinctive feeling for this: to go with a boy of the same age is agony. That's why they prefer older men. They know what's what. They know how. After all, girls are only human too, and want to enjoy it as well. And if an accident happens sometimes—well, an adult always has his connections, doesn't he? Whereas a kid just starts to pray or runs to mummy to confess.

With people of my age it's the same story. Most of the girls I met were not only too stupid to talk to, but they were also too stupid even to *do* it. I ask you now: who's got time nowadays to teach a girl the baby steps? No, thank you! Waiter, bring me a thirty-year-old, please! I'll take them older than that too.

Now try and understand my nervousness. For I *am* nervous as I'm sitting behind the wheel, driving up to the Frankfurt entrance of the Autobahn. I mean, while I don't exactly have beads of sweat on my forehead, I must admit I really am nervous. It's because of Lady Verena. I can't help glancing in her direction.

I take a look in the rearview mirror.

The Italian beau keeps watching us for a bit, then shrugs his shoulders and returns to the airline building.

"He's given up now," I say.

Again no answer.

From where I'm sitting I can at least see part of her eyes, in spite of her stupid sunglasses. I think her eyes are black. Her nostrils are quivering. Her hands tremble. I can't help noticing that the clip of her bracelet—a tiny platinum loop—is open. But I'm unable to tell her that. I can only stare at her.

Beautiful. Beautiful! She is so beautiful. Everything about her. Her body. Her posture. Her hair. I've got the feeling that if you stroked it with a comb, it would rustle. And if you ruffled it with your hands——

Wow-eee!

Damn it!—that was close. I overlooked the stop sign by the entrance to the Autobahn. Almost drove into that Cadillac. If the driver hadn't jerked the wheel around. . . .

It won't work that way. If I want to really hit the road, I'll have to concentrate and stop looking sideways at her. I say: "I'm sorry."

With that smoky voice of hers she asks: "What?"

"Oh, nothing in particular. It's just that we came to within a hair's breadth of being killed."

Do you think she answered, even when she heard that?

Not a word. Not a single word.

There's a little traffic on our side of the highway leading north into the Taunus. On the opposite side, going toward Kassel–Frankfurt, the traffic is bumper-to-bumper. Of course. Sunday afternoon. The whole town is returning from excursions. Papa. Mummy. The kiddies. Back from the picnic in the woods. Autumn leaves all over the place. Now they're sitting in their cars, all those tired but happy families. Family—I just have to hear that word . . .

I drive in the left lane. The needle is already touching 160 kilometers. Now and then, even in my lane, another car tries to overtake us. But right now there's that fat captain in blue. He won't move over to the right. So I come close and blink my lights.

What's your problem, Shorty?

The guy at the wheel shakes his fist and honks his horn at me.

Don't get so mad, baby! The lady's in a hurry . . .

And what a lady!

After we've been on the road about three minutes, she says at last:

"It would be all the same to me."

"What?"

"If I were dead, I mean."

"Yes, yes," I say.

"Seriously," she replies.

"And I was serious when I said yes, yes."

Suddenly her jaw juts forward, and her voice sounds as if she were choking on her tears. "I just don't care any more. About anything. Anything at all. It all disgusts me."

"Now, now," I say, casting a glance (Moral Outrage Department) on the five-carat stone and the bracelet with the emeralds and diamonds.

"Oh that," she says, "that junk. Do you think that this is enough to make you happy?"

"Bravo! Straight from a grade-B movie," I say. "So go ahead and throw the stuff out of the window! The clip on the bracelet is already open. It would just take a flick of the wrist."

But she doesn't hear me. And the clip stays open. She should have listened and closed the little platinum loop, right then. A great deal would have turned out differently. Maybe everything.

Right now I have worded that very nicely. We're always so smart afterward. But at the moment, when it really counts. . . .

And I don't think any longer about the open clip. Suddenly I feel angry at this woman. Spoiled brat! Only a spoiled brat could talk such nonsense. Money alone doesn't bring happiness. We know that.

Hold on. It's getting better: "You are very young, Mr. Mansfeld."

"Sure, Madame," I answer, "sure I'm still very young. And that's why I beg of you to think a bit of my young tender life. For things are not all the same to me." Pregnant pause. "And neither are they to you, really."

"But they are!"

"And because you don't care any more, you have to get to Friedheim in such an awful rush."

Now she does something that really drives me out of my mind. She places her left hand on top of my right one. Hers is cold and mine is hot. Her hand, her hand. I can't stand it.

She says: "You're right. I do talk nonsense."

I say: "You have beautiful hands."

She withdraws it immediately. Thank God. That's what I wanted. That's why I said it. How else could a fellow keep his car on the road at a steady 170? It's difficult enough. She sits very close to me. The car is so narrow, so small, so low. I can smell not only her perfume, but also her skin, her powder, and her make-up. It must be a good lipstick she's wearing. No smudges.

180. 185. 190.

"How lucky I am," she says, suddenly becoming hoarse.

"You mean because the highway isn't crowded?"

"No."

"Then what?"

"I mean, because you too have to go to Friedheim."

Luck? How do you mean luck, lady?

If you had said Heidelberg—I would have taken you to Heidelberg. Or to Düsseldorf. Or to Istanbul. I would have taken you anywhere. You see, those between thirty and forty are just my size.

[ 5 ]

I've got to say something right now. Three things. It's about time. Number one: I could tell the story in a different way, of course. Not exactly like Thomas Mann, but in a more classical style and using longer sentences. Sure I could. Let me tell you a secret. That's how I started out, and that's how the first version looked! Longer sentences, no slang words. More emotion. Less speed. And do you know what? After twenty pages I found out something: this is going to be a cold cup of coffee.

And I can explain to you why. Because I'm wet behind the ears. Just like in the book (described by the so much more refined adults): lazy, fresh, sloppy. A smart aleck. I know every new book, every new record, every new orchestra. And all that stuff bores me, bores me to death. (Sagan gives us that message over and over again.) I'm Third Class Mail. I can help nobody, and if I could, I wouldn't. When I and my kind grow up, God have mercy on the human race! For our generation will send this world to the grave, don't worry. (Isn't this exactly what you think, beautiful or ingenious readers? Aren't you convinced of this?) On the other hand, we adolescents harbor really serious fears that you yourselves might accomplish that. Now don't get on your high horse, angry old men. It wasn't meant nastily. Just honestly. Yesterday eighty-seven people were killed in Algeria. That's not bad for a Saturday's work, eh?

Mind you, I too would prefer to be wise and clever and to write like Thomas Mann. But no dice. I am an adolescent, so I've been told many times, and if an adolescent wants to be understood, all he can do is write like an adolescent. And I do want you to understand me, right to the very last word. For I have lived through a story which has been harder on my kidneys than anything I've ever experienced before in my life. It is—you will laugh—a love story.

Please, no. Please, don't laugh.

I thank you. And you do see my point about the style, don't you?

Number two: On the fifty-six pages I have written so far, I have again and again cursed my old man. I have called him a pig, a criminal, a crook. And now may I add that I wish cancer on him, on him and sweet Aunt Lizzy.

You read all this. Now there are two possibilities. Either you think: This is repulsive; the boy is repulsive; the story is repulsive. Or you think: If he really hates his father then he should come to the point and tell us why. Precisely and clearly. So that we can decide whether he is right or just plain pathological.

Let me assure you that I am not pathological. And you will agree with me when you know what my father has done. But I can't put it down on paper. Word of honor. I've tried. It just doesn't work. I either start crying or I get plastered. You see, it isn't only the things the courts have charged my father with. It's more. Much more. After we knew each other for a while, Verena asked me what my old man had done and why I hate him so much. And believe me, she is the one person I could tell it to. I cried then too. But I was able to tell Verena everything. The whole stinking truth.

This is my first book, and I find it very hard work. So I ask you: Give me a little time, time enough to reach the place Verena wants me to go to. It'll be easier for me then. Then I'll have to describe a scene, and write down what she said and what I said, and so on. Then I'll become a third party, so to speak, and not so much involved. Then it will work, I'm quite sure. So will you be a little patient with me?

A little? Yes?

I thank you.

Finally, of course, there is number three:

Time. In the first version, I wrote down everything in the past tense. The usual way. She *was* the most beautiful woman I *had* ever seen. She *placed* her hand over mine. And so on. But I couldn't keep it up. Even in the first draft I found myself continually slipping into the present tense. Unconsciously. I noticed it only when I pulled the paper out of the typewriter and read it through.

It doesn't work. I just cannot write in the past tense about what is my life, my breath, everything that I have and want and that I'm fighting for. Because what I want to talk about is my present. I'm right in the middle of it. I must remain in it. The day on which I saw Verena for the first time is as much present as the moment in which I now type the letter *t* in the word *that*. For me, everything is present. Everything that has happened since that Sunday afternoon. I would kill myself—no—that is too great a word, too splendid a word for me. That word should be reserved for great and splendid writers. Well, I would do away with myself if this present were to become past. I know that it will not become past as long as our love endures. So let me continue to write in the present—even for the sake of superstition.

Yes?

Once again, I thank you.

## [ 6 ]

195. 200. 205.

"Well," I say, "what did I promise you?" And I risk throwing a glance. "If it didn't go so steeply uphill, I'd be able to do 220." She is watching me. And for the first time she smiles. If only I could see her eyes! She is still wearing the dark glasses. But in spite of them, her smile is wonderful.

You know, when I was fourteen and attending boarding school, we made a trip to the Zugspitze. (Right after that I was kicked out of that particular institution. But that is another story, as Kipling says.) In a cabin up there somebody woke me up at three o'clock one morning so that I could see how the sun rises. At first I gave him a kick. But later on, when I saw how the sun rose, I apologized and thanked him. For years afterward I thought that this sunrise was the most beautiful thing you could ever experience. I thought that until today, goddammit, right up to this very moment. Now I don't believe it any more. Verena Lord's smile is more beautiful than a million sunrises.

I'm finding it gradually more and more difficult to accept all this talk about our being cynical and blasé, forever bored and disgusted by everything around us. A few men of letters have been busy propagating this idea and making a lot of money from it. Bravo! Good luck to them, I say. I don't begrudge them a thing. But what's really going on here? Who believed Hitler, who screamed *Heil!*, attacked half the world, and gassed six million Jews—and yet can't remember a thing today? Who was that? Not us!

*Consider that for a minute!*

*Consider,* for example, that we cannot reproach our dear parents for having done that. Believed? Yes, that they did. Our elders believed all right, a little bit too much. In any case, they keep telling us that. And we believe them when they tell us that they believed. Unfortunately, they did too little thinking. In fact, a little less believing and a little more thinking might have been somewhat preferable. That's why they don't care for us. Because with us half-strong ones it's the other way round. We believe only a little of the twaddle they dish up to us; but that's because we do a little bit more thinking. Naturally, not all of us. But at least those who don't think don't believe either. I think that represents enormous progress. And I would much rather they dance the twist and wear leather jackets and take the mufflers off their motorscooters than that they sign up spontaneously for a community sing, and have tears in their eyes whenever they hear The Hymn. Of all the boys I know—and I know a lot—not one signed up voluntarily! Each one did it only because he had to. And you should have heard what they said before they did. Of course there are always idiots among us. Where are there none? But let me tell you: Most of them do a little more thinking than ever their parents did.

I, I have done my share of thinking too.

I've been thinking all the time she's been sitting beside me. All the way to the Taunus.

Schwalbach exit.

Weisskirchen exit.

I've been thinking whether or not I'd be successful in laying her. I mean, that's a natural consideration. Being a normal man I think you'll agree with me. She is so beautiful. She cheats on her husband. With an Italian like that. Perhaps she does it with others too. So why not with me? Then, after the Bad Homburg exit, something strange happened. Something that very rarely happens with me. I was embarrassed. For myself. For the thoughts I was thinking. Even though it was the only sensible thing to think. What can I do?

I was ashamed. I think that was the moment when I started to love her. After the Bad Homburg exit.

Then I say to her: "That scarf, the one you're holding, I think you'd better put it round your head."

"Why?"

"If your husband is already at the station and we overtake him now, he might recognize you—in spite of the glasses. But with the scarf nobody will recognize you. And keep looking over slightly in my direction."

She turns red and her lips move soundlessly, but she takes her scarf, ties it over her hair, and pulls it forward so that her face becomes invisible for anyone who looks at her from the right.

"Okay," I say.

What a glorious fall this is. The trees along the roadside are bearing red and yellow and brown leaves that glow in the sunlight. There is a blue haze in the distance, and the forest through which we are driving is bathed in gold. This is so lovely. So lovely. But already the shadows are growing longer.

She has half-turned toward me now, but I've got the car up to 210 and have to look ahead. The car is trembling as the white dividing line on the road rushes toward us.

"At the airport you said you know more about me than just my name."

"Correct," I say.

"What else do you know about me?"

"That you're the wife of the banker Manfred Lord from Frankfurt. Your husband does business with my father. I don't know your husband. But I do know my father. So the business they do together can't possibly be very legal."

"There are many people called Lord, Mr. Mansfeld. I don't have to be the banker's wife."

"But you are."

"Yes."

"You have an illegitimate child."

"Its father died before it was born. We were going to be married."

"Of course," I say as I think: I wonder what you were before that. A bar girl? Never! Secretary? Never. I do know a little about people. And you weren't a model. No, you were none of these things. I can't really tell what you were or where you came from. I've got a feeling there's something secret about your past. What kind of secret is it? What kind of background do you come from? Where did the honorable Manfred Lord find you?

"Don't feel offended," I say, "but you asked me if I knew about you, and I'm answering. The child's name is Evelyn. Your husband has resigned himself to it, but he doesn't want to adopt it."

"How do you happen to know all this?"

"My father told me. He's talked about you several times."

"What did he say?"

"Nothing but good." This is a lie, Verena. He said nothing

but bad about you—dirty, degrading things. As far as my old man's concerned his business friend's wife is at best "that person" and at worst "the little bitch" and "the gold-digger." My father is in the habit of saying things like "It's a pity a man like Manfred Lord slipped up so badly." And my Aunt Lizzy, my dear, sweet Aunt Lizzy, says things that are even worse. But can I tell all this to Verena Lord? There are times when we can tell people only part of the truth, if we want to be decent about it and don't want to hurt their feelings.

"What kind of car does your husband drive? A Mercedes?"

"Yes."

"Black?"

"Yes."

"There are two of them in front of us. I'll overtake them now. Turn toward me a little more."

She does so. We are both silent for quite awhile. When she finally speaks I can feel her breath on my cheek.

"What are you thinking about, Mr. Mansfeld?"

It's really strange. If she had asked me this question at the Schwalbach exit or the Weisskirchen exit or even before the Bad Homburg exit, I would have probably given her a fresh answer. Or a charming one. As it is, we've already passed the Friedrichsdorf exit and everything is quite, quite different. As a matter of fact, I don't think it'll ever be the same again as it was before the Bad Homburg exit.

No, it'll never be the same again. But then, I'm—full of complexes, perhaps?

"I've just asked you what you're thinking about."

Pompously, the way we young folks sometimes do, I answer: "I was just thinking that a classless, international society is the only hope left for humanity, but that one cannot constitute such a society without an atomic war, and that such an atomic war would wipe out mankind. *Voilà:* the Circulus Vitiosus."

After that she only asks: "And what is your first name?"

"Oliver," I answer.

Now I know that I love her.

## [ 7 ]

I love her.

Isn't that insane? Me—in love! And with a woman I've never seen before in my life and who's been sitting beside me for only half an hour. Who has a child. Who has a lover. Is that insane or isn't it?

"Look out," I say, "another black Mercedes."

Obediently she turns her head in my direction. I overtake the car.

"This time there was a woman at the wheel," I say. "Look straight ahead again or else you'll get a stiff neck."

But she keeps on looking at me.

"What do you honestly think, Mr. Mansfeld?"

Well, what do I honestly think?

I think: I will stay with you always, always.

But can one say something like that to a woman one has known only for half an hour?

"I don't want you to get into trouble," I answer. "Your friend was listening at the Information Bureau when the lady was explaining to me the way to Friedheim . . ."

"And?"

"And I was listening while you were phoning. I couldn't help it. You see, you didn't close the door of the telephone booth properly. And you were talking too loudly. Far too loudly."

"It was really an unimportant conversation."

"That's not true."

"You only heard what *I* said."

"It's possible to reconstruct a whole conversation from the answers, you know."

"And?"

"Somebody was calling you from Frankfurt. Somebody you can trust. Perhaps the cook. Or the chauffeur."

"And?"

"Whoever it was knew that you were at the airport—with

your friend. He called to tell you that your husband had returned from his trip much sooner than expected, and that he is looking for you right now. The person who called must have lied to your husband that you are in Friedheim. Possibly you have a villa up there. That's why you've got to get there so quickly. So that you'll be there before your husband. Then you can tell him that you've been taking a walk."

Then she faces the front, throws back her head and says: "There's another exit. Turn off here. Let's get it over with quickly."

"I don't understand."

"You're a blackmailer. Well, all right. It's my bad luck, I suppose. Slow down and turn off now. It's lonely country here, and the bushes are high. I'll give you fifteen minutes to help yourself, Mr. Mansfeld."

I'm so surprised that I can't utter a word. Then she screams hysterically: "Go on, turn off! Take what you want!" She grabs the wheel and pulls it to the right.

The Jaguar starts to skid, and goes within a hair's breadth of another car to the right of us—and at 210!

My reflexes make me lash out at her. I strike her arm and body. Something clatters—probably her bracelet. I must have hurt her very badly, because she screams out some more, lets go of the wheel, and presses a hand against her breast.

Has your car ever gone into a skid? Yes? At 100? At 140? Will you ever forget it? I was doing 210. I've never known anything more terrifying. The Jaguar is now on the two left wheels. I wrench the steering wheel. Now it's on the two right wheels. The tires are screaming. Brake slowly. Brake very, very carefully. Keep your hands slack on the wheel. Now your car is showing more intelligence than you are. Back onto the road. Back onto the curb. And on the opposite road there's a column of cars. Everything whips past as in a horrible dream. Terrified faces. Stones. Cars. Back onto the road.

At first Verena had screamed. Now she's quiet and holds

on to the upholstered dashboard. Momentarily the Jaguar spins so rapidly that I think we're going to turn over and that will be the end. It jumps ahead again. I step on the gas so that it'll at least go forward. It keeps dancing like a drunk. Sweat is pouring into my eyes. But all I can think of is this: if we come out of this I'm going to kick her teeth in. Behind us, in front of us, and next to us a wild cacophony of horns has broken out. But it's all over now. The car is only oscillating slightly. And I increase the speed.

"O God," she says.

"Don't ever speak that way to me again," I say with difficulty as I wipe the sweat from my forehead. "Never, never again."

"I'm sorry. I'm so very sorry."

"Be quiet."

"It was mean, what I said. It was crazy of me to grab the wheel like that. I'm insane."

"I told you to be quiet."

"I'm absolutely out of my mind. I don't know what I'm doing any more."

By now the car is quite safe on the road.

"Can you forgive me?"

"Why not?"

"I was mean."

"You're unhappy," I say, "that's all."

"You just can't imagine."

"I've got an imagination. I can imagine quite a lot. Look out. Another Mercedes."

She turns her head again. And this time she lowers it and it touches my shoulder. I can feel her hair. It smells wonderful.

We were passing the Mercedes.

"Did we pass him?"

"No," I lie, "wait a little."

Although it's only five o'clock, it's becoming dusky. Up high, in front of us, the sun still forms a golden circlet, but the light is becoming dim and the forest is not as colorful as it was a short time ago. The foliage is already withered, brown and brittle, and in the meadows it's becoming shadowy and cold. And Verena's head is still on my shoulder.

[ 8 ]

"Five o'clock. There's music on the AFN." I press the button that starts the car radio. Piano and violins. A plaintive trumpet. We both say at the same time: "Gershwin—Concerto in F."

"The second movement," she says.

"The second movement is the best one."

"Yes," she says, lifting her head and looking at me, "it is for me too."

"Are you feeling better?"

She nods.

"How long have you been married?"

"Three years."

"How old are you?"

"One doesn't ask that question."

"I know. How old are you?"

"Thirty-three."

"And your daughter?"

"Five."

"And your husband?"

"Fifty-one. That was mean of me too, wasn't it?"

"What was?"

"To marry a man eighteen years older—and now to deceive him."

"You had a child," I say, "and probably no money. Listen—that piano—" She puts one hand on my shoulder and we both listen for a long time to the music of this great artist who had to die of a brain tumor at thirty-eight while there are generals who are still growing roses at eighty.

"How old are you, Mr. Mansfeld?"

"Twenty-one. And so that you don't have to ask, I'm going to Friedheim because there's a boarding school up there and I'm still going to school. I got busted three times. Now I'm about to get busted for the fourth time."

"But why?"

"Just for fun. Understand? Now we've got to get off the Autobahn." I turn the wheel to the right.

EXIT OBER-ROSBACH / PFAFFENWIESBACH / FRIEDHEIM

After the names of the villages are the distances.

FRIEDHEIM—8 KM.

A large curve takes us to a bridge that crosses the Autobahn. I can see birches, elders, and a few oaks. The road narrows. Pylons of cross-country electric cable. The wires gleam silver high up there as the sun hits them. Meadows and forests. A small village. A tiny wooden bridge crosses a tiny river. On both sides of the street are poplars, then come the houses. An idyllic scene. I'm passing a roofed-over passage between two white-and-brown framework houses now, then we can see the marketplace, the town hall, and a thick-stemmed church tower with a baroque cap—all of it shiny, white plaster, gilded and painted. More and more framework houses, clean and old, painted with colorful paints. I must drive slowly—fifty now, since there are a lot of cars on this road.

Opposite the church tower stands a very old house with artistic carvings on its front, a motto which I forgot immediately, and an old shop on the ground floor. TRAVEL NECESSITIES it says above the entrance. On display are not only suitcases and handbags, but also saddles and riding gear. Here they still use horses for traveling. Past the marketplace. We're in the back alley now, and even here there are old framework houses with painted gables, and old shops. WHOLESALE HAIRDRESSERS ARTICLES—OMNIBUS HIRE—SPECIALTY BAKERY A. WEYERSHOFENS AND SONS. The façades of the houses are very light, while their woodwork is very dark. A nun is crossing the street wearing a starched cap and carrying a prayer book in her white hands.

"Is there a second road leading up to your house?" I ask the woman sitting beside me.

"If you turn off now to the right. But it's a very bad one."

"That doesn't matter. I can't get ahead on this one. This is the one that probably goes to the boarding school. Today's the end of the vacation, so all the parents are taking their children back. There are supposed to be over three hundred."

"Have you ever been there?"

"No, I'm a newcomer. To the right now?"

"Yes, but I could walk . . . I don't want to detain you. You have to get to the boarding school."

"I've got time. You don't."

I turn off to the right. The road is getting terrible. Potholes, ruts, and stones. The autumn flowers in the grass by the road are dirty and dusty.

"Why are you doing this for me after what I said?"

"I don't know," I say.

And that's such a lie.

## [ 9 ]

I have to go down to thirty, or my axles and springs will break. The path—it can't really be called a road any more—climbs steeply. It's getting darker. Around me, in parks and gardens, I can see magnificent villas, small castles, a restored citadel.

"Who lives there?"

"People from Frankfurt," she says. "During the summer, on weekends. In ten minutes you'll see our house."

Is it possible that one can actually feel, from one moment to the next, such a murderous, mad craving for love? For real, true, honest love?

The light is fading faster and faster.

The day dwindles to an end. She is still sitting beside me. Only ten minutes more. And then? Suddenly I feel cold.

At the side of the path a sign appears. I read:

PHILANTHROPIC SOCIETY

(THE ANGEL OF THE LORD)

CONVALESCENT HOME

A path leads down to a white painted farmhouse. In front of it stands a green pump. Children are dancing around it.

"Who called you at the airport?"

"The cook."

"You can trust her?"

"Definitely."

"How many employees do you have up here?"

"A gardener and his wife. One servant."

"How about them?"

"They're with my husband. They hate me. To them I'm—" She stops herself.

"Dirt, right? I thought as much. I can well imagine."

"O no, Mr. Mansfeld, no! You can't imagine what it's like!"

"Yes," I say, "yes I can. We've never seen each other before. You live here. I'm from Luxembourg. Yet I believe . . ."

. . . that we are so much alike and could understand each other so well, I wanted to say. Naturally I don't say it.

"What do you believe?"

"Nothing. I'm talking nonsense. You are right. Naturally I can't imagine anything."

"Now right again, please."

The path is getting worse still.

"At what time did you leave the villa?"

"About half past two."

"Is your daughter at home?"

"Yes."

"Did you tell them at home that you were going to take a walk?"

"Yes."

"Then stick to that story. Under all circumstances. I'll leave you off before we get to the house. We have never met. You have to stick to that. No matter what happens. Even if someone insists on having seen you in my car. You have to stay with one lie. Only then will he believe you."

"Who?"

"Your husband. You should never change your lies. Once you've picked one, stick to it."

"What kind of man are you?"

"A good one—at heart."

"Where did you go to school before the holidays?"

"In Salem."

"And?"

"And nothing. I had to leave."

"Because of a woman?"

"Because of a girl."

"Have you had many girls in your life?"

"Yes. No. I don't know."

"Have you . . . have you ever loved one—once?"

"I don't believe so. No. Definitely not. And you?"

How we talk with each other. How we understand each other. I knew it. And now only five minutes left. Five minutes at the most. It's becoming darker and colder. Mists are rising from the valley, and above the dark forest the small circle of the crescent moon is standing out in a colorless sky.

"And I what, Mr. Mansfeld?"

"Have you ever loved?"

"The father of my child, yes. And Evelyn."

"The man at the airport?"

She shakes her head.

"Really not?"

"Really not. He is only my . . . I just sleep with him. That's something entirely different."

"Yes," I say, "that's something entirely different. You'll have to show me where I should stop."

"Straight ahead by the big oak."

"I . . . I would like very much to help you."

I've never said anything like that before, never!

"You can't do that, Mr. Mansfeld."

"Maybe I can. Who knows? I'll probably be living up here if they don't throw me out again."

She says nothing.

"Are you going back to Frankfurt tomorrow?"

"No, I'm going to stay on with my child. Until the beginning of October."

Why does that make me happy? Why does that fill me with such joy? Only because she'll be somewhere close to me until the beginning of October? Close to me. Somewhere.

Tough guy? Sentimental idiot.

"You're right," I say. "Nobody can help anyone else."

There's the oak tree. I stop the car. And then it becomes stronger than I am. "May I ask you for something?"

"O God," she says. "No. Please. I am so glad I was wrong about you awhile back."

"It's nothing terrible."

"What is it?"

"I would like you to take off your glasses for a moment. I would like to see your eyes."

She hesitates. Then she does it. And now at last I can see her eyes, the loveliest, the most beautiful part of her. They are really much too large for the narrow face, they are black, with long lashes. There is a very sad expression in those eyes. They know a lot about many things, probably about many ugly things at that. There's also a helpless look in her eyes, a look showing very little hope. Strange eyes, yet with so much passion in them. And longing too, so much longing. I think that no one who has ever looked into those eyes could ever forget them.

"Get out," I say, "go away. Quickly. And don't turn around again."

She climbs out of the Jaguar and puts on her glasses again.

"Thanks," she says hoarsely.

"Go."

"And you will never . . . to anyone . . ."

"To no one. Never."

"Mr. Mansfeld, I—"

"You must go away. *PLEASE.*"

Then she goes. And I'm still looking at her, the woman with the beige-colored pants, the beige-colored sweater, the scarf on her hair, the woman with the small waist and the wide shoulders which now—tired and weak—are hunched forward.

Sometimes, though not often, I know exactly what's going on inside other people, or what absent people are doing. It happens very rarely to me. But when it does, I am always right.

Now at this moment I know with absolute certainty that Verena Lord's eyes, those wonderful eyes, are filling with tears. Tears for whom?

Behind the oak the path makes a turn. There she disappears, the woman with the blue-black hair. She really didn't turn round again. AFN is playing "Brandenburg Gate," by Dave Brubeck.

There's room to turn where I stopped, so I turn. I go back and forth three times before I've turned the car and start driving down the path to the crossroads, across the potholes, stones, and ruts. The old white farmhouse below in the valley—there it is again. And there too is the road sign with the strange inscription:

PHILANTHROPIC SOCIETY
(THE ANGEL OF THE LORD)
CONVALESCENT HOME

The children are still playing happily there near the green pump in the yard. Now I've wound down the window on my side and hear shouting:

"Brother Walter! Brother Walter!"

"Sister Claudia! The rabbit is getting away from us."

Philanthropic Society. The Angel of the Lord. Convalescent Home.

The scent of lily of the valley has already disappeared, blown away.

Diorissimo.

Verena Lord.

Sunday, September 6, 1960.

That's how it all started.

## [ 10 ]

Now I'm back at the turnoff and squeeze into the row of cars which are going up to the boarding school.

The cars are full of adults and children, big and small, boys and girls, and are covered with dust, having come from such distant places as Vienna, Zurich, Paris, Lille, and Hamburg. I'm able to tell that from the license plates. I can also see a couple of American cars. And they are all crawling up the mountain in one long, endless chain.

Verena's eyes. I can still see her eyes. She's arrived home by now. Did we make it? Or was her husband already waiting for her? And will her nerves be strong enough to stick to the one and only lie one must stick to when one lies?

The road coils up the mountain like a snake. Ancient trees cling to the curb. In the distance I can see some broken walls and the ruin of a tower. Were there fortresses here once? Steep cliffs rise up on both sides of the road. There are warning signs:

CAUTION FALLEN ROCK ZONE

Now it's really getting dark. I switch on my headlights. In front of me a chain of red taillights start to flicker. Wait for me. I shall not fail to meet thee in the shadowed vale.

What is it? Marlowe? Yes, I believe so. I wonder why that suddenly comes to mind?

Wait for me. I shall not fail to meet thee in the shadowed vale.

Her wonderful eyes.

And "Brandenburg Gate."

Road signs:

DR. FLORIAN INSTITUTE—THE WATERLILY

DR. FLORIAN INSTITUTE—THE OLD HOMESTEAD

INSTITUTE DR. FLORIAN—TO THE MAIN BUILDING

What does it really mean, always referring to him as Doctor? I thought he was a professor. The path to the main building is the steepest of them all. That's the one I have to drive up. I know that already. It was the same in Lugano, in Salem, and in Bayreuth too. Usually about six or eight villas stand around a main building like this. Girls' dormitories and boys' dormitories. Now they're driving up in their dusty cars to deliver their children, to unload them—to get rid of them. And then they will drive away again. It's the same story everywhere on the first day of school. I've seen it now for years. The only difference for me being that for years I've been arriving at school alone, wherever the school may be.

The main building must have been a castle at one time or other. A huge old chestnut tree stands in front of it. Everything is dark. I see nobody, not a single car. Naturally they're all in "their" houses, already squabbling over rooms and beds. Who rooms with whom? Where are the old friends from last year? What are the new ones like? Mountains of suitcases. Radios. Tennis racquets. Travel bags. Worried mothers. Fathers looking at their watches. How long is this going to take? Tomorrow morning at eight I've got to be in court. Come on, now, Trude! Goodbye, my little sweetheart, promise your mummy you'll be good. You've got to study hard now, for you know how expensive the Institute is. A good deal of yelling, quite a bit of laughter. And a lot of tears.

There's sure to be a lot going on right now in the villas. Most certainly all the toilets are locked and little children are standing inside, crying secretly—for crying is frowned upon here. I know all about it, I can imagine what's going on. I locked myself in too the first time. I was fourteen then. And I had no car, no driver's license. It was in a boarding school near Bad Vilbel. Teddy Behnke, our pilot, had taken me there. You see, my mother isn't allowed to come to Germany either. She's on the wanted list too and is to be arrested as soon as she crosses the border. Teddy gave me a kiss at that time. Can you imagine that? "From your mother," he says. "She asked me to give you this kiss. And I'm to ask you to forgive her." "Tell her there's nothing to forgive, when you see her, Mr. Behnke." "Yes, my little one. I'll be flying back today, and tomorrow I'll visit your mother in the sanatorium. Shall I give a message to your father too?"

"Yes, please. To him and Aunt Lizzy too."

"What is it?"

"Tell them I wish they would both die. Both of them. Slowly. And that they should suffer while they're dying. Do you understand that, Mr. Behnke? Die!" And that was when I ran away and locked myself in the toilet. That's how childish one can be at fourteen. Fortunately, we grow older.

I get out of the car.

They wrote to Luxembourg that on my arrival I was to go to the main building. To Professor Florian. Apparently he wants to talk to me. He can wait a few more minutes.

I don't lock the door. I stretch and stretch my legs. Good air up here. I leave the car and walk in front of the castle, which has balconies and carved figures and niches with sandstone statues standing in them with books in their arms or orbs in their hands or crowns on their heads. You know, the usual.

What is that?

I turn round quickly. Somebody has slammed the door of my car. Who could it be? Dammit, it's so dark here. There's no light in the building. I can only see a shadow. It's the shadow of a girl.

"Hey!"

The girl comes down. Her skirt flies up as she starts running. I tear after her. She's about as tall as I am, but that's all I can see of her.

"Stand still."

She plunges into the dark house. I stumble, fall, almost just manage to get to my feet and finally reach the school. The front door is open. It's dark in the hallway. So dark that I can hardly see my hand in front of me.

Deathly silence.

"Hello." Not a sound.

What shall I do? She's hiding here. Where? I don't know this house, of course. I don't even know where the light switches are, dammit! Now I bang my head against a pillar.

Where is the wretch? Again I bang into something, this time a bench. What's the use? I might as well give up. What good would it do even if I found her, the nosy bitch? Or was she stealing something?

Darkness streams through the front door like black milk. I go back outside and open my car door. No. As far as I can see she hasn't stolen anything. In any case, I lock the Jaguar. Better safe than sorry.

## [ 11 ]

Now I stand in front of the school for a long time and wait and wait. For what? I don't really know. For the girl to reappear? Idiot! You'll probably wait a long time. She undoubtedly knows her way around here and has left some time ago through a different entrance. But this Professor Florian might even appear, right? Or somebody else for that matter. What kind of a junk heap is this, anyway? Annoyed, I walk into the main building. My steps resound loudly in the pitch-black hallway. I can't find my matches. I grope my way along the wall and feel that the hall is round, with a staircase in the middle. At some time or other I'll probably find a light switch or a door. I fumble for the doorknob and turn it. The door opens. The drapes are drawn in the room beyond. Under a tall lamp a little boy is sitting at a table playing with dolls and singing, "Captain, captain, how is your wife?" The room is furnished like a living room. Antique furniture. The soft light is concentrated on the boy and on the table.

"Hello," I say.

Nothing. The little one keeps on playing and singing. "She doesn't comb her hair, she doesn't wash herself, she is an old pig."

Now I can see how small he is. He's like a dwarf. He's sitting as if he were continually trying to touch his chin with his knees. I suddenly feel rather sick when I notice that he's not trying to do that at all, but that his whole spine is bent. Man, really bent!

He even holds his head crookedly, with his left cheek almost touching his shoulder. Or one might even say that his left shoulder has moved up to his cheek. He's completely deformed, the little one with the blond hair, the pale cheeks, and the radiant blue eyes. I can see his face after I've said "hello" for the second time. Startled, he lifts his hands to his face. Naked fear stares out of his blue eyes.

Where have I landed? What is this? A lunatic asylum?

"Listen," I say, "I'm not going to hurt you."

But he remains there as if paralyzed, his hands in front of his face and his knees drawn close to his body.

"Did you happen to see a girl?"

He shakes his head.

"Wearing a skirt. As tall as I am. She must be here somewhere."

His crooked shoulders start twitching. Then his lower lip starts to tremble.

"What's the matter with you? Why are you so afraid?"

"I'm always afraid," he says in a very quiet and very high-pitched voice.

"Afraid of whom?"

"Of everyone."

"Why?"

"They're all pigs," the little cripple replies. "You can't be careful enough." Finally he drops his hands and looks at me. His glance is unsteady. "Who are you? A new boy?"

"Yes."

"I've been here for two years."

"What are you doing here alone? Didn't you go home for the holidays?"

"No," he says, and kicks the dolls he had been playing with, the pretty little dolls.

"I stayed here."

"The whole summer?"

"Yes. A few others did too. Santayana. Noah. And Chichita. But it was simpler for them, since they couldn't go home. Me, I had to slash my wrists before they understood."

"Understood what?"

"That I wanted to stay here."

"You slashed your wrists?"

He stretches out his skinny left arm and I see two fresh red scars. "With a piece of glass," he says. "In the bathtub. The Romans used to do it that way, right? In hot water. We learned that in history. But I forgot to lock the bathroom door. Somebody came in. I was almost gone. Dr. Farber put me together again. And then the chief said that I don't have to go home. Great, eh?"

"Yes," I say, "you did a good job there."

"I would really much rather have died."

"Why?"

"Because of my mother."

"What's with her?"

"Well, if I had died she would have had to cry for me. Right?"

## [ 12 ]

An old lady comes in. That's to say she gropes her way in. It's quite scary, the way she appears out of the darkness of the staircase, looking for the way by touching a chest and a chair with her right hand, which is shaking. She isn't much taller than the little cripple, and is certainly a lot older than sixty. She is wearing spectacles. The lenses are so thick that the eyes behind them seem to be bulging from their sockets. The old lady must be half-blind. So far I find everything somewhat dismal here. If it goes on like this I'm going to take off at once. Well, can you blame me? Shadows, cripples, and mummies—all for six hundred marks tuition a month? I feel as if I'm a guest at Frankenstein's place. Maybe it would be even cozier there.

The old lady's movements, and the certainty with which she

moves, show that she knows this room well. She smiles. Her face is kind and cheerful. "Well, who is that?" she asks when she's close to me, in a tone of voice one uses when speaking to six-year-olds. "Excuse me, but I can't see too well in artificial light."

"You don't know me, Mrs. . . ."

"Miss. Miss Hildebrand." She tugs at the white collar of her severe, high-necked dress. She smells of lavender soap. "I'm a teacher here."

"My name is Oliver Mansfeld."

"Oh, Oliver! We've been expecting you. Dr. Florian wants to speak to you."

"Now you say *Doctor* too!"

"I beg your pardon?"

"On all the signposts it said 'Dr. Florian.' On his visiting card it says 'Professor Florian.' "

"He is a professor."

"Well?"

"But he doesn't want to be called that."

"We just call him 'The Chief,' " says the cripple without looking up.

The old lady smiles and strokes his hair.

"The chief, yes. He will be here, the chief. There's a lot going on here today. Look, Oliver, what our Hansi has done!"

On the table in front of Hansi are dolls, trees, fences, kitchen utensils, building blocks, furniture, a colorful world in miniature. There are men, women, children, and babies, all in three categories: beautifully, moderately, and poorly dressed. There are harmless animals and dangerous animals. There are cars, a toilet, railway cars, gates, and ropes. And there is a very gorgeous prince, together with a beautiful princess. The boy, who is apparently called Hansi, has created chaos with all these things. The dolls are lying across and under benches, chairs, and cupboards that have been toppled over. The walls of one room have collapsed. Only one out of the three shiny blue painted door jambs is left standing. Through it marches the beautiful prince pulling, with a red cord, a huge, dangerous-looking crocodile with a horrible, gaping mouth and threatening teeth.

"For God's sake," cries Miss Hildebrand, clapping her hands with feigned horror, "whatever happened, Hansi? When I left, the whole family was having supper, and everything was perfectly in order." "Yes, when you left," says the little cripple, holding his head even more crookedly, an evil smile playing round his narrow lips. "But then—then the crocodile came in. Through this wall here. It just kicked the wall over. And then it bit all of them to death." He points to the dolls. "Heinz, Karl, Mister Fahrenschild . . ."

"And the mother? She's stuck with her head in the toilet bowl!"

"And she has to stay there too."

"But why?"

"Because she always wets her bed and chews her nails, and she's so mean."

"How come, mean?"

"I don't know. The crocodile said so."

"And you? It didn't do anything to you?"

"No, Ma'am. First it killed them all and stuck the mother's head down the toilet. And it said to me: 'You must promise me that you'll leave her stuck there even after I've left.' I promised him. Now I'm taking it back to the zoo. Its name is Hannibal. I'm building the zoo too, aren't I?"

"Yes, Hansi, yes, a beautiful zoo. But tell me, wouldn't you like to do me a favor? Pull the mother out of the toilet!"

Hansi shakes his head mysteriously.

"But how long should she be stuck there?"

"If the box of toys belonged to me, she'd stay there forever!" says little Hansi. Then he turns his crooked back to us. "I have to make the zoo. Hannibal wants to go home."

"Well then, we can't detain you, of course," says the old lady, who has now bent down over the toys.

"Come, Oliver, we'll wait next door for Dr. Florian." And

she walks toward the second door, again touching chairs and the edges of tables, and opens it. The room beyond must be Dr. Florian's study. A desk lamp is lit. All four walls are covered with bookshelves. A large globe stands by the window. I can see a lot of pictures painted by children, as well as many things that have been built by them. There are few deep armchairs.

"Take a seat," says the old lady.

We both sit down.

"Have no fear, Oliver. Don't think you've landed in a psychiatric institution instead of a school. Hansi is an exception. Most of the three hundred children we have here are mentally healthy. You will meet the sons and daughters of famous actors and writers, architects and maharajas, pilots, businessmen—and even a little Persian prince."

She toys with a book that she's carrying with her. "Doctor Florian is conducting an experiment in our institute—with the approval of all the parents, of course. From time to time we mix a few difficult and even very troublesome cases among the normal children and that way try to help the sick ones."

"And are you successful?"

"Almost always. But we don't take all the credit."

"Who does?"

"The others, the normal children. The healthy heal the sick," says Miss Hildebrand with a smile.

"And what about poor little Hansi? He mentioned that he had tried to take his life before the holidays?"

"That's right," says Miss Hildebrand quickly. "Through fear of his mother and Mr. Fahrenschild."

"Then there really is one?"

"Unfortunately yes. I have a few difficult children, but with Hansi it's really terrible. For more than a year I've been spending my time with him and there is no improvement. Would you believe that he's the cruelest child in the entire Institute?"

"That blond little cripple—" I interrupt myself.

The old lady nods.

"Yes, little Hansi. This morning he tortured a little cat to death. We heard the screaming. But by the time we found Hansi, the cat was already dead. That's why I let him play once again."

"Play? Do you mean he's not going to be punished?"

"Punishment will get you nowhere with him. Playing relieves his aggressions. You have seen the battlefield he created. Every human being is aggressive at times. There are a lot of perfectly normal children here who throw knives or axes or hoes into the beautiful old trees."

"And you do nothing about that?"

The little lady shakes her head. "No," she says, "because it's still better for trees to get killed than people."

At that the book she's been toying with falls out of her hand. She bends down and gropes around on the carpet, but doesn't see the book that's lying almost in front of her. Startled, I suddenly think: She's not only half-blind—she's completely blind!

Quickly I pick up the book and give it to her. She smiles.

"Thank you very much, Oliver. This awful electric light. I really can see quite excellently. But with electric light . . ." Her smile vanishes, and for a few seconds she sits there, lost in thought. Then she sits up very straight and speaks very rapidly. "Hansi has gone through terrible experiences. He was born in Frankfurt. His father left his mother in the lurch and just took off. Hansi was three at the time. The mother looks good—even today. First she was a belly dancer and then a streetwalker. Then she caught some protracted disease or other and couldn't work any more." Miss Hildebrand is talking quite matter-of-factly, and smiles quickly once more. "Naturally she needed help. I know her well. She is asocial and a bit feebleminded. In any case, during the time she was badly off, the thought occurred to her to bind Hansi's hands and feet and to leave him lying like that for three hours in the morning and three hours in the afternoon. Sometimes even longer."

"But why, for heaven's sake?"

"Well, to make a cripple of little Hansi, of course. And she really succeeded. His spine is never going to be straight again. And he will never again be able to hold his head upright."

"It makes me feel sick," I say, "yet I still don't understand."

"But it's so simple, Oliver. His mother wanted to send him out to beg. And once he was so nicely crippled, she did it too. He always stood in front of the best restaurants and night clubs. She dressed him in the oldest rags. During that time he brought in a lot of money. Everyone finds a crippled child such a touching sight, isn't that so?"

"Didn't anyone in their house see any of this going on?"

"Much too late, unfortunately. The mother sent the boy out begging only at night—and secretly at that—and everyone took the curvature of the spine to be a natural affliction. Hansi never betrayed her. You see, his mother had warned him that she would beat him to death if he ever opened his mouth just once. Only when he was five the Children's Welfare Department intervened. Somebody had informed them."

"And?"

"She went to court, because in spite of his fear, Hansi had told the truth to a case worker. But during the trial he denied everything again. So there was no proof against the mother. She only had to pay a fine for sending her son begging."

"And nothing else?"

"Hansi went into an institution. In fact he went to many institutions. His mother got a job as a maid with a certain Mr. Fahrenschild. She was healthy again. And still pretty, as I said before. Three years ago the two of them got married. Now the mother wanted to have Hansi back. But it isn't that easy." Her voice is low. She bends toward me, and whispers as if nobody was allowed to hear: "You won't tell on me to the chief?"

"Tell?"

"About what happened with the book?"

"Definitely not."

"He wants to retire me. My eyes are getting worse, he says. And he doesn't believe it, about the electric light, I mean. But I've spent all my life with children."

Through her thick glasses the old lady looks out into space. I feel so sorry for her, and ask quickly:

"And then what happened to Hansi?"

She smiles, as if relieved, and answers: "To Hansi? Oh, yes. This Mr. Fahrenschild is wealthy. He's in the construction business. Mr. Fahrenschild wanted the boy to go to a boarding school, a good school. He was willing to pay whatever it cost. Well, that wasn't so easy. No boarding school wanted to accept Hansi. You know the sort of thing—bedwetter, bad scholar, and so on. Very disturbed. So then *we* took him in. And everything went well up until the Christmas holidays. There we made a mistake."

"What was it?"

"Mr. Fahrenschild came up himself and pleaded with us so fervently to be allowed to take Hansi that we finally gave in. We were deceived, the chief and I. Mr. Fahrenschild made a good impression . . ." Again she looks as if she were lost, and says to herself: "I always thought I could tell a man's character by his face."

"Can't one do that?"

"Well, I can't. Someone might impress me as being an angel yet turn out to be a devil. You haven't seen the welts."

"Welts?"

"They cover Hansi's entire body. I let the boy play with the toy box—and gradually everything came out, everything that had happened during the Christmas holidays. This Mr. Fahrenschild had treated Hansi horribly. That's why the little one had tried to commit suicide before the summer vacation. That's why we kept him here. But it's difficult, very difficult with him. And now he's reaching puberty . . ." So much friendliness, so much warmth radiates from Miss Hildebrand. I think: And nobody knows of this almost blind lady, who is up here in the forests of the Taunus and who has spent all her life with children. Nobody bestows a medal on her as they do to the great butchers of mankind—no fanfares blare for her, there is no cross of distinction for her: nothing.

I ask: "This toy box—do you use it with all the difficult children?"

"Yes, Oliver. This is a so-called Szeno Test. Modern child therapy is a play therapy. We watch: How does the child play? We reason: Why does it do that now? We listen: What ideas is it expressing? We observe with which object and person the child identifies. When evaluating the test it is not the point to establish the IQ, character traits, or talents. We want to gain insight into the nature and depths of the conflict the child is suffering from. You have seen yourself what's going on inside Hansi: The crocodile killed Mr. Fahrenschild. And all the other people too. It stuck the mother in the toilet. Because of bedwetting and nailbiting! And because she is *really* mean. The only person the crocodile didn't do anything to was Hansi himself—and Hansi is the tall, beautiful prince, the nicest doll of all. It was even willing to allow itself to be tethered to a rope to be led back to the zoo."

The lady nods. "Yes. But also his hope, his longing, his wish to be grown up one day, to become strong and mighty and to wreak revenge on everyone, on the whole world!"

I say, "He *will* be grown up someday. Certainly not strong and mighty. But at least adult. And then what's going to happen?"

"Yes," says Miss Hildebrand, moving her glasses. "What's going to happen then? Perhaps our Hansi's going to be a criminal, a murderer."

"What do you believe?"

"I believe he's going to become a good human being," she says quietly.

"In spite of the incident with the cat today? In spite of everything?"

"In spite of everything. If I couldn't believe that, always and with all my children, then I couldn't practice my profession. Then I would only have failures. But I've been practicing my profession now for more than forty years, Oliver, and I've had successes—many, many successes!"

"More successes than failures?"

"Oh yes," she says, and now she smiles again. "But they were never *my* successes, for other people have always helped me. We have to help each other. 'No man is an island.' "

"A what?"

"Turn around. Behind you on the wall there's a quotation. Read it."

I get up, and this is what I read:

*No man is an island, entire of itself; every man is a piece of the continent, a part of the main; if a clod be washed away by the sea, Europe is the less, as well as if a promontory were, as well as if a manor of thy friends or of thine own were; any man's death diminishes me, because I am involved in mankind; and therefore never send to know for whom the bell tolls; it tolls for thee.*

—JOHN DONNE 1573–1631

"For whom the bell tolls . . ."

"Yes," says the old lady, "that's where Hemingway got it from." For a time we are both silent, then she asks me: "Would you help me? I mean, with little Hansi. Would you look after him a little?"

I don't answer.

"So that he won't become a criminal, a murderer. If I were to ask you . . ."

The little cripple tortured a cat to death. What about help? What about care? I seem to have landed in rather a peculiar school.

"You probably have your own troubles too, Oliver. And undoubtedly you will find friends here who will help you. I would be so glad if . . ."

The telephone rings.

The old lady rises and gropes her way to the desk, and I feel so sorry for her that I take the receiver and hold it out to her.

"O thank you, how attentive of you." She answers the phone. As she does so her face registers surprise. "Yes, he happens to be here. You can put the call through here." She holds the receiver out to me.

"For me?"

"The telephonist has been trying to contact you in the Quellenhof."

Who could be calling me here? Perhaps it's my mother. But even before I put the receiver up to my ear I know that it's not my mother. For I can smell the lily of the valley, I can see those huge black eyes, I can hear "Brandenburg Gate."

And there it is, the smoky, throaty voice, low and hurried. "Mr. Mansfeld?"

"Yes."

"Do you know who this is?"

"Yes."

"I must see you."

"Where are you?"

"In the Hotel Ambassador. At the entrance to Friedheim. Could you come down?"

Well, this is a fine start. Maybe I'll get kicked out of here before I've even seen my room.

"Something has happened."

"I'll come at once," I say quickly. Otherwise she might even tell me on the telephone what happened. I don't know how it happens, but I just have to meet one woman and I'm in trouble.

"Think up some excuse."

"Okay," I say, having already thought up a good lie. "Okay, Madame, I'll hurry, so that you can start for home." I replace the receiver before she can reply. "I'm sorry," I say to Miss Hildebrand, "but I have to leave for a short while. A friend of my mother's is dining at the Hotel Ambassador, before leaving for Frankfurt, and would like to see me for a few minutes."

"That's understandable," says the old lady, smiling gently. "I'll explain to you the quickest way to the A. The children call the hotel the A. By the way, it is strictly forbidden to stay at the A—even for the older ones."

"The lady is about to leave. I won't be staying at the hotel."

"No, of course not, Oliver." That smile. She doesn't believe one word. Why should she? I wouldn't believe one word either if I were in her place. What could have happened?

"Please apologize to Professor Florian for me, if he should come meanwhile."

"Of course." And then she explains which road to take. As I'm leaving, I have to pass through the room where the little cripple is playing. He has built a zoo and destroyed it just as he destroyed the living room. Animals are lying around, and fences are broken.

"Hannibal," he says, grinning.

"Hannibal what?"

"He did it. Everything. Opened cages. Bit the animals to death." The crocodile sits in the middle of the table. The beautiful prince is riding on its back.

"But I, I can do with him whatever I want, Hannibal said. He loves me!"

"Well, that's nice," I say.

It's funny, but everybody wants somebody to love him. Even if it's a crocodile. Hansi, Verena. You and I. And Müller's cow. And Müller's donkey too.

## [ 13 ]

The A is a blast! Do you know the Carlton in Nice? Well, it's something like that.

Three parking lots. Golf course. Tennis courts. Water fountains with colored lights. Mercedes, Mercedes, Mercedes. BMW. Another Mercedes. You can see nothing else here. The uniformed doorman opens the glass doors for beautiful ladies in evening dresses and for distinguished gentlemen in tuxedos. Band music wafts toward me as I drive along the front of the huge building. So this is where the cream of Frankfurt society meets, the nobles who own houses up here. And this is probably a first-class place for managers and directors in need of recuperation. They probably keep their girl friends here. So convenient. Only half an hour away from Frankfurt. And so big. You can always tell your wife it's a convention you're attending. There must be some kind of convention always going on here.

And look at those mink capes! Man, all that mink, mink, mink! Each one more beautiful than the last.

When I think that twenty-three years ago we started the most terrible war in history, that fifteen years ago we lost it. . . . Now a bellhop is bringing a cellophane box. Inside it are well over thirty orchids. The thing can hardly get through the door. It's just as well we lost it. The war, I mean. Who knows whether or not we would have butter for our bread otherwise?

But where is Verena Lord?

It's clear to me that she wouldn't stand smack in front of the entrance door. I guess there are a few people here who know her and Mr. Banker. But I've passed the entrance, I've circled the whole hotel. The road is dark again.

What now, lady?

Just a moment!

A little girl is standing there by the side of the road, and beside her there's a huge, light-brown boxer with its tongue hanging out. The little girl is waving. Cute little thing. Blond hair, braids, blue eyes. Blue cardigan, white blouse. Blue-and-white stockings. White shoes.

I stop the car and roll down the window. The little one looks at me seriously and asks:

"Are you Uncle Mansfeld?"

"Yes, Evelyn," I say.

"How do you know my name?"

"Well, that wasn't really very difficult, was it? A little bird told me. Climb in."

"May Assad climb in too? This is my dog, you know."

"Come in, Assad," I say. I flip over the right seat and Assad climbs in behind me, panting hard.

"You too," I say to Evelyn, putting back the seat. She gets in. I drive on. Evelyn has a bar of chocolate in her hand. "Would you like some?"

"No, thank you. You eat it. I'm sure you like chocolate a lot."

"O, yes," she says, biting off a piece. "But I like marzipan. I like marzipan most of all."

"I can understand that," I say. (I feel sick when I just hear that word.)

"Good evening, Uncle Mansfeld," she says sweetly, offering her hand. "When I'm sitting down I can't curtsy. I always do."

"Me too," I say. She laughs and laughs.

"Yes, I believe it now," she says, after almost choking on a piece of chocolate.

"What?"

"What Mommy said."

"And what did Mommy say?"

"That I was to take you to her because you're a good uncle and that you will help us."

"Help you?"

"Yes," she says quietly. "You know. Because of Daddy.. That's why nobody must know you are meeting her."

"No. No one, Evelyn."

"And most of all Daddy. He isn't actually my real daddy, you know."

"Yes, I know all about it."

"You're great, Uncle Mansfeld. I like you."

"I like you too, Evelyn."

That happens to be true. I like all children. Many of my friends have cracked silly jokes about it. But it's true: I know nothing nicer than little children.

"Well now, where is Mommy?"

"Straight ahead there's a road that goes to the right. We have to drive up there. Mommy's waiting for us there. She couldn't wait here. Because of the people, you know."

"Yes."

"And I had to accompany her. Because of the gardener. And the servant. So that they don't tell Daddy that Mommy has gone away again by herself. We told them we were taking another stroll."

"You have no secrets from each other, do you?"

"No. We tell each other everything. She only has me, anyway," says the little one. "There she is."

I have been driving up a rather narrow path on both sides of which stand some old trees. Further up I can see some ancient ruins. What is that? A lookout tower?

There she is, standing halfway behind a tree. She is still wearing the scarf, but no longer the dark glasses. She has on a dark blue raincoat with upturned collar, with the belt pulled tight. Her face is very pale. Or is that just caused by the headlights? I draw up beside her. Evelyn gets out at once.

"Assad!"

The boxer jumps out after her.

"I'll leave you alone until you call me."

"All right, my love."

"But please, at least leave the small lights of the headlights on or else I'll be afraid. Come, Assad."

The boxer follows her as she skips up the path toward the old tower.

"What's up?" I ask.

"Oh, God," says Verena. "You didn't find it, then?"

"Find what?"

"My bracelet."

"You've lost your bracelet?"

She nods, pulls flashlight from the pocket of her raincoat and searches the floor of the Jaguar. I get out. I turn up the seats. I also have a flashlight. For at least five minutes we search the entire car. Nothing. I can hear all sorts of birds and other animals calling. There are many sounds in the forest. In front of us I can see little Evelyn and her dog as two tiny silhouettes. Evelyn is collecting stones and throwing them, and Assad picks them up and brings them back to her. Sometimes he barks as he plays the game.

Now we are sitting in the car beside each other. The doors are open and I can smell her perfume.

"Do you have a cigarette?" she asks so quietly that I can barely hear her. I give her one, take one myself, and we both smoke. I feel sick for a moment when it occurs to me that she thinks I stole the bracelet. But I feel better when she puts her hand on my shoulder and says hoarsely, "With me you only have a lot of trouble."

"Don't talk like that. I'm very sorry. I told you in the car that the lock was open. Do you remember?" She nods. "When you grabbed the wheel and I hit you I heard something clatter. I guess that's when it fell."

"But where is it now?"

"Maybe when you got out at the oak tree?"

"I searched everywhere."

"Perhaps somebody found it before you."

"Yes, perhaps," she says. "Have you been at school already?"

"I had to wait for the director. But I locked the car. No one could have . . ."

And now I remember!

"Dammit!"

"Dammit what?"

"The girl," I say. "That damned girl!"

## [ 14 ]

After I've told Verena everything, she sits quite still, smoking and looking ahead where, some distance away, her little girl is playing with the dog. Verena exhales the smoke through her nose and asks: "Do you believe the girl stole the bracelet?"

"Definitely. She ran away when I called to her."

"Switch on the radio."

"Why?"

"So that nobody can hear us."

"There's no one here. You mean so your daughter doesn't hear?"

"Yes."

"But she's on your side. She says there are no secrets between you."

"She doesn't like my husband. He doesn't like her. She believes she knows everything about me. She would let herself be killed rather than betray me. But naturally she doesn't know everything."

And I am thinking that there is so much to know, but I say nothing and turn on the radio.

"Do you have any inkling who the girl was?"

"Not the slightest."

"Then we don't have the slightest chance of retrieving the bracelet."

"Not neccessarily. I have to think. There must be a way. There's always a way. Please don't get upset. Just stay calm."

"There's no way. There's never a way," she says. "But I won't get upset. I'm very calm. Don't be afraid."

"Evelyn said something a short time ago which I didn't understand. Didn't your husband come home?"

"No. Only . . ."

"Only?"

"Only—he telephoned. He intends to do something. He's planning something."

"What is he planning?"

"I don't know."

"You mustn't be afraid."

"I'm not afraid. I have no fear." But her hand is shaking so much her cigarette drops.

"Oh, God," she says, "I wish I weren't so afraid."

I put my arm around her shoulder. She lets me—she even presses close to me and says in a choked voice: "You don't know the position I'm in, Mr. Mansfeld. You just can't imagine. This business with the bracelet is all I need."

"I'm driving back to the school. I'll notify them of the theft. Then they will have to search all the girls' rooms. Or I'll think of something. I'll definitely think of something else. I'll find the girl and I'll find the bracelet. No, please don't cry."

"I'm not crying," she says, but since her cheek is touching my cheek, her tears are wetting both our faces, and the little girl up ahead on the lonely path near the old tower still jumps and dances and throws stones.

"What did your husband say on the telephone exactly?"

"That he is not coming up tonight as intended, but that he's staying on in Frankfurt."

"And when is he coming?"

"Tomorrow night."

"Then we still have a whole day."

"If he doesn't come in an hour. If he isn't here already—"

"You really must stop crying."

"You don't know him. You don't know him! For quite some time now I've had the feeling that he distrusts Enrico . . ."

Enrico? O yes, the . . .

"And now the bracelet too. When he arrives and finds out that the bracelet's gone, he'll have one more reason. Lost? He'll never believe me! He's already said he thinks Enrico's a gigolo."

"Be quiet!"

"What?"

"I can't believe such a thing. Do *you* have to give money to have him make love to you?"

"Oh, what do you know about anything!"

"Nothing," I say; "naturally I know nothing."

The woman I'm holding in my arms as if she were my beloved says: "You are rich. You were always rich. Not I. Once I was so poor that I had no bread for Evelyn and me. Do you know what real need is?"

"I've heard tell of it."

"You know nothing. Nothing at all! The night I met my husband . . ."

Just at this moment Evelyn and the boxer come running down the path toward us. Verena straightens up and interrupts herself.

"What is it, sweetheart?"

The boxer barks.

"Quiet, Assad. Excuse me for interrupting, Mommy. But do you believe that Uncle Mansfeld can really help us?"

"If he can . . ."

"Will you be able to, Uncle Mansfeld?"

"Definitely, Evelyn, quite definitely."

"O good." She gives her mother a kiss. "Don't be angry. But I was so curious that I couldn't wait any longer. Now I'll stay away until you call me. Come, Assad!"

And again she and the dog run away. Verena and I sit there watching her.

"She is all I have," says Verena.

"Then you have quite a lot. What happened the evening you met your husband?"

Verena laughs. She sounds almost hysterical.

"That evening, dear Mr. Mansfeld, I had nine marks eighty pfennig—and thirty tablets of Veronal."

"Where did you get that stuff?"

"From a pharmacist. I made a pretense at love for a few weeks, slept with him, you know, always when he was on night duty."

"And then you stole the tablets?"

"Yes. So that I could kill myself."

"And Evelyn?"

"Evelyn too. Anyway, that evening I took those nine marks eighty and went out with her. It was intended to be our last meal. Afterward I was going to do it . . ."

"But you didn't do it."

"No. On the way home Evelyn almost ran into a car. *He* was behind the wheel." And suddenly she screams: "I'm not going back to poverty, to no bread, no light, no gas. Never again. Never again! I still have those thirty tablets. If he throws me out I'll do it!"

She is screaming so loudly that Evelyn is looking. And if somebody is walking below on the road he'll hear every word. I have to do it. It isn't an easy thing to do. I slap her face. Twice. Right. Left. She is breathing heavily. Her mouth is open. But she doesn't scream any more.

Above my rear mirror there's a small lamp which I switch on. Then I turn the mirror toward her and say: "Fix your face. Nobody must see you like this." Obeying me like a child, she pulls a compact and lipstick out of her raincoat and repairs the damage. As I watch her I'm thinking: nine marks eighty, nine marks eighty, thirty tablets of Veronal. How beautiful she is, how beautiful, how beautiful. I say: "You were poor then. But you weren't always poor."

"How do you know that?"

"I don't know it. I feel it. Your family must have been very rich once. Only someone who has known wealth and lost it for a time is so afraid to lose what he has gained through fear of becoming poor again."

She is silent.

"Won't you tell me where you're from?"

"No." She sounds angry, aggressive, and loud.

"Then don't. Now, are you going to be reasonable?"

She nods. I really believe she is going to be reasonable now, otherwise she wouldn't be making up her face.

"I'm going to drive back to school. You're going to go home. I'll tell Professor Florian that a bracelet belonging to my mother was stolen. I'll say she'd given it to me to take to a jeweler in Frankfurt. The girl—whoever it is—can't have gotten very far with it. All the children have to be in their houses at eight P.M. So there will have to be a search in all of the houses. I'll insist on it. Or I'll call in the police."

"Police!" She stares at me.

"It's my mother's bracelet. Don't forget that! So I have a very good reason for getting upset. If your husband doesn't come home until tomorrow night we'll have lots of time."

"And if he's bluffing? And if he comes earlier?"

"My God—surely this can't be the only piece of jewelry you own—can it?"

"No, he . . . he gave me a lot."

"There, you see! Maybe he won't even notice that you're not wearing that particular bracelet. And if he does notice, you can always say you've lent it to a girl friend. Surely you can think up a few lies by yourself. You weren't born yesterday, you know."

"You must have a nice opinion of me."

"I'll tell you what I think: you and I are as similar as a face and a mask, like a key and a lock. And that's why I have a good opinion of you—yes!"

She doesn't answer.

"Whereabouts is your villa?"

"Directly beyond the old tower."

"I'm supposed to be living in the Quellenhof. Do you know it?"

"Yes."

"Can you see the house from yours?"

"From my bedroom window."

"Do you sleep alone?"

"Yes. My husband and I haven't . . . for ages."

Just once I'd like to meet a woman who doesn't say that. And I'm not even her lover. Surely it must be a trick, even with men. Yes, men are the same. Intimate relations with my wife? Not for years!

"You have a flashlight. I have one too. Tonight at exactly eleven o'clock you watch out of your window. If I signal once every five seconds, that means I haven't found out anything and things look bad. In that case we will meet here again tomorrow morning at eight and plan something else."

"But at eight you have to be in school."

"I don't have to do anything," I say. "You signal back once to let me know you've understood my signal. Now: if I signal twice quickly, one after the other, I already have the bracelet. Then too you'll come back here at eight A.M. and I'll give it to you. You mustn't leave the house this late at night—whether or not your husband is there. But at least you'll be able to sleep better."

"Never in all my life has anybody ever—"

"Okay, okay, it's all right. If I blink three times in succession, it means that I know who the girl is and where the bracelet is, but that I need more time. We've got to think of all the possibilities. In that case you flash back that you have understood. And then I'll signal the time when I hope to be able to give you the bracelet. So—eight times means eight o'clock, thirteen times means thirteen hundred hours and so on. Clear?"

She nods silently. Now her face is all right again. The light from the little lamp above the rear mirror is shining on both of us. She looks at me and her huge black eyes make me dizzy. I don't want to do it. I really want to behave properly, but it's her eyes, her wonderful eyes. I pull her toward me to kiss her. Then she takes my hand and presses it to her lips with a gesture which is as tender as it is refusing—and more beautiful than the most memorable kiss I have ever received.

"I'm sorry," I say quickly. "Don't lose your nerve. We'll make it. It would be ridiculous if we didn't make it. I've been through a few things like this."

"You are marvelous," she says.

"I'm a piece of dirt and nothing else. But you, I like you. I . . . I would do anything for you, anything."

"You're doing a lot for me already."

"But I'm demanding something in return."

"I noticed that."

"The attempt to kiss you, you mean? That was pure reflex action. Routine. I always do that. But when I find your bracelet I'll demand something."

"Demand what?"

"Thirty tablets of Veronal."

She doesn't answer.

"If you don't agree, we just won't do business."

"Mr. Mansfeld, you really have no idea the position I'm in, apart from the bracelet."

"I don't want to know that. I want the thirty tablets. Do I get them or not?"

She looks at me for a long time, until I start feeling dizzy again. Once more she pulls my hand to her lips and nods.

"Exactly at eleven," I say once again.

And she goes off, up to the old tower where her little daughter and her boxer Assad are playing. They start running toward her, and the mother and daughter both turn and wave to me. I wave back, but only once. Then I get back into the car, switch on the headlights, watch Verena, Evelyn, and the dog disappear into the dark forest behind the old observation tower, while I let the car roll back onto the road. Just before I reach the crossroads, I lift up to my face the hand she raised to her lips. It smells of Diorissimo, of woman, of make-up and powder. I close my eyes and touch my face with this hand while birds are calling and the animals of the forest are talking to one another and cars are whizzing by on the road in front of me. The scent of her perfume, her lips, her skin envelops my whole face. I open my eyes again, look at my hand, and clench it as if to retain the sweet scent a little longer. Then I remember that Milton (I believe his name was John—anyway, the great English poet, you know), that Milton had spent half his life in Italy. He loved the country so much. He called it his paradise. He became blind in his old age. Then some friends of his took him back to cold, foggy England, and he sat there in his house at night, beside the open fire, holding in his hand an old dried-up olive. The housekeeper told the neighbors that Milton was always smiling then. He had brought the olive from Italy. And once he told his housekeeper: "Whenever I hold this little fruit in my hand I am once again where I was so happy. Then I can once again see everything, Florence and Naples, Milan and Rome—my paradise. Now I am holding my paradise in my hand."

Now I'm holding my paradise in my hand. . . . Does everything lovely disappear so quickly? Certainly. With all people. Only the evil, the horror is lasting. The tenderness which drives tears to your eyes because even you need someone else, this smile, this touch of fingers on lips, this memory, all that passes, blows away, is soon forgotten.

I must make sure that I turn up with that bracelet. I might be able to use those thirty tablets of Veronal myself sometime.

I step on the gas. Back to the school. It's sickening to think how sentimental I can get sometimes. Thank God it's over. No. Why should I lie?

It is not over. I'm afraid it'll never be over. No, not with Verena. Not with this woman. Illogical, isn't it? Just now I wrote exactly the opposite of what I really feel.

## [ 16 ]

He shoots out from behind the signpost like a bullet, like a satyr, like a fugitive from a nightmare. I get a terrible shock, step on the brake and stall the engine. Bang! I am thrown across the wheel. When I straighten up he is standing in front of me, crippled, tiny, scary. A dwarf. A ghost. A nonghost. And there it is again, the malicious smile that distorts his thin lips.

"Did I scare you?" asks little Hansi.

"You can say that again."

"I was lying in wait for you."

"You *what*?"

In an ironically complaining tone of voice he says: "Everybody here takes me for an idiot. Naturally I was listening when you were on the telephone. I was also listening when Miss Hildebrand was talking about me. What did you tell this woman?"

"What woman?"

"Well, the one you just met. By the way, the chief came up. He told me to stop playing and to go to the Quellenhof. Well, what did you tell her?"

"Now look here, I've had about enough of you! Buzz off! I've got to go and see the chief."

"Everybody takes me for an idiot," he complains again. "Did you tell her you'll find her bracelet again?"

"What bracelet?"

"Let's cut it short," he says, grinning. "I lied to you."

"When?"

"Well, you asked me if I had seen a girl, one wearing a skirt. I said no. But I did see her. I heard a noise, opened the drapes, and there she was. And I saw too how she stole the bracelet—it glittered and sparkled."

I get very excited, grab his pitifully skinny arms, and pull him close to me.

"Ouch, let go of me! You're hurting me!"

"Then you did see her!"

"I told you yes."

"You know what her name is?"

"Sure."

"What is it?" Now he is silent.

"What's her name?" I ask as I shake him.

Suddenly I notice that his lips are twitching. I hope he's not going to start crying. He murmurs: "I'll tell you. But on one condition."

"Condition?"

"That you are going to be my brother," he says quickly.

"What kind of nonsense is that?"

"That is no nonsense." Now he suddenly becomes soft. "You see, none of the children have their parents here. Or they don't like them. The children are quite alone. They form their own families so that they won't feel so alone. They've been doing that for a long time, for many years. Noah is Wolfgang's brother. Walter is Kurt's brother. All of them have brothers or sisters. Or cousins. Not fathers or mothers. They don't exist. You see, they've had enough of fathers and mothers—like me." Now he talks eagerly and quickly and is holding onto my arm with his tiny hands. "You can confide in a brother or a sister. You can even cry when you're alone with a brother or sister like that. Everybody here has sisters and brothers. Only I haven't. I've begged all of them. Nobody likes me."

"Why not?" I ask, though I know why.

"Well, because I look so horrible. But I would so much like to have a brother. A bigger one. You're the tallest one here, and the oldest. The others would flip! Will you be my brother if I tell you who has the bracelet?"

If I answer no, this little cripple will probably warn the girl. And the jewelry would disappear before the search even begins. And of course it's not exactly advantageous to me to arrive at Professor Florian's with the police. It would be best to soft-pedal it. But if the little one is lying?

"Can you prove that she has the bracelet?"

"In five minutes."

"What?"

"I said in five minutes. If you will be my brother. Will you?"

What's five minutes. Give him the benefit of the doubt.

"How old are you really, Hansi?" I ask.

"Eleven," he grins.

"Yes," I say. "I'll be your brother."

He runs around the car and climbs into the seat next to me. "Take the road on the right. To the Alte Heimat. That's where the big girls live."

The forest is so crisscrossed with roads that it looks like a labyrinth. I feel as if I'm driving into a tunnel carved out of ancient trees. And again I hear the animals of the forest. What an evening. I wonder if the chief's angry already at having to wait for me for such a long time? Little Hansi keeps looking at me. It's making me terribly uneasy. Do you know that moist-eyed look children have? Full of trust, full of love? Good God, what am I getting myself into?

"I know this girl very well," says the cripple. "I even know how she looks naked. Most of the girls draw the drapes when they undress, but some leave them open. Then I watch them."

He whispers: "I came here when the chief sent me away. She was in her room and played with the bracelet."

"Does she have a room to herself?"

"Yes. No other girl wants to room with her. Every girl here hates her because she steals their boy friends. We call her the luxury whore because she dolls herself up like a film star. Costume jewelry and bead necklaces and medallions and jangling bracelets. Everybody here knows that she steals. And she hides it so well no one has ever found anything again. Perhaps she is still wearing the bracelet. Maybe we're in luck. Don't talk now. And leave your shoes here. One has to be careful not to make any noise. You'll have to take off your shoes. Stop here, or somebody will hear us."

So I park the car between two trees in the woods, cut the engine, and switch off the lights.

"That's disgusting, watching girls get undressed, and things like that. A nice boy doesn't do things like that," I say.

He says in all seriousness: "I'm not a nice boy. I'm not dumb enough to be good. I'm bad! You heard it a while ago. Walk behind me."

I follow him.

"This is the tree where I always take off my shoes."

On stockinged feet we walk through the woods toward a villa with its windows lit. The parking space in front of it is empty, since the parents have all left already.

I step on a dry twig. It snaps. Hansi turns around. "Watch it, man!"

"I'm sorry."

"I'm sorry! If I were as clumsy as you are, I would never have seen a bare breast."

He doesn't use the word *breast,* however. This eleven-year-old's going to be really something. But aren't we all? Suddenly I get excited. If what he says is true—if it is true. . . . Now we've reached the Old Homestead. It's a playfully built old house with bay windows and little towers and balconies and I think to myself how easy it would be to climb up to one of those balconies and wonder how many boys might have done that very thing. From the inside of the house I hear the voices of girls, laughter, running water, and at least ten record players. Although it's an awful racket, it's a good thing for us! Hansi has taken my hand and pulls me into a low hedge that runs behind the house. Windows with drapes. More windows with drapes. There, a window without a drape. The little cripple pulls himself up onto a sill. I'm tall enough to look through the window into the lighted room. A bed. A table. A chair. A cupboard. A washbasin in a corner. On the walls, pictures of film stars cut out of magazines. Brigitte Bardot. Tony Curtis. Burt Lancaster. O. W. Fischer. Elizabeth Taylor. All the walls are bedecked with these icky, candy-colored pictures. On the table is a record player. I can hear the record it's playing: "Love Is a Many-Splendored Thing." From the film. I have it too.

A girl is slowly circling around the room to the sound of the sad music. She's wearing a blue skirt, a petticoat under it, a white blouse, and flat shoes. The girl must be seventeen or eighteen. She has lion-colored hair, rather long, teased very high, and brushed back from a high forehead. At the nape of the neck it is caught in a black clip. Below the clip it cascades down over the girl's shoulders and back. She has her arms stretched out and—on her right wrist she's wearing the bracelet! The diamonds and emeralds are sparkling in the light. The girl is looking at the piece of jewelry as if she were looking at her lover. She doesn't take her eyes off it. Suddenly she turns. I think she might have noticed us and duck down.

"It's nothing," whispers Hansi. "Somebody knocked."

True.

The luxury whore calls: "Just a moment, please, I'm just dressing." Hurrying over to her bed, she moves it away from the wall, kneels down and slowly, carefully pulls a brick out of the wall. I can see things glittering in the little hollow. The girl slips off Verena's bracelet, places it in the hollow, and pushes the brick back into its place. She moves the bed back, straightens herself, and goes to the door.

"Now we know," whispers Hansi.

We sneak away from the house back into the woods. Hansi aims exactly for the tree where we left our shoes. While he's putting them back on, the cripple says: "You'll have to wait until tomorrow."

"Do you think I'm crazy? I'm going back now!"

"Yes," says Hansi and laughs again. "And then what?"

"I'll get that bracelet."

"Now let me tell you something. If you go about it that way you'll never get the bracelet. The main door is locked now.

That means you have to ring. So the housekeeper opens the door. Do you know what she would do? She would either throw you out right away or she would tell you to wait while she phones the chief. Until he comes you'll never get into that house, never in your life. And during the time all that takes, the luxury whore had hidden the stuff so well that nobody will ever be able to find it."

"There's something in that."

"Tomorrow," says the little cripple, "tomorrow morning when everybody is in class you have to get the bracelet. Which class are you in?"

"The senior."

"Why, that's great. The luxury whore is too. All you have to say is that you feel sick."

"And then?"

"You race over here. The best time is just after twelve. In the mornings all the houses are open and empty. The children are in class. The housemothers are either in the village or at lunch. And just after twelve the cleaning women have gone too. You know now where her room is. So get over there and get the bracelet."

I think for a bit and the more I consider it, the more sense he makes.

"You're right."

"I'm always right," he says, walking through the woods beside me. "But here everyone believes I'm an idiot."

"I don't."

He gropes for my hand and I'm holding it tightly. Because he's my brother now, and man, has he done me a service!

"She's a real sharp one, isn't she?" he says.

"Yes. And if she gets rid of that bracelet—"

"Impossible. No one is allowed out any more tonight."

"What's her name?"

"Geraldine Reber."

We've reached my car.

"I thank you, Hansi," I say.

"Nonsense. I thank *you*," he says, giving me those moist,

little-boy eyes again. "I've always wanted a brother. Now I have one. You don't know what that means."

"Okay," I say. Okay. Now I have to get rid of him. I look at my watch. It's eight-thirty already. At eleven o'clock Verena is expecting a signal from me.

"This is the happiest day of my life," says Hansi. "Now I've got a brother as well as the best bed in our room. I've always had to sleep next to the door. In the draft. Now I have the bed below the window in the corner, next to the radiator. Isn't that great? I have to thank the OAS for that."

"Who?"

"You're not stupid, Oliver, are you? The OAS! The French terrorist organization that throws all the bombs around."

"What's that got to do with your bed?"

"Everything. You see, last year that nice bed belonged to Jules. Jules Renard was his name."

"Was?"

"The chief got a letter from Jules' father today. Apparently Jules had been playing in his room in Paris. A car full of OAS people was driving down their street. The window in Jules' room was open. They threw in a plastic bomb. He died instantaneously. So now I'm getting his bed. Isn't that a stroke of luck? Just think. They might have thrown the bomb somewhere else. Then I would still be sleeping by the door in the draft."

He pressed my hand.

"I'd better be off now or I'll be in trouble with the pedagogue. By the way, he's new here. But you must admit, this is an awful lot of luck for one day."

"Yes," I say. "You really have to be congratulated, Hansi."

## [ 17 ]

Do you know James Stewart, the American movie actor? Well, that's how the chief looks. Taller than average, with limbs longer than average, short graying hair, uncertain gangling movements. And because he's so tall he's always slightly stooped forward.

How old? I would say forty-five at the most. Definitely not older than that.

He always speaks in a friendly way and in a low voice which he never raises. He is calmness personified. Wearing a faultless gray flannel suit, he is sitting behind an expansive desk, with his fingertips together. He looks at me in silence for quite a while. He has gray, scholarly eyes. I'm sitting in front of him, lower than he is, in a deep armchair. I'm returning his look. He'll have to start talking sometime. He does. He asks me: "Do you smoke?"

We light up. He talks, always low, always quietly: "It's very simple with you, Oliver. You're twenty-one. You've been kept back three times. You were bounced out of five boarding schools. I've been reading your report. Always in trouble with girls. I know that no other boarding school will accept you. So don't look on our school as a bus stop. This is the end of the line. After us there's nothing."

I'm silent because suddenly I don't feel at all well. Actually I had intended to get kicked out of here too—because of my father. But now I have met Verena.

Smiling, the chief says: "In any case I don't think I'm going to have any difficulties with you."

"But I am difficult, Doctor. It says so in the reports."

He smiles. "I like the difficult ones especially well. You know why? A normal boy is quite boring. But when I have a difficult one I always think to myself: there must be something behind this."

Man, is he crafty.

"We use different methods here."

"Yes, I've noticed that already."

"How?"

"I've seen the toy box you use for testing. Miss Hildebrand explained it all to me."

His face becomes sad and he touches his forehead with his

hand. "Miss Hildebrand," he says, lost in thought, "yes, there is a really marvelous person. My oldest colleague. Only her eyes . . . her eyesight is very poor. Didn't you notice that?"

"That her eyesight is poor? No, not really. I didn't really notice, Doctor."

"Oliver," he sighs, "that was a very kind lie. But I don't like even nice lies. That's why I'm not going to ask you what you were doing at the A and why you came to me so late. Because you would lie to me. I only ask very rarely. But don't run away with the idea that you have somebody who will put up with anything. Certain things are the same here as in other boarding schools. If somebody becomes intolerable he gets kicked out. Understand?"

"Yes, Doctor."

"That goes for you too. Clear?"

"Yes."

"My boarding school is expensive. With the few exceptions who are on scholarships, only children of rich parents come to me." Now he becomes a little ironic: "The elite of the international world."

"Like me, for instance?" I say, just as ironically. "My father hardly belongs to the international world."

"That's not the point. My job is to educate you, not your parents. Someday you and the others here will be taking over your father's factories and dockyards and banks and whatever else. You will be on top then. And then? How much disaster are you going to cause, you chosen ones, rich ones, snobs? That's my responsibility."

"What is?"

"That you won't cause any disasters. Or at least not too many. All of us here, Miss Hildebrand, all the teachers, pedagogues, and I, are trying to straighten you all out to prevent the worst from happening. It's because your parents have money —most of them have anyway—that you will be held up as an example or a *model* for many, many people. That's why I throw out anyone who doesn't do well. Do you understand that?"

"Yes, Doctor."

"Tell me why."

"Because you don't want to be guilty of having produced some pretty bad examples in about ten or twenty years' time."

He nods and smiles and presses his fingertips together.

"And do you know too why I became a teacher?"

"Well, because of that."

"No."

"Well?"

"Now listen. I was once taught by a teacher who was an idiot."

Man, is he ever clever. First the lecture, then the anecdote. So that I won't think he's just a piece of shit. No, but really, I like the man. I wonder if he likes me? To test him I change my tone.

"An idiot? I didn't know there were any of those among teachers."

"Of course. Listen. At nine years of age I was a complete nit-wit at orthography. And because my teacher was an idiot he put me across his knee and whacked my backside. Every day, Oliver, every day. It was like the 'Amen' in a prayer. The others at least had a breather, but not me. No, he whacked me every day."

"Poor Dr. Florian."

"Hold back your sympathy and listen. There'll soon be tears running down your cheeks. The thrashing in school wasn't the half of it. At home, when my father looked at my books, it started all over again. My father was very quick-tempered because he suffered from high blood pressure."

"I know all about it," I say and think to myself: Never have I felt so much at home with somebody so quickly. "My old man too. But he—well, you know yourself what's the matter with him, Doctor."

He nods.

"One can't help wondering," I say—and I'm being honest now, not fresh—"that after all that you became such a responsible man."

"I had to pull myself together. It was a terrible struggle," he says, " and besides, you don't know my true character." He hits his chest. "In there, it's terrible, as Schiller remarked."

"Down there, Schiller said."

"Wherever you will—have your choice," he says.

If I were a girl I'd fall in love with the chief. The man is charming. Is he married? I don't see a ring. I'm telling you, this fellow could have any girl he wants. That's the way I'd like to be. Quiet yet strong at the same time. Wise yet merry. But that's not likely to happen. "Now listen," says the chief. "My father, an insignificant civil servant, didn't take out his anger only on me. He also thrashed my two brothers and insulted my mother. Let me tell you, when I was nine there were stormclouds above the house of Florian." The way he smiles and talks and does gymnastic exercises with his fingers, I have to think: I wonder if he's very unhappy? Because I can feel that he is unhappy. Very clearly. Very sharply. More than sharply. I sometimes know what others are thinking and feeling—and I'm always right. What's troubling the chief?

He continues: "My mother was in despair. Then we got a new teacher. He was different from the first one. He took me aside and said: 'I know all about your troubles, with orthography and at home, I mean. I'm not going to correct the mistakes in your work at all. You are a hopeless case anyway. Just go ahead and write.' "

"No, really?"

"Yes, really. Do you know what the result was?"

"Well, presumably peace and harmony returned to your cosy home."

"That did too. But because he said I was a hopeless case, my fighting spirit was roused. His remark made me furious. Nobody likes to be looked on as a fool, right? So I pulled myself together. What should I tell you? In three months' time I was writing faultlessly. And do you know what I made up my mind to do then?"

"To become a teacher."

"Now you know it. I wanted to be a teacher like this one was.

Seelman was his name. We always called him The Soul. I wanted to have my own school and my own methods. And I didn't want to take only rich children, but also poor ones, because my father was himself a poor man and had never been to high school. Why are you looking at me that way?"

"Oh, for no particular reason."

"Go on, tell me."

So I tell him. I believe I can tell this man anything. "Of course that's a splendid idea to give scholarships to the gifted poor. There's just one drawback to that, Doctor."

"What's that?"

"You say: 'I don't want only rich children in my school, but also gifted poor ones.' "

"Well, yes."

"There will never be any justice that way."

"Why not?"

"Justice—or let's call it balance—could only exist if you also took in nongifted children. Because the way things are, the gifted poor who are getting the scholarships have to excel in intelligence, diligence, and good marks, right? Where does that lead to? To sycophancy and intrigue. To meanness. You want to do good things for the poor, Doctor, but at what price? Really, I've thought about that often. It's the same as everywhere else where gifted minorities have to accomplish twice as much."

He smiles again, says nothing for a while, then answers quietly: "You are right, Oliver. But unfortunately the world is not set up the way we want it to be. What should I do? Give scholarships to poverty-stricken idiots? I can't afford to do that. I would go bankrupt. And would that help the gifted ones?"

"You're right," I say.

"We must talk more often," he says. "Would you like to visit me sometimes?"

"Very much, Doctor."

Dear God, if only my father had spoken to me like that just once!

"And because one can only do a job with sixty per cent or at the most seventy per cent efficiency, I also took on all those difficulties."

"As an alibi for one's self, so to speak."

"Yes, as an alibi," he says suddenly, getting up. "That'll be all for the moment, Oliver. Oh yes, one more thing: of course you have to remove your car. There's a garage in Friedheim. You can take it there. Up here no student is allowed to keep a car. So of course you can't have one either. That's quite clear, isn't it? I'm sure you'll understand that, since you've done so much thinking about balance and justice."

What could I say to that?

My first reaction is to be insolent.

But what do I say?

"Yes, Doctor, tomorrow I'll take the car away."

"Good. Your luggage is already at the Quellenhof. You can drive down now."

"I'll be staying in the Quellenhof?"

"Didn't I write to your father?"

"Yes, but . . ."

"But what?"

"But a short time ago I met Hansi. He also lives at the Quellenhof. That's the house for *little* boys, isn't it?"

"Yes," he says. "And I'm putting you in there for that very reason. You see, we've arranged for a few of the older ones to live in the houses set aside for the younger children. They can assist the pedagogues and help to take care of the little ones. We are very conscientious in our selection of the older ones, naturally. This time we selected you."

"Without knowing me?"

"After I heard you were kicked out of five schools, my choice was made."

"Doctor," I say, "you are the wisest man I know."

"Passable," he answers. "It's nice of you to say so. But what do you mean?"

"Why it's as clear as day. While entrusting me with looking after the little ones, you are also obligating me."

"Obligating?" he asks innocently.

"To behave myself properly . . . to be an example and . . . and . . . well, you know exactly what I mean."

"Oliver," he says, "I must return your compliment. You are the wisest boy I have ever met."

"But difficult."

"I like that especially; you know that."

"Just you wait," I say. "We'll see if you'll really like it."

"You have one weakness. Everybody has one. Me too. So does Miss Hildebrand. I wouldn't like to have people around me who have no weaknesses. People without weaknesses are inhuman people. You tell me what your weakness is."

"Girls."

"Girls, yes," murmurs this scary teacher. "And in your case they will soon be women. Do you drink?"

"Just a little."

"Now drive to the Quellenhof. See your pedagogue. His name is Herterich. He's new here, like you. Your room is on the second floor. There are two more older boys there whose names are Wolfgang Hartung and Noah Goldmund. They are good, old friends. The Yanks hanged Wolfgang's father in 1947. As a war criminal. Apparently he'd let off steam in Poland."

"And Noah?"

"Noah is a Jew. When the Nazis rounded up his parents, friends of the family took him in and hid him. He was a year old then. He doesn't remember his parents at all. Nor does Wolfgang. He was three when they hanged his father. The mother had committed suicide before then. Relatives are paying both boys' tuition. Noah's relatives are living in London."

"And these two are friends?"

"The best you can imagine. It's quite natural, really, Oliver."

"It is?"

"Just think! Wolfgang's father was an important man among

the Nazis. In history lessons his name is always mentioned. We have a very radical history teacher who spent not less than three years in a concentration camp."

"Must be pleasant for Wolfgang," I say.

"Exactly. Nobody wanted to have anything to do with him when they found out what his father had done. Only Noah. Noah said: 'It's not his fault that he had this father.' "

That's a sentence I'll have to remember. How can a boy help it? For example, what fault is it of mine . . . no—I must not think about it.

"And then Noah said to Wolfgang: 'Your parents are dead and my parents are dead and we both can't help that. Do you want to be my brother?' You see, here we . . ."

"I know how it is. I already have one too."

"Who is it?"

"Little Hansi. He asked me. A while back."

"That's nice," says the lanky chief, rubbing his hands. "That makes me very happy, Oliver. Really, that makes me happy."

## [ 18 ]

"No, he is not married," says Miss Hildebrand. She's sitting beside me in the car. I'm taking her home. She asked me when I left the chief. I met her in the school hall. ("It would be very nice of you, Oliver, I can't see quite as well at night.") We are driving down to Friedheim. I hear the old lady has a room there. A very comfortable room with nice people, an innkeeper and his wife. Above the bar. "You know," says Miss Hildebrand while we are driving through the dark forest, "he had been in the war from the beginning, the poor man. And right at the end it got him."

"He was wounded?"

"Yes, very badly. He . . . can never have children."

I'm silent.

"Many of the students know about it. I don't know how. Nobody has ever made a nasty remark or a silly joke. All the children love the chief."

"I can imagine."

"But do you know why? Not because he is free and easy and talks the way they do. No! They say he is always fair and just. Children have a very good feeling for that. Later, when they grow up, it gets lost, unfortunately. But nothing impresses children as much as justice."

And again there are many noises in the woods, together with the ancient trees, bizarre shadows, a tiny fawn standing frozen by the roadside, and a rabbit that runs ahead of the car until I switch off the headlights for a moment. It takes about ten minutes to get to Friedheim. During this time Miss Hildebrand tells me about the children I will be getting to know: Indians, Japanese, Americans, English, Swedes, Poles, Germans, the tall Noah and the tiny Chichita from Brazil.

I read a book once called *Hotel People,* and as I listen to Miss Hildebrand I feel as if I've landed in some Grand Hotel, an international hotel in which children are the guests.

Miss Hildebrand asks me to stop the car in front of a well-lit inn. On an old plaque above the entrance appears the word *Rübezahl.* Because it is Sunday, there is still a lot of activity, and from inside I hear laughter, men's voices, and a music box.

"Doesn't it bother you?" I ask.

"Well, you know, Oliver, of course I can hear it. But it is so difficult to get a room around here. I don't mind the noise. I would sleep in a grove or in a garbage dump as long as I'm allowed to stay with my children. He didn't say anything, did he? I mean, about my eyes?"

Of course I say, "He didn't say a word." How happy we can make people by telling a lie! I help her out of the Jaguar, and the old lady beams at me.

"That's nice. I knew it. He would never do it . . ."

"What wouldn't he do?"

"Send me away because of my eyes. The chief is the best person in the world. I'll tell you something now, if you promise never to tell anyone. Word of honor?"

"Word of honor."

And to the accompaniment of the music from the Rübezahl—trara-ra-boom-di-a!

"Once we had to send away a child. The father came and got terribly excited. Finally he yelled at the chief: 'What do you know about children? How can you sit in judgement when you don't have one yourself?' "

"And?"

" '*I* have no children? I have and have had and will have hundreds and hundreds of children.' He was somebody important from Düsseldorf, bloated and well-fed."

"I know the type."

"He calmed down," said Miss Hildebrand. "And when he had left, the chief said to me: 'Never get mad—just get surprised.' Good night, Oliver."

"I'll see you to the door."

"That won't be necessary," she says, taking two steps, stumbling, and almost falling down at the curb. I hurry up to her and lead her tenderly to the old entrance next to the inn's new entrance.

"That was kind of you," she says. "As I mentioned before, this electric light . . ." And she looks at me through the thick lenses of her glasses, imploring me to believe that she can see all right.

"Sure," I say. "The lighting is terrible. I can hardly see my hands in front of my eyes."

"And now, good night, Oliver."

Two drunken farmers are coming out of the bar. They are singing the song that's coming from the music box: "What are you doing with your knee dear Hans, while you're dancing . . ."

Everything in Friedheim is neat and trim. The main street even has neon lights. There's a traffic light up ahead. This is surely a very pretty little old town with a lot of decent people who go to church on Sunday morning, who laugh at Saturday-night TV shows if they're funny enough, but who can also be serious and solemn when they're watching *Don Carlos* or *The Death of Wallenstein.* Dear people, good people. They believe what they read, what is told them. They vote. If it has to be, they go to war (that's usually about every twenty-five years in this part of the world). And those who survive play Beethoven's Ninth Symphony when they've lost the war. And the chief, who had his parts shot off the last time, tells himself he has hundreds of children because he can't have a single one.

Well, which one of us doesn't try to convince himself of something or other?

## [ 19 ]

9:30 P.M.

I'm standing in my room in the Quellenhof unpacking my stuff and hanging it in the closets. (I've already said that a friend sent my luggage ahead.) Noah Goldmund and Wolfgang Hartung are helping me unpack. Noah is a pale, delicate boy with black hair which is too long and black, almond-shaped eyes. Wolfgang is tall and strong with blond hair and blue eyes.

Both of them have a very comfortable room. Noah is interested in music, Wolfgang in books. Records are strewn all around. On a shelf are Wolfgang's books. Many foreign books are in first editions. Malraux, Orwell, Koestler, Poliakow: *The Third Reich and Its Servants* and *The Third Reich and Its Thinkers.* Ernst Schnabel: *Power Without Ethics.* Picard: *Hitler in Ourselves.* John Hersey: *The Wall.*

Noah has just found Tchaikovsky's Piano Concerto No. 1 and asks if he can play it.

"Sure," I say.

They have a record player. Noah switches it on. "It's funny about Tchaikovsky," Noah says. "My father loved him as much as Wolfgang's father did. My father listened to him the night before they came to get him. And Wolfgang's father wanted to hear it before they hanged him."

"Did the Yanks play the record for him?"

"No," says Wolfgang. "But not out of meanness. They just couldn't find the record in such a hurry. You have to take things into consideration. After all, it was 1947 and things were still pretty confused at that time. And they couldn't postpone a hanging just because of a record."

"Yes," I say, "we have to take such things into consideration."

Wolfgang is putting shirts into my closet.

A young man with a sparse blond mustache comes in and says: "Lights out in fifteen minutes."

"Yes, Mr. Herterich," says Noah, bowing deeply.

"But of course, Mr. Herterich," says Wolfgang. "May I introduce Oliver Mansfeld? Oliver, this is Mr. Herterich, our new pedagogue."

I shake the young man's hand (which is quite moist) and say that I'm glad to make his acquaintance. The door is left open and I can hear at least a dozen record players and radios. Only jazz. We are of course in the "house for little boys."

The teacher hands a few letters and newspapers to Noah and Wolfgang. "These came this afternoon."

Again both of them behave like clowns, bowing with exaggerated smiles and excessive politeness. "Many, many thanks, Mr. Herterich! It is extremely kind of you to take so much trouble and bring us the mail today, Mr. Herterich!"

The slightly built teacher turns quite red and backs out of the door.

"All right," he says, "all right. But as I said, lights out in fifteen minutes."

"But of course, Mr. Herterich."

"Certainly, Mr. Herterich."

The door closes behind the little teacher. I ask: "Why are you crawling to him like that, fellows?"

Wolfgang explains: "This Herterich is new. We don't know what he's like. We have to test him. We do this with everyone new. Listen to that piano! It's enough to drive you crazy! Who's playing?"

"Rubinstein," I say. "What do you mean by 'test him'?"

"Well, what we were doing just now. 'Yes, Mr. Herterich' and so on. Just too polite. But not so much so that he can say we're trying him out. That's the quickest way of finding out his character."

"How?"

"If a teacher is an idiot he tells us to stop it and says that we're mocking him. That way you can recognize the idiots among them."

The blond Wolfgang starts warming up to the subject: "We wind the idiot round our little finger. But the ones that enter into the spirit of it are more dangerous. Then you have to put them to the test again. I don't really know whether it's honesty or just plain trickery, but what I do know is that in about two or three weeks you've got a completely clear picture. Do you want your pants on a hanger or a stretcher?"

"Stretcher, please."

"As I said, you've got a clear picture then. Either a teacher is nice and doesn't snitch on us, or he gives way to weakness and informs on us. Then we change him."

"Inform about what?"

"Man, I've heard that you've been bounced out of five schools. Surely you must know what I mean."

"Oh," I say, "so *that's* what you mean!"

"Of course. Each one of us sneaks out at night or else has a visitor, right? So if the teacher's okay or if he toes the line we'll make friends with him. On the other hand, if he doesn't improve or if he squeals on us, we get back to work on him so thoroughly that he usually leaves of his own accord. You've done the same sort of thing where you've been, haven't you?"

"Yes. Only we didn't do it with all that politeness. The dumb ones lose their nerve more quickly."

Wolfgang has put away my clothes. Noah is reading.

"This Tchaikovsky's really great," says Wolfgang. "I'm glad we've got the record at last."

"You're both great," I say. "And I'm glad I'm rooming with you."

"Yes," says Noah, "this is all right."
"Go and take a piss," says Wolfgang.
This is how they hide their feelings.

[ 20 ]

The doors of the young boys' rooms are closed already, but jazz is still coming from them. The hallway I'm walking is deserted. When I reach the toilet door I find it's locked. Okay, I can wait. There's a note pinned to the door, written in red pencil:

*The children have no ability as well as being lazy and without knowledge. While I worry day and night about how I can improve this situation, yet I cannot introduce them to a decent visitor because of their clumsy behavior. They are unable to lift one morsel of food to their lips in a civilized way, and they live in their rooms like pigs.*

*Achim von Arnim to his wife in the year 1838.*

Suddenly I hear a boy's voice whispering on the other side of the door. It sounds like a little Italian with a dreadful accent. You know what I mean. Every word has an *a* tagged on to the end.

"Anda inna our towna, understanda, you just cannot get a house, yes? So many families, anda no houses." (Let me write what he says in decent English.) "Then finally they managed to finish a few more new houses, a kind of social housing project, yes, but before they could move in the families who had been waiting for years for the apartments, a whole pile of families up and took over the new building—mama, papa, and children."

"What do you mean, took over?" asks a different voice. This time it has an arrogant tone to it, with a clipped accent. I keep rattling the doorknob. On the other side I can hear the toilet being flushed. But the door stays locked and the conversation goes on.

"Well, they took over the apartments without permission. Us too. Then we erected barricades and nailed up the doors and the downstairs windows. The Carabinieri couldn't find any way to evict us the next day."

"Why didn't they just open fire?" asks a third, very thin voice with a peculiar accent.

"Because they were good people," says the second voice.

"Nonsense. All people are pigs," says a voice I recognize. It's little Hansi. So there are four of them sitting on the toilets talking. "They didn't shoot because it looks bad—shooting at poor people, I mean. I bet there were photographers there too, right?"

"Loads of photographers," says the Italian. "And they were just waiting for the Carabinieri to shoot or for a woman to collapse or something like that. They were all keyed up for that sort of thing."

"And what did the Carabinieri do?" asks the boy with the strange, thin voice.

"They surrounded the building and wouldn't let anybody in or out."

"Starving them, right?" says Hansi, my so-called brother.

"Yes, but understand, it wasn't that easy. Our parents pushed us through the basement windows and we ran off to get bread and sausage and cheese. The Carabinieri caught a few of us—but not all of us. When you're as little as that you can run damned quick."

"And then?"

"Then we went shopping."

"But did you have any money?"

"The men from the newsreels and TV gave us some."

"Sure," says Hansi, "the *good* people! So that they could get a few pretty pictures."

"A few of us also did a little bit of begging," the Italian says. "Me for instance. And then we went back and threw the food over the Carabinieri's heads to where our parents were."

"Didn't you miss quite often?" says the one with the haughty accent.

"A few times, yes, and that was just too bad. But most times we were right on target."

I start pushing the door again. And in answer that fresh kid Hansi calls out: "It's occupied. Can't you read?"

"I can read," I say, "but if it's going to be occupied much longer I'm going to bust in the door, you creep."

"Wait a minute," says Hansi. "I know that voice. Don't get mad, Oliver. We're just having a shithouse party and smoking a cigarette. Go downstairs. There's a john down there as well."

"You're supposed to be in bed. I'm supposed to be looking after you. I gave my promise to the chief."

"Just five minutes more, okay?" says Hansi. As he speaks he unlocks the door and I can see four boys inside. Two are sitting on the toilets and one on the floor. Hansi is standing. "This is my brother," he says proudly to the other boys, who are all smoking, just as he is. The small window is open. All four of them are in pajamas. Hansi points to a boy with black, curly hair with a gleam in his eyes.

"This is Giuseppe," he says. Then he points to a tiny Negro who is sitting on the toilet, and who is as black as night. "This is Ali." Then he points to a boy with a delicate bone structure and a sensitive face. "This is Rashid. He's a Persian prince."

"How do you do, Sir?" says the prince. He's the one with the funny accent.

"Okay, okay," I say.

"I have to speak English to them," explains Hansi. "None of them know any German as yet."

"Oh, really?" But irony is wasted on Hansi. The tiny Negro, who is wearing a broad gold necklace with a large golden cross hanging from it, looks at me furiously and says: "Now get the hell out of here and leave us alone!"

"You must be crazy," I say, intending to slap him.

"Dirty white . . . ," he says, and I take a step forward. Hansi moves in between us.

"He doesn't mean it like that!" he shouts. "In his native country everything is different from here. I'll explain it to you tomorrow. Why don't you go downstairs?"

"Well, all right," I say. "But you've got to be in bed in five minutes. Understand?"

"Word of honor," says Hansi. I close the door, which Hansi locks again immediately. Then I walk away for a few paces, stamping my feet loudly, but return on tiptoe to hear what they're talking about now.

Hansi's voice: "This is MY brother, understand? Whoever says anything against him is going to get a rap in the mouth from me."

The little Negro's voice now: "Okay, okay. Forget about him. Then what happened, Giuseppe?"

"For a few days everything went well. We children slept in the doorways and during day we bought bread, cheese, and sausage and threw it up to our parents. The people from the TV and newsreels took films of us when we ran away from the Carabinieri or when one of us was caught or when we threw the food."

"And?"

"By the third day they had enough pictures and left. And we didn't get any more money. Two days later our parents came out of their own accord, because they were hungry."

"I tell you—all people are pigs," declares Hansi.

The prince inquires politely: "And how did you get into the school, Giuseppe? It costs a lot of money here."

"I was lucky, understand, yes? I was the best in my class. My father drew nine months."

"Nine months? For the business with the house?"

Giuseppe's voice sounds ashamed: "Not only for that business. He was already on probation for something else. Now he's got to serve that sentence, too."

"For what?"

"He was involved in some strike or other."

"Your father is a Communist?" The Negro asks this question in a disgusted tone of voice.

"Yes, he's a Communist. But he's not my real father," answers Giuseppe quickly. "He's just my foster-father, understand? I'm adopted."

"What does that mean?" asks the prince in his thin voice.

"That's a child who doesn't have any parents and then strangers look after it," explains my "brother."

"But every child has to have parents," says the prince.

One of them flushes the toilet to make Mr. Herterich believe that someone is really busy in there, and above the noise I can make out Hansi's voice: "You're right. But some of them don't give a shit. The mothers abandon it somewhere. How did it happen in your case, Giuseppe?"

He says, in a voice full of shame: "Yes, I was abandoned too. In front of a church."

"An adopted child," says the Negro, nastily. "That's something really nice, isn't it?"

"Be quiet," says Giuseppe bravely. "Your parents *had* to have you, because you just arrived. But my parents had to *choose* me."

"Please continue," begs the little prince. "How come you're here?"

"The chief read the story in the papers and wrote to the director of my school saying that he would take the best one in for nothing—if he wants to come, that is. *Mama mia,* did I want to! You better believe it!"

"Do you feel as cold as I do?" asks the little prince.

"Yes, but that's the only thing to complain about. Apart from that, it's marvelous here. I have my own bed. My own bed! For the first time in my life!"

## [ 21 ]

By the time I return to my room from the lower floor, Noah and Wolfgang are already in bed. My Tchaikovsky record is still playing, though quietly, and only two bedside lamps are lit. While I was coming upstairs I heard the toilet party breaking up. It's slowly becoming silent in the house. I have found a balcony at the end of the hallway from which the old tower can be seen in the moonlight. Behind it a large white villa stands in front of the dark woods. Verena's house.

It's ten-thirty.

In half an hour I'll go to the balcony. I made sure I took the flashlight from the car when I arrived. Noah Goldmund is still reading. He is reading the *Times*. Wolfgang Hartung is reading *There Were Many Eichmanns*. Both are smoking.

"So how is it here?" I ask as I start to undress. "Are we allowed to smoke here or not?"

"We are. Not the little ones."

"I see. That's why they hold parties in the john."

"They all do that," says Noah, laughing. "The girls even wear gloves so that the governesses can't smell it on their hands. In all of the houses the little ones have loads of that spray stuff which eliminates the smell."

"They even throw eau de cologne around," says Wolfgang. "We have the best-smelling johns in the whole world."

"Afterwards they gargle with mouthwash," says Noah, as he scans the *Times*. "And they lock themselves in two at a time."

As I'm washing myself I tell them what I've been listening to.

"I eavesdropped on two girls once," says Noah. "In school. They were talking about *Gone with the Wind*. They must have just read it. One of them was crying terribly. You could hear her sobbing all the way down the hall: 'Do you really believe they're going to get one another? Do you really believe that?' The other one was consoling her: 'Sure! Quite definitely. You can bet on it. Otherwise it wouldn't have been such a success.'

" 'My God,' said the one who was crying, 'I hope so, I hope so.' " We all laugh.

"Listen," says the boy whose parents were gassed to the boy whose father had let them be gassed and was hanged for it. "There's the theme again. Isn't that great?"

"First-class," says Wolfgang.

And we listen until the record is finished.

"Play the flip side again, Oliver, and then hop into bed."

That's fine with me. I turn over the record. Both boys are lying in bed smiling at me.

"Why are you smiling?" I ask.

"Oh, it's nothing much, nothing bad," says Wolfgang.

"It's because you probably feel miserable tonight," says Noah.

"I'm not miserable."

"All the new ones are miserable on the first night."

"I'm not. I'm used to it, you know."

"Of course it's an advantage if you change schools a lot," says Noah.

"Man, is your father some character!" says Wolfgang.

"Stop it," I say, "or I'll get sick."

Then I turn to both of them and ask: "There was a little Negro in the john as well as a prince. I believe Rashid is his name."

Noah puts down the *Times* and grins. "His full name is Prince Rashid Dschemal Ed-Din Runi Bender Schahpur Isfahani." He sits up in bed and talks to me while I'm cleaning my teeth: "I interviewed him as soon as he arrived."

"How did he arrive?" asks Wolfgang.

"In a taxi. From the airport. From Cairo. He has relatives there."

"What kind of relatives?"

"He has an uncle in Cairo. The young prince's family is one of the noblest and oldest in the country. I looked it up in the encyclopedia. What he says is right."

"What does he say?"

"His oldest progenitor, Ismail, founded the dynasty of the Safawides which became the 'new Persia.' It happened in A.D 1501, gentlemen."

I'm putting on my pajamas now.

"He introduced the doctrine of Shiitism—whatever that is —into Islam, and left his son an enormous empire. He and his descendants conquered new lands, but—as it is expressed so nicely in the encyclopedia—they not only promoted trade and the arts, but they also created a residential town enormously rich in treasures which, in honor of the little pipsqueak from your W.C. party, was called Isfahan. In the centuries that followed, the ancient family was again and again noted in the most honorable, patriotic, and historical ways. End of news flash." Noah falls back onto his bed.

"And how did the little kid get here?" I ask.

"Rashid's father seems to be an opponent of the Shah's. I heard he attempted a revolt with a few thousand students and officers, which proved to be unsuccessful. You should never agitate—that's what I always say. The result? The Shah had the father locked up and Mama was put under house arrest. At the last moment friends took the kid out of the country. I imagine the family has money in Germany—that's why he's here. He's now waiting for the Shah to be overthrown. Otherwise he can't go home. You should have heard what he said about the Shah when he arrived here!"

Suddenly we hear a tremendous noise.

"What's that?" Wolfgang jumps up.

"They're probably messing about with the new pedagogue," says Noah.

"I promised the chief I would watch out for the little ones."

"We did too," says Noah. "But in the middle of the night?"

"I'm going to have a look."

"Okay," says Noah. I put on my slippers, look at my watch (10:45; I have another fifteen minutes), and slip into my robe. The yelling is coming from the main floor. I run down the stairs. A door is open. In the room beyond I see a pale, trembling Mr. Herterich, my grinning, screeching "brother" Hansi, the little Negro, and the little Rashid. The prince is holding a small carpet in his hands and is crying. The other two boys are dancing around him. Mr. Herterich is shouting in a shaky voice: "Silence! I want absolute silence!"

"You're not getting anywhere that way," I say, as I grab the cripple and start shaking him. Then I pull him close to me and say softly: "Down!" He becomes silent. His eyes glint menacingly. But he is quiet.

"That's the way to do it," I say to Mr. Herterich. I feel as if I've won a big battle. It would be better if I hadn't done anything.

"What's going on here?"

"Rashid wants to pray."

"Is that so funny?"

The Negro and Hansi look at each other.

"Laugh, if you think it's so funny, you idiot," I say, and I can feel how grateful Mr. Herterich is for not having to say that himself.

"Go ahead. Laugh if you've got the guts."

Of course they're not laughing now because I've raised my hand and am looking at them in such a way that even I wouldn't be brave enough to laugh. The little Negro says: "Rashid is a heathen. That's why we laughed."

"What's your name, anyway?"

"Well, you know. Ali. I'm the son of King Faharudiged-schimala the First."

"*Whose* son are you?"

The pedagogue says quietly to me: "He's the son of one of the most powerful men on the Kakao Coast. Where he comes from only the very, very rich people have white servants, white chauffeurs, and white tutors for their children. It is a sign of great wealth to be able to have white employees. Ali's father has. That's why the boy has a superiority complex."

"Now I know why those gentlemen down there need foreign aid," I say.

"What can we do? To Ali a white man is dirt. He was brought up like that. We'll have to straighten him out slowly."

"Slowly?" I ask. "It's going to happen very quickly." Then I ask the superior Negro: "And you, you aren't a heathen?"

"I'm a Christian," he says proudly.

"Aha. And Rashid is a heathen because his religion is different from yours?"

"There is only one religion. Mine."

"There are many religions. I'm surprised at you, Hansi. I thought you were smarter than that."

"Well, it was just funny because of the carpet," says my "brother," smiling softly.

The little prince with the olive skin, the delicate bone structure, and the black eyes which are large and sad and shaded by long, silky eyelashes, answers: "I asked where the East is. I have to say my evening *sure*. On the carpet. And I have to bow to the East."

"I have a watch with a compass," I say. We find out where the East is. It's exactly where the window is.

"Now," I say to Mr. Herterich, because after all he's the one who is supposed to be in charge, not I, "I've helped him enough. Now you do some talking."

This teacher isn't going to be with us for long. He must have grown up in very poor circumstances. Even now, after I've arranged everything so neatly for him, he speaks haltingly and insecurely: "Put your carpet down by the window, Rashid. And say your evening prayer."

"It is not a prayer, it is a *sure*," answers the little prince, and looks at me with a look full of gratitude.

"Say your *sure*," Mr. Herterich murmurs, embarrassed. I feel I've got to help him out once more. "Yes," I say, "say it, Rashid. Out loud. In your language. We'll all listen. Nobody is going to make a sound. And if Mr. Herterich or I ever hear—it doesn't matter when, in the morning or at night—that you're not left in peace, these two boys can look forward to something!"

The little prince arranges the carpet, kneels down, bows his head to the floor and talks in his native language. Later he translated for me what he had said that evening:

"Allah alone knows the secrets of heaven and earth, and the last hour, the raising of the dead, takes only one moment, or even less, because Allah is all-powerful. He brought us forth out of the bodies of our mothers and we knew nothing. He gave us ears, face, and an understanding heart so that we may be thankful. Do we not see how the birds fly in the air of the heavens without anyone else but Allah holding them there? In this too are signs for believing people. Allah it is who gave us houses for places of rest and the skins of animals for tents which we can take down on the day we leave and erect the day we settle again; and their wool and their fur and their hair for many purposes. He too gave us some things for shade, trees for instance, mountains for the sun and their caves and grottoes for refuge and clothes for protection from cold, and armor in war. His mercy is so great that we give ourselves to him. Allah is great, Allah be praised, Allah be thanked."

## [ 22 ]

That was it.

After that he straightens up, the little Rashid, rolls up his prayer mat and crawls into bed. Ali and Hansi do the same.

"Good night," says Mr. Herterich.

"Good night, gentlemen," I say. No one answers. Only Rashid smiles at me and I notice that Hansi too sees the smile and suddenly he smiles too—this terrible, skull-like smile. But I don't realize what I had done here in the space of five minutes. If only I could have kept my big mouth shut and let Mr. Herterich muddle through on his own, the poor little jerk.

Now he's walking out into the hallway with me and gives me his cold, sweaty hand as he stutters: "I thank you, Oliver . . . I . . . I. . . . You see, today is my first day . . . I feel quite sick with excitement. So many boys. . . . The little boys are all devils anyway. . . . I'm afraid, yes, I admit it, terribly afraid, and if you hadn't helped me just now—"

"You have to grow thick skin around your soul, Mr. Herterich. Otherwise the boys will wear you out."

"Thick skin around my soul," he murmurs sadly. "That's easily said . . ." He nods at me again and shuffles down to his room. I don't believe anybody can help this man.

10:50 P.M. It's time now!

Upstairs on the second-floor balcony it is cool, but not cold. The moon is behind the house, so the balcony is in the shadow. There's the old tower. And there is Verena's house.

11 P.M. exactly.

I fish the flashlight out of my robe and point it toward the distant villa. I flash it three times. Then I count to five. Then I flash three times again.

In an upper window of the large white house a light flashes quickly, but very, very brightly. Verena has understood me.

I have already decided. School in the morning. Then I'll fetch the bracelet. We are off between two and four and then have lessons until six. So I can meet Verena at two-thirty at the earliest. Better make it three. You never know what can happen.

I flash fifteen times.

Fifteen times it flashes back from the white villa. Just to make sure, I signal another fifteen times. Again comes her signal: Understood.

Now I can go to sleep.

Why don't I?

Why am I still standing on the balcony looking up toward the large, white house in the forest? Suddenly I become sad, sadder than I have ever been before in my life. And I have often been sad. I am longing for something I know is impossible to get.

In the house I can hear a few children crying. I know that sound very well. The children are crying in their sleep. They bite into their pillows and sigh, and many cry because they have nightmares. Some of them will be sitting by their windows staring out into the night. A boarding school is a world of its own. Perhaps you aren't really interested in the kind of world it is. I'm sorry about that. Of course it's of interest to me because it is my world, the world in which I still have to live. That is also why I now remember the stories about the children in this school that Miss Hildebrand told me when I took her home.

There's the eleven-year-old Tania from Sweden. Her mother died when she was six years old. Her father married again. The second wife died in a car crash the following year. Now the father married for the third time. Tania refuses hysterically even to meet the third wife. She cannot make friends in school. Death has twice taken from her what a child needs most: a mother. And Tania is convinced that death will do it a third time. That is why she won't even recognize the existence of her father's third wife. She recognizes it less and less as time goes on. Miss Hildebrand says: "Tania is sickly. She doesn't eat. She learns poorly. She is absent-minded. We are afraid of schizophrenia."

And then I think of what Miss Hildebrand told me about Thomas. He is eighteen years old, so he will be in my class, and I'll be meeting him tomorrow morning. Thomas' father was a famous general during the Third Reich. Today he holds an important position in NATO headquarters in Paris. His name is mentioned all the time in the newspapers. Many envy Thomas for his father, whom Germany's former enemies have chosen to be one of its modern leaders (apparently they couldn't find anyone more suitable). Thomas hates his father for doing what he has always done.

I think of Chichita, the fifteen-year-old girl from Rio de Janeiro. Her father is building a dam in Chile, and her mother is dead. Chichita will stay in school for three years without seeing her father. She says that makes her happy. Because every time she sees her father, he has a different girl friend whom Chichita has to call "Aunt." When Miss Hildebrand asked her once what was the most terrible thing on earth, Chichita from Brazil answered: "Children. My father always says that."

I think of what Miss Hildebrand told me about the thirteen-year-old Fred. His parents are divorced. As the guilty party, his father has to pay a great deal of alimony to the mother. The mother lives in Frankfurt, quite nearby. But she lives like an adventuress. Her son is always in her way. Most times he comes home, an "uncle" is there and he's sent away again. His mother gives him money. A lot of money. Fred ought to have a good time, yes? Only never at home. When he feels very lonely he goes to see his father in Hamburg. But there, too, he's in the way of his father's girl friend. The girl friend seduces the thirteen-year-old. The father finds out. Now Fred is no longer allowed to go to Hamburg.

I think of what the old, almost-blind lady told me when I

took her home, about a sixteen-year-old girl called Santayana. Her father is a Spanish writer who cannot go to Spain for political reasons. After the war he wrote a few great books. Now he only indulges in great scandals. In Ceylon he and a married woman became lovers. They were both thrown out of the country. Santayana was born a Eurasian. She has no home. She has never known a home. But she knows most of the world's capitals and their best hotels. She knows the meaning of a diamond coronet, a bounced check, or a bailiff. Because her father, uprooted and in despair, sometimes has too much money and at other times none at all. Santayana knows and understands almost everything. She is very clever, very beautiful, very vain. She will probably become a very prominent whore. . . .

So I go back into the house and hear the little ones talking and crying and sighing in their rooms, I enter my room quietly and see that Noah and Wolfgang have turned off the lights in the meantime. They are both asleep. I get into bed. Wolfgang is breathing deeply. In the forest the owls are hooting. I fold my arms behind my head and think that I'll be seeing Verena again tomorrow at three o'clock. Her narrow face. Her blue-black hair. Her wonderful, sad eyes.

Tomorrow at three I shall see her again and take her bracelet to her. Perhaps she will smile.

She is beautiful when she smiles.

The owls.

Verena Lord.

# Chapter Two

[ 1 ]

*"Germania omnis a Gallis Raetisque et Pannoniis Rheno et Danuvio fluminibus, a Sarmatis Dacisque mutuo aut montibus separatur; cetera Oceanus—"*

"Stop," says the polecat. "That's enough. Please translate, Miss Reber." So here we are. First day of school, last hour of instruction.

Latin. Fifth of September 1960. I glance at my watch. 12:10 P.M. And the lesson finishes at 12:30 P.M. . . . My grade has twenty-two students: twelve German, three French, one English, three Swiss, one Japanese, and two Austrian. We are in a light, modern furnished classroom whose steel chairs are arranged in a half-circle. There is no old-fashioned desk on a rostrum. The teacher has the same kind of table and steel chair we have, and is on the same level.

"Now, Miss Reber, would you be kind enough to start?"

Miss Geraldine Reber. The luxury whore. In daylight I can now have a good look at her. I can understand how she came to get her nickname. It's not that she is overwhelmingly beautiful. Only her legs and breasts are terrific. Yet she's provocatively sexy. She has teased out her tawny hair to such an extent that it looks almost ridiculous. Her lips are painted brightly, her eyelashes are thick with mascara and the lids painted green. She is wearing a white wide-meshed sweater which is at least two sizes too small. Naturally she has one of those endlessly long glass-bead necklaces (green), a jangling bracelet with a lot of junk on it, and a ring which is as large as it is worthless. It is a very large one. Again she is wearing a pleated skirt, a green one this time, and since this morning I know why Geraldine prefers pleated skirts. Since this morning she has been flirting with me.

At breakfast I met the crippled Hansi and he said: "The luxury whore is hated by everyone because she can't bear to see a couple going together. She is after the boy until he gets rid of his girl and goes with her."

Hansi knows everything.

"But she doesn't only do that. If she has someone and a new boy arrives, she makes a play for him. It's funny. As soon as she has him he does not interest her any more and she treats him like dirt when another new one arrives."

So since eight this morning I'm the "new one" for the luxury whore and I'm sitting directly opposite her. And so I see her legs. Geraldine knows that she has beautiful legs. She is wearing very high-heeled shoes which, according to Hansi, is forbidden, but she does it nevertheless, and she is wearing sheer, dark textured stockings, too—the latest fashion! She is forever crossing her legs. She shows everything she has; the skin of her thighs, the black panties. And she looks at me in such a funny way that would probably turn me on if I hadn't had quite a bit of experience.

Naturally she is a poor student. Behind her sits a tall blond boy who is trying to help her. Walter Colland is his name, Hansi told me. "He goes with her. That is, before the vacation he was going with her. Now it's your turn. Whether you believe it or not; in at least three days Walter will be rid of his luxury whore."

I believe you, Hansi, I believe every word. Poor Walter. He hasn't even noticed anything yet. Or seems not to. Geraldine cannot understand what Walter is whispering to her. The polecat yells: "Colland, one more word and I'm going to report you." Walter is quiet now and Geraldine stutters hopelessly: "Germany . . . well. Germany in its entirety . . ." By now I know this Tacitus by heart (I got stuck in the same form twice). I could help the luxury whore quite easily, but first of all she sits too far away from me and then there is still the small matter of the bracelet, right? So I had much rather look at her legs and black panties.

"Stop," yells the polecat. He is always yelling.

"I told you to be silent, Colland! Once more and I will report you!"

Perhaps I should say a few words about the polecat. His name is Dr. Friedrich Haberle and he is the Latin teacher. He is new, just as Mr. Herterich is, and consequently the class is trying him out. He brought his nickname with him. It was unfortunate for the polecat that a boy who was kicked out of the school where he himself taught and is now in the sixth form here gave us exhaustive information about Dr. Friedrich Haberle. "He is a real asshole. You can wind him around your little finger. He has a wife and three small children. His life's dream was a house. He slaved and saved and never allowed himself anything or his wife or his three little children—everything for the house. A few months ago he found something in Friedheim. It is a house that was built around the turn of the century. It's reasonably priced, and worth the money. I wouldn't be buried there. But he is happy. So because of the villa he also changed schools and came up here."

"His Achilles' heel?" inquired Wolfgang.

"He doesn't have one."

"Nonsense. Everybody has one. Girls?"

"For goodness' sake! He doesn't look at another girl. He is an ideal family man, he loves his wife, his children . . ."

"And the house, yeah," said Noah impatiently. "But how can we wind him around our little finger if he has no weaknesses?"

"I didn't say he had no weaknesses. He is weakness personified! You'll see. He puts up with anything. He threatens and does nothing. He is as gentle as a lamb. For a few weeks you'll be doing everything you want—and then stop of your own accord. You get tired so quickly if there is no opposition. Last but not least, he is a first-class teacher—in case one of you is interested in Latin. Which I don't expect."

"Yes, I am," said Noah. "So your report is interesting to me."

"If you can learn your Latin, he is even nice to you. But one thing you can tell your girls: if they don't know anything—and none of them do—the polecat gets rid of them! It doesn't do the girls any good to behave like Circe and to wear low-cut blouses and make eyes at him. The polecat is strictly monogamous!"

Seems to be right. Geraldine is trying with no effect to show everything she has to offer to the polecat. He is sitting in front of her and she is doing everything she can to win him over, but the polecat does not even look.

By the way, polecat is a lovely name. He is small, our Dr. Haberle, has button eyes and round, protruding ears. But that is not all: the whole face seems to come to one point, an aggressive bulbous nose. Below that you can see a small mouth with sharp, ugly teeth. The poor guy! He also has inflamed red eyes!

And now the main thing Dr. Haberle has in common with a polecat. He stinks! In his case he stinks of sweat.

It is not that he doesn't wash. I'm convinced that he scrubs his armpits and everything else until he's sore—morning and night. Even if it is with the cheapest soap. (The little house, the little house!) Because he is saving so hard he is wearing a double-breasted suit with heavily padded shoulders which is at least ten years old. For ten years he has sweated in this suit, when he became excited, when he was overworked. Have you ever known a suit like this, soaked in sweat, I mean? I'm sorry for the polecat. He is a poor slob. The class has classified him. All are of the same opinion: a nothing.

That is—and I have to say that for the polecat—at the beginning of the lesson things looked different. You must realize we are all giants compared to the little teacher who is probably not very healthy any more and certainly not very brave. When he entered, one of the French boys—Gaston—took a snuffbox out of his pants pocket, opened it, and took some snuff with great flair. Then he passed it to Wolfgang and he did the same. (As I said already, every new one is being given the treatment.)

The polecat stood there, turned pale and red and didn't say a word. I saw how desperate he was. At first he could think of nothing. The girls giggled. The box arrived at the third boy. The polecat said: "We will begin with Tacitus' *Germania*. Please open your books."

That was not really the best way to start. Promptly the following happened: none of the twenty-one pupils opened his Tacitus. The box was passed from one to the other. One after the other took some snuff. Apart from that there was silence. We said nothing, he said nothing. He looked at us without a word. There are six girls and sixteen boys in the class. You can imagine how long it took for all sixteen boys to use the box. The sixteenth got up and returned the thing to Gaston. All this time I was watching the polecat. At first I was afraid he would burst into tears. Then came a period of time when I could see that he was planning something! And sure enough, just as Gaston was going to put away the box the polecat said to him: "I am new here but I must say: You have some manners! You've never heard of offering some to a guest, eh? Do you do this sort of thing at home all by yourselves and let the others watch? I thought it would be different." Such an approach has to be admired, right? The others hadn't watched him as closely as I had. Gaston got up quite disconcerted, took a step forward, and offered the box to the polecat.

"Excuse me, Monsieur, we didn't know . . ."

"Yes, yes," said the polecat, "you don't know a whole lot of things." And then he took some snuff. I could swear to it that he was taking snuff for the first time in his life and he was disgusted by it, but he did it and he knew how: he had just seen it done sixteen times.

"Thank you very much, Gaston, " said the polecat. At first everybody was speechless. Then Wolfgang said to Noah very loudly: "That boy gave us the wrong information. He is not so stupid."

"Just wait," answered Noah.

And he was right. A few minutes later his control was shot because of an insolent remark Walter made. And he started to yell. He had controlled himself so well. He had been so clever. All for nothing. He didn't stop yelling. He is still yelling.

"How long must I wait, Miss Reber? Germany in its entirety —what does that mean?" Of course, she has no idea. "Does someone else know?"

Twelve past twelve.

Now it is time for me to move. I raise my hand.

"Well, Mansfeld?"

"I don't feel very well, Doctor."

Much laughter. The polecat grows pale. All right. One more enemy. He can't hurt me in Latin. After all, I'm doing it for the third time. The others think I want to take advantage of the polecat. So I have one enemy and twenty-one friends. With one sentence! I say: "I'm afraid I have to leave the room."

He just nods silently and looks quite sick. I go to the door while Friedrich Südhaus raises his hand. He is the first in the class, an unpleasant boy with a hypocritical face and a nervous twitch to his mouth.

"Please, Südhaus."

"Germania onmis, Gemany in its entirety . . ." and he finishes the translation.

"Excellent, Südhaus, I thank you."

Wolfgang told me the boy's father is a former Nazi and a very important man—Chief Attorney-General, in fact. I almost wrote naturally that he is now a very important man.

I have to hurry. I must get to the girl's villa.

## [ 2 ]

Little Hansi was right: about twelve-fifteen it's the easiest thing in the world. The entrance door is not locked, the cleaning women have left already and the teachers are at lunch or still in the village or heaven knows where. Nobody seems to be in the house.

I try to remember where Hansi and I had stood last night, then I open the last door in the right hallway—right the first time. I'm in Geraldine's room.

Now everything happens very fast. I leave the door open and open the windows just in case someone should come. Then I'll be able to hear him in time and have a second way out. I push the bed away from the wall and feel for a crack, because Geraldine had put the brick very nicely back into the wall and filled in the joints. Of course! Otherwise her hiding place would have been discovered by now. I still know about where the place should be. There it is. I dig out the brick with my pocket knife. And then, then I see it: Verena's bracelet. It is on top of a watch, two rings and a silver necklace which Geraldine had stolen too. I leave the stuff, I only take the bracelet.

Funny—now that I hold it in my hand, in my imagination I see Verena, naked, completely naked. I'm standing on some beach on some island in the south and she comes running toward me, laughing, her arms stretched out and naked, as I said, completely naked.

I feel a little dizzy as I'm pushing the brick back and start as I hear the voice. "Oh, so that's the way it is."

I turn around.

Geraldine is standing in the doorway.

## [ 3 ]

She looks like a ghost, ash-gray in the dimly lit hall, almost unreal. Very quickly her polished nails glide up and down the pearls of her long necklace. Her breath is panting, her eyes glitter.

"Yes, that's the way it is," I say and push back the bed. "Did you think you could keep it?"

"How did you know where it is?"

"That's none of your business."

Now she comes toward me, with half-closed eyes and half-opened mouth. She has seen that in the movies.

"Stop that. How come you are here?"

"I got sick too. I wanted to follow you."

"Why?"

"Because I like you," she says and touches me. I push her back. "I really like you. I thought you were still in the school. Then I didn't find you and came here. That stupid school is almost finished anyway." I feel hot. I must get out of here. Immediately!

"Let me go."

"No."

"You don't have to be afraid. I won't tell the chief."

"I'm not afraid. For all I care tell him! But stay."

"You're crazy!"

"Please!" Now she puts her arms around my neck and holds her hands tightly closed and presses close to me, breasts, abdomen, thighs, everything! She wants to kiss me.

I turn my head.

"Yes, I'm crazy, crazy for you! Didn't you notice how I stared at you all morning?"

"Yes. But I'm not crazy for you! Understand?"

In answer to that she puts her tongue between my lips.

I grab the teased hair and pull back her head. Now she is smiling a mad smile and whispers: "Come into the woods!"

Now I have enough. I give her a push and hurry out of the house. Just get away! I'm taking the lonesome path into the woods. The bracelet is in my pocket. Slowly. That's done with. Now I have time. I think. I have not walked one hundred yards and I hear steps. I turn around. She is following me.

It is very warm on this day. The sun is shining. I am not walking faster. She doesn't either. It's really ridiculous. She is following me like a dog, always at the same distance. No one says a word. So we wander over the colorful leaves, through the autumnal woods as the slanting rays of the sun shine upon us through the treetops. No one is in sight. Once in a while I turn around. She has the same facial expression: tightly closed lips, a double crease between her brows and completely mad eyes. She follows me that way for perhaps ten minutes. Then, when the path curves and leads through a small grove, she disappears.

She's had enough, I think.

The trees grow closely together here and in between them there is heavy shrubbery. It is very lonesome here in the little grove. The path curves again. Geraldine is standing in front of me.

She knows her way around better than I and must have used some shortcut. She is leaning against a tree and looks at me with open mouth and half-closed eyes and this crazy expression in her eyes. She has taken off her sweater. She has taken off her skirt. And now she is not wearing any panties.

## [ 4 ]

When I started to write this book I promised myself: It must be honest, completely honest. Now I have reached a part where it would be easier for me to lie. But then, would there be any reason for writing this book?

I was kicked out of five boarding schools. Every time girls were the reason. I have a flaw in my character. Situations arise and I have no reason any more, no brain. Blackout. It's been like that since I had my first girl. Then I'm simply not responsible for my actions. Damn it, I had felt it already in her room, like an epileptic fit. I just managed to get out of the room in time. I won't be able to do that here. I won't be able to pass that tree.

When I look back on it today I have the feeling that I was completely drunk and she, too. We were raving mad. Perhaps five yards away from the path, in the thicket, on the ground warm from the sun. I tore her stockings, she my shirt because I did not undress quickly enough. We scratched and bit each other. We did what I could not write down because it would not be printed. Our bodies grew bloody from stones and thorns we rolled on, convulsed in each other. We weren't aware of the pain.

And there is no end, it starts again and again.

For days after it I could feel the scratches of her long fingernails on my back. When she reaches the climax her eyes turn so I can only see the whites and she makes sounds like someone undergoing torture. She clutches me and everything spins round and round.

In my life I have had quite a number of girls. But never one like this. This madness is infectious, and two raving maniacs are clawing at each other.

This must be an honest book. I have never loved Geraldine. But never have I experienced with any other woman anything like I did with this man-mad girl, which has filled me with disgust from the first moment on. Which I cursed the moment the red mist came down over my eyes. Which I hated when she withdrew from my arms exhausted. She was lying on the ground, very still, looking at me with that crazy look and sighed: "I love you." And again and again she moaned: "I love you . . . I love you. . . . Never before was it like this, as it was with you!"

This must be an honest book.

When finally everything is done she lies there without moving. Her lips are blue. She is still trembling. And suddenly with horror I remember what she said, with this rigid look and with a weak child's voice: "This was the first time in my life."

Silently I'm sitting next to her.

"I have tried it so often. Again and again. Since I was fourteen. I had surely more boys than you had girls. It never worked, whatever we tried. I went almost crazy. I put on an act for the boys . . . I have tried it with myself. It never worked. And now you. . . . Oh, you, it was so wonderful . . . I love you!"

Geraldine loves me. And I loathe her.

[ 5 ]

2:15 P.M.

We dressed. I had to help her, she was so weak. At three o'clock I have to be at the old tower. Verena will be waiting. How can I get rid of Geraldine?

"What are you thinking of?" she asks suddenly. "Of you," I say of course. At that she presses herself close to me, real close. "I love you. It was so wonderful. I thought I would die. So wonderful. Like never before. Only now I know how it is. I will never be able to get away from you."

And she is serious. One can see that. Something like that just had to happen to me!

"Do you love me too?"

"No."

This is senseless, she has to know that from the start. There is really no sense in this. "I don't mind if you don't love me. You will sometime."

"No!"

"You don't know me, you don't know how I can be. You will love me, sometime, definitely. I'm so happy, Oliver. I have never been so happy. You'll see how nice I can be."

She gives me many kisses, caresses me, and I think: Verena, Verena, Verena.

[ 6 ]

I say: "You must go back to your house."

"I don't want to."

"Then go to lunch."

"I can't eat now."

I couldn't eat either.

"They will be looking for us."

"They won't find us."

"But I have to go back to my villa."

"Just another quarter of an hour," she says, begging me with eyes like a faithful dog. It's enough to make me quite sick. "Then I'll be very good. Then I'll go back and leave you in peace. Fifteen minutes?"

I nod.

"Now that I belong to you . . ."

And that too!

". . . and we both belong to each other . . ."

Ho. Ho. Ho!

". . . now I will tell you what's wrong with me."

"What do you mean, what's wrong with you?"

"Why I'm like this . . . so crazy. And if you hadn't come and set me free . . ."

That is what she says! These words! Just as I write it. Once again: *set me free!*

". . . then I would have ended up in the nuthouse. May I put my head on your chest?"

"Of course." She does it, and I stroke her ridiculously teased hair, which now looks as if she had been in a fight. She talks as if in her sleep as she caresses me: "I'm eighteen. And you?"

"Twenty-one."

"We used to live in Breslau. My father was a physicist. In 1946 the Russians took us. Him as a scientist and us for pleasure. Father was to work for them. We went to Novosibirsk. That is where my father worked. In a huge institute. There were many other German research workers there. We had a little, pretty house outside of town."

"Then you were four years old."

"Yes. And it started in kindergarten."

"What?"

"Wait. The Russians were nice to my father and to my mother, and the grown-up Russians were nice to me too. All of them! They brought us food. For me they brought dolls and toys. We celebrated holidays with our neighbors."

"And who was not nice?"

"The children! I told you, it started in kindergarten, and then when I started grade school it got much worse. Even though I spoke fluent Russian! I could only speak German at home. My father had committed himself for ten years. So I had to go to school for eight years. I can tell you, it was hell."

2:25 P.M.

Verena, Verena, Verena.

"Children have no reason. They heard I was German."

"Oh, that."

"A German, you understand? We had invaded their country, and many children in my school had no fathers any more or no brothers. Because they had died in the war, in the big Hitler war. Now they took revenge."

"On you."

"On me, yes. They beat me up. Every day, sometimes so badly the doctor had to come."

"Awful."

"My parents had to take me out of the school finally. Then in 1956 the contract which my father had signed expired. Well, then we went to West Berlin. Father worked at the Max Planck Institute. And I was beaten up again."

"By whom?"

"By German children."

"What?"

"It's quite simple! My father had worked for the Soviets for ten years. The children talked about that at home. So some father said to his son: This man has betrayed secrets. He helped the Soviets. Perhaps he is a Communist. In any case he is a traitor! The next day the boy said it in school. Then it began. They called me 'traitor' and 'pig.' Here they call me—"

"Yes, I know."

"But that's not so bad."

"Poor Geraldine," I say. And that is honest.

"Well, you know, then I was bigger. And stronger. I hit back, bit, threw stones. And then it got really bad and a bunch of them came for me. I had a marvelous trick to protect myself."

"What kind of thing?"

"I yelled at them in Russian. As loud as I could. Russian!

Whatever came to mind. Sometimes even poems. Didn't matter! When I yelled in Russian they got scared. All of them! Always! Then they crawled back and left me in peace." She lifts her head and smiles: "That was a great trick, wasn't it?"

"Great. And then?" Her face darkens. She bows her head and places it on my knee.

"Father is a very accomplished scientist, you understand? For instance, in Siberia he thought of something which the Soviets built into their jet planes. In the very fast ones."

"What kind of a thing?"

"Of course I don't know exactly. In such a huge plane which flies at such great speed the pilot cannot watch all the instruments any more. That would be more than any man could do. So my father built in something electronic which watches all the important instruments in the plane. Let's say for instance it watches fifty possible danger spots. If there is something not working right a loudspeaker switches itself on and tells the pilot: Attention, Attention, this or that is not working right."

"Great," I say. And I think it is great.

"But the greatest is that my father had those fifty warnings recorded on tape by a woman. A woman's voice! That impresses me the most. Because a pilot usually talks by radio only with men. So if he hears the woman's voice he knows: This means danger! He cannot miss hearing it, the woman's voice!"

I say: "And now I can finish telling your story."

"Yes?"

"Yes. The Yanks made a fantastic offer to your father and today he is working in Cape Kennedy or some other place which means you can visit your parents in the summer. Right?"

She tears off a blade of grass and chews it and says quietly: "Only partly. The Yanks made an offer to my father. We were all supposed to go. But my father flew over alone."

"Why?"

"My mother got a divorce. She maintained that she could no longer live with a man who helps, year after year, to build worse weapons for destruction."

"That is certainly a point of view," I say.

2:30 P.M.

Verena, Verena, Verena.

"But she lied. All human beings lie. My mother got a divorce because she had met a very rich businessman in Berlin! My father did not know that. He does not know it even today. I have spied on them, my mother and this fellow."

"Why didn't you tell your father?"

"Why should I? I always liked my mother better! Father knew that too. That's why he agreed that I would stay with my mother when they were divorced."

"Well, that turned out well."

"Very well indeed. My father had hardly left when my mother married again and stuck me in this boarding school."

"Why?"

"My stepfather does not like me. Always, when we see each other, there are fights. I am only allowed to go to Berlin very rarely. Mother shakes with fear every time I come. But my father is happy that I'm being raised in Germany. I'm flying over there to him for the summer vacation. He really does work in Cape Kennedy. Now he is building rockets."

"I understand," I say. Then I look at her. She whispers: "The fifteen minutes are up, are they?"

"Yes."

"I'll go now. I won't cry. I won't keep you. I won't make trouble for you, I swear it. I won't ever make trouble for you!"

"Okay," I say. We both get up. "All right, Geraldine. Wait, I'll fix your hair a little." She cuddles close to me and kisses my hands. "And you have to fix yourself up a little before you go back to the others," I say. "Or else everybody will be able to tell what happened."

2:40 P.M.

"You have to go back to the villa."

"We have history at four. We'll see each other then."

"Yes."

"I want to be with you always. Day and night. Until I die."

"So long, Geraldine."

"Won't you even give me one kiss?"

We kiss. She smiles sadly.

"What is it?"

"Is she beautiful?"

"Who?"

"Don't ask. The woman the bracelet belongs to."

"No."

"Of course she is beautiful. She is much more beautiful than I. And now you are going to her. Please don't lie to me!"

"Yes," I say. "Now I'm going to her."

"Do you love her?"

"No."

"You're lying. But it doesn't matter to me, word of honor. It doesn't matter as long as you're with me too. Because you are the first man in my life."

"Well, until four in the history class."

And then she leaves, stumbling in her high heels, flushed with a smudged face and a blouse which slips out of her skirt. She disappears in the bushes. It is growing quiet. I am starting on my way to the old tower, which I can see above the treetops. One hand is in my pocket, and in the hand I hold Verena's bracelet.

After three steps I hear a noise and stop. Someone is running hurriedly through the undergrowth. I cannot see him, only hear him. I don't think I can catch up with him because his steps fade away. Someone has been listening to us. For how long? What did he hear? What did he see? Everything? Who was it?

## [ 7 ]

Two minutes to three.

I am punctual. Fortunately, there was a small stream nearby and I took time to wash. It was pleasant, the ice-cold water.

Two minutes to three.

And nobody around.

So I sit down on a step at the entrance to the dilapidated ruins next to which is a sign:

DANGER. ENTRANCE PROHIBITED.

An old thing, this tower! Renovated the last time by the Most Gracious Elector (Grand Duke) William IX, A.D. 1804—which I read on a tablet which is also falling into ruin. Suddenly she's standing in front of me, like Little Red Riding Hood in the forest. This time she is wearing a little red dress and a red cap. Her mother dresses her like a little doll.

"Good day, Uncle Mansfeld," she says sedately.

"Hello, Evelyn! Where did you come from?"

"I waited for you behind the tower. Mummy is waiting upstairs."

"In the tower?"

"Yes. You are to go up."

"But if that thing collapses—" I point to the sign.

"It won't collapse. We have to be careful, Mummy and I. No one must see her alone with a man. That's why she takes me along every time."

Every time. . . . Does she take you along often, little one? Very often? To the tower too? Does she meet her Italian lover here too? And other gentlemen? So many questions. None asked.

"Wait," I say and give her something I have been carrying around with me all day. She utters a cry of delight: "Marzipan!"

"You like that best, don't you?" I had bought the little package this morning at breakfast in the school cafeteria.

"How do you know that?"

"You told me yourself, last night."

"Really?" She looks at me, unbelieving. So she can't remember very well yet. Too little. Verena is lucky. And a good accomplice.

Even if it was not very nice what she is doing. Apropos this business of not being nice: Are you so great, Mister Mansfeld? What were you doing two hours ago?

Because I'm yellow and don't want to think of it I ask quickly: "How is your dog?"

"Assad? Well, thank you."
"Why didn't you bring him?"
"He is sleeping now."
"Oh, then one can't disturb him."
"No. Besides, he wants to be alone sometimes, you know. Like everybody."
"You're quite right, Evelyn."
"I'll disappear now. Go on up. If somebody comes I'll sing. Mummy knows that already."
"Oh, really?"
"Yes. Up there you can hide."
"Has Mummy been up there before with another uncle?"
"No, never!"
"Then how do you know that you can hide up there?"
"Well, because I've been up there! With Mummy! We often go up there. It's very beautiful up there. You'll see."
"Bye," I say. She hesitates. "Anything else?"
"May . . . I give you a kiss, Uncle Mansfeld?"
"For the marzipan?"
"No."
"Then why?"
"Well, because you'll help us."
"Oh," I say. "Because of that," I say. "Of course you can give me a kiss," I say, bend down to her and she puts her little arms around my neck. I get a kiss on my cheek that is surely the wettest I ever got. Then she runs away very quickly. I wipe off my cheek, enter the old tower, and go up the spiral staircase, which creaks and groans at every step, higher and higher, and the thought that every step brings me a few inches closer to Verena brings the sweat to my brow. This is a huge thing. I wouldn't have thought so. Ninety-seven steps? When I finally arrive at the room at the top of the tower she is standing in front of me, serious and straight and her wonderful eyes are looking at me, those black eyes, much too large for the narrow face, those eyes in which so much sadness and knowledge can be seen, so much longing for love, those eyes which I cannot forget and will not forget until I die.

She is wearing a light, low-cut dress on this day, sleeveless, made of white linen on which are printed flowers in bright colors. I know about dresses: as simple as this one looks, it had cost a small fortune. And how it fits! I must not look at it for too long. In this dress she looks more exciting than if she weren't wearing it.

Verena. Verena. Oh, Verena!

I pull the bracelet from my pocket and give it to her. Then I go to a corner window in this room which is filled with rusty tools, broken furniture, sacks full of straw, and rotting wood. I look out over the brown and red and golden leaves of the trees. The sun is shining on everything. A light blue haze obliterates the distance. And again those silver threads drift by in this Indian summer.

"It's pretty here," I say and feel how she steps behind me. "I know this part of the country. I have lived in Frankfurt." I keep on talking and it is becoming more and more difficult to continue because now she's standing close behind me. "The little river down there, this is the Nidda. Over there, that's the Vogelsberg; that huge thing there, with the three humps, that is the Winterstein; and there, where the sun is shining on a piece of meadow between the black trees, there is the Hohenrodskopf. There I once—"

"Oliver!"

"Yes."

I turn around and everything is there again: Diorissimo, the lily-of-the-valley scent, the scent of her skin, her blue-black hair, the eyes, the eyes . . .

"Thank you," she whispers.

"Oh, ridiculous," I say. It is supposed to sound vigorous but I'm almost crying. "What a beautiful dress you are wearing!"

"My husband is really coming home tonight. Don't we have tremendous luck?"

"Yes. Tremendous luck."

"Why are you staring at me like that?"

"I still get something from you."

"What?"

"You know quite well what. Give it to me."

She doesn't move.

"Come on! Or I'll take the bracelet away from you again!"

She reaches into a small pocket in her dress at the hip and extracts a small round box.

I open it.

"What are you doing?"

"Seeing if there are thirty. And all Veronal."

There are thirty. And all Veronal.

I put the little box away.

"Will you throw them away?"

"No."

"Then what?"

"Save them."

"What for?"

"What did you save them for?"

"Oliver . . ."

"Yes."

"You are very . . ."

"Very what?"

"Nothing."

And then we both look out of the window and I feel bad and I tell myself that I am an idiot, an idiot, an idiot three times damned, and that I should go for Geraldine or somebody else, but that I should leave this one here, this Verena Lord, in peace. And I see little villages, castles, farms, black- and brown-spotted cows, and hear railroad trains which whistle loudly and quickly disappear into the haze. I see Bad Homburg, Bad Mannheim and Frankfurt, and Verena sees all that too. So we stand next to each other for perhaps three minutes and neither speaks. Then I feel suddenly how her left hand tries to find my left one. I am embarrassed because my hand is damp with excitement but when she entwines her fingers in mine I notice that she feels the same as I do. Her hand is damp too.

Whatever I'm writing down now we said without looking at

each other even once. The entire time we are looking out of the tower window across the treetops, down to the railroad trains, cows, castles, villages.

"How did you find the bracelet?"

"A girl stole it. A little boy watched her doing and told me her name."

"Is she pretty?"

"No." (Simple question.)

"How did you get the bracelet back?"

"The girl is in my class. During school I ran to the villa where she lives and in her room I got the thing."

"Has she missed it yet?"

"No." (Simple question.)

"Your collar is full of lipstick."

"Then I'll have to change my shirt before the afternoon school starts. I thank you for pointing it out to me."

"I thank you for the bracelet."

"Can we meet here again?"

No answer.

"I am free every afternoon between two and four. But of course I can come at any other time too. I just take off then."

No answer.

"I have asked you something, Madame!"

"I heard."

"And?"

Silence.

"I did help you, right? Help me too. Please!"

"Help? I? You?"

"Help. You. Me. Yes."

"By meeting here?"

"Yes. Just meeting. That's all. To look down there. To talk with each other. To stand next to each other, the same as now." She lets go of my hand.

"You are twenty-one. I am thirty-three. I am twelve years older than you!"

"I don't care."

"I am married."

"I don't care. And unhappily married."

"I have a child."

"I like children."

"I have a lover."

"I don't care." (Lie.)

"Before him I had another one."

"I'm sure you had many. All that is completely unimportant. Verena, just why didn't we meet a few years earlier?"

And from now on to the close of this talk we look at each other. We talk calmly and quietly. A slight wind starts and it whispers in the trees.

"That would be madness," she says.

"What?"

"If we were to meet here again."

"I swear, I won't do anything! I just want to look at you, just talk with you. Yesterday on the Autobahn, didn't you have the feeling that we would understand each other very well? I don't mean in bed. I mean our opinions, our thoughts. Didn't you have the feeling that we are very much alike? Very, very much like each other?"

"Yes. You are just as rotten and lost and alone as I am."

In the distance a locomotive whistles. Rays of the sun come through the window and light on Verena's dress. The flowers are as bright as if they were alive.

"Did you sleep with the girl who stole my bracelet?"

"Yes."

"But not out of love?"

"Truly not out of love."

"I know that. Oh, how I know that!"

How she talks. Her bearing. Her walk. Every movement. This woman has a secret. She will not tell me where she is from. She speaks ill of herself, runs herself down. All that is disguise, all that is his.

Who are you, Verena?

From where did your path lead you?

Why do you load yourself down with jewelry?

Why do you tremble at the thought of being poor again—and still court danger by deceiving your husband. Why?

I will never ask you why again. Perhaps you will tell me, sometime.

"And we will meet here again and talk with each other?"

"On one condition."

"Which one?"

"That you give me back the Veronal."

"Never! If that is the condition we forget about it."

"I don't want the tablets. I don't want you to have them."

"And I don't want you to have that stuff!"

"Then destroy it, now. I must see it."

"How shall I destroy it?"

"Perhaps it will burn."

This time I have matches. I hesitate before I strike one, because I would have liked to have kept the Veronal.

The box burns brightly. The tablets only char and fall apart. I throw what is left on the floor. Verena steps on it with her shoe until everything is smeared, destroyed and rubbed into the thick boards.

Then we look at each other.

"And when one thinks that for this you slept with a pharmacist!" I say.

"And when one thinks that now neither of us can kill ourselves with it," she says.

"And when one thinks that I satisfied your condition. When do we see each other? Tomorrow?"

"No."

"The day after tomorrow?"

"Not the day after tomorrow either."

"Then when?"

"It will be possible in a few days again."

"Why?"

"Because I'm pregnant," she answers. "I have told you that you have no idea in what kind of a situation I am, with all that is wrong with me. You know nothing. Nothing at all!"

## [ 8 ]

"Pregnant?"

"You heard me."

Funny, with anyone else I would have thought at once: Well, boy, that is *the* opportunity! This book has to stay honest. A while back, when I wrote about Geraldine, I didn't make myself appear better than I was. Now I'm not making myself appear worse. With Verena I did not for one second think what a golden opportunity this would be. Not for one second? I did not even have the thought!

"By whom are you pregnant?"

"I don't know."

"By this Italian?"

"By him. Or by my husband."

"Last night you said—"

"I lied. A woman has to sleep with her husband if she has a lover, right? In case something happens."

"You are quite right. I just did not want to contradict you last night. Of course you told Enrico that there has been nothing between you and your husband for a year."

"Of course."

"All women tell that to their lovers."

"Did a woman ever tell you that?"

"Yes."

"And?"

"I didn't believe it. But I didn't say that I didn't believe it. One must not be unjust. Men behave the same when they have a mistress."

For a while silence. Then I ask:

"Do you want the child?"

"Good God! In my situation?"

"Does Enrico know?"

"Enrico is married. Nobody knows. I only told you. I wonder why?"

"Because we understand each other. One day . . ."

"What?"

"One day you will love me."

"Stop it."

"With the kind of love you are longing for. I know it for certain. Sometimes there are moments when I know exactly how everything will be. Do you have a doctor?"

"I cannot bring the child into the world." She bends her head. "After Evelyn's birth the doctor told me another one would endanger my life. So now I have to go to a hospital. That's one of the reasons, too."

"Reason for what?"

"That my marriage is so bad and that I am so . . . that I am like that."

"I don't understand you."

"You know that Evelyn is an illegitimate child."

"Yes."

"You know that my husband does not like her."

"Yes."

"But he always wished terribly for a child of his own, you understand? A son who would one day take over the bank. When I met him in poverty I concealed from him that I could never have another child. Later I told him. That was mean of me, wasn't it?"

"You were in need?"

"No. I ought to have told him. Under any circumstances. You see, this way we were becoming more estranged each day. He never reproached me, directly reproached me, I mean."

"But indirectly."

"Yes. He . . . loves me, in his way; he is attached to me but he cannot forgive me that I will never be able to fulfill his greatest wish. He looks at me in a different way. No longer as he would at a . . ."

"A real woman."

"Yes, that's it."

"And that is why you have embarked on leading this life."

"Why?"

"To prove to yourself that you are still a woman."

She looks at me for a long time. "You are a strange boy, Oliver."

"That's why you did it, right?"

She does not answer. I would really like to know if there are happy people in this shitty world, too. Only now I notice that Verena is not made up. I tell her. She answers: "I had intended to give you a kiss."

"But you own a fantastic lipstick which does not come off. You wore it when you kissed Enrico."

"That's why I didn't want to use it."

"You will see, there will be love between us."

"Never, never. Impossible."

"The lipstick," I say. "The lipstick proves it. And now just wait. I have time. All the time in the world."

She looks straight at me. Then I ask her:

"When are you going to tell your husband?"

"Tonight."

I ask: "Which hospital are you going to?"

She tells me which one. A hospital in the western part of Frankfurt.

"When is it going to be done?"

"If I leave tomorrow, the day after."

"Then I come to visit you Thursday."

"That's out of the question! That's not possible! I forbid you to come."

"You cannot forbid me anything."

"And if you endanger me by it?"

"I won't endanger you. You have a private room, of course. At the desk I'll give a false name. And I'll come in the morning."

"Why in the morning?"

"Because then your husband is at the Stock Exchange—or . . . ?"

"Yes, that's right, but . . ."

"Thursday, Verena."

"It is madness, Oliver. What we are doing is complete madness."

"It is sweet madness. And some time it will be love."

"When? When I'm forty? And Evelyn twelve?"

"And if you're sixty," I say. "I have to go back to school; it is three-thirty. Who goes first?"

"I will. Wait a few minutes, all right?"

"Sure." She goes to the staircase and there she turns around once more and says: "If you come Thursday make believe you're my brother. Otto Wilfried is his name. Can you remember that?"

"Otto Wilfried."

"He lives in Frankfurt." Now she is smiling. "And tonight at eleven you come out on the balcony."

"Why?"

"Because I have a surprise for you."

"What kind of a surprise?"

"You'll see," she says. "You will see. Tonight at eleven."

"Okay," I say. "Otto Wilfried and tonight at eleven."

I am leaning against one of the old rotting beams which support the arched roof, and look at her walking down the spiral staircase, slowly, carefully, even though she is wearing flat shoes. At a bend of the staircase she turns around once more.

"And it is still madness," she says. Then she is gone.

Down below I hear her talk to Evelyn, then the voices fade away. I don't walk to a window. I don't look at them leaving. I hold the hand which Verena had held in hers to my face and smell the scent of lily of the valley which disappears so quickly. After three minutes I go down the staircase too. Outside again I remember that I have to go to the Quellenhof because the collar of my shirt is smudged by Geraldine's lipstick. So I start and run because I don't have much time left. And I don't want to be late for school the first day. At the moment I start to run something cracks in front of me and I see a figure running through the undergrowth. It happens so quickly that I, the same as the first time, couldn't say at once who was running there. But it's strange: this time I was prepared for something similar, this time I almost waited to be watched. And so my eyes react quicker and I recognize who is running away there. It is the blond, crippled Hansi, my "brother."

[ 9 ]

"Nowhere else as in Germany does one believe so fervently that war is the best political tool. Nowhere else is one inclined to overlook its horrors and disdain its consequences. Nowhere else is the love of peace equated so thoughtlessly with personal cowardice." These words of journalist Carl von Ossietzsky, who chose to die in a concentration camp rather than give way to force, Doctor Frey read to us at the start of the history lesson. This Doctor Frey is the best and most intelligent teacher I've ever met, believe you me! And I've met a lot of them. He is lean and tall, perhaps fifty years old, and he walks with a limp. Probably they broke his bones in the concentration camp. This Doctor Frey always speaks quietly, doesn't yell like that stupid polecat, he smiles, he is friendly, and he conveys an air of authority which one can only call unbelievable. Nobody ever talks in his class. Nobody gives fresh answers. I get the feeling in this first hour that everybody loves him, this lame Doctor Frey. There is one who doesn't love him, I notice: the top boy in the class, Friedrich Südhaus, the boy with the nervous twitch of his mouth.

Ah well, if I had a father who is an ex-Nazi and now Attorney-General somewhere I wouldn't love Doctor Frey either. One has to be reasonable: a human being is the product of his environment. On the other hand: don't you think that is terrible? What a great guy Südhaus could have become with a different father, with this Doctor Frey, for example?

After he quoted Ossietzsky Doctor Frey said, "In history we have reached the year 1933. In most schools and with most teachers there is a large gap here. In fact from 1933 to 1945. There is nothing to tell about in those years. It starts again in

1945. That is to say, with the so-called collapse of Germany, the way the fact is unabashedly transcribed, that this country, which started the biggest war of all time, had to capitulate unconditionally to its enemies. Then comes another smaller gap and we arrive at 1948 and the economic miracle. I don't want to tell you anything you don't want to hear! So tell me now if you want to hear the truth about the Third Reich or not. I'm warning you! The truth is not nice. Most of my colleagues take the easy way out and just don't talk about it. I'm going to talk about it. I'm going to tell you everything, the whole dirty truth —if you want. Whoever wants it, raise your hand."

After that, everybody raised a hand, the girls too—all except two boys. One boy was Friedrich Südhaus. The other, you won't believe it, was Noah Goldmund!

Geraldine sits opposite me and looks at me as she raises her hand. She stopped the business of wearing pleated skirts and crossing her legs. She looks as if she is going to burst into tears any moment. Once in a while she shapes her mouth to a kiss, and then closes her eyes. Meanwhile, Walter, with whom she was going before the vacation, must have noticed what's up. I think she is deliberately trying to make him notice. She doesn't care about anything. She wants everybody to know that now she belongs to me. To me! To me, who can only think about visiting Verena on Thursday in the hospital.

I think if I had not raised my hand Geraldine would not have raised hers. She does whatever I do. She is pale. She has dark circles under her eyes. And again and again she shapes her mouth to the shape of a kiss and closes her eyes. I feel sick. What did I get into? How can I get out of it? I feel sorry for her, this luxury whore. She has as much longing for a real, true, great love as Verena and I have. But can I help Geraldine? No. Never. Not at any time.

By the way, it is interesting to note what Noah and this Friedrich Südhaus replied when Doctor Frey asked them why they were against his telling in detail about the Third Reich and its causes.

First Friedrich Südhaus: "Doctor, I think there ought to be

an end to this eternal business of German self-accusation. Even our Western Allies and all foreign countries are fed up with that! Who are we catering to? Only East Germany, only the Communists!"

This is a strange boy. Wolfgang hates him. This morning at breakfast he quoted opinions Südhaus had supposedly uttered. For instance:

"They should have let Hitler carry on, but good! There were not nearly enough Jews gassed."

"They let him do enough," Wolfgang had answered. "Six million is a pretty good figure."

"Nonsense. It was never more than four. At the most!"

"Ah well, excuse me. Of course there is a tremendous difference if four or six million Jews were murdered."

"Jews have to be eliminated. They are the poison among nations."

"You were going with Vera for a year. She is half Jewish. You knew it. It didn't make any difference to you?"

"No, on the whole, half-Jews have to go. But you see, they also have fifty percent Aryan blood in them. Be reasonable."

Be reasonable. . . . A strange boy, this Südhaus. You know what Wolfgang (who hates him) told me, too? Friedrich's model is Mahatma Gandhi. Can you believe that? I tell you, the boy can't help it. It's the parents, the damned parents who have raised him like that. (I know exactly what happens if parents like Südhaus' should ever read these lines. They will throw the book on the floor and start ranting and raving. But I said this is to be an honest book and so now I just cannot start to lie or leave out passages. Just hold your breath. It's going to get worse yet.)

## [ 10 ]

Just as interesting as Südhaus' answer was the one Noah gave. He said, stammering and with bowed head, as if even he should have a guilty conscience: "Doctor, you know how I admire your stance. You know that I know what you went through in the concentration camp. I'm sure that you want to do only good by your report about the Third Reich. But you also want to do something impossible."

"Such as?" Doctor Frey said, friendly, quiet and limping around in the classroom.

"You want to instruct people who don't want to be taught."

"You mean Südhaus?"

"Yes, him for instance. You won't succeed. You know what will happen? He will just be furious at us and hate us again."

"That is not true, Goldmund."

"That is the truth, pure and simple, Doctor. I admire you. I respect you. But you are on the wrong track. You're going to run into difficulties if you carry on like this. This nation just won't listen to reason. It's all completely senseless. You can see: whoever says anything against the Nazis is immediately a Communist! Do you want to be called that?"

"Yes, Goldmund. Gladly, if it's like that."

"Excuse me, Doctor, but I thought you were smarter than that. What reason is there for abstract truth?"

To that Doctor Frey answered with a sentence so beautiful that I have to write it down here. He said: "The truth is not abstract. The truth is concrete."

[ 11 ]

Wolfgang Hartung gets up, the son of an SS thug who let thousands of Poles and Jews be shot, and says: "I don't care if truth is abstract or concrete. I want to hear the truth! And with the exception of Noah and Friedrich, everyone in this class wants to hear it. We are glad to have a teacher like you. Please, don't give up on us! The vote was two against twenty. Start. Tell us the truth, the whole truth! Don't leave out anything! Somebody has to tell us the truth! How can things get better if no one will tell us how it was?"

"Wolfgang, you don't understand," said Noah.

"What doesn't Wolfgang understand?" asked Doctor Frey.

"He means well, Doctor. He just doesn't see the consequences. If you start discussing now what Hitler did, from every angle, then Friedrich—and perhaps a few of the others—will say: he was right! Don't you understand?" (Never have I seen Noah so excited.) "With the best intentions in the world you are starting something terrible! Let's forget the whole thing! Let's talk about the Emperor Claudius. Tell us again how Mister Nero burnt down Rome. Harmless stories, please! This is not the time to talk about Jews."

"And the six million?" cried Wolfgang.

"Don't yell," replied Noah. "Were any of your relatives involved? Well?"

"I can't forget it," Wolfgang said. "No, no relatives of mine were involved. But my father let your people be killed, Noah. And as long as I live I won't be able to forget it. Unto my death. What happened between thirty-three and forty-five is for me and will continue for me to be the most enormous crime of history. My father was an accessory to the crime. And that is why I want to know everything, everything, everything about this time, because I have to know all, all, all of it if I want to atone for something. And I would like very much to atone for something."

Noah smiled and said, "You're a nice guy. But you have no sense. There is nothing to atone for, not on this earth, believe me."

"I don't believe you," Wolfgang replied. To that Noah was silent and only smiled. And from this smile all of us had to turn away: Wolfgang, I, Doctor Frey, and even Friedrich Südhaus. We couldn't bear this smile.

But then Doctor Frey began to talk. About the Third Reich.

## [ 12 ]

Perhaps he is a nice guy, this Walter Colland—but he isn't fair, no, not at all. He was waiting for me in the woods and when I leave the Quellenhof to go back to school—about 7

P.M.—he jumps me from behind and hits me in the neck with his fist so that I stumble and fall. Then he is on me and hits me wherever he can. And he connects damned good and often. He is stronger than I.

Did my "brother" have a hand in that? Or did the blond Walter think of that himself? It's already quite dark in the woods. Now I'm doing a bit better. He isn't all that strong. We are rolling around on the ground, back and forth on the stones.

I give him one on the kisser. I'm lucky and hit him properly. He moans and slides over to the side and I'm able to get up. Just to be sure I give him one more kick. He stays down and in the moonlight I see that he is starting to cry. That too!

"Leave her alone," he says.

"Who?"

"You know who."

"No idea."

"You can have any girl you want. I'm the only one that has her."

"Get up." He gets up.

"I'm not such a grand kid as you are. I don't have such a rich father. My parents are poor."

"What has that got to do with it?"

"At home we always have arguments. I tell you, Geraldine is all I have."

I just want to answer: Who is taking her away from you? and *her* voice says: "You *have* me? You have *had* me. It's finished. Finished. All over."

Both of us turn around fast. There she is in her green pleated skirt, a jacket around her shoulders, leaning against a tree, smiling that wary smile.

"What are you doing here?" I ask.

"I wanted to pick you up for dinner."

Walter is moaning.

"Did you watch the fight?" I ask her.

"Yes. Why?"

Now I notice that my nose is bleeding. Blood has already dripped onto my jacket. What a mess! I like this leather jacket. So I take a handkerchief and hold it to my nose and say: "Why didn't you make yourself heard before that?"

"Why should I have done that? I have seen everything, and heard everything."

The poor guy, the blond Walter, moves over to her and wants to lay a hand on her shoulder, but she pushes him away.

"Geraldine, please . . . please. Don't be like that."

"Stop it."

"I'll do anything, anything you want. I'll apologize to Oliver. Oliver, please forgive me!"

My nose is still bleeding and I don't answer.

"I love you, Geraldine. I love you so madly . . ."

He says that, really, the idiot!

"Stop it!"

"I can't stop it."

"You disgust me."

"What?"

"Yes!" she yells suddenly, as it echoes through the woods. "You disgust, disgust, disgust me! Did you understand now? Did I make myself clear enough?"

"Geraldine. Geraldine . . ."

"Get going."

"But what shall I do without you? I only have you. Please, Geraldine, please! I don't mind if you go with Oliver, but let me be with you too . . . just be with you . . ." I'm beginning to feel sick. A man can't talk like that!

With every one of his words she grows more and more into her regal role.

"We are finished," she says. And I have to think that his parents are poor, and are at loggerheads with each other, and that her parents are divorced, and what poor creatures they are, and how they hurt each other more, more, more. Often, often, often I wish I had never been born.

Geraldine whips the air with a stick she holds in her hand and yells: "Now are you going to go away and leave us alone or not?"

Walter slinks away in the dark, between the trees. At once she drops the stick and I have her hanging on my neck. She kisses me. She glows.

"Come . . ."

"Not now."

"Please. Please, now. Please."

"No," I say. "We have to go to dinner."

She presses close to me. "We don't have to go and eat."

"Yes. We must. Especially I. I have to do everything to avoid any attention. I was kicked out of five schools. This one is the last one. No other one will take me any more. You have to show some consideration for me."

"I'll do it . . . I'll really do that . . . I'll never create difficulties for you, my darling, never. I'll only do what you want me to . . . if you just stay with me."

Now I ask you: Do you find life beautiful? Two minutes ago Walter spoke just as obsequiously and helplessly as Geraldine does now. It is a pure accident that I come off better in this thing. Just because I'm not in love.

"After dinner, yes?"

I nod.

"In the canyon again? In our canyon?"

I nod. I'm quite determined to run to the Quellenhof right after dinner. I'm not going to the canyon. I am not going to the canyon. I do not want to go to Geraldine again. Never again. Never again. During the fight, during the entire talk, during the history lesson I was thinking of Verena. What lies ahead of her. And that I will see her again, Thursday morning in the hospital. Verena. Verena. Verena.

"I'm so happy. You don't know what kind of a day it has been for me," says Geraldine.

"Come and eat now."

"Yes, let's go quickly and eat. And then to the canyon! The

moon is shining . . . I have left a blanket in school. If you knew . . . if you knew . . ."

"What?"

"I'm almost ready if you just touch me, Oliver. If you look at me. I love you, Oliver, I love you so very much."

"If we don't go and eat now it will look suspicious. And I just can't afford that now. Especially with a girl. The chief will just be waiting for something like that."

"Yes, Oliver, yes, I'm coming. You are quite right. And I know that you don't love me."

Should one answer that? No!

"But this woman you've given the bracelet to . . ."

To that I have to answer: "That is not true!"

"Yes, it is true! I don't know who she is. I don't even want to know—as long as you don't say to me what I've said to Walter."

"What?"

"Go away. Disappear. Leave me alone."

Poor Walter, if you only knew!

Poor people. If they all knew.

It is good that one knows so little, isn't it?

## [ 13 ]

Three hundred children eat dinner. The dining hall is in the basement of the main building. Many long tables. We have to eat in two sessions, one hundred fifty each time, because the hall does not hold more.

The tables are nicely set, and pedagogues or teachers are watching that no one eats like a pig. Most often the chief sits down with us and eats too. I heard that last year he let girls and boys eat together in the hope that they would pull themselves together and develop better manners, I guess. But it didn't help. Now the chief tries a different system. The girls sit on the left, and we sit on the right.

You have no idea how many employees a boarding school

has. The cooks. The waitresses (because we are being waited on), the dishwashers, the potato peelers. Food for three hundred children! Three times a day. The chief says to me as he is showing me my seat: "I'm becoming more and more depressed, Oliver."

"Why?"

"No more personnel. Everybody runs away from me. Below in Rosbach is a barracks. They take my people away. I can pay whatever I will—the Army pays more and more! Well, and the girls are crazy with all the boys down there anyway. If it keeps on this way you will soon have to peel potatoes and wash dishes and serve yourselves!"

At this dinner the incident with Hansi and Rashid, the little prince, takes place. You have to imagine it this way: older and younger boys are sitting together at the long tables. Noah and Wolfgang and a few older boys are sitting at my table and just one chair happens to be empty. I can't help it! It is the chair next to me.

Of course, Hansi walks toward it at once and is about to sit down and the chief says: "No, Hansi. You have been here longer and you have friends among the little boys. You sit over there. Besides, you will make Ali happy by doing that."

"Shit on Ali," says Hansi through his teeth.

"I didn't hear that," says the chief. "But the next time I'll hear it, Hansi. Understand?"

The little cripple nods, looking at me all the time, his eyes glittering.

"Rashid will sit in this chair," says the chief." Mr. Herterich reported to me that he asked for that. Because apparently Oliver had done something for him last night. Isn't that correct?"

"No idea," I say and look at the little prince, who is dressed as impeccably as if he were going to a state reception.

"I don't want to tell tales," says the prince in English.

"I don't want you to tell tales," says the chief. "I already know what happened. Mister Herterich has told me. That was really disgusting behavior, Hansi and Ali. Please, Rashid, sit down."

"Thank you very much," says the prince and sits down between Noah and myself.

"And you go to Ali's table," says the chief. Hansi takes off. In leaving he murmurs to me: "After dinner we'll see."

Like a bad thriller! Just the same I have a very peculiar feeling in my stomach.

Next to my plate is a red rose. Wolfgang and Noah have already made their jokes about it, before Rashid and I sat down. It amused them a lot, that rose.

"Please, leave Oliver in peace," says the prince.

"We don't mean it badly," says Noah. "Love—love is a divine gift."

"I have no idea where the flower comes from," I say lamely.

Then Wolfgang and Noah look at each other and then look across to Geraldine, who is sitting at a girls' table quite a distance away from us and whose face is now turning red. Did I deserve that?

I have to arrange it so that Rashid and Wolfgang and Noah and I will walk together to the Quellenhof.

It's really stupid, but I'm slowly becoming afraid of this Geraldine. She isn't right in her head, and she's quite likely to do anything. Now she's smiling at me again with that crazy, man-mad smile, and everybody sees it.

I just don't want any scandal. I take the rose and smell it and smile back. Then she bends down over her plate and eats, and I have my peace. More and more I think what a horrible life it would be if there were no Verena. Verena, Verena, whom I will see again the day after tomorrow, Thursday.

The waitresses go from table to table and offer platters and we behave quite properly, and when I look over to Geraldine I meet her glance. That's why I look very rarely, but I do look sometimes, because I don't want to make enemies, and I don't know how much Hansi knows; he is sitting at the table looking at me as if he wanted me to drop dead if looks . . . and so on.

Now each of us receives a plate on which are three radishes and four different kinds of cheese. Wild exchanges spring up at table. "Give me your Emmentaler, and you will get my Gervais."

"I'd like the Gorgonzola. You can have my Emmentaler."

And so on. It seems to be the custom here. "You like Camember," says Noah to Wolfgang, pushing his piece over to him and receiving from the nodding Wolfgang a slice of Harzer Roll. "I like Harzer the best," declares Noah. And now Geraldine looks at me again. She is beaming.

I see Walter throwing his napkin on the table and leaving.

I see how the little humpbacked Hansi looks at me. I see how Geraldine looks at me. I choke on my cheese.

## [ 14 ]

"For God's sake, the *chief* said you could not sit next to me, not I, Hansi!" I say. I say it for the third time. We are standing in front of the main building under the old chestnut, and the moon shines poisonous and green through the branches. All the other students have gone to their houses, and dinner is now over. I read a book once with the great title: *Poor, Ugly and Nasty*. I can't help thinking of this title now that Hansi, the hunchback, is looking at me with his hate-distorted face. Poor and ugly, apparently that equals nasty.

"I don't give a shit if the chief sat me somewhere else or not! You are my brother. You should have defended me!"

"Defended you? How?"

"You should have said I insist that Hansi sits next to me. But no. You kept your mouth shut! Of course, a prince is something better than I am! And that's why you defended him against me last night!"

"I didn't defend him because a prince is something better, but because you were nasty to him."

"But you are my brother!"

"That's not the point here!"

"Yes, it is! You always have to help and defend a brother or sister—what other point would there be in this game?"

Owls are hooting.

Verena Lord.

Maybe now she has just told her husband that she is expecting a child?

"And now I'm going to tell you something else, Oliver! The red rose, I put it next to your plate."

"You?"

"Did you think Geraldine is that stupid? Do you think she wants to get kicked out? Didn't you notice how red she became when the others saw the flower? That," says my "brother," "was only a little taste of what is going to happen to you if you don't behave properly with me."

I can just stare at him.

"I am small. I am weak. I am humpbacked. I'm only eleven. But I have a brain. I can get very unpleasant, Oliver. Very!"

One just cannot put up with something like that.

"Now I'm going to tell you something, Hansi! I don't give a damn about you! Find yourself another 'brother.' Anyway, I don't need one who is always spying on me."

To that he hums the march from the *River Kwai* and pushes little stones away with his feet.

"Did you understand me?"

"Exactly, Oliver. And that's why you have to stick to me whether you like it or not. I'm not going to have my brother taken away by such a shit of a prince now that I finally have found one!"

"What does that mean?"

"I know everything," he says and pushes little stones.

"Such as?"

"I have seen everything."

"There was nothing to see."

"Well, now. . . . I saw everything with Geraldine, and everything at the tower."

I don't care about that with Geraldine! But I have to know

exactly what he saw at the tower. "What happened at the tower?"

"You gave marzipan to the little girl, she kissed you, you went upstairs, then the lady came down and then you."

"But you don't know who the lady was."

"Yes, I do."

"Nonsense."

"No nonsense."

"Well then, who was the lady?"

"The mother of the little one."

"Some news! But you don't know her name."

"Oh yes. I know her name too."

"No!" I feel cold.

"Yes."

"How?"

"During the summer the little one came to the pool very often, below, next to the A. She can't swim as yet. I played with her and held her in her float. Her name is Evelyn Lord. So the mother's name is Lord too. I just don't know her first name. But there can't be that many Lords up here, don't you think?"

## [ 15 ]

Do you know that dream (if you've eaten too much), when you're in a room whose walls slowly come toward you, and the floor rises and the ceiling lowers itself, and the air becomes less and less, thinner and thinner—and there is nothing you can do, nothing, nothing, nothing?

I lay my head against the chestnut tree, light a cigarette, and say to the little cripple: "You are quite mad. Never in your life was that little girl from the swimming pool—what, by the way, did you say her name was?"

"You know exactly what her name is, and she was the one."

"No."

"Well, all right," says Hansi.

"What do you mean: 'Well, all right'?"

"First let me have a puff of your cigarette." I give him the cigarette. That's how low a human being can sink.

He gives it back to me; now the mouthpiece is wet, and he blows smoke through his nose and says: "If you don't promise me now, here, that you will be my brother, my real brother, forever—no matter what I do—then I'll tell Geraldine that I saw you at the tower with Mrs. Lord. And then I will tell the chief. And then I will tell Walter. And if all that is not enough, I'm going to find out where these people live, and then tell her husband. Lord. Because if the woman has a child I guess she must have a husband, right? Will he be happy!"

"You pig," I say.

"You see that I'm right."

"Why?"

"If you weren't afraid that I would really do that you wouldn't have called me a pig. But you don't have to be afraid. *As long* as you're my *brother,* I'll be on your side. I promise you, too, to watch out later so no one will catch you."

"Who? Where?"

"Geraldine and you. In the canyon. Where you are supposed to meet."

"Why?"

"I was around when she spoke to you earlier. I'm always around," he says, and now he smiles this terrible, small-lipped, death-head smile. "So that you know that I'm serious," he continues, "I will also tell you that Geraldine is convinced that she will see you tonight."

"How do you know that?"

"I have promised her that you will come."

"You have—"

"Yes. I have. Another little taste of things to come. Like the rose. You must realize that I will not have you taken away from me. Never! By no one!"

"Hansi, you are mad!"

"Of course. What did you think? I'm a cretin. I'm a cripple. But that's why I need you so! Geraldine, she would be someone for me! But I'll never get one like her! Anyway, I'll never get a beautiful girl, crippled and ugly as I am. But I did get a kiss from Geraldine!"

"When?"

"When I told her that I knew something about you and that you would be coming to the canyon. That you must go to the canyon. And you have to! Or I'll tell Geraldine the name of the woman you met in the tower."

Well now, just a minute! He is eleven. I'm twenty-one. It must be possible that I, who am so sure of my intelligence . . .

"Hansi! If you've already been spying on me all the time, then you know also how this thing with Geraldine happened."

"Sure. She caught you as you got the bracelet and followed you and in the woods she threw herself at you."

"Exactly. But I don't love her!"

"Did I say that? You love this other woman. You love Mrs. Lord."

"I don't even know a Mrs. Lord!"

"Oliver," he says, "we'll never get any further this way. I don't want to know whom you love and whom not. I don't care about it one way or the other. I want to sit next to you at meals and I want you to behave as a real brother would."

"And if I can persuade the chief to let you sit next to me, and if I am your real brother—then what?"

"Then I'll keep my mouth shut."

"Word of honor?"

"Real word of honor." With that he gets out a pocket knife and scrapes his wrist a little and a little blood spurts out. "Drink!"

"Why?"

"You swear to me that you will be my brother, and I swear to you that I will not spy on you any more."

And we will both break our oaths, I think. Apparently that is the way it is! The adults do it with state receptions and documents and solemn contracts; the humpbacked Hansi does it with a pocket knife and a little blood.

He holds out his thin arm to me. I lick his blood and think my dinner is coming up. Hansi takes my right wrist, scratches the skin and licks a little of my blood.

"Now," he says then and puts the knife away, "and if one of us breaks the oath he must die." If it is nothing worse than that. . . .

"Go to the canyon. Geraldine is waiting for you. I swear I won't follow you. But if you come to the Quellenhof later you have to go to my room and shake my hand and say: 'Sleep well, Hansi.' Only to me."

"Why?"

"So that Rashid doesn't imagine anything, understand?"

"Understood," I say. David and Goliath. Goliath and David. I will lose Verena and endanger her if I don't do whatever this little beast says.

The little beast says: "I have to be like this, Oliver. For the first time in my life I have a brother. I will never be able to get another one. And I don't want to lose you to this prince."

"You're not losing me."

"I can see how he acts with you."

Now he cuddles up to me. "And I love you so much—"

"Stop it. I don't like that."

He lets go of me. He finally leaves. The little Hansi.

## [ 16 ]

"This time was even more beautiful."

"Yes."

"For you too?"

"Yes."

"Really?"

"Really, Geraldine."

"Don't lie. You surely have experienced it lots of times. With the woman the bracelet belongs to, too."

"No!"

"Why are you getting so upset?"

"Because—because there has never been anything between this woman and me!"

"But there will be."

"No!"

"Why not?"

"Because I don't want to."

"You lie. You want to. I know it. But perhaps it is impossible. I hope . . ."

Has this damned Hansi kept his promise? Probably not. He's hiding in the bushes somewhere again and saw and sees and hears and heard everything. Good Lord, what a spot I'm in!

The green moon is shining into the little canyon, and everything casts strange shadows, including Geraldine and me. We are sitting next to each other on a rock, she with one arm around my shoulder.

It is warm. The owls and other animals are screeching. Geraldine's body is aglow. I can feel it through the dress.

"You know, Oliver, that I lied to you?"

"When?"

"This afternoon. When I said it didn't matter to me if you loved this other woman. That was a lie."

"Yes, naturally."

"Don't be so superior. I am serious! I . . . I couldn't stand it if you loved someone else. If I ever find out that you love her and who she is . . ."

"You'll have to see Hansi."

"What?"

"Clever Hansi, who knows everything. By the way, it was he who managed the thing with the rose."

It is ridiculous, but I'm still holding it in my hand, the red rose, and turn it round and round.

"That was Hansi?"

"Yes," I say loudly, so that he'll hear it if he should be close by, "that was dear Hansi, your confidant. And you are going to have a few more surprises if you don't put him in his place. And now I have to go home. And you too."

Immediately she starts whining again.

"It was just in fun!"

"It was in earnest."

"No, fun! I would lose you altogether! So, if I'm reasonable I still have a part of you. Oliver, Oliver . . . you are not going to leave me?"

Perhaps Hansi *and* Walter are nearby.

"I'm going now!"

"Just another ten minutes. It's still early. Please, please." She kisses me a lot, on the cheeks, on the mouth, on the forehead.

"Can you seriously imagine that I would ever make trouble, make difficulties for you, that I'd ever get in your way?"

"No, Geraldine, of course not." Yes, Geraldine, of course yes! Only difficulties. Only troubles. Only be in my way. How is this going to go on? Now she is stroking my face. "You trust me, don't you?"

"Yes, Geraldine." Not in the least, Geraldine.

"Nobody trusts me, you know. Only you. None of the girls like me." That's no surprise.

"Walter trusted you," I say.

"Oh, him," she says. Never in my life have I heard anyone say two words with such contempt. "You trust me, I trust you. I want to tell you everything."

"You already did."

"No, not just about me. About all the other girls. How things are in our house. You'd laugh yourself to death."

Laugh yourself to death.

I look at my watch.

Nine o'clock.

"Shall I . . . may I tell you a few stories?" With Hansi perhaps in the bushes! Perhaps Walter in the bushes?

"Please, Oliver. Just talk. I don't want anything else any more. Just to stay a little longer in your arms. I'll only tell funny stories, to laugh at—all right?"

Suddenly I feel sorry for her. Only funny stories. How funny are your funny stories, sad Geraldine?

"So tell a few," I say and caress her, and she cuddles up close to me and sighs with happiness.

"I can tell you who goes with whom, if you like . . . almost everyone of us has a. . . . But no one has one like I have! The nicest couple we have are Gaston and Carla. You know Gaston already. Carla is only fifteen."

"Carla is only fifteen, you say?"

"Yes."

"But Gaston is eighteen!"

"Well, so? It's always that way. All the girls go with older boys. The ones of the same age are too dumb."

She has a point.

"Don't you think Gaston is sweet?"

"Sweet."

"They are going dancing in the A on Thursday."

"But it is forbidden to go to the A."

"Everything is forbidden here! Nothing is allowed! If you knew how sick we are of the whole mess! Many go to the A intentionally! They want to get caught! They want to get kicked out!"

"Why?"

"Because they want to go home, home to their parents!"

"But the others," I say.

"Which ones?"

"Those that don't want to get kicked out."

"What about them?"

"I heard the chief has his informers everywhere. Even among the waiters. If one of you shows up there one of those waiters telephones the chief at once. Is that true?"

"Yes, that is true. But Gaston and Carla don't care. They want to get kicked out."

"They want to get kicked out?"

"Yes. And get married. Gaston plays the piano beautifully. He could work in a band right away. And they love each other so much, right?"

And they love each other so much, right?

# [ 17 ]

"But you wanted to tell me funny stories, Geraldine!"

I have to get away. I have to get away. And if I can't get away right now I have to talk with her about things which have nothing to do with love. Or everything will start from the beginning again. Or she will compare Gaston and Carla with us. Or . . .

"Come on! Tell something funny, Geraldine!"

And she tells about all sorts of gossip, tells how comical it is when all the girls fix themselves real "beauty facials" or when Chichita sings "Pigalle, Pigalle, that is the great mousetrap of Paris. Pigalle, Pigalle, there the bacon tastes so sweet!" And so she prattles on with her silly chatter. I hardly listen to it, but think of something quite different and finally say: "Now we must go."

"Yes, Oliver, yes."

So we walk hand in hand (what can I do, she just took my hand) through the autumn forest to the signpost where our paths finally separate, and there we kiss once more. While we are kissing I think of where Hansi could be hiding now, behind which bush, and where Walter is, and what could happen if Hansi gives me away.

"Good night, Oliver."

"Good night, Geraldine."

The owls are screeching.

"Are you so happy, too?"

"Yes."

"That is not true."

"It is."

No. I can tell by your face. I know it. You only think of the woman with the bracelet."

"No."

"Yes. A woman can feel these things. A woman knows these things."

"It is really not true."

"Then say that you are happy. Only a little bit happy."

"I am happy, Geraldine."

"You don't have to have any fear. Of course it is going to come out that we go together. But no one will tell the chief. Not even Walter. Otherwise he will be sent to 'prison.' "

"Prison? What is that?"

"We organized that. If someone informs he is sent to 'prison.' Then nobody talks to him, nobody takes notice of him, he is just nothing for everybody, even for the littlest ones! In minutes everybody in the school knows if we send someone to 'prison.' And it is so bad, the 'prison,' that up to now no one has told tales. No one!"

"So we don't have to be afraid."

"No fear at all. You know what, Oliver?"

"What?"

"Before you came I was always afraid. Not of the 'prison.' Of much, much worse things."

"What kind of things?"

"I won't tell. But now I'm not afraid at all any more. Isn't that beautiful? Isn't that wonderful?"

"Yes," I say, "wonderful."

"Are you afraid too, Oliver?"

"Mhm."

"Of what?"

"Of many things," I say, "but I don't want to talk about it either." And I kiss Geraldine's hand.

"You are my love," she says. "My great love. My only love. You are the love of my life."

I think: that was the last time. This is the end. I don't know how I'm going to tell her that it is finished, but it is finished. And the luxury whore stumbles on into the darkness. I stay on a moment longer, because from where I am standing, I can see Verena Lord's villa. There is light in many of the windows. The drapes are drawn. Behind one drape I see the shadows of a man and a woman. The man has a glass in his hand. The woman is talking to him. He nods. Walks toward her.

It is really stupid to write something like this, but I notice suddenly that I have tears in my eyes.

"Love," it says in that damned sentimental song, "is a many-splendored thing." Is it really? No it is *not*. I throw Hansi's red rose away as far as I can, away into the bushes.

## [ 18 ]

Now I have read once more what I have written up to now, and I believe it is indeed time that I say something: this is not a book against boarding schools. I am not writing to advertise that no one should send his child to a boarding school because he reads what I have written.

I really don't want that. That is not my intention. On the contrary, sometimes I think that a few teachers and pedagogues who read this book will be a little grateful to me because I show how mean some of us are to them, and how difficult it is for them. I very much hope that a few teachers and pedagogues will think that way.

Furthermore I want you to realize: I was kicked out of five boarding schools because I behaved abominably. So you can see: the boarding schools take care themselves that people like me don't corrupt their entire institution. No boarding school in Germany wanted me any more. Because of my reputation. The boarding schools have reputations to lose themselves. They cannot afford to keep characters like me. Only one thought he could afford it and change me: Doctor Florian. He did it because he, as I mentioned, employed different methods; because he was afraid of no one; and because he kicks out characters like me when he cannot put up with us any longer. Naturally, you have to consider that with a man like Doctor Florian, who is so trusting and optimistic—I would almost say dangerously optimistic—more characters of my kind collect here than anywhere else. He is something like a collecting post for all those no one wants any more. In this way his boarding school is not a typical boarding school.

And finally: even at Doctor Florian's there are hundreds of pupils who learn like completely normal students, who behave well and work properly. The teachers are satisfied with them. The parents are satisfied with the school. Everybody is satisfied. If I write little (or not at all) about these normal, good-natured, properly adjusted children, it is because in this story I want to tell I had no contact with such children. And that again is my fault. Birds of a feather. . . . Were I normal, good-natured and decent I would have made contact with this majority—oh yes, surely! But with an almost frightening instinct, those people who are similar always gravitate toward each other. That is the way it is here too.

Boarding schools are a necessary, good institution. In England all parents who can possibly afford it send their children to boarding schools. I say it again: what I portray here are the exceptions, not the rule. It would be terrible if you didn't believe that. Otherwise I would appear mean because of our fine chief, Dr. Frey, the polecat; mean to those other teachers and pedagogues who tried their utmost to make decent people of us—and meanest toward the good old Miss Hildebrand, the mentor who has helped so many children here for so many years.

I am bad, I and a few others, *not* the school! When I was a little boy I loved it most when I could play in the mud after it had rained. In those big puddles, you know? And of course I always became terribly dirty. My mother despaired. Not my father. He just got mad and whipped me at once. That of course didn't help at all.

Then my mother bought me the nicest toys. Dominos, trains, and so on and so on. And said: "Why don't you stay indoors when it rains, darling, and play with your nice things? You have so many of them!"

"I'd rather go outdoors."

"But why? Doesn't all this interest you?"

To that I answered: "No, Mommy, I am interested in dirt."

I was still so little that I was not able to pronounce some

words properly. My mother often told the story, and many people laughed at it.

When I think of the story today I cannot laugh about it any more.

[ 19 ]

When I reach the Quellenhof I see a shadow next to the entrance, under the trees. A few steps more and I recognize Walter. I bend down and pick up a stone. As I said before, he is stronger than I am, and I'm going to make sure he doesn't beat me up again.

As I bend down he says: "Put down the stone. I'm not going to hurt you."

"Then what are you doing here?"

"I wanted to apologize to you."

"What?"

"Apologize, yes. Because of what happened. You can't help it. She alone is to blame. Or maybe not. She is just as she is. When I came it was just the same. My predecessor was Paul. She left him the same way she is leaving me now. And the way she is going to leave you some day because of some other new one. Do you forgive me?"

It's awful when someone asks one something like this, isn't it?

"Sure I forgive you," I say.

And then I even have to offer him my hand.

"Thanks."

"It's okay."

"And be careful. If the chief finds out even the tiniest thing, he's going to kick you out. Both of you."

"Yes, Walter." And I bring myself to say: "If she's the way you say, then you really shouldn't feel so bad!"

Then he turns his head to the side, and his voice sounds choked when he answers: "That's the damned trouble. She can be any way she wants. Worse. Much worse! I couldn't care less what she is! I . . . I love her!" And he runs into the house.

I stay outside for a moment, then I follow him and look into the room in which Rashid, Ali and my "brother" live. Ali and Hansi are sitting on their beds, quite still and solemn, and the little, frail prince is kneeling on his prayer mat saying his evening sure. "In the name of Allah, the all-compassionate! Glory and praise to Allah, the master of all people on earth, the gracious, merciful Lord, who will prevail on the day of judgment! We want to serve only you, and only you we beseech for help. You show us the right path. The path of those with whom you are angry or those who have gone astray."

He bows low three times, then he gets up and rolls up the little carpet, all the while smiling at me. Hansi smiles too, and I'm slowly getting rather afraid of this smile of my "brother." Now is the time. A while ago in the woods he made a demand I must comply with or endanger Verena Lord; I have to comply, even if I hurt Rashid by doing it.

What kind of a life is this, in which we always have to hurt people? A good one?

No, thank you.

The three boys are looking at me now, Hansi and Rashid full of veneration and the longing that I might be their friend, the little Negro with a contemptuous attitude springing from his superiority complex. (What luck—or at least it will be easy with one of them!)

Rashid smiles.

Hansi smiles.

Ali says to me: "What kind of a pigsty is this here! I put my shoes outside the door so they will be polished and this Herterich—"

"*Mister* Herterich."

"What?"

"It's *Mister* Herterich, you understand."

"Ridiculous! I should say *Mister*. To him! He doesn't even earn five hundred marks a month."

"If you don't call him Mister, I'll report it to the chief."

"Tattletale!"

"Call me what you like. What happened with Mr. Herterich?"

"He said I should polish my own shoes."

"He's quite right. We all polish our own shoes."

"Not I! I've never done that in my life! At home I had a white servant for that sort of thing."

"Yes," I say, "but here you're not at home. And here you have no white servant for that. You will polish your own shoes."

"Never!"

"Then go around dirty. I don't care. You should be ashamed. You—the son of a king!"

That does it.

He looks at me for a moment with glinting eyes and pulls at the large gold cross which hangs from the heavy gold necklace round his neck, then he says something African, nothing nice, I'm sure, throws himself on his bed, turns his head to the wall and pulls the blanket over his head.

Now comes the worst moment. I have to do it. Or I'll endanger Verena.

I shake the cripple's hand and say: "Sleep well, Hansi." And then I leave the room. As I turn I see Hansi looking at me with a triumphant expression. The victor. The hunchbacked victor. The forever oppressed, mocked, despised one—tonight he is the victor. That is why he is beaming.

And next to him stands the little prince, with sagging shoulders, the prayer mat still under his arm, looking at me sadly with his liquid, dark, long-lashed eyes. I close the door very quickly behind me.

## [ 20 ]

I go into a bathroom, stand under the shower and soap myself for a long time, because there is still time. It is only nine-thirty. And Verena said I was to go to the balcony at eleven.

After the shower I go to my room. The record player is playing again. I hear the Piano Concerto No. 2 by Rachmaninoff. Wolfgang and Noah are already in bed. Both of them are reading. As I enter they look at me, then at each other, and grin.

"What's so funny?"

"You?"

"Why?"

"Well, you're just funny," says Noah. "You walk funny, you talk funny, you come home funny and late. This is just your funny day. Maybe I find you funnier. More than Wolfgang does."

"What does that mean?"

"Well, we made a bet."

"Don't think I find him less funny just because I had to pay ten marks," says Wolfgang.

"What kind of a bet was it?"

Noah grins again: "Whether or not the luxury whore would make you the very first day."

"And how do you know?"

"Instinct," says Noah with a resounding laugh.

"Nonsense," says Wolfgang to me. "Just on instinct I would never have paid ten marks. Hansi told us."

"Hansi?"

"Sure. He always talks. He tells everything. To everybody. This afternoon at two in the small canyon. Right?"

I am silent.

"You see. One can always rely on Hansi," says Noah. "By the way, he gets one of those ten marks, that was the arrangement."

"Is it always done like that?"

"Of course. If someone wants to know something about somebody he calls Hansi and promises him a certain commission. He will always be well taken care of by Hansi."

"Well, he must be quite wealthy by now," I say.

"He is. He had a huge piggy bank crammed full even before the vacation. Now he's bought a new one."

"Where's the old one?"

"Buried in the woods," says Noah.

Hansi again. Always Hansi.

I get into bed.

## [ 21 ]

Eleven o'clock. Noah and Wolfgang are already sleeping, and it's dark in the room. I get up quietly, find my robe and sneak out onto the balcony. Clouds are covering the sky, the moon has disappeared, the night is black and gloomy. I cannot even see the white front of Verena's villa. I just stare in its direction.

I wait. I freeze. I step from one foot to the other.

Eleven-five. 11:10. 11:15. I have just decided to go back into the house because I think that perhaps Verena's husband had prevented her from doing what she had wanted to do to surprise me, when a tiny light springs up in the darkness. There it is again. And again. I'm so excited that I can hardly breathe. Because after those three light-signals Verena begins to signal.

She has learned how to signal! Not very well yet. But she has only had a few hours. And she learned. For me. My heart beats wildly while I decipher the letters that come to me through the night, hesitant and blurred.

That is a D. And an O. And two MS. An E. An R. An S. A T. An A. A G: DOMMERSTAG!

Of course she means Thursday. She got the N mixed up with the M, but what does it matter? Thursday I am going to visit her in the hospital and she is looking forward to it or she wouldn't have picked such a difficult word. She begins to signal again.

D . . . O . . . M. . . .

I run, as quietly as I can, back to my room and take my flashlight from my bedside table. I go back outside onto the balcony where Verena is signaling the second word: D . . . A . . . Y. . . .

I lean back against the cold wall of the house, and now I signal, and because I'm afraid that she knows only the letters of this one word, I signal the same as she, but correctly.

D . . . O . . . N . . . N . . . E . . . R . . . S . . . T . . . A . . . G. . . .

If only it doesn't hurt her too much.

Five seconds' interval.

Then she signals again.

D . . . O . . . M . . . M . . . E . . . R . . . S . . . T . . . A . . . G. . . .

We signal the only word she learned; she incorrectly, I correctly.

DOMMERSTAG.

DONNERSTAG.

Dear God, dear God above, please take care that she won't have much pain.

# Chapter Three

[ 1 ]

I don't think I will ever be a writer, because I can't ever describe Verena Lord's face on this Thursday morning. I can find no words, no expressions to describe how I feel when I enter her room. It is a large, beautiful room, and outside the window is an old sycamore tree, whose leaves are beautifully colorful, red and gold, yellow, brown and orange. Verena is in a bed next to the window. She is very pale, and there are dark circles under her eyes. That's why her eyes seem twice as large, enormously large. The entire face, with the bloodless lips, the sunken cheeks and her hair drawn back and fastened at the nape of her neck, seems to consist only of eyes, those sad, knowing eyes, which I will never, never be able to forget; of which I dream; the most beautiful eyes in the world; the most passionate; and perhaps the saddest. I don't believe that real love can ever be anything else but sad.

"Hello," she says. But only her pale lips smile, not her eyes.

"Was it very bad?" I ask and forget even to say good day.

"Not at all."

But I can see that she's lying, because she still smiles distortedly. "Are you in great pain?"

"They gave me injections and pills immediately afterward. Really, Oliver, it was nothing!"

"I don't believe you. I believe that it's very painful."

"But you prayed for me."

"Yes."

"Really?"

"Yes."

"Do you usually pray?"

"No, never."

"You see, and in spite of that it helped. I thank you, Oliver."

I still don't believe her. I say nothing, but place a bunch of flowers on the bed.

"Red carnations!" And now—for a moment—her eyes smile too. "My favorite flowers."

"I know."

"From whom?"

"Yesterday, in my free time, I walked up and down in front of your house until I finally saw Evelyn. I think she likes me."

"Very much! You are the first uncle she likes."

"She told me you were in the hospital to have your tonsils out and I asked her then what your favorite flowers are. It was very simple."

"Oh, Oliver!"

"Yes?"

"Nothing. Please ring for the nurse. I would like to have the flowers next to my bed."

"But if your husband—"

"You did register here as my brother?"

"Sure, the way you said."

"Well, my brother could really have visited me here and brought my favorite flowers for me! He lives here in Frankfurt. And he even looks a little like you! My husband arranged a job for him. In the Exchange at the Main Station. By the way, imagine: he had to go to Hamburg this morning, my husband, very suddenly. We have as much time as we want. He will come back at night. Isn't that wonderful?"

I can only nod. These black, sad eyes make it difficult for me to breathe, to talk, to be.

"Sit down."

I take the chair and pull it toward the bed.

"How did you get here?"

"By car."

"Nonsense! Of course not by walking. But you have school now!"

"Oh, that. That was quite simple! This morning I told the pedagogue that I felt sick. So he got a thermometer. In my room there's a nice boy—Noah is his name—who showed me how it's done with a thermometer after I explained to him that I had to get away in the morning."

"How is it done?"

"You hold the end where the mercury is between two fingers and—"

Door opens.

A nurse appears, all in white.

"You rang, Madame?"

"Yes, Nurse Angelica. My brother, Otto Wilfred . . ."

I rise and say: "How do you do."

". . . brought me a few flowers. Would you be so kind as to bring a vase?"

"Of course, Madame."

Nurse Angelica leaves. She takes the flowers with her. As soon as the door has closed behind the nurse Verena says: "So you hold the end between two fingers—and?"

"Well, and then you rub. The mercury rises in no time at all. I rubbed it and it rose to *42*. We had to shake it down again."

"A marvelous remedy. I'll have to remember that."

"Why?"

"You know, sometimes my husband wants something from me and—"

"All right," I say quickly. "All right."

[ 2 ]

"Verena?"

"Yes?"

"Monday night, with your Morse code, you made me very happy."

"That's what I intended. Did I signal very badly?"

"You signaled wonderfully! Always *Dommerstag* instead of *Donnerstag!*"

"I mixed up *n* and *m?*"

"Yes."

We both laugh. Suddenly Verena stops, holds her abdomen, and makes a face.

"Are you in pain!"

"Not at all! Only when I laughed so hard! Carry on! Now, how high was your fever?"

"39.5. The pedagogue wouldn't let me go to school. He called the doctor. But he could only come at night."

"And then?"

"By then the fever will have gone down. Until the day after tomorrow! Because I can't stand not seeing you any longer than that."

"I'm going to be discharged from here tomorrow. I'll be able to walk a little by then. My husband wants me to recuperate in the villa. Because the weather is still nice."

"Well, if only the weather would stay nice like that for a while longer! Then I can rub the thermometer every other day, and maybe I can meet you in our tower on Saturday."

"I hope so, Oliver, I hope so. Now go on." She talks quickly, like someone who only talks to prevent the other from saying something the first one does not want to hear. "What happened after they saw that you had a temperature?"

"Easy as pie. I waited until the others were in class, then I got up and saw Mr. Herterich, the pedagogue, and talked seriously with him."

"Seriously?"

"You see, this Herterich is new in the school. Unsure of himself. Weak. I helped him once when he couldn't manage a few of the little boys. He hopes that I will help him again. So I said to him: 'Mr. Herterich, I rubbed the thermometer.' 'That's what I thought,' he says sadly. 'Now there are two possibilities,' I say. 'I really must get away for a few hours. Possibility number one:

You don't know anything and I promise you that I will be back in my bed at twelve-thirty at the latest, before the others return. That is one possibility. The other is that you call the chief now to tell him what I just told you. In this case I swear to you that you will voluntarily leave here within a month—fit for a mental institution. I have a lot of friends here and you haven't got one.' Of course he was reasonable and said I could take off and that he knew nothing as long as I was back by twelve-thirty, before the others returned. He was even grateful."

"What for?"

"That I promised to help him with the little ones. There's a crazy Negro there who imagines all whites are dirt and—"

"Oliver?"

"Yes?" I lean over to her. She leans over. There is a knock. We jump back. Nurse Angelica returns with a vase with my carnations. She places it on the bedside table and admires the flowers and my good taste and congratulates Madame on her charming brother. She's enough to turn your stomach, this Nurse Angelica!

After she leaves the room I bend forward again. But Verena shakes her head and pushes me back. "No," she whispers, "not now. You don't know what I'm risking. I bet she's outside looking through the keyhole and listening," she whispers. "She'll never believe that you're my brother."

It makes sense to me. And I whisper as quietly as she, "Funny beginning, isn't it?"

"Funny beginning for what?"

"For love," I whisper. "Perhaps not for you. But for me."

After that she is silent for a long time and then she says: "Dreadful! Nothing scares me more."

"What scares you?"

"Love. Real love."

"But why?"

"Because all my real loves ended terribly. They started beautifully and ended terribly. I don't want any new love. I've had enough!"

"You don't love your husband."

"No."

"That's why."

"That's why?"

"That's why you're longing for love, even though you are afraid of it."

"Nonsense."

"It isn't nonsense. Everybody needs someone he can love."

"I love my child."

"A child is not enough. It has to be an adult. Perhaps I'm not the right one for you. You are definitely the right one for me."

"How can you know that?"

"One knows if it is true love. Instantly. I knew it instantly."

She takes my hand and her eyes, her wonderful eyes look directly into mine when she says: "I have told you how miserably off I was when I met my husband. You know a lot about me. I know nothing about you."

"But about my father!"

"Not even about him."

"How can you not know? The scandal he caused made headlines in all the papers in the Federal Republic!"

"At that time I had no money to buy newspapers. I had other problems. Sometimes when I asked my husband later what about this Mansfeld he always said: 'You wouldn't understand that anyway, so there is no point in my explaining it to you.' "

"Because he worked with him."

"What?"

"And he's still working with him! That's how I knew your name at once at the Rhein-Main Airport."

"What did your father do, Oliver? Why do you hate him so?"

I'm silent. Outside the maple leaves are stirring, the golden, the red and the brown leaves, in a gentle south wind.

"Oliver!"

"Yes?"

"I asked you why you hate your father so much. What did he do to you?"

"I'll tell you," I say softly. "I'll tell you everything."

She reaches for my hot hand. Her hand is ice-cold.

"It started on the first of December, on a Monday. Yes, that's when it started. For me, anyway. On that Monday the Homicide Divsion of the Frankfurt Police Headquarters was informed that a tragedy had happened in the main office of the Mansfeld Works. A certain Emilie Krakel called. Her voice . . .

[ 3 ]

. . . was shrill with horror. "I'm one of the cleaning women here . . . and just as I entered Mr. Jablonski's office, there he was sitting, sitting in his chair at his desk—slumped, with his head on the desk. He had a hole in the temple. Blood everywhere. Somebody must have shot him. Come—come quickly!"

The homicide squad came quickly. Quarter of an hour later they were there. The name of the man in charge was Hardenberg. His men got straight to work. The fifty-year-old chief clerk met his death by a pistol, .38 caliber. The bullet had entered his head through the right temple and on its way out had torn away a part of the left temple. The bullet was found, not the pistol. The police examiner explained: "Naturally, I cannot be sure until after an autopsy. But one thing is certain: this man has been dead quite a few hours." "More than twenty-four hours?" asked the Police Inspector Hardenberg.

"At least thirty-six," answered the doctor.

According to that estimate, death must have occurred in the hours of Saturday afternoon. It was known that Jablonski, though happily married and the father of two children, often spent Saturday afternoons, even Sundays on occasion, in the empty building at work in his office. On this particular weekend his family had gone to relatives in Wuppertal. (This explained why his wife had not contacted the Missing Persons Bureau.)

Police Inspector Hardenberg and his staff found that the chief clerk's office had been completely ransacked. Cupboards had been broken into, the contents of drawers partly burned on the floor, partly thrown around the room, and the door of the safe was open. I can remember it well when my father was informed by telephone, just as I was getting up to go to school.

I was thirteen years old then, a poor scholar, an awkward boy with spotty skin and clumsy movements who was afraid of all the other boys and ashamed in front of girls. I preferred to spend the time alone. My father was a massive man with the florid face of a wine-drinker and the ruthless manner of the man of big business. In 1952 he was the owner of one of the largest radio and television manufacturing concerns in Germany. He was a millionaire. In the hall of our treasure-laden villa at Beethovenpark hung a Rubens, which my father had bought at an auction for 600,000 Deutschmarks; in the drawing room were two Chagalls (DM 250,000), in the library a Picasso (DM 300,000). We owned three cars, a plane and the pilot to go with it, a man called Teddy Behnke, who had flown bombing planes during the war. I liked Teddy very much, and he liked me too, I think.

My father was an electrician by trade. In 1937 he met my mother. In 1938 they married. In 1939 I was born. They say that all children think their mothers are beautiful. I've never done that. I love my mother, I feel very sorry for her, but I've never thought she was beautiful, never. She wasn't. She was too skinny, too bony, her features were always blurred, her figure was bad. She had dull blonde hair. She cried easily and often. She was never able to dress elegantly—not even when she had millions.

My father had learned his trade in the radio factory that had belonged to my mother's parents. He only married my mother because of the factory. I'm quite convinced of that: this way he hoped one day to be owner of a small but well-functioning business. But then the war upset his plans. In 1940 he was conscripted into the Army and was a soldier until 1945. In 1945 my mother's parents were killed in a bombing raid, the little factory was half destroyed, and it was a great joy, a gift from heaven for us, that the Americans released my father from the POW camp and that we saw him again, and in good health. I was six years old then. We didn't have a dime. The only thing we had was the half-destroyed factory which now belonged to my mother. Toward the end of 1946, my father had already started working in this ruin. He had two people who helped him, two women: my mother and a certain Miss Lizzy Stahlmann. This Miss Stahlmann was in every way the opposite of my mother. She was beautiful. She was much younger. Even in the hard times after the war she was elegantly dressed. She could cope with any situation. My father brought her home one day and gave a very short explanation: "Miss Stahlmann is an old friend of mine, whom I met again by accident. I suggest we all say *du*. After all, we are working together, right? You, Oliver, will call her Aunt Lizzy."

"Yes, Papa," I answered.

The Mansfeld Works—this pompous name my father gave to the ridiculous ruin which once had belonged to my mother's parents—was registered in 1946 in Frankfurt's Trade Register as a limited-liability company. My mother and my father were equal owners. The essential stock of 500,000 marks my father received for a promissory note from a banker in Frankfurt. This banker's name was Manfred Lord.

[ 4 ]

Now my old man sat with these two women, who were so different from each other, in the dirty, awful hall of the small factory. Through its roof rain and snow found their way, and the women wound condenser coils by hand while my father assembled the first primitive radios. The parts he needed—tubes, fuses, switches, casings and things like that—he acquired laboriously on the black market. Sometimes he had to travel to Munich or Bremen for a few meters of copper wire.

Our apartment had been destroyed by bombs, as had my mother's parents' house and Aunt Lizzy's apartment. So it just happened that all of us lived in the factory. I had a small room, Aunt Lizzy slept in a bare storage room, my parents in another one. For the time being they adhered to the general custom whereby the husband sleeps in the same room as the wife. For the time being, I say. In misery. In a half-destroyed factory. 1946. By 1952 my father was employing more than two thousand laborers and employees, the pathetic ruin had changed into a skyscraper, the central office in Frankfurt had branches in Munich, Stuttgart, Hanover, and Hamburg. In each of the branches, in accordance with an exact rationalizing plan, single parts were manufactured and shipped to Frankfurt. There they were assembled and dispatched to foreign countries.

Now we lived in a villa next to the Beethovenpark. My father owned the Rubens, the Chagalls, the Picasso; owned the Cessna, the pilot; owned millions. One small thing had changed. My father no longer slept in a room with my mother.

My mother cried much and easily. She did that mainly at this period. My father sent her to important doctors. These again sent my mother to sanatoria in Bühlerhöhe, Bad Hamburg, and Bad Wiessee. The different cures had no effect. My mother became quieter and more emaciated. Now she looked like an old woman.

Politicians and artists, scientists and racketeers came to the parties which my father frequently gave. Most of them despised my old man, who very often got drunk at these parties, tore open his dinner shirt and poured champagne over his hairy chest, which amused him—only him—no end. But everyone flattered him, because many people needed him and many of them were afraid of Walter Mansfeld. In their eyes, I think, my father was a parvenu, a brutal cutthroat. But his factories were doing tremendous business and whoever opposed him he destroyed. His favorite quote consisted of the only two words of Latin he knew: *Non olet*. No, apparently money didn't stink!

My mother attended my father's parties more and more infrequently. Most often she developed migraine and had to stay in bed. At those times, Aunt Lizzy, beautiful, young, and desirable, substituted for the hostess with complete charm. Sometimes both women were present. They wore the most expensive clothes and the most precious jewelry. The circumstances surrounding this jewelry were peculiar. On the day of the party my father would have the precious stones taken out of his bank vault; after the party he took them back and the next day they would go back into his vault. The jewelry didn't belong to the two women. My father only dressed them up with it.

I believed.

Many believed.

Only the police inquiries after the death of Chief Clerk Jablonski brought to light that Aunt Lizzy too had access to my father's vault and full power of attorney.

## [ 5 ]

On this first day of December 1952 I was in school particularly late and returned home by two in the afternoon. I noticed that several black cars were parked outside the gate and that this stood open. I walked up the gravel path to the villa. Here too the door was open. In the hall were men I had never seen before. Our servant, Victor, stood next to the stairs that led up to the first floor and didn't bat an eyelid when he saw me.

Strangely, I noticed at once that the Rubens was not hanging in its usual place. What could have happened? With my bookbag in my hand, I stopped and watched the strange men who hurried back and forth, into the library, into the drawing room, into my father's study. It took quite a while before Victor woke from his torpidity and said to a tall, slim man with white hair: "That is he."

Thereupon this man came to me and asked, friendly: "You are Oliver Mansfeld?"

"Yes."

"My name is Hardenberg. I'm a police inspector."

"A detective?"

"You mustn't be afraid. I—"

"But I am afraid!" I cried. "What is going on here? What happened?"

He was silent.

"Mr. Victor!" I called.

But the servant was silent too, and silent men kept walking through the hall, into the drawing room, into my father's study.

Inspector Hardenberg smiled.

"First put down your bookbag."

I let it drop to the floor, onto the thick Smyrna carpet.

"And now we'll sit by the fireplace; I'll explain everything to you." With gentle force, he led me to the cold fireplace, in front of which we both sat down on huge, old and very valuable wing chairs.

"Where's my mother? Where's my father? Who are all these men?"

"That's just what I want to explain to you," answered Hardenberg in a friendly way. "You must not get excited. What has happened has happened. Now you must be a brave, clever boy. And in certain situations one must be able to face the truth, as much as it might hurt."

"Inspector," I said, "what could have happened?"

He shrugged his shoulders (a nice man, one could see; how embarrassing it was to him and how difficult it was for him to have to explain to me, especially to me, a child) and said: "They are gone, my poor little one."

"Who are gone?"

"Your father, your mother and Miss Stahlmann. I believe you call her Aunt Lizzy."

"Because I have to."

"Because you have to?"

"My father says he'll slap my face if I don't. What does it mean, they are gone?"

Hardenberg took a draw on his cigar.

"Don't look at me like that! It's not my fault! Your father withdrew his entire banking account, his valuable paintings and the jewelry which belonged to Aunt Lizzy and your mother; and then the three of them got into his plane and—*ssst!*" In his embarrassment he made a descriptive movement with his hand.

"Where to?"

"Luxembourg. That's just a cat's jump from here. We were too late. They have already landed in Luxembourg. It's my fault. I made one mistake. I let your father go. This morning, after the first interview."

"I don't understand that."

"You know that his chief clerk was found dead?"

"Yes. I was just getting up to go to school when my father was called because of that. He left for the plant immediately." Suddenly I noticed that my knees were shaking. "For God's sake, my father didn't kill Mr. Jablonski and escape because of that?"

"Mr. Jablonski committed suicide. Your father just got rid of the gun and several papers and arranged things so it would look like murder."

"How do you know that?"

"Many men worked many hours to establish that. I can't explain it so simply to you. It is true."

"But . . . but if my father didn't kill Mister Jablonski, then why did he get rid of the pistol? Why did he withdraw all his money? Why did he take the paintings and jewelry and take off with my mother and this witch?"

"Perhaps I will be able to explain that to you tonight. Or tomorrow. But more than likely you won't be able to understand it, my little one."

"Please, Inspector, don't always say 'my little one' to me. I'm not so little any more! And I will understand it; rely on that, Inspector."

"I didn't want to hurt you, Oliver. But may I say *du?*"

"Of course, Inspector."

"And you call me Hardenberg."

I felt tears rising, and I swallowed hurriedly, because I didn't want to cry. "And they left nothing for me? No letter? No message?"

"I'm afraid not."

"Oh, yes," our servant said at that point.

"Mr. Victor?"

"I beg your pardon for interrupting this conversation, but your mother left a message for you, Oliver." He fished out a few tissues and while doing that, he said quietly and quickly to the inspector (but I heard it anyway): "Madame did not want to leave. There was a terrible scene. Mrs. Mansfeld locked herself in the bathroom. Mr. Mansfeld yelled and raged. Finally he broke down the door and dragged Madame out. At the last moment she gave me this." And Mr. Victor handed me the tissues. I unfolded them carefully. Inspector Hardenberg got up, stood next to me and read what I read.

The words were written in disorderly letters, probably with an eyebrow pencil, all smudged and smeared. My mother didn't seem to have found anything else to write with in the bathroom. I read and over my shoulder Hardenberg read, too.

"My poor, poor child! One day you will understand what happened here today. I have no choice."

Second tissue.

"I have to go with your father; we cannot wait for you. As soon as everything is sorted out, you follow"

Third tissue.

"us. I will call you Tuesday evening. You know how much I love you. But I have to leave you alone for"

Fourth tissue.

"a little while. Please forgive me. Thousand kisses. Your unhappy Mommy."

"That's all?" I asked.

"That is all," said Victor.

And strange men walked through the house, and Inspector Hardenberg was called to the phone. When he got up he stroked my hair.

## [ 6 ]

The detectives stayed the whole day. Hardenberg left, came back, left again. Late last night he returned once more, and when he heard that I had not eaten and could not sleep, he gave me two pills. I swallowed them, drank some water, and Hardenberg said: "Now you'll sleep very well. Tomorrow you don't have to go to school. I'll call your teacher. Why are you laughing?"

"Because tomorrow we have a very, very difficult test in mathematics!" Five minutes later I was asleep. I slept for twelve hours.

The next day the same detectives were in the house and a few new ones too. They searched every corner. I was everywhere and in everyone's way and so I went to my room and sat by the windows and read again and again my mother's last message, written on those four tissues. It was by now very blurred. Only one sentence remained legible:

"You know how much I love you."

About seven o'clock my mother called from Luxembourg.

"My poor darling, can you hear me clearly?"

"I can hear you well, Mommy, and Inspector Hardenberg can hear you well, too. He is holding the receiver very close to his ear."

"That's why I can't explain everything to you."

"Then write it."

"The mail would be opened."

"Yes, but . . ."

"It won't be much longer, darling, it won't take much longer, then you'll be with me and I'll explain everything to you."

"Yes, Mommy. How long will it take?"

"Not much longer, not much longer at all, my heart."

But there she was wrong. One day after the other passed. I didn't receive any news. New men appeared in our home. Mr. Victor told me they were internal revenue men. "They are working everywhere, in the plant, in the branches in Munich, and Stuttgart, in Hanover and Hamburg."

"What are they looking for?"

"You wouldn't understand that," said Mr. Victor. Everybody I asked at this time what really had happened told me I wouldn't understand anyway. From my mother I received pretty picture postcards. On them was always written how much she loved me. A few times she called me and told me so, but she did not tell me when I would be allowed to come to her.

"You have to have a little patience, darling, only a little patience, then everything will be all right."

All right?

On the fifteenth of December another postcard arrived. This time it was from "Aunt" Lizzy! "My dear little Oliver, your poor mother unfortunately is in a very nervous condition and had to be taken to a sanatorium. Hopefully she will be better soon. And hopefully you will be with us soon. Consider yourself hugged and kissed by your loving Aunt Lizzy and Papa."

The word *Papa* my father had written himself. It was the first and last word written to me by him which I have read in all those years.

## [ 7 ]

Inspector Hardenberg arranged that for the time being I did not have to go to school at all.

"Aunt" Lizzy called and asked what I wanted for Christmas.

"To be allowed to go to Mommy."

"But Mommy is in a sanatorium, my treasure, you know that."

"Then I don't want anything."

Nevertheless a few days before Christmas three huge packages arrived, addressed to me.

"Do I have to accept them?" I asked Hardenberg, who came every day and looked after me.

"You don't have to."

"I don't want them," I said.

So the three packages were returned to Luxembourg.

Christmas Eve I spent with Victor and our servants. My father telephoned but I hung up at once, and a little later my mother called. She spoke with a weak voice. The connection was bad and my mother told me that she would be leaving the sanatorium soon and everything would be all right. I just must not lose heart.

"No, Mommy, I won't lose heart."

"And you know that I love you very much?"

"Yes, Mommy. I love you very much too. I hope you feel better. And a Merry Christmas."

On the twenty-eighth of December one newspaper carried the headline:

RADIO MILLIONAIRE MANSFELD FLED
DEFRAUDED STATE BY 12.5 MILLION MARKS

Underneath this fat headline in a long article was written—and the next day underneath a few thousand fat headlines in a few thousand long articles in a few thousand other domestic and foreign papers—how my father was the most notorious tax evader of the postwar era. The investigators had finished their work and made public the results of their search. I read a few papers, but I didn't understand what they meant. I kept them anyway, those papers. I still have all of them today, and today I understand what they said.

Briefly this is what they said:

Using fraudulent business sale numbers, false balances, allegedly unmarketable but in fact very salable radios, but mostly through simulated deliveries and transactions abroad, it was possible for my father, between the monetary changeover in the year 1948 and December 1952 to defraud the German Internal Revenue Department by 12.5 million marks. That kind of enormous manipulation he of course was not able to do by himself, but had assured himself of the assistance of his chief clerk, Jablonski. When in October 1952 it became apparent that in December there would be a tax audit (actually completely harmless), Jablonski lost his head and shot himself in the early afternoon of the twenty-ninth of November 1952 in his office. My father, who by pure chance was still in the plant, discovered the suicide and arranged it so that it would seem to be murder—and also destroyed important papers. When he realized, after the first questioning by Inspector Hardenberg in the early morning hours of the first of December 1952, that Hardenberg did not believe it to be murder but assumed suicide, he escaped with all his ready money, his most valuable art treasures, my mother and Aunt Lizzy to Luxembourg, where in the beautiful village of Echternach he had owned a splendid house for a considerable time.

The newspapers of the twenty-ninth of December 1952 reported that on the day before my father had held a press conference, via his own transmitting system, with fifty-seven domestic and foreign journalists. My father was in his house in Echternach. The journalists were in an office of a press agency in Frankfurt. They were allowed to ask questions. My father could answer them if he wanted to. If he didn't want to, he didn't have to answer them. Because I kept the old papers I only have to copy the way this question-and-answer game took place:

*Question:* Mr. Mansfeld, you know the serious accusations against you. Do you have anything to say to them?

*My father:* Lies, from A to Z.

*Question:* Why then did you escape to Luxembourg, a country which, as is well known, does not extradite people because of tax evasion?

*My father:* I did not escape. I'm here on business.

*Question:* For how long?

*My father:* For an indefinite time.

*Question:* Is it true that the Mansfeld Works have defrauded the German Internal Revenue by 12.5 million marks?

*My father:* If that is so *I* have nothing at all to do with it.

*Question:* Who does then?

*My father:* My chief clerk Jablonski. That's probably why he shot himself.

*Question:* Do you expect us to believe that a chief clerk

could, without the knowledge of his superior, manipulate such adventurous transactions?

*My father:* Believe it or don't believe it. I don't care. I knew nothing about it.

*Question:* But you know that Mr. Jablonski leaves behind a wife and two children?

*My father:* I offer them my condolences.

*Question:* Why don't you face the German authorities if you are innocent?

*My father:* Gentlemen, after years of hard work I have built up my radio factories, which number among the largest in Germany. I will not return to Germany because I will not let my life's work be destroyed! I know that an arrest warrant has been issued for me and my wife and that we can be arrested as soon as we set foot on German soil. Well, we will not set foot on German soil soon. We are very comfortable here in Luxembourg.

*Question:* You talk about your life's work, Mr. Mansfeld. Is it not in even greater danger if you don't return to Germany voluntarily and face an investigation?

*My father:* No. Why?

*Question:* Do you not know that the German authorities can take your factories and villa in pledge up to 12.5 million marks?

*My father:* That is just what they cannot do!

*Question:* What is that supposed to mean?

*My father:* With the exception of the aforementioned villa and its contents I have no possessions in Germany. The gentlemen may have the villa. Good luck to them!

*Question:* And your factories? What do you mean you have no possessions in Germany?

*My father:* I'm sure it has not escaped the attention of the august tax authorities that I have had the status of the Mansfeld Works altered into a joint stock company with an original stock of 30 million marks.

*Question:* Where is the new company located? In a foreign country?

*My father:* No comment!

*Question:* But the tax authority can impound your shares.

*My father:* It cannot, because neither I nor any member of my family owns even a single share.

*Question:* And who owns the stock shares?

*My father:* My old friend Manfred Lord, the well-known banker from Frankfurt, who has helped me build my plants, and who owns nineteen per cent. Of course, this nineteen per cent cannot be impounded since Mr. Lord bought them properly.

*Question:* Who owns the remaining eighty-one per cent?

*My father:* The remaining eighty-one per cent I have sold to a Belgian banking association.

*Question:* Which one?

*My father:* That is none of your business.

*Question:* Did you sell them as repurchasable?

*My father:* No comment.

*Question:* How are your factories going to continue working?

*My father:* The same as before. The authorities know exactly that they are not allowed to impound one screw in the factories. Being general director I shall direct the work of the plants from here.

*Question:* For how long?

*My father:* Perhaps for a few years. Tax fraud falls under the statute of limitations even in the Federal Republic.

*Question:* So one day you intend to return to Germany and continue working without paying back even one penny of the 12.5 million marks?

*My father:* I don't even know what you are talking about. I don't have to repay even one single penny.

*Question:* Why is your little son Oliver still in Germany?

*My father:* Because I wish it. He will remain in Germany, matriculate in Germany and then join the management of the business. He can do that in seven years.

*Question:* You mean, you can't do that in seven years and that's why he should stay?

*My father:* This is a remark I use . . .

[ 8 ]

. . . to terminate this interview: Good evening, gentlemen, said my father and replaced the receiver. With that the press conference was ended.

After I told all this to Verena, both of us are silent for a long time, and we still hold hands. Hers, meanwhile, has become warm. A jet plane flies above the building. From afar I hear children singing: "Let the robbers march underneath the golden bridges . . ."

Asks Verena: "And what else?"

"Oh, nothing else that's special. All the employees left and the tax authority impounded the house."

"But you had to live somewhere!"

"Inspector Hardenberg continued to look after me. At first I lived for a while in a hotel, in a good one too, because my father, who with his swindled money was sitting pretty, was transferring money somehow. But then came the Young People's Welfare Office."

"Welfare Office?"

"Sure! Because I was a child without parents. Under age. The parents escaped and were impossible to reach. So I had a guardian and he put me in a home."

"That, too."

"I really don't want to complain, but it was a damned miserable time! Now can you understand why I have such warm feelings for my father?"

She is silent and strokes my hand.

"By the way, I was in this home only for a year," I say. "Then I went to my first boarding school."

"Boarding school—but that is terribly expensive!"

"Meanwhile things had settled down to a routine. Your husband transferred money to my guardian's account every month."

"*MY* husband? But how—?"

"To appear as if he acted out of compassion and to help an old friend. The old friend was my father. The authorities had to be satisfied with that! In truth these two are still in cahoots, as I have already told you, and your husband still receives the money he transfers. I don't know how, but he gets it. My father will have thought of something. Terribly funny, really! Your husband still pays for me every month, and we are sitting here, and you are stroking my hand, and I . . ."

"Stop it." She averts her head.

"What is it?"

"I have never loved my husband," she says. "I was grateful because he took Evelyn and me out of poverty. I was grateful for the good life which he offered me, but I have never loved him. But I have respected him until today. Manfred, to me, was until today something like . . . like his name! A lord. A gentlemen! One who does not do dirty business."

"I'm sorry to have destroyed an illusion."

"Oh."

"For consolation: we have a little cripple in the boarding school who is very cunning. You know what he says: All people are pigs."

"Do you believe that too?"

"Mhm."

"But . . ."

"But what?"

"But . . . but one can't live if one thinks like that!"

And now she again looks at me with those black, knowing eyes.

I feel hot. I bend forward, kiss her neck and say: "Excuse me. Excuse me. I don't believe that."

Suddenly she puts both arms around me and holds me tight.

I can feel the warmth of her body through the cover, I smell the fragrance of her skin and my lips stay on her neck. Neither of us moves. We stay like this for a long time. Then she pushes me away, fiercely, with both fists. It hurts me.

"Verena!"

"You don't know what I have done! With how many men I have—"

"I don't want to know. Do you think I'm an angel?"

"But I have a child . . . and a lover!"

"No lover. Only somebody you sleep with."

"And before him I had another! And another! And another! I'm a whore! My life is rotten. I'm worth nothing! I'm not worth a penny! Calculation made me get married, and from the first moment on—"

"Now let me say something!"

"What?"

"You are wonderful," I whisper and kiss her hand. "To me you are wonderful."

"I'm already inducing my little child to help me with my deceit. I . . . I . . . I . . ."

"You are wonderful."

"No."

"Well, all right, then you are worth as much as I. I always said, it's scary how similar natures attract each other, find each other, perceive each other. Isn't that wonderful?"

"You think so?"

"Yes, Verena, I think so."

"But I don't want to. I don't want to!"

"What?"

"I don't want to start again. With you. I don't want to deceive Enrico too."

Suddenly she starts to laugh. At first I think it is an attack of hysteria, but no, it is quite a normal laugh. She laughs until once more she has pain and presses her hand to her abdomen.

"Ouch," she says. "Now I know that I have to watch out.

You're right, Oliver, it is very funny. Terribly funny! Life as a whole."

"There, you see," I say. "That's what I say."

[ 9]

The children are singing in the distance again. There must be a playground somewhere. *"A little man stands in the woods, quite still and silent . . ."*

Verena and I have looked at each other for a long time. We spoke the last words unflinchingly, she with an expression as if she were seeing me for the last time. Now we are both talking at once and are both looking elsewhere, she at the ceiling, I out the window. You know? As if we were afraid of each other. No, not of each other; as if we were both afraid of ourselves.

"My father is . . ."

"And from this first boarding school you . . ."

*". . . it has a little coat the color of my scarlet . . ."*

"What did you want to say?"

"No, what did you want to say?"

"I was going to say: My father is a slave to Aunt Lizzy. He is a masochist. I'm always going home for the holidays, right? I don't stay in the villa but in a hotel. Only if my mother is not in a sanatorium am I living at home." I shrug my shoulders. "At home!"

"Is she often in a sanatorium?"

"Almost always. I only go home for her sake. Otherwise I would stay in Germany."

"Of course."

"Of course, right? And once, when my mother was not in a sanatorium but at home, I searched Aunt Lizzy's room when she was out. And lord! It took two hours. Then I found them."

"What?"

"The whips. Dog whips, riding whips, whatever you want. In all colors. At least a dozen. Carefully hidden in her clothes closet."

"She whips him?"

"For at least twenty years! In my opinion."

"Really!"

"I tell you, she's an old flame! When I discovered the whips everything was clear! She is the only man among the three of them! My mother is only a poor little skeleton. And my father? Always: Lizzy! Lizzy! She has full power of attorney over his accounts. I tell you, she thinks up every new trick, every new dirty business deal. I tell you, my father today is just a miserable nothing, a nobody in her hands. She is a sadist."

"Awful."

"Why? He wants abuse. He gets it from her. That's love."

"Don't talk like that."

"More than likely he offered it to my mother. And she declined. Or did it badly. To satisfy masochists does not seem to be so easy. Well, and then she who could take care of him so well reappeared. He was well satisfied, and probably she was too. You should see her. A really competent woman."

"Revolting."

"I'm telling you the truth. That's always revolting."

"There can be nothing between us."

"Why not?"

"Because you are like this."

"But you are the same."

"Yes," she says, and laughs again, like a child. "That's true."

"It is going to be the greatest love in the world," I say. "And it won't end until one of us dies."

"Sentimental fool."

"You speak excellent English. I know. After the war an American boy friend for every German woman."

"Have you gone crazy? How you do talk to me!"

"Oh, excuse me, dear lady. You never had one?"

Now she laughs again.

"Three!"

"Only?" I say. "Well, where was I?"

"Your father's masochism," she answers, still laughing. "Oh, God, oh God, this is some conversation!"

"Right. I tell you, he is the typical masochist! I have watched him, closely and for a long time, after I found the whips. I have watched my Aunt Lizzy. How she commands. How she looks at him. How he lights her cigarette when she wants to smoke. Then she fusses for such a long time until he burns his fingers. And they enjoy that, very much, both of them."

"Oliver, this world is disgusting. If I didn't have Evelyn I would commit suicide."

"Ah, nonsense! Very few commit suicide. You'll never guess how often I toyed with this idea! You and I, we're much too cowardly. Besides, you are well off! You are a rich woman. You have a lover. And now you have me too. If you like, you can experiment which one of us is the better."

"Oliver!"

I say a lot of things I don't want to say.

"Please excuse me. I'm behaving pretty badly. I say a lot of things I don't want to say."

"I do too, I do too! All the time! Perhaps you're right and it will be love. That would be terrible!"

"No, no. One thing I'll tell you right now. I'll never be something like Enrico for you! I won't kiss you, not even touch you, if we are not *really* in love."

Again she averts her head and says quietly: "Those were the most beautiful words any man has ever told me."

## [ 10 ]

She doesn't look at me; she has turned her head to the side. She stays that way. She is even more beautiful in profile. She has very small ears. The ears alone could drive one mad.

"Well," I say. "That's the whole story. In thirteen years my dear Aunt Lizzy has gotten everything. Today she is the queen. She beats my old man. She decides what is going to happen. My father is only a marionette. You know what kind of a man he is by the way he treats his employees: ruthless, unrelenting. The smallest detail; you are fired! That is typical of such men. A slave to a woman but a tyrant to his employees. Only: the true chief of the Mansfeld Works today, not just today but for many years, is Lizzy Stahlmann. Stahlmann, a nice name for the lady, right? I'm sure that she did her part in evading the taxes. Because of her I was not allowed to come to Luxembourg. You understand? She had already made a wreck of my mother. She completely dominated my father. Only I was still in her way."

"Poor Oliver," she says, and looks at me again.

"Poor Verena," I say. "Poor Evelyn. Poor Mommy."

"Poor humanity."

"It is awful."

"What?"

"How similar we really are."

"Why is that awful? I am going to say something ridiculous, something absurd. Shall I?"

"Yes."

"You are all I have in this world, and all I believe in, and all I love, and all I want to be decent for if I could. I know that both of us could be happy with each other. We—"

"Stop it!"

"Your child would be my child—"

"Stop it!"

"And never, never, never would one deceive the other. We would do everything together: eat, go on trips, attend concerts, go to sleep, wake up. Tomorrow you are going to be discharged. Will you come to our tower on Saturday at three o'clock?"

"If I'm able to come."

"If you can't come then give me a signal on Friday night. At eleven. Three times short. That means you can't. And three times long means you can."

"Oh, God."

"What does it mean again, 'Oh, God'?"

"And I'm twelve years older!" She looks at me for a long time. "Oliver . . . Oliver—you know what is strange?"

"What?"

"That in spite of it I'm so happy."

"But I am too, I am too!"

"Yes, but with me it's the first time in my life." She opens the drawer of the bedside table. "Look," she says, "how mad I am. How crazy!"

I look into the drawer. In it are a flashlight and a small book. I read what it says on the front cover.

*"The Morse Code."*

"We are both insane, Oliver!"

"Naturally."

"And we shall have to atone for what we do."

"Naturally."

"There is no happy love."

"Naturally, naturally, naturally," I say and bend forward to kiss her mouth, her wonderful mouth, when there is a knock and immediately after it Nurse Angelica enters the room, smiling, deceitful and lascivious.

"You'll have to leave, sir. Your sister is still very weak."

"Yes," I say. "I must go." (Also because of Mr. Herterich; it is eleven-thirty.)

I get up and plant a brotherly kiss on Verena's cheek and say: "Well, until soon, Sis."

"Until soon!"

"Why are you smiling, Nurse Angelica?" I ask.

"Oh," she answers with the smile of a Madonna, for which I would gladly kick her in the teeth, "it is so touching to see brothers and sisters so close."

"Take care," says Verena. "And thanks for the flowers."

Nurse Angelica watches her patient as a python would a rabbit.

Verena closes the drawer of her bedside table. Isn't it ridiculous how a man can be half crazy with happiness because of a flashlight and a Morse-code manual?

"So long, little sister," I say. And leave the room feeling like a man who has just drunk five Scotches.

## [ 11 ]

It is twelve-forty-five. I am in bed. Noah brought my lunch in two aluminium containers. I got back in plenty of time. Mr. Herterich had looked at me sadly when I returned and said, "I'm going to end up in hell's kitchen because of you."

"You won't," I said. After lunch I go back to bed and tonight I'll be examined by the doctor. The fever will have gone down by then. Upset stomach. Such things happen. "By the way, I've heard that Ali was rude to you again last night."

"Yes, he is a dreadful child. He demanded that I wash his feet!"

"Never mind, Mr. Herterich, I'll see to him."

"Really?"

"And how," I say.

Now he beams, the poor slob.

Ah well, if necessary the little Negro will get a paddling! Mr. Herterich's friendship may soon be a vital necessity to me. I'll probably have a temperature quite often in the mornings to come.

Noah tells me: "The chief threw out Carla and Gaston this morning! They've left already. The ten-fifty train. He left for Paris and she went to Vienna."

"What happened?"

"Miss Hildebrand caught the two of them in the woods yesterday. She can hardly see as it is, but she reported it to the chief. At night they had a teachers' conference. The chief telephoned Carla's and Gaston's parents and explained to them that he had to throw them out effective immediately, and why."

"Was Gaston very upset?"

"Not really."

"But they left this on the bulletin board." And he hands me

the pages, one line written in a girl's handwriting and one in a boy's handwriting.

*"To you just and reasonable Adults!"*

*Is love a crime?*

*Then why do you condemn the love of a fifteen-year-old for an eighteen-year-old?*

*One can't possibly be in love at fifteen!*

*You ought to get your backsides tanned. What happens if you have a child? Such understanding!*

*Parents say: "We should have such problems!"*

*O.K. You have different problems. Money. With us it's love and trust. Don't you have any understanding? Why do you forbid us what you did yourselves? Why do you punish us though you always tell us that we are more grown up, more adult at an earlier age?*

*We know the Chief is afraid Carla might have a baby and his school a bad reputation!*

*You'll never know that we need you!*

*We shall try to understand our children and to defend them.*

*Our children shall be happier than we are.*

Carla Honingstein and Gaston Latouche

"Well," I say, "even in their haste they managed to relieve their souls!"

Noah says: "Now that you've read it, I'll put it back on the board for the edification of our dear teachers. Chichita is arranging a Macumba. At three o'clock."

Noah laughs. "Chichita comes from Rio, right? And in Brazil they have this superstititon. The Macumba is to persuade the good spirits to watch over Gaston and Carla."

"But that's nonsense!"

"Anyway, I'm going. And at least a hundred other children will too."

"I'll get up for an hour and come too."

"But you have to bring some cigarettes or tobacco, matches or liquor."

"What for?"

"As an offering to the spirits. I'll bring a small bottle of liquor."

"I'll bring cigarettes," I say. "Does it matter what brand they are?"

"No, the spirits smoke and drink everything, Chichita said."

"That's a relief."

"Don't be funny. Gaston and Carla were fired."

"I'm not being funny. I'd really want the spirits to protect them. I want the spirits to be satisfied."

"A love is a love is a love," declares Noah. "See you later, Alligator."

## [ 12 ]

Three o'clock. Sunshine, south wind, small clouds in the blue sky. One hundred twenty children are watching the tiny Chichita light at least fifty candles and open packets of cigarettes and bottles of liquor. Next to me is Geraldine. She stands very close. Across from me, Hansi. He doesn't take his eyes off us. A little while ago somebody told me that Hansi is thirteen and not eleven years old. I asked him. He said: "Sure, that's right. But I'm a cripple, a dwarf, right? I'm always laughed at. I was held back twice. If they knew that I'm so little and puny at thirteen —boy, it's pure self-defense."

So he is thirteen.

That's why he talks so cleverly.

Geraldine whispers: "When will I see you?"

I know that I have to finish with Geraldine but I need time to think. Perhaps I'll even have to talk it over with my "brother."

I whisper: "Not today. I'm sick. I have to go back to bed. I just got up for the Macumba."

"I love you, I love you, I love you."

Something comes to mind: "We have to be careful or we'll

get thrown out like Carla and Gaston. The chief has spies everywhere."

"You are right." She steps aside. "Oh, God!" she says. "Imagine if we were separated! I—I would kill myself!"

"Nonsense!"

"No, I would really!"

Fortunately at this moment Chichita gets up and behaves like a great witch doctor in Africa. She moves her arms imploringly, her body writhes, and she speaks in Portuguese with the spirits, here, in Germany, thirteen thousand kilometers away from her homeland. I look at the children, the big ones, the small ones. Some praying silently, some audibly. I'm praying too, silently of course. Dear God, let there be love for Verena and me. Real love. And let no one and nothing separate us. I'm old enough. I can work. I can support the three of us, Verena, Evelyn and me.

Geraldine whispers; "I prayed that we'll be happy. Is that very bad?" She looks at me imploringly.

"No," I say, "not at all."

What am I going to do with Geraldine?

Chichita raises both arms and says: "This is the end of the Macumba. Leave now. Singly. Don't talk or turn around. Think only of Carla and Gaston or the Macumba will have no effect."

The children leave and the candles are burning, cigarettes and matches are left for the spirits. The bottles of liquor are opened, ready for the spirits. Because they have no corkscrews, the spirits.

## [ 13 ]

The door of my room is open and I can hear the chief talking via the loudspeaker system to the children in the dining room and the children who are already in their houses. I'm in bed. The doctor had advised me to stay in bed until the next morning. Miss Hildebrand had brought my dinner and now she is sitting near my bed and listens to Her Master's Voice.

"I'm very sad, gentlemen. I know of your Macumba. You have disappointed me and all the teachers who are taking care of you. I have read Carla and Gaston's note. Do you really believe that Miss Hildebrand and all the other teachers are your enemies? Do you really believe that we could think of nothing more pleasant than to raise three hundred children, among them very difficult ones who are intolerable somewhere else? My teachers become ill, ruined by you. Yes, by you. They never receive one word of thanks. Many are hated and tormented by you. Why? For their efforts to shape you into decent human beings. Your parents bring you to me. My colleagues and I are responsible for you. We adults thought you were ready for more freedom. And we gave it to you. There have never been young people who have had more freedom than you!

"I did not sleep last night. I thought about whether or not I made the right decision about Gaston and Carla. And I tell you, it was the right one. I hope you know how much I like you in spite of everything and I still believe that you will grow up to be reasonable, just human beings. I feel sick. Sick to death. Good night."

The loudspeaker clicks.

"Oh, God," says Miss Hildebrand, and tears are trickling from her half-blind eyes. "Now I'm a tattletale for the entire school. But I had to report what I saw!"

"Of course, Miss Hildebrand, of course."

"Sometimes I think that they are all so crazy and hungry for life because they feel they will be dead in ten years' time because of an atomic war. So they want to live, live, live!"

And then out of context: "Oliver, I want to thank you for being so nice to Hansi. He told me . . ."

This lying bastard!

". . . and you are a good decent boy" (such words!). "It will be a year before I'll be able to help a child again, before a child will trust me again."

"Miss Hildebrand," I say, "I will help you. I'll explain to the children why you couldn't act differently, and they will listen to me." I feel sorry for this old lady! I can feel sorry for somebody if I want to—right?

Miss Hildebrand rises.

"Thank you, Oliver, I thank you."

"It's okay. Don't mention it."

Then she leaves, the dishes in her hand, and of course she runs right into the door. She makes a superhuman effort to control herself. She even smiles as she turns to me.

"Always this electric light," she says.

"Yes," I say. "Sure," I say. "I hope you didn't hurt yourself," I say.

## [ 14 ]

I'm a coward. I know that I have to talk with Geraldine.

Friday morning I had to go back to school. And sat across from Geraldine. For six hours. At lunch she asked me when we would see each other again.

"Please give me another day or two. I still feel lousy."

"Of course! Naturally. Get quite well first."

Geraldine . . . Hansi . . .

Verena . . . Hansi . . .

Hansi. . . .

That's the danger! How did Hansi threaten me when he was not allowed to sit next to me at mealtimes? "I'll find out where these people live and tell Mister Lord!"

I must talk to the chief.

I visit him in his apartment and obtain his permission.

And then the little cripple sits next to me at mealtimes and beams at me and swells and stretches with pride and Rashid sits next to the arrogant black Ali who does not speak to him and looks at me sadly, devoid of understanding. Somebody else is looking at me unceasingly: Geraldine.

I hardly manage to get my food down. I leave the dessert.

"Can I have your dessert?" asks Hansi.

"Sure."

"Don't make such a face, man," says the little cripple. "Everything is great! And if you do what I want you to do you'll be surprised what a big shot I'm going to make of you."

"Shut up," I say weakly while he is eating my dessert. Because Geraldine is looking at me. And Rashid is looking at me.

[ 15 ]

That night I'm playing chess with Noah (and lose; he plays spendidly) and wish for eleven o'clock to come and hope for one thing: that I shall see three long light signals which mean that Verena will be able to come to our tower at three on Saturday.

"Man, you play awful!" says Noah.

"I'm not feeling too good yet."

"Then I'd rather play with Wolfgang."

"Yes, you do that."

It is ten-forty-five. I walk out onto the balcony. The moon is shining. From a window of the white villa above the tower and the trees a light flashes—long. And again—long. And once more—long. This time I have my flashlight with me. Now I signal back, three times long. Tomorrow at three, Verena, tomorrow my love. In the old tower. In our tower.

[ 16 ]

"I . . ."

"I . . ."

"No! Don't say it! Please! I won't say it either!"

This is our greeting. We embrace one another, we kiss one another. This time I was there first. She is wearing a cornflower-blue dress and a beige flannel coat because it is cold and raining on and off.

"But I knew what you were going to say!"

"What?"

"And I wanted to say the same thing!"

"It is enough that we know we both wanted to say it, right?"

"Yes."

Today there is more color in her face; she is made-up again. She still looks a little peaked. But already okay again. If one were to look out of the windows of the room in the tower one could see hills and villages in the rain, in this thin, sad September rain. This time she does not do that, this time I don't do that. This time we are a giant step farther. Farther to what? To being happy? To being sad?

"Where is Evelyn?"

"Down below."

"In the rain?"

"She has my umbrella. She doesn't mind the weather. She is playing with Assad."

"How are you, my sweetheart?"

"Fine. And you?"

"I'm fine only when I can be with you," I say.

"Don't be sentimental. I don't like that."

"You don't like that? You are sentimental yourself."

"Well, maybe. But don't be, anyway."

"All right," I say. Assad is barking. Evelyn is laughing. I hear them through the forest.

"Did your husband notice anything?"

"What do you mean?"

"My visit. The flowers."

"No. My brother, of course, didn't come. Even though he knew that I was there. My brother doesn't care about me. We only see each other when he wants to borrow money from me." She looks at me with her huge black eyes and her lips tremble a little. "Oliver—"

"Yes?"

"Are you still involved with this girl?"

"No."

"Don't lie. I'd rather you say yes; that's not as bad then."

"I'm not lying. I did have something with her. But now I'm going to tell her that we are finished."

"When?"

"Tomorrow. I'm such a coward."

"Coward," she says, "take the hand of a coward," and kisses me again, more gently, sweetly, more ardently than the first time. She whispers: "I'm not going to kiss you until you have told her. This was the last time."

"Okay. Okay. Do you really have no more pain?"

"No, really. But this is madness," she says. "It's going to come to a dreadful end."

"Of course."

"If I lose everything, then what happens?"

"I'll take care of you and Evelyn."

"You? You're still a boy! You have nothing! You have no profession. You are worth nothing," she says.

"No," I say.

"You are a tramp."

"Yes."

"I'm a tramp, too."

She walks over to one of the windows and looks out into the rain. I don't even dare put a hand on her shoulder, even though I stand very close to her. Now she turns and looks at me and shivers run down my spine. I have never felt like this when a woman looks at me.

No, no, this *must* be love.

"Are you brave?"

"I?" I answer. "I'm a born coward, you know that."

"Don't be silly," she says, and her eyes begin to glow and her narrow face seems even narrower. "I have told my husband."

"Verena! You are crazy!"

"I told him that I met you. You were with other boys. Quite by accident. Your name was mentioned. So I thought: Mansfeld? Mansfeld? And talked to you. And it was you: The son of his old friend and business partner."

"You are crazy!"

"Of course. That's what we've said all along! I want to see you more often. Not always secretly! Not always in this tower. Did you ever think what is going to happen when winter comes?"

"Go on."

"The unexpected happened. My husband was delighted! He asked me to phone you at the school and ask you to be our guest for dinner tomorrow. That's why I asked you if you were brave."

"I think I am."

"I thought that if you came to us once then you could come more often. To Frankfurt too. We'll be leaving here soon."

"I thought of that last night. I was afraid of it."

"What would you like to be, Oliver?"

I don't answer because I am embarrassed.

"Don't you know yet?"

"Yes, I do, but it sounds stupid."

"Tell me."

"A writer. Possibly I'll never be one. And besides . . ."

"Have you written anything yet?"

"Just silly love stories for girls. Nothing else."

"Why don't you write our story?"

*"Our story?"*

"Our story! How we met. What has happened so far. And. . . ." She interrupts herself. So I ask: "Were you going to say 'and what is going to happen'?"

She nods and looks out into the rain.

"All right," I answer. "All right. I'll try. I'll let you read it all. And if it is bad you'll tell me. Agreed?"

"Yes. And if I like something especially well I'll tell you that too. Oliver."

"Yes?"

"Enrico is going to be there tomorrow too. He is back from Rome. My husband invited him. Now are you still brave?"

"Why should I need to be brave? It will probably be more embarrassing for Enrico to see me again than for me to meet him."

"Do you trust me?"

"Of course not," I say. "Nonsense. Of course I trust you, Verena."

"Do you have a tuxedo?"

"Yes."

"Then wear it tomorrow. Are you allowed to go out at all?"

"I'll have to ask the chief. It would probably be very impressive if your husband were to call the school and say that he has invited me. Otherwise the chief might think I'm going to the Kakadu in Friedheim to pick up a girl."

"Would you like that, Oliver?"

"You know, up to now I wanted to sleep with everything that was feminine."

"And now?"

"Only with one."

"Is that true?"

"On my life. No, on your life. On Evelyn's life."

"Really and truly?"

"Really and truly."

She says directly in front of my mouth: "It really must be true, you know."

"I know. It is really true."

"I must be crazy but I like you so much. It's going to come to a bad end. I'm twelve years older than you."

"Don't always say that."

"But I really am twelve—"

"Be quiet."

And just as I am going to kiss her the dog starts barking and Evelyn begins to sing. *"All my little ducks swim on the lake . . ."*

"Somebody is coming," Verena says hurriedly. "I must go. Tomorrow at eight, all right?"

"Yes. Don't forget to have your husband call the school."

She kisses me lightly on the cheek, walks quickly to the stairs and says: "Hide if somebody comes up here. Otherwise wait a few minutes."

"All right. And tonight at eleven?"

"Tonight at eleven."

She has gone. Looking out the window I see her leave the

tower, and with Evelyn and the dog walk into the woods, through the rain, away from me, without looking back.

A fat man and a woman are looking at the tower for a while and then leave. More than likely the warning had persuaded them not to climb the tower. I sit down on an old box and cup my head in my hands, which again smell of Verena's perfume.

Tonight I'm going to start writing our story. Dear God, to whom I only turn when I need something for myself or for others, please, please, let it be a good story.

[ 17 ]

At eleven o'clock I'm standing on the balcony in the rain and through the night, through the dark, through the rain this message comes to me from the villa beyond the tower:

TOMORROW—EIGHT—LOOKING—FORWARD.

And I signal back: LOOKING—FORWARD—TOO—TOMORROW—EIGHT.

Through the dark come these signals: SLEEP—WELL—OLIVER.

I answer: SLEEP WELL—MY LOVE.

Yes, I'm going to write the story of our love.

I go to my room. Noah and Wolfgang are still awake.

"Man, you're completely soaked," Wolfgang says. "Where have your been?"

"Leave him alone," says Noah. "Don't you see he is in love?"

Yes—I'm in love.

Tomorrow at eight.

Verena Lord.

Verena.

[ 18 ]

The first thing I see when I enter the villa is the Rubens which belonged to my father. A fat, blond, naked woman washing her feet. Here it is in Mr. Manfred Lord's wood-paneled hall. Funny, isn't it?

I think it's so funny that I forget to give to the butler the paper in which the flowers I brought are wrapped. This servant has a smooth, long face, cold eyes and lips which are so thin that at a glance it looks as if he had no mouth at all. He is short and lean, arrogant and sure of himself. What a difference between him and our Victor. I wonder where he might be working now!

So this butler, and the couple here, are the people who hate Verena. She told me the night we met. The night I took her home. I have to be careful with this butler. Friendly. Very friendly.

"Excuse me, please, sir, the paper."

"Ah, yes." Smile, always smile. "If you would."

He would. He takes the paper.

"Thank you—"

"My name is Leo, Mr. Mansfeld."

"Thank you, Leo. Oh, and there is something else. Sometimes when I have been invited I have completely forgotten to leave something for the people who took so much trouble to make things pleasant. That's terrible, isn't it? I expect you will be serving dinner tonight?"

"Yes, sir."

"And who cooks?"

"The wife of the gardener."

"So may I give you this now for both of you?" I give him thirty marks. At first I only intended twenty marks, but then he would have had to split it. This way he can keep ten. It is a trick of mine to tip the help at the start of the evening. I look at this butler again. Have I made a friend? Who could tell? So many rich people come to Mr. Manfred Lord's.

"But I can't possibly accept this, Mr. Mansfeld!"

"But I would like you to have it."

"Well, all right, thank you very much."

He bows slightly and smiles.

The sliding mahogany door opens.

"My dear Oliver—I may call you that—I'm truly happy to welcome you in my house!"

This man looks great. He is at least a head taller than I am.

His tuxedo must have cost a fortune. His smile is blinding. His blue eyes sparkle. The hair is white, brushed back, and shows a high forehead. I think: This man is clever and dangerous. His nose is noble and well-formed. He smells of after-shave and wealth, wealth, wealth.

His voice is resonant, fascinating. "What lovely flowers! And red carnations are my wife's favorite flowers. How did you know?"

"I . . ." Careful! ". . . I didn't, Mr. Lord. They are my favorite flowers too."

"Of course!" He laughs and puts his arm around my shoulder.

Does he know anything? Does he suspect anything? It seems to be this gentleman's forte that it is impossible to tell by his face what he thinks or feels.

"My wife will be very pleased." He notices my look toward the picture and laughs again. "The Rubens? Your Rubens! I bought it at an auction in Luxembourg. Your father suddenly didn't like the picture any more."

Now I am composed again. "If you have pictures like this here I'd like to see your apartment in Frankfurt."

"You will, my boy, you will. I'm delighted that Verena found you! My friend's son . . ."

Boy, oh, boy, is this man dangerous!

"Aren't you afraid of burglars when you are not here, Mr. Lord?"

"There is always someone here. And the protection agency. And little surprises in the park for anybody who would try to sneak in here." Suddenly his blinding smile is wiped away and he looks at me with blue eyes which have become hard as steel. A frightening man, this Manfred Lord. I have a premonition of unpleasant events ahead.

## [ 19 ]

Verena is wearing a very tight-fitting black evening gown. She is wearing a diamond necklace, a diamond bracelet, diamond earrings and a diamond rose on her dress. She is very made-up. As Manfred Lord and I enter the drawing room she advances toward me, a cocktail glass in her hand: "Mr. Mansfeld! Welcome! May I introduce you to Enrico Sabbadini?"

The Italian beau from the airport seems nervous. He also wears a tuxedo, dark blue.

"I'm happy to make your acquaintance," he says with his slight accent. His left hand opens and closes nervously. He holds a glass in his right hand.

"Imagine," says Manfred Lord, "Oliver likes the same flowers you do, darling!" And he smiles again. I kiss Verena's hand and hand her the flowers.

"But Mr. Mansfeld! So many flowers!"

"I like to give flowers."

"There you are, Verena, he likes to give flowers."

He presses a button and Leo appears. "A vase for the flowers, please."

"Yes, sir."

"What will you have to drink, Oliver?" The drawing room is furnished with antiques. Thick carpets. Dark furniture. An enormous tapestry. The bar is an old armoire.

"Scotch, please."

"Ice and soda?"

"Yes, please."

He prepares the drink carefully. The way a pharmacist fills a prescription. I drink the Scotch quickly and he refills my glass almost immediately. Manfred Lord is taller than anybody here, and seems to enjoy this evening.

"Let's drink to Verena finding our—no, my—Oliver. Little Oliver! Now he is a man. And isn't he handsome? Don't you think so, Verena? Don't you agree, Enrico?"

"He looks marvelous," says Enrico.

Verena says nothing, just looks at me.

Now I must say something quickly.

"Nonsense," I say. "Let's drink a toast to our hostess. *She* looks marvelous. I . . . I . . ." I look at Verena and think: I'm not going to put up with everything! ". . . I have never seen a more beautiful woman than you, Madame!" I raise my glass.

We drink.

"What a charming young man," says Manfred Lord. "Really, Verena, I can't thank you enough for having found him."

We sit in huge old chairs in front of a fireplace. A fire crackles in the grate. Verena looks into the fire. Enrico stares at me. Manfred Lord looks alternately at me and Enrico, amused and pleased. He doesn't look at his wife at all. Rubbing his hands he says, "There is nothing more cheerful than a fire, is there, Oliver? Did you find your way up here without any difficulties?"

"Oh, yes." Damn, that was a mistake.

"Very good! Most people who come here for the first time usually lose their way. Cheerio, everybody!"

We raise our glasses.

"I know my way around fairly well, Mr. Lord. My school is not too far from your house."

"Of course," he says, smiling. "I forgot about that. You are practically our neighbor. Isn't that wonderful, Verena? When I'm not here and Oliver is free you can go for walks or go to the Ambassador for tea or play tennis on our court!"

"I have only two hours a day, Mr. Lord. There is no time to play tennis. And I'm not allowed to go to the Ambassador."

Glass in hand, Manfred Lord settles back into his chair: "Isn't that crazy, darling? He is not allowed to go to the Ambassador, he doesn't play tennis, he only has two hours a day! And Enrico plays tennis, he can go to the Ambassador, and he has time—and now he is going back to Rome! Poor darling!"

Manfred Lord, the husband of the woman I love. Sitting

across from the man she sleeps with. Just then little Evelyn enters. She wears a robe over a pale blue pajama and little pale blue silk slippers.

"Excuse me," she says politely. "I just wanted to say Good night." She embraces and kisses her mother. I notice that Evelyn's left hand is closed into a fist.

"Good night, sweet dreams."

The little girl offers her hand to Mr. Lord. No kiss. "Good night!"

"But don't I get a kiss?" Lord seems to be very amused.

"Yes," whispers Evelyn. She kisses her stepfather quickly on the cheek. He stops smiling for a moment and gives her a little tap.

Evelyn curtsies in front of Enrico. Now she comes to me.

"This is Mr. Mansfeld, Evelyn," says Lord.

Evelyn curtsies and shakes my hand. "Good night, Mr. Mansfeld," she says and leaves. Something soft and warm is now in my hand that was in Evelyn's right hand the moment before. What could it be?

Leo appears with the vase and places the carnations on a marble table. He looks at me, his smile a sneer. Enrico looks at me as if he would like to kill me. Leo says: "Dinner is served, Madame."

## [ 20 ]

"We must not have any illusions, Enrico. The time of the great, wonderful, golden miracle of our economy is *passé,"* says Manfred Lord as he helps himself to two more lobster claws, which Leo, wearing white gloves, offers to him on a silver platter. "Thank you. A friend of mine—you really ought to take some more mayonnaise, Oliver, it's delicious. Our cook is really excellent—well, anyway, this friend said something yesterday I thought was interesting. . . . Aren't you interested, darling?"

"But of course, Manfred!" Verena sits next to me. There is no electric light, only candelabra with many candles. And while she answers she steps hard on my foot under the table.

"What makes you think that?"

"I had the impression, forgive me. Well, he said: 'The time has finally passed when we had to keep trimming the golden hair because it grew so quickly. Now we have to be careful that we don't end up with a bald head.' "

Enrico laughs, Verena laughs, I laugh. Mr. Lord laughs.

Flickering candlelight. The lobster is excellent. And I press Verena's little foot gently, again and again. When I get up I shall have to clean the shoe on the back of my pants or somebody might notice something! Verena seems experienced. As passionately as she presses my foot, her face is completely calm. The respectable hostess. The wife of a millionaire. A lady.

I'm afraid to look at her. And I know why.

Because of her husband. Because this Manfred Lord is a personality. I expected him to be one of those cold sharks who attend my father's secret conferences. But this man is a gentleman, an aristocrat; his family must have been wealthy for the last five generations and not like mine, just for the last ten years. After the lobster there is Cordon bleu, French fries, mixed green salad. Champagne, 1929. Pears Hélène. Demitasse. Cognac. And then we are back in the drawing room.

The only one who talks and enjoys himself is Manfred Lord. At least Verena and I ate. Sabbadini hardly touched his food.

He only exhibits some interest when his business partner is talking. About money, of course. He says many clever things, some I don't understand. To sum it up: The miracle is over. Minister Ehrhard built it up. Industry and government and the unions will tear it down. Now it is each man for himself. Possibly he is right. It's just that people without fine Napoleon, candelabra, jewelry, carpets, and nice houses will feel the effect first. The thought bothers me and I get up to find a bathroom. Verena's smiling husband takes me through the hall to the right door. There I look at the little package Evelyn had pressed into my hand when she said good night. It is a piece of the marzipan

I had given her and a piece of paper on which she had written in awkward letters:

> DEAR UNCLE MANSFELD!
>
> YOU LIKE MARZIPAN TOO. PLEASE HELP MOMMY AND ME. IT IS VERY URGENT. PLEASE!
>
> EVELYN

## [ 21 ]

After flushing away the paper and marzipan I return to the drawing room. Manfred Lord talks, but all his sentences seem ambiguous.

He says: "You have to be very careful, Enrico, very careful!"

He says: "Your father is my friend, Oliver. My friends' friends are my friends. Do you want to be my friend?"

"My father is not my friend, Mister Lord!"

He smiles indulgently and answers: "In spite of that shall we be friends? Everybody needs friends, you'll find. Well?"

"All right," I say. Ought I to have said *no?*

*HELP MOMMY AND ME. IT IS VERY URGENT.*

Lord refills the glasses.

"To our friendship, then," he says brightly.

The cognac makes my head swim. I can't take very much.

Apparently Enrico can't either. His face is red, his eyes don't focus. It seems this Manfred Lord wants to get us drunk. Does he want to see how we will conduct ourselves, what we will do, what we might say?

His smile. His charm. His superiority.

"Another drink, Oliver?"

"No, thank you, I have to drive."

"It's not far!" He again refills our glasses. Mr. Sabbadini is drunk now. "And Enrico stays overnight."

Verena is worthy of admiration. She drinks and drinks, and shows no effect. None! That of course gives rise to the thought that she might have been a barmaid or something similar. But I know she couldn't have been! The secret of her life. . . .

Manfred Lord kisses Verena's hand and says: "It's been months since you looked as beautiful as you do tonight, dearest."

10 P.M.

11 P.M.

11:30 P.M.

The room begins to spin. I'm not used to so much liquor. Enrico repeats himself the way all drunks do. He is ridiculous. When will he say something incriminating? I've got to get away from here! If I have one more drink I'll get up and tell everybody that I love Verena!

"No, no, I . . ."

"Nonsense! Leo is making some strong coffee. So cheerio—to our beautiful hostess!"

And so we drink to Verena and she smiles but her black huge eyes are serious.

Her hand touches me. A small white tablet is in my hand. Without anyone noticing I wash it down with some champagne. At the same moment there seems to be an atomic explosion in my head. I feel dizzy and bathed in perspiration. And then I am sober. Almost completely sober.

## [ 22 ]

At midnight the butler Leo appears.

"A call for you from Rome, Sir."

The fifty-one-year-old host jumps up quickly.

"My broker. Come along, Enrico. I'll take the call in the library, Leo."

"Very well, Sir."

Lord kisses Verena's hand again: "Excuse us a few minutes, dearest. Oliver will keep you company." And to me: "I'm sorry, but as I said, business is not as it used to be. One has to be on the ball."

Enrico follows him quickly, holding himself erect. He seems to be almost sober too. Well, if there's money to be made!

The door closes.

We are alone, Verena and I. We look at each other.

"Thank God that we're alone at least for a few minutes!"

She moves a little closer.

"They might be back in a moment."

"They're talking about stocks. That always takes a while."

Her eyes! Her face is close to mine, and she whispers: "I finished with Enrico." Her husky voice. Her closeness. The scent of Diorissimo. "Did the tablet help you?"

"Yes, thanks, very much."

"He tries to get you drunk. Enrico too. He is a cynic. He knows I've finished with Enrico."

"But did he know that?"

"No. But he felt it. Intuition! Now he wants to see what is going to happen next. Don't ever drink too much in his presence! Next time I'll give you more of these pills. They are marvelous."

"You . . . you told Enrico that you are finished with him?"

"Yes."

"But what reason did you—?"

"That I don't love him any more."

"But you have never loved him!"

"No! But he believed I did. That's why he couldn't eat tonight. His vanity has been hurt."

She sits close to me. I want to hold her, crush her, kiss her. I don't dare.

"I don't want to lie any more. I'm too old for that."

"But you lie to your husband! Continually!"

"He keeps Evelyn and me. I have to lie to him."

Some conversation! I have to laugh. Is it the champagne? Is it fear?

"It is funny, isn't it? You know the real reason why I told Enrico that it is finished? Because I like you so much."

I am silent.

"I'm a little crazy, you know that. Now I'm crazy for you. I want you."

I am silent.

"Only a whore talks like that, right? Well, I'm a whore. Now, do you still want me?"

"I love you."

"Shut up! I'm not talking about love. I'm talking about the other. That's nothing to do with love! Love? Love is just a word! I don't want to be in love! I want you! I want that! Do you understand?"

I nod my head.

"I'm not able to love. So it will never be love. Mustn't be love. We have to be very careful. He must never know or he will throw both of us out—Evelyn and me. And we'll have to go back to where we were. It's not very nice there." Her voice fades; she lowers her head. I caress her soft, cool hands. "We'll be very careful, won't we? He must never find out. I know him. He seems so superior, doesn't he? Well, I know him. He isn't superior. No one is. I've lived like a—forgive me! But I know men. That's why I can't love a man any more. Which doesn't mean that I don't need men. Is that quite clear?" She has had quite a lot to drink. Now it is noticeable. Was she a whore after all? So what? Why should that bother me? It will change into love!

"You better take one of those pills."

"Yes, I think I had better." She swallows the pill and empties her glass at one gulp. Her eyes are glowing now.

"I should be ashamed of myself, shouldn't I? Twelve years older than you. A whore!"

"Don't say that any more!"

"God, can you look angry!"

"You are not a whore!"

"Then what would you call what I am?"

"Now stop it!"

"All right. Do you know that I feel like a young woman when I'm with you?"

"You *are* a young woman!"

"Yes, thirty-three!"

"So what?"

"If you weren't twenty-one. It's complete madness! But it happened. I want you. That's all I can think of. You know since when I felt this way?"

"Since when?"

"Remember when you said to me in the hospital 'You are all I have in the world, and all I believe in, and all I love'? It drove me crazy! Because no man had ever said that to me." And her face comes closer, her mouth comes closer, still closer. I can feel her breath when she speaks. "Tomorrow at three in the tower?"

"At three."

"Kiss me."

Her dress is disarranged, I see her beautiful legs, the deep decolletage of her dress, her catlike face, whose eyes are now half-closed. Her mouth. Directly in front of mine. Now I don't care. I bend over to kiss her, and then I hear a noise.

We pull back quickly. Leo brings a tray with coffee and cups and saucers. He smiles.

"Have you decided not to knock any more before entering?"

"I did knock, Madame. Madame and Mr. Mansfeld must not have heard it," answers Leo and begins to set the table. And says: "Probably the logs in the grate are crackling too loud."

Verena and I look at each other, and suddenly I know with absolute certainty: Verena will be the one real love of my life. And I will be the one true love in her life. There will be nothing after this love. Not for her. Not for me. Nothing!

## [ 23 ]

It is a very warm night.

All is quiet when I return to my villa at one-thirty. After collecting a pencil, paper, and flashlight from my room I sit down on a bench on the balcony. I hang the light on a nail so its light shines on my paper. What did Verena say to me tonight? "Love is only a word!"

Love is everything. It's all. All.

And I'm a romantic fool. I sit here and write:

*LOVE IS JUST A WORD*

*A NOVEL*

And on the next sheet of paper:

*FIRST CHAPTER*

That was simple enough!

And now how do I start? That is simple too. I start with my arrival at the Rhein-Main Airport. I write:

*If you couldn't cry about it, you would most certainly have to laugh over it. Every time I return to Germany, it's the same story. . . .*

Something distracts me. I look up. Above the black treetops I can see Manfred Lord's white villa. In one of the windows a light signals; again, again, long, long, short, long, short. Verena! She must have seen my light:

G-O-O-D N-I-G-H-T D-A-R-L-I-N-G, she signals.

And "Good night, darling!" I signal back.

After that I feel so sentimental that I just finish the sentence I had started. I switch off the flashlight. Now it is dark in the villa too. I'm thinking about the things she said tonight. That she is a whore. Why shouldn't one be able to love a whore? Couldn't she change? Will she really never be in love again? Does one always do what one intends to do? I believe that no one really longs more for love than she. On tiptoes I go back through the house.

There is a light in one of the rooms.

There is a glass window at the top of the door through which I can see into the room. Mr. Herterich, in shirtsleeves, is sitting on his bed, head in both hands, motionless. He is a picture of complete, utter hopelessness.

I wonder how many million men in this world sit in their rooms like this, men who did not reach their goal, who were destroyed by what is called the "force of circumstances."

They all aimed high. They fought many years to realize their ambition, they ruined their health, they disavowed facts. And then they gave up. Why? Their own inability. Personality defects. Family. Children. Not enough money. Too many commitments. Too much alcohol. I'm sure Mr. Herterich too had dreamed of being a benefactor of humanity. Now he knows he will be nothing. He will go from one school to the next and be tormented by a thousand Alis, helpless, underpaid, poorly dressed, little respected, not at all respected.

I sneak back to my room, slowly, silently. Will I have to realize at some time or other that I will never be a writer, never, never? Will it happen after this book? After the eleventh book? When?

# Chapter Four

[ 1 ]

The morning after the night before at Mr. Manfred Lord's! I have a terrible headache, swollen eyes, and no appetite. Hansi next to me doesn't even notice that I feel sick and only drink coffee.

"I need your advice, Hansi!"

"What's the matter?"

"Not now. Later."

A little later we are standing by the old chestnut tree. We still have ten minutes. I say: "A brother has to keep another brother, right?"

"I'd do anything for you! What is it? Geraldine?"

Three hundred children are laughing and yelling, running around. No one can hear what I say or what Hansi says. At the entrance to the school Geraldine stands motionless. Hands behind her back. She is looking at me. But I am not looking at her. I am talking to Hansi, quietly, hurriedly.

"Yes, Geraldine."

"Can't you get rid of her?"

"No."

"I thought as much. You'll have to wait until a new boy comes."

"No. Well, you see, it's much more complicated than that. She . . . she is very attached to me. I—I don't want to hurt her . . . but I must get rid of her!"

"I understand," he says, and shuffles his feet.

"Mrs. Lord, huh?" I ignore that.

"Hansi, you helped me recover the bracelet. Couldn't you help me get rid of Geraldine?"

"Maybe. I'll think of something. An easy way."

"Nothing brutal, you hear?"

"You can rely on me, Oliver."

He shakes my hand.

"Bye. I have to go now and copy my homework from the head boy in our class. One has to look out for oneself."

And the little cripple limps away hurriedly, poor, ugly, mean. I shall find out soon what Hansi terms "an easy way."

[ 2 ]

Eight o'clock.

A bell rings. Three hundred children pour into the school.

The first period is Latin. Geraldine intercepts me at the stairs. Now I have to face her.

"What's the matter with you?" Her lips are wet; she is excited. She walks along with me.

"With me? Nothing! Why?"

"Why are you hiding? Why can't we meet?"

"Geraldine, I—"

"You have another girl!"

"No."

"Yes, you do!"

"No."

"Yes, you do. And when I find out who she is I'll create the biggest scandal that has ever been. No girl is going to take you away from me! Do you understand? No one!"

Her voice is shrill now. Boys and girls stop, listen, grin and whisper.

"Geraldine! Geraldine, please be quiet!"

"Why should I?"

"Because I say so!"

From one moment to the next she seems to crumble, her shoulders sag, and there are tears in her eyes.

"I . . . I didn't mean to—"

"Okay. Okay." Boy, oh boy!

"Really." Now she obediently whispers: "I can't sleep at night. I just lie there and think about how it was in the little canyon. I love you, Oliver . . . I just love you so much."

Only ten more meters. How long ten meters can be!

"Do you love me too?"

"Of course."

She holds my hand.

"When shall we meet? At three in the canyon?"

Today is a lovely day, the sun is shining. White streaks of clouds are traveling across the blue sky and colorful leaves drift down from the trees.

"Not today. I'm on restriction," I lie.

"Tomorrow?"

"Well, maybe tomorrow."

Hopefully tomorrow Hansi will have a plan.

She squeezes my hand. "Then I'll just think of tomorrow. Then I'll just look forward to tomorrow. You too?"

"Yes, me too."

Why did this have to happen to me? Why? Miss Hildebrand passes touching the wall from time to time as she gropes her way along. We say good morning. She smiles kindly. I'm sure she didn't recognize us. She probably doesn't know who we are. And she does not know that she will be here only another twenty-four hours. I do not know that. No one knows that. Perhaps only one. Hansi.

[ 3 ]

We have reached our classroom. She looks at me with the same hazy look she had in the canyon and goes to her seat.

On this day our poor, pitiable Latin teacher, Dr. Friedrich

Haberle, the little man with the old suit reeking of perspiration, manages to become the best-hated man to the class for the remainder of the year. He split the class into two groups. One group, A, translated Horace; the other group, B, Tacitus. He arranged for an A man to sit behind a B man, which means it is positively impossible to cheat.

Damn and damn again!

At first before I met Verena I wanted to get thrown out of this school to spite my father, but now everything has changed. Very much.

I'm a B man.

Thank you, dear God! I know Tacitus almost by heart. This is my third year. I'm finished with this stuff in half an hour.

When I look up I can see the red, brown, yellow and golden leaves falling from the trees. Fall is approaching, winter. During this hour, while I'm translating the *Germania,* I have this feeling for the first time—and it will come again, not too frequently, but it will come again.

It is not an unpleasant feeling, not frightening. It is really no feeling at all. It is a certainly. During this lesson in Latin for the first time in my life I have the premonition and I am certain, absolutely sure, that I will die soon.

Crazy, isn't it?

## [ 4 ]

We kiss . . . unendingly!

We are in the old room in the tower; the afternoon sun shines through the tiny windows, leaves drift in on a gentle breeze and we kiss. I have never kissed a girl like this, never a woman. I wrote in this book as mad and as wild as it was with Geraldine it would never be again. It is the same with this kiss. But with Geraldine it was only lasciviousness, sensuality. Now with Verena, something is added, something as gentle and soft as the southern breeze coming through the little windows.

We adolescents do not like big words, impressive phrases. But an adolescent tells you what there is in Verena's kiss: tenderness, longing—and love.

I remember Verena said "Love is just a word." But Verena now is just a woman, helpless and impetuous. It reminds me of Rudyard Kipling's "God ha' mercy on such as we . . . Damned from here to eternity."

Damned to eternity! That is what we are—Verena and I; we all are. And here we are, high above the trees in the Taunus, on a sunny September afternoon and we kiss each other the way I have never kissed before.

Slowly the tip of her tongue caresses my tongue. Both her hands are holding my head and I am holding her close to me. Love. Naturally, it is love! And in time she will realize it.

"I am happy," I say and, bending down to kiss her again, my hands slide under her sweater. But she pushes me away.

"Don't!" she says.

"What's wrong?"

"Let's stop. I'm . . . I'm half crazy after this kiss."

"Come . . ."

"Where? Here? In this dirty hole?" I look around. Dust, dirt, junk. We would have to lie on this filthy floor. No blanket. No water. No soap. Nothing.

"But I want you. . . ."

"Do you think I don't want you?" She walks away from me quickly and leans against a window. "Don't you think I want you too? But not here! I need a bed! I want you to be tender and no one to disturb us. Any moment somebody can come up here. I want us to have time. You have to be back in school in an hour."

She is perfectly right.

"Then we shall have to wait until your husband goes on another trip."

"Leave it to me. I'll find a place for us. I've always managed to find a place up to now."

You see, that's the way she is. As soon as there is any sentiment, destroy it! Love is only a word.

"Besides, this is exciting, too," she adds.

"What is?"

"This getting worked up, waiting for the première."

And she says that too, you see.

[ 5 ]

Verena wears a black suede jacket, a red skirt and sweater.

Her blue-black hair falls to her shoulders.

"Oliver, who taught you to kiss this way?"

"I don't know . . . no one. You kissed me. When will it be, Verena, when?"

"Can't you wait any longer?"

"No."

"Say it."

"I can't wait much longer." Her foot taps the floor quickly. It seems to excite her.

"You are good-looking, Oliver."

"Nonsense!"

"Really. Do the girls chase you?"

"No."

"Yes they do. And you already have one girl."

I must not lie to Verena. Never! "I . . . I just slept with her—that's all."

"For you. And for her? Does she love you?"

"Yes. But I told her then that I don't love her."

"And you'll never go to her again?"

"Never again."

"Does she know that?"

"I'm going to tell her. Today. Tomorrow. You know, she is a bit crazy. I have to be careful she doesn't go off her head completely."

I tell Verena about Geraldine. She listens silently. At last she says, "So that's the girl who stole my bracelet. You'll have to tell her, Oliver. Why are you looking at me like that?"

"I . . . naturally I'll tell her. It's just so strange for you to insist on it."

"Why should that be strange?"

"Usually you are so uninterested."

"I am. But for as long as someone is my lover he is not to have another girl."

"Where is Evelyn?"

"I have left her at home. I said I was going shopping in Friedheim. So Leo and the servants won't become suspicious. By the way, since the party Leo is actually friendly. He has never been pleasant to me before."

Leo. . . . I shall remember these words.

Verena tosses her head. "Oliver, I have bad news. We're leaving here tomorrow to return to Frankfurt. My husband told me this morning."

Once I had taken boxing instruction. During the first lesson my sparring partner gave me a kidney punch. They carried me from the ring. That's how I feel right now.

"Do you think he noticed anything?"

"Perhaps. Maybe not. He frequently makes inexplicable, surprising decisions. I live in constant fear, never knowing what will happen next, whatever my lord and master will do."

"Your lord and master!"

"I am dependent on him. And Evelyn too. Could you take care of us?"

"I . . ." Damn, why aren't I older? Why can't I do anything?

"Not yet. But when I finish school . . ."

"Poor Oliver," she says. "Don't be sad. I have cheated my husband so many times. It is only a half an hour by car to Frankfurt. The address is Miquel Drive, and you have a car."

"Yes . . ." I feel like crying.

"You see! I'll find cafés for us, I'll find a little hotel. And we'll meet."

"But it will be always for just a few hours. Verena—just a few hours!"

"That's better than nothing, isn't it?"

"I want to be with you, for always, day and night."

"You go to school, little Oliver. But we will be together

—nights—till morning comes—— Wonderful nights . . . my husband will take another trip."

Below, people are passing, we hear them talk and are silent until the voices have died away.

"Damn," I say. "The day after tomorrow we are going on a three-day trip. So I can't go to Frankfurt. I won't be able to see you for six days."

"What kind of a trip is it?"

I tell her.

[ 6 ]

This is the way it happened: Today we had history with the emaciated, limping Dr. Frey. He said: "I don't want any of you to believe that I'm telling stories about the Third Reich or that I am exaggerating. That is why we are taking a trip on the fifteenth to visit the concentration camp at Dachau. We shall take the bus to Munich, stay there overnight and on to Dachau the next day. It is very near. The concentration camps were always close to villages and towns. Only the people living there didn't know. Yes, Südhaus?"

The head boy in the class, Südhaus, whose father was an old Nazi and who now is Attorney-General, gets up and says: "I think a former concentration camp is hardly the right destination for an excursion!"

"But we are not making an excursion, Südhaus. Last night I read: *Wallenstein: At Stralsund he lost twenty-five thousand men.** I could not sleep any more thinking: What does that mean? He lost? Did those twenty-five thousand men belong to *him?* Twenty-five thousand men are twenty-five thousand lives, twenty-five thousand hopes, fears, loves, expectations. The Field Marshal did not lose those men—twenty-five thousand men died," says Dr. Frey and limps through the classroom. "And they left behind their wives, their children, their mothers, their families, their brides! Twenty-five thousand—that is

* Drama by Johann Friedrich von Schiller, 1799.

quite a number, I think. Many probably didn't die right away and were in pain. And apart from the dead there were probably a lot of cripples, with one arm, with one leg, with one eye. History books or Schiller do not mention them, and you won't find much about how Dachau was and how it is today. You will find I have my own method of teaching history. If someone does not wish to go just raise your hand."

Noah is the only one. Dr. Frey looks at Noah, whose parents died in the gas chamber in Auschwitz.

"I understand, Goldmund," says Dr. Frey finally. "That's all, then. We are leaving at nine o'clock on the fifteenth."

[ 7 ]

All this I tell Verena in our tower.

Suddenly she smiles.

"You know, first I had bad news and now I have good news. I'll be in Munich on the sixteenth! Alone! I'm going to be a witness at the wedding of an old friend of mine. The ceremony is at nine o'clock. If Dachau is so near Munich I guess you'll be back in the afternoon, won't you?"

"At the latest."

"Then you'll come to me—to the hotel. We'll have the afternoon—the evening—and the night, the entire night!"

I swallow with difficulty.

"Four more days, Oliver! In a city where no one knows us! Where we don't have to be afraid!"

She embraces me and looks into my eyes: "I'm so looking forward to it."

"I am too."

Then we kiss again. The same way we kissed the first time.

The way we shall always kiss. Because it is love.

And while we kiss one thought is in my mind: Verena and the concentration camp. A great combination, you think, right? In bad taste, you think? Horrible, you think?

I'll tell you what it is!

Love in the year of our Lord one thousand nine hundred sixty.

[ 8 ]

During the next twenty-four hours I make three mistakes. Each one will have its consequences, its terrible consequences!

To start at the beginning:

Verena leaves first and I follow a few minutes later. Walking away from the tower, about a hundred yards ahead, I see Leo, the butler, coming toward me: short and skinny, arrogant and assured. He has Assad on a leash.

"Good morning, Mr. Mansfield." His bow is exaggerated.

"Good morning."

"You have been visiting the tower, I assume?"

"Yes."

Leo is dressed in an old gray suit. His face seems even longer and smoother than usual. The lips two narrow lines.

"It's quite old. It is said the old Romans built it."

"Yes, we learned that in school."

He sighs. (Did he see Verena leave?)

"The way you say that, Mr. Mansfeld! Quiet, Assad, quiet! You learned that in school. You learned it in an *expensive private school,* Mr. Mansfeld!" And he proceeds to tell me how unhappy he is, how poor his parents were and how to further himself he had wanted to buy a restaurant but had been cheated of his life's savings by a confidence man. What is this man getting at?

"Well, I'm sorry, Leo, but I'm afraid I have to go."

But he holds onto my arm. His eyes are cold and cunning.

"I'm afraid you are going to have to help a poor man. You are going to give me five thousand marks."

This man is not only dangerous, he is mad!

"I don't understand."

"If you don't have the money, Mr. Mansfeld, you could take a loan and use your car as collateral. A rich young man like you . . . you could pay off the loan in instalments."

"Why should I, a stranger to you, give—?"

Then he tells me that he had listened to Verena's and my conversation at the party. How he knew that Verena and Enrico Sabbadini had been lovers, and of Verena's fear of ever being poor again.

"I'm sure Mr. Lord would not hesitate to start divorce proceedings if he found out. And now you are—"

"This is ludicrous! Not one word of all this is true!"

"But there is proof, Mr. Mansfeld. Letters and tape recordings of telephone conversations." He pulls out three letters addressed to a box number in Frankfurt and hands them to me. I read one of them. That is enough. Damn! Why wasn't Verena more careful?

"How many letters?"

"Eight."

"And how many tapes?"

"Eight."

"How do I know that you are not lying? After all, you are a blackmailer."

"Of course. But then how do I know that you're not going to notify the police? Perhaps your sympathy for Madame is not—?" Mistake number one: I reason: I must get possession of those letters and tapes. On no account can I tell Verena of this. If I tell her she will never want to see me again! She will be faithful to her husband, for a time anyway—maybe for always! No, I must not tell Verena.

Immediately after this I make mistake number two: "If I get the money for you, naturally I get all the letters and tapes?"

"Naturally."

"Yes, naturally. And then you'll say there are not just eight but fifteen letters and tapes and . . ."

"I swear to you—"

"You will also give me a receipt for the money."

Later it becomes evident what an idiotic demand that was!

"But with pleasure, Mr. Mansfeld."

Is there any point in telling a creep like this what a filthy swine he is?

Not the least. What difference would it make? One letter would be sufficient.

He pulls out a piece of paper.

"This is the address of the best finance company in Frankfurt. I thought that if you saw them tomorrow you would probably get the check the following day." He speaks very quickly now. "And could you make it cash, please? A check could always be canceled, couldn't it?"

Just like an idiot I walk into his trap.

"I would wait for you here the day after tomorrow at three o'clock."

"But Mr. Lord is returning to Frankfurt tomorrow."

"He has his own staff there. The gardener and his wife and I are staying on here. If you knew how lonesome it is in the winter . . ."

"All right, all right."

"Excuse me, please. At three the day after tomorrow!"

Verena. She must never know or I'll lose her. Mistake number one. This swine, I have to pay him to get the letters and tapes. I must pay him. Mistake number two.

"Yes."

"May I say that I would be extremely sorry not to find you here at three o'clock the day after tomorrow, my dear Mr. Mansfeld? Come, Assad, come! Find the stick, Assad, get the stick!"

[ 9 ]

It is eight-thirty.

Ali, Hansi and Rashid are in their beds.

Hansi had not spoken to me all evening.

"Did you think of something?" I asked him at dinner.

He shook his head. Later he had mysteriously disappeared. Now he is in bed staring at the ceiling.

Before coming in here I took some chocolate to Giuseppe. He beamed at me, the little, starved boy, and in his terrible English said, "Thanka you, Oliver!" The black Ali (there is only one God, *my* God) and Rashid are praying:

"Our Father who art in heaven . . ."

"Allah is merciful and compassionate or he would never absolve even one of you of his sins . . ."

Of his sins.

I read the second letter, I couldn't read the third. I burned the three letters in the woods and scattered the ashes.

". . . and forgive us our trespasses . . ."

Our trespasses!

What kind of woman is Verena? Why didn't she destroy these letters? Leo must have stolen them. She really ought to have taken better care. Now I have to watch out for her. She must not be unhappy.

I'll have to pay that bastard and hope he does not have any more letters and tapes. Verena couldn't have been that careless! Strange that I'm not at all jealous of the other men! My allowance will never be enough to pay off the loan. I shall have to write to my mother.

At this moment the gong rings in the hall. The chief is going to make an announcement. Both boys stop praying. Hansi does not move. Dr. Florian's voice sounds strained. He summons all teachers to come to a conference at once and exhorts us to be punctual at breakfast for an announcement. It is foggy and cold the next morning. The children are in the dining room punctually at seven-fifteen. The chief arrives a few minutes later. His face is gray and there are dark circles under his eyes. Next to me Hansi's face is completely expressionless. I look across to Geraldine's table. Her seat is empty! Right away I have the explanation.

"Geraldine Reber had a very bad accident last night. All you children know that the narrow path along the canyon is very dangerous and that you are not allowed to use it."

Hansi stirs his coffee.

"Geraldine disobeyed instructions. She fell into the canyon. Both arms are fractured, she has a concussion, and the doctors say there is a possibility of her having fractured her spine."

Fractured her spine!

"Did you hear that?"

"Well, I'm not deaf," says Hansi.

"Geraldine is in the hospital in Frankfurt. She is in critical condition and is not allowed visitors. I telephoned her mother and she is on her way." He pauses for a moment. "Oh, yes, there is something else. Miss Hildebrand has resigned. She asked me to say goodbye to you for her and say that she will never forget you. She has already left the school and is now living in Friedheim."

A voice asks: "But why did she resign?"

"Miss Hildebrand was quite old and not always healthy. The doctor prescribed rest. She has helped many of you and I shall always be grateful to her for all she has done. Goodbye." On his way to the door he passes my table and, stopping for a moment, asks me to come to his office.

On his desk is a pitcher of water. He pours some into a glass, takes two tablets from a package, swallows them and drinks. "Headache," he says. "I have a terrible headache. What I'm about to tell you is confidential, Oliver. You must never talk about it. Word of honor?"

"Word of honor."

"I'm only telling you this because Miss Hildebrand asked me to. She especially liked you because you looked after poor little Hansi. Well . . . to make it short: Miss Hildebrand used the forbidden path too because it is a shortcut not only to the big girls' house but also to Friedheim. Last night Miss Hildebrand was taking Geraldine to Friedheim, to conduct a few tests, and to talk in a neutral atmosphere."

"Why?"

"Geraldine was very unstable and difficult in recent weeks. Miss Hildebrand was walking ahead of Geraldine when suddenly she heard a scream and, turning around, saw Geraldine had slipped and—"

"Fallen into the canyon?"

"No! She was hanging over the precipice and clinging to a root. Miss Hildebrand tried to pull her to safety by grabbing Geraldine's hands."

"And?"

"The old lady could hardly see. It was also dark. She didn't grab Geraldine's hands but the root. The root was white. With a hard pull she had pulled the root out of the earth—and Geraldine fell into the canyon."

The chief rises and walks to the window. "Miss Hildebrand hurried back to the school. I called a doctor and an ambulance. It was only after Geraldine had gone that she told me the entire story. She collapsed and the doctor gave her a sedative." Suddenly his voice is clear and hard: "It is my fault. If Geraldine should. . . . It is my fault. I should have let Miss Hildebrand go years ago. I knew she could hardly see. She was a danger to herself and to others."

"You knew how much she loved the children."

"If Geraldine does not recover completely it will have been my fault. Don't say anything, Oliver. Go now. Goodbye." He stares out into the fog and from the side I see how his face is working.

In the hall outside the children stand in groups talking about Geraldine. My books under my arm, I head for the exit. I need some air. Someone pulls my sleeve. It is Hansi. He whispers, "Well, how did I do?"

"Do what?"

"Well, *that.*"

"You did . . . ?"

"Sh! Not so loud! You told me you had to get rid of the luxury whore and I should help you—didn't you? Well, I did!"

## [ 10 ]

"I knew the old woman always took the short cut because of her bad legs."

We locked ourselves in a bathroom. Hansi is elated, and I feel I am going to be sick.

"I heard her tell Geraldine: 'Tonight you come with me for a little while. The other girls and the teachers say you're so restless. You cry in your sleep. You daydream in school.' He grins: That's because you . . ."

"Shut up."

He lights a cigarette and inhales deeply.

"What do you mean, shut up? Don't speak to me like that! Didn't you say you wanted to be rid of her?"

I don't answer. I did say it. I'm no better than he is.

"Well, all right then." Now he is satisfied and grins his horrible grin.

"I stole some wire from the gardener."

"What for?"

"What for, he wants to know! And you are twenty-one? So she'll fall into the canyon, your sweetheart."

"You planned a murder?"

"Nonsense, murder! I hoped she would break a few bones and would have to go to the hospital so you'll have some peace."

He inhales again!

"Hansi."

"Well, what's the matter? You'll be rid of her for months now. And if her spine doesn't heal quite properly she won't be able to chase you. Or anyone else. Finished! Look at me! I'll never get a pretty girl. Can't you even say thank you?"

## [ 11 ]

"You. . . ." I'm going to be sick. "You took the wire—"

"And tied it to a tree. I waited in the bush and pulled the wire taut after the old Hildebrand passed. I was furious when Geraldine didn't disappear into the canyon right away. But luckily Miss Hildebrand fussed around and then she went down. The wire is back where I found it. Anyway, you're rid of Geraldine until Christmas at least. And as I said, maybe she'll look like me then. What's the matter? You're horrified, aren't you?"

"Yes."

"I thought so. First a lot of talk and then you have your pants full. I'll tell you another thing. I did it mainly for my protection. The more I have on you the more I'm sure of you. We both know of Madame Lord. Now this. If you tell the chief I'll tell Mr. Lord."

"And if Geraldine had died?"

"Well, then she would be dead. You would have cried terribly, wouldn't you?"

"You are . . . you are a devil."

"A lot of people have said that; that's no news! Didn't I take care of you? Tell the chief ! I can think of other things, not just the wire! I'd like to know how Mr. Lord would react to a visit or a letter from me!"

Hansi. Leo. It gets worse. I don't want to do wrong and do it all the time. For Verena!

"Don't you even feel sorry for Miss Hildebrand?"

"Why did she choose the path? It was time the old bag retired. Don't worry about her. You will never tell the chief because you care more for Mrs. Lord than the luxury whore." I don't answer. I know he is right. I am a coward. Verena would become involved. I would get kicked out of the school if they found out what had happened between Geraldine and me. I am no better than Hansi. I will keep my mouth shut. And I will pay Leo.

"Okay, Hansi." And that's my third mistake—the worst one!

"Hansi, get out of here. Now!"

"Why?"

"I'm going to vomit."

## [ 12 ]

I went to Frankfurt and borrowed money. I have to repay the five thousand marks at 321 marks a month. I met Leo and gave him the cash. He gave me a receipt stating that he had received five thousand marks on September 14, 1960, from me. He would not be more explicit than that! Anyway I feel somewhat protected having this receipt. Some protection! !

Leo then gave me the five letters and eight tapes, and to be sure they were the right ones we played them back in Mr. Lord's deserted house. They were the real ones, all right. I burned them and the letters in the woods.

Maybe Leo has duplicates! I don't know. For the moment I've done all I can. I have sent flowers to Geraldine. Was that another mistake?

Probably!

## [ 13 ]

The entire world has heard of Dachau. It was the Concentration Camp No. 1. This is where the murder started. You can get to the camp in only thirty minutes by bus from Munich. But neither the inhabitants of Munich nor the inhabitants of Dachau knew what was happening inside the camp. Nobody knew! The barracks are still there. People live there. A yellow telephone booth flanks the entrance to the camp. So the people who live there today in 1960 can telephone. The people who lived there until 1945 could not. The progress of humanity! There are clotheslines between the barracks. Women with headscarves, children playing. A small chapel. The walkways are surfaced with black slag. Our bus stopped at the entrance. A man who had been a prisoner at the camp is our guide. He told us that many people came, especially foreigners.

"And Germans?"

"They, too. About one German to thirty foreigners," he answers. He limps the same way Dr. Frey does.

It is a beautiful day. Blue sky. Very clear. No wind. We are walking toward the crematorium. Barracks. Thousands and thousands of people have suffered here. Thousands and thousands of people have been tortured and murdered here. The crematorium. Thousands and thousands of bodies have been burned here. Half an hour away from Munich. I shudder at the horror of it.

A building attracts my attention. A sign above the door of it reads RESTAURANT.

"They have a restaurant here?" I ask.

"We have two," the guide answers. "The people who live here have a beer or two there at night. This was the disinfection building."

"What was?"

"Well, the restaurant! I'll show you the museum now. It used to be the crematorium."

Inside are tables with picture postcards and brochures. A few showcases with horrible reminders of this hell.

Wolfgang is crying. Walter tries to calm him.

"But why are you crying?"

The guide says: "Here is one of our visitors' books," and points to a desk. "If you're interested I'll fetch a few more." He leaves and returns with a half dozen gray books.

Americans, Spaniards, Dutch, Chinese, Japanese, Israelis, Arabs, Persians, Belgians, Turks and Greeks, but mainly British and French, and, as expected, Germans, have signed their names and addresses and some added comments. Wolfgang stands by the window, his back toward us, but by the convulsive movements of his shoulders one can still see that he is crying. He doesn't want us to see it. But it is noticeable. He reminds me of the chief when he stood with his back toward me and said: "If Geraldine does not recover completely it will be my fault."

Of course, that is nonsense.

Just as much nonsense as if Wolfgang now thinks he is guilty or implicated in what had taken place here just because he had such a wretched father. The chief and Wolfgang: although innocent, they feel as guilty as the guilty ones themselves. If only Noah were here now. He would surely know the right thing to say to Wolfgang. I can't think of anything. I take out my notebook and copy some of the comments. Here they are:

That people are capable of this!

Honte aux millions d'Allemands qui ont laissé ces crimes s'accomplir sans protester.

After all this time I think these installations should be removed.

It is a disgrace to have restuarants in such a place.

Terrible things have happened here but it ought not to be brought up again and again. Sometime or other we ought to be able to overcome the past. Besides, there ought to be a memorial to the Russian POW camps. Where, oh where were the thinking Germans?

Someone else had written:

*What did you expect them to do about it?*

"If you will follow me to the crematorium," says the guide.

We follow silently and enter a large room. We stand in front of the ovens. There are many and wreaths are in front of all of them.

[ 14 ]

Large and small wreaths, many of them dusty.

"Wreaths were hanging on the open doors," I tell Verena.

It is five o'clock and beginning to get dark. Verena had taken a suite in a hotel at the Karlsplatz. Verena wears tight-fitting pants and an overblouse. We sat on a couch in front of a large window and drank tea. I have told Verena what I had seen and heard in Dachau. When I arrived we kissed but she must have sensed something had upset me because she broke away from me, took my hand and led me to the oversized couch.

Verena does not look at me. She looks down from the fifth floor of the hotel onto the traffic thronging the Stachus.

The first lights are visible. Large advertisements in neon lighting.

Thousands of people crowding into trams, hundreds of cars.

It is quitting time. Now they are going home. I have never seen as many people or as many cars in such a large square.

So many people. How many of the older ones among them have perhaps been. . . . No, No, No, don't think about it. Yes, yes, yes, always remember! I shall never forget what I have seen today. I shall never be able to forget. Verena still stands motionless by the window. The hotel suite is air-conditioned, everything is new, everything is nice, and I smell Diorissimo.

"Only half an hour away!" I say.

She nods. Suddenly she looks at me. In the twilight her huge black eyes shine like stars. With her throaty, husky voice she says: "Don't say it, Oliver."

I stutter: "I'm so sorry. I was looking forward to it so much."

"I was, too."

"But I didn't think it could be like that. So horrible!"

I should have known.

I sit down next to her and caress her knee.

"Verena, if you had been there."

"I didn't have to be there. I understand you. I understand very well, darling."

"I just can't, Verena . . . I can't. I'm afraid I'd start crying when I hold you in my arms . . . and ruin everything."

"I understand. I understand."

"How awful. We are alone in a town where no one knows us. We have time. We both want each other. And then this happens."

"Don't talk. It is all right. How wonderful to have you sitting next to me."

"Verena, I love you."

"You musn't say that."

"Verena, I love you."

"My husband was a member of the Party too. He had nothing to do with Dachau. But he was in the Party."

"How many of those people down there, in cars and buses and trams, were Party members, do you think?"

"Your generation is innocent. But I knew that Manfred Lord

was a Nazi when I married him. Evelyn's father was not. I married Mr. Lord for certain reasons."

"Because you didn't have anything to eat."

"Is that an excuse?"

"Yes. No. I don't know. I think for a woman it is."

"Oliver?"

"Yes?"

"Was your father a Nazi?"

"Naturally! Why do you think I feel so awful?"

We hold hands in silence and outside is quiet dark. The sky became cloudy in the afternoon. Now it is starting to rain gently, very gently. Shimmering drops trickle down the window. The window seems to be crying. For whom?

## [ 15 ]

We must have stayed like that for at least an hour, holding hands in silence and watching the people down below.

Her voice sounds hoarse when she finally says: "You know our arrangement. You know what kind of life I've led. But if everything had been different, then I would have fallen in love with you today, Oliver."

In a little while she says: "Shall we take a taxi and go for a ride?"

"Yes, I don't know Munich."

"I don't either."

We hold hands in the taxi, and from time to time we look at each other but we don't talk. It is raining heavily now. The driver acts as a guide once he knows that we are strangers to Munich.

We drive down wide roads, past many department stores, past the Town Hall with the famous chimes.

Rain. The windshield wipers work hastily.

A floodlit arch.

"This is the Victory Arch."

Victory Arch. Because we were so often victorious.

Schwabing, the Bohemian quarter.

We drive through narrow cobblestoned streets. We drive through a huge park, whose old trees shine wet with rain in the light of the headlights.

"This is the English Garden," says the driver. We swing around and reach a wide road behind the park. The road leads to a tall column topped by a figure with wings and a raised hand.

"That's the Angel of Peace."

*THE ANGEL OF PEACE!*

And half an hour from here. . . .

At the same time Verena says: "And half an hour from here."

We drive through a new suburb. Modern high-rise apartment buildings, gardens, rows of garages.

"This is Bogenhausen. They just finished building it."

We drive back to the center of town.

Verena presses my hand.

Heavy traffic, many traffic lights, many people. A black obelisk.

"Napoleon had it made of molten-down German guns. After the war. The one we lost. Well, I don't remember which one it was."

The railway station.

"They are still building it! Fifteen years after the war and not finished yet! The roof was halfway finished when they found a fault in the construction. So it was torn down again. Corruption, I tell you! Now another firm is making millions rebuilding it."

"Are you hungry?"

"No!" I say.

"I'm not either." She pushes a little vial in my hand.

"Sleeping tablets. So we'll be able to sleep."

Not a word whether or not we should spend the evening together. I'm grateful for the sleeping pills.

"How can I get in touch with you?"

"I'll write to you; you write to me care of General Post Office."

"No! I never write letters! One never knows. Someone might find them. Someone might blackmail you or me."

"That's true," she says. "I'm a bit careless too. I've lost a few letters, you know. I usually burn them immediately but I've saved several and now they've disappeared. I hope no one finds them."

"I hope not, too."

"I shall call you."

"You must be very careful. Make the calls from a post office between two and a quarter to four. I'll wait for your call every day at that time at the garage in Friedheim."

"And if I can't get away?"

"I'll wait anyway. You must not even call the school. It's too risky."

"Why are you so careful, Oliver? Why are you so suspicious? Did something happen?"

"Yes!"

Alarmed she cries: "What?"

"Not with us. With another woman . . . we were careless."

"Oh!" And then: "Don't be sad. Please don't be sad. It will only take a few days. Not even a week! By then . . ." her lips are close to my ear . . . "I'll have found a place where we can meet. A hotel."

She holds my hand tightly.

"I can't even send you flowers," I say.

"It doesn't matter, Oliver. I don't need flowers. You. . . . I need you. You'll see . . . it will be wonderful. For you and for me."

We are back at the hotel.

The doorman hurries over with an umbrella. There is no time left to talk, to kiss.

"Take care. I'll call you the day after tomorrow."

"All right."

I kiss her hand.

She smiles at me and, under the protecting umbrella of the doorman, walks quickly into the hotel. She does not turn around. Back in the taxi I give the driver the address of the little hotel where my classmates and I are staying. Now the rain is torrential.

## [ 16 ]

Naturally she cannot call every afternoon. But each day at the appointed time I'm waiting in Friedheim. The garage belongs to an old lady named Liebetreu and has a neglected garden. There is a table and chair where I sit when the weather is nice and write this book—my book. I have told Mrs. Liebetreu that I am waiting for telephone calls. I have given her money. When Verena calls she always apologizes for not being able to call every day. She tells me what she has been doing. She went to the theater. She had a fight with her husband. She longs for me.

"And I, darling, I long for you."

"Be patient. Just a little, little patience. My husband is impossible right now. He doesn't let me out of his sight. I wonder if he suspects anything? But I'll find someplace for us. Maybe tomorrow, maybe the day after tomorrow."

"Maybe in a year's time!"

"Don't say that. I want it as much as you. Don't you believe me?"

"Yes, I do. I'm sorry."

"Do you think of me?"

"Always."

"I think of you. I think of you all the time. And of the ride in the taxi. Be patient. Write our story. Are you writing it?"

"Yes."

"I kiss you, darling."

"I love you."

This is the way it is. Day after day. I'm patient. I wait. I write. When it rains I write in the office. I stare at the telephone and when it rings I'm happy and at least I hear her voice. Verena's voice. Comes a Sunday. Visiting day. The dear parents drive up in their expensive cars to visit their dear children. They bring presents and food packages and have dinner with their beloved children in the A. No one comes to visit me. Many other children have no visitors. Either the parents live too far away or they don't want to come or they are not able to come.

"I'm glad; I don't have to see my old lady," says Hansi. Could that be true? He creeps into his bed and stays there all day.

Only one couple came by train. They brought sandwiches. They say goodbye early in the afternoon. They seem distressed. I am sitting around watching this circus and Walter tells me: "I think our marriage has had it."

"Why?"

"No money. Father is broke. He is a little auditor, you know? He says he can't stand the poverty and hopelessness any more. He wants to emigrate. To Canada. He already has all the necessary documents."

"That's super, kid!"

"Super? Shit, that's what it is!"

"But why?"

"Mother wants to stay in Germany at all cost."

"And you?"

"They told me to choose. Some choice, eh? In any case I'll be leaving here Christmas. Father can't pay the school fee any more."

"Wouldn't you get a scholarship?"

"I'm not good enough to get one."

He leaves and hides some place like a wounded animal.

Funny, his parents' marriage breaks up because of insufficient money, my parents' because of too much money.

Obviously money can't be the reason.

About six or seven o'clock the adults are suddenly in a terrible hurry. Embraces. Admonitions. Kisses. Tears. Visiting day is over. The parents have done their duty. The children remain. They fall upon their packages, overeat, and some throw up the same night, some the next morning. It is always the same.

[ 17 ]

I can't complain. I receive mail from my mother. My father never writes, nor does Aunt Lizzy. The letters contain the money I asked for. Her writing is shaky and all letters are short and similar.

> *My dear Oliver:*
>
> *I think you know that I am in the Sanatorium again but I feel much better already! I am looking forward to Christmas when I shall see you again. Maybe I shall even be allowed to go home for the holidays. If only these eternal depressions would stop. And the insomnia. One day when you will be really grown up and have finished school I will explain a lot of things you would not understand now.*
>
> *I hug and kiss you a thousand times.*
>
> *Always yours,*
>
> *MOM*

No need for an explanation, Mom. I have understood everything for quite a while now. Congratulations, Aunty Lizzy! A few more sanatoria and you'll be in command.

Apropos mail: Geraldine is still not allowed visitors. Walter tried to see her but was refused. So I forced myself to write a few inconsequential lines while waiting for a phone call from Verena. Time passes. It is already October. A lot of rain falls, the trees are bare and bleak. A cold wind blows. Wolfgang and Noah belong to a newly formed jazz band which often has jam sessions in the basement of the villa. It is always a complete success.

Dr. Frey allowed pupils of the sixth grade and upward to

watch a series of documentaries on television. The Third Reich.

Many pupils, teachers and pedagogues are there.

The seizure of power.

The extermination of the intelligentsia.

The book burnings.

The preparation for war.

The invasion of Poland.

The invasion of Russia.

The concentration camps.

The invasion . . . and so on.

Sometimes pupils look at the adults, for instance when Goebbels asks: "Do you want total war?"

And the frenzied screaming of the mob: "Yes! Yes! Yes!"

Those were our fathers.

Those were our mothers.

Those were the German people.

Not all of them, certainly, but a large number of them.

The children look at them not with contempt but with astonishment, devoid of understanding. It seems the children ask: "How was it possible for you to be taken in by such screaming, ranting, pot-bellied gangsters?"

They say nothing.

Their eyes ask.

And the adults lower their heads.

Friedrich Südhaus is never there. I hear he writes letters.

No one knows to whom.

Soon we shall find out.

Mr. Herterich is becoming increasingly paler and thinner. No one pays any attention to him. Pupils of the third, fifth, seventh, and eighth grade have formed a choir. One of the best singers is Giuseppe. My favorite song is: "Stand still Jordan! Stand still Jordan! But I cannot stand still."

But I *have* to stay still.

Every day I wait to hear Verena's voice.

"Patience, just a little more patience. . . . He watches me every moment. I can't even go out with the child. He just left for the city for an hour. I have to go, darling, don't be angry, darling. Till tomorrow, I hope."

I wonder if she has someone else?

No, then she would not call at all any more.

"Write our story and be patient," she said. The two weeks seem like two years. I write. But every new day seems bleaker than the one past and I feel worse after every telephone call.

Until the eleventh of October.

It is a Tuesday and it is pouring.

Verena's voice sounds breathless: "The time has come! My birthday is on the fourteenth! And my husband told me this morning that he has to leave for Stockholm on the thirteenth and he won't be back until the fifteenth! Darling, sweet darling, I'll invite you to my birthday party!"

"But there will be others there, won't there?"

"They will leave by twelve at the latest. I've invited a lot of older people. You'll leave with them and come back and we'll have the entire night to spend together!"

"The servants—"

"They sleep on the upper floor. My room is on the main floor. We just have to be quiet. Isn't it wonderful? Why don't you say anything?"

"Because it is so wonderful. It is so wonderful that I can't find words."

## [ 18 ]

*Love is just a word*
*It does not mean a thing. . . .*

The provocatively babylike voice of the singer is accompanied by piano and drums. The little record spins. We dance to Verena's favorite song.

*. . . It's a fancy way of saying*
*Two people want to swing.*

Verena wears no jewelry except a beautiful ring. Her dress accentuates every curve of her body. We are all a little tight.

Verena said the way we dance would not attract attention. Our arms are around each other. Her body presses close to me. I can feel Verena's excitement. She too can feel my excitement. She does everything to excite me even further.

*Love is just a word,*
*And when the fun begins*
*A word we use to cover mountain-high with sins . . .*

Eleven-thirty.

"What are you thinking?" Verena whispers.

"Of that."

"I am, too. They will go in a minute. They'll be gone in half an hour, at the latest." She presses closer to me. We dance, hardly moving from the one spot. Her eyes huge as never before. She is more beautiful than ever.

*Love is just a word*
*That's dropped all over town.*

Now we don't move at all.

We just sway to the rhythm of this sad song.

*. . . an active little word—*
*And most improper now.*

"Do you like the song?"

"No."

"Too bad. I do. It's my philosophy."

"It won't be for much longer."

"Oh, darling!"

*Love is just a word*
*But let me make it clear . . .*

"Hold me tight. Tighter. Real right, Oliver."

"We are being watched by this Dr. Fielding."

"Ah, him! He is just jealous."

"Why?"

"He has been paying court to me for years. He is a close friend of my husband. You can see the wife he has. He is not allowed to . . . He watches me at every party, no matter whom I dance with, no matter whom I talk to."

"That's what I mean."

"It doesn't matter. I tell you I don't care. Tonight I don't care!"

"Not so loud. He'll hear you."

"Let him! It's my birthday." Now she whispers, "and in one hour . . ."

*Though I know, we know, it's really insincere*

Dr. Fielding doesn't take his eyes off us. Did Manfred Lord ask him to watch?

*Love is just a word . . . a word . . .*
*A word we love to hear. . . .*

Piano. Drums. A melancholy trumpet. The song is ended.

Dr. Fielding fixes a cocktail. Somebody says that after this last drink it really is time to leave. General agreement. The gentlemen have to be in their respective offices in the morning. We drink to Verena. The servants have already gone to their quarters. Evelyn has been in bed for hours.

Verena had invited fourteen guests. They all brought little gifts. Antique pewter ashtrays. Something useful for the kitchen. I brought fifty-one red carnations. Commented Dr. Fielding: "You must have a lot of money, young man."

Yesterday Verena had received a new ring from Manfred Lord—it must be at least two-carat. He also gave her a light beige Tourmaline mink coat. Verena wears the ring, it sparkles and glitters. Manfred Lord's expensive presents have shocked me. This man loves his wife. An hour ago he called to congratulate Verena once more. He asked to speak to me. "I'm glad you are there, Oliver. Look after Verena a little. Dance with her. They are a lot of older people. You are the only young man there. And Verena longs for youth. You see, dear friend, I'm a bit too old for her, too. . . ."

"Cynicism," said Verena, who had listened to the conversation, when I replaced the receiver.

"His own particular brand of cynicism."

"But the mink . . . the ring. He must love you."

"Certainly he does. In his way. But I don't love him. I told you I'm a—"

"Be quiet."

This was the evening. Cocktails. Delicious food. Coffee, cognac, whisky, champagne. Verena is an accomplished hostess. It is a beautiful house. The atmosphere is one of respectability, dignity and tradition. Walking through the house I realize how nouveau-riche our house had been, what an upstart my father is.

That's what I think, little realizing that not only people but houses too can be deceptive.

## [ 19 ]

Everybody is talking and finishing the last drink (and Dr. Fielding stares at us and I hear his wife say sharply: "Don't stare at her continually! You look ridiculous!") when Verena calmly asks me: "Have you told Geraldine?"

"I couldn't."

"What do you mean?"

Strangely enough Verena believes me at once when I tell her what happened to Geraldine. I say nothing about Hansi or Miss Hildebrand.

"Just like two love birds," says Dr. Fielding pointedly.

Boy, must he be crazy about Verena. Not hard to believe. His wife must weigh a ton.

"What do you mean, dear Doctor?" Verena smiles.

"How much you enjoy each other's company! I've noticed it all evening! You must have much in common."

"Our families are friends, dearest Doctor. Especially my husband and Oliver's father." Verena does not rattle easily.

Mrs. Fielding has had enough by now: "Come on, Jürgen, enough now. You have to be up early." And to all of us, that's her revenge: "Tomorrow he'll complain how terrible he feels. With his liver he oughtn't to drink at all." The other ladies are almost replicas of Mrs. Fielding and the gentlemen all seem to resemble Dr. Fielding. Most probably every one of them would like to be rid of his wife and marry a chic, slender young thing who is not always angry and nagging. Too bad! We have equality. A moneybag like that would have to fork out a load of loot to procure a divorce. Who needs it? Better to have hell at home, millions in the bank and somewhere in the city a love nest with a sweet young thing. The girl friend naturally has a few of these old boys on a string and a timetable.

The guests are saying their goodbyes. Embraces. Kisses. I hope Evelyn does not wake up. Or one of the servants. Walking down the driveway to the parked cars I see the lights going off one by one.

Dr. Fielding just has no peace of mind: "You have a long drive ahead of you, young man."

"It's not too bad, old man," I feel like saying, but I say: "It takes me just forty minutes, Doctor."

"Which way are you going?"

I don't think fast enough and reply: "The way I came. The Miguel Drive to Rheingau Avenue across to Wiesbadener Street to the Autobahn."

"That's marvelous. I'm sure you don't mind being our guide. We'll follow you. Our address is 144 Wiesbadener Street."

Damn!

Well, I'll have to go out of my way. I just intended to drive around the block and park the car somewhere. A good thing I know my way around Frankfurt. I drive past his house but he is still following. He wants to see if I am really driving back to school. I drive fast now, not using my indicators and without any trouble manage to lose him. When I'm sure I have lost him I park the car in an all-night garage. From here it is only five minutes' walk to Verena's house. The streets are deserted and it is just fifteen minutes past midnight. When I reach the villa light shines through the shutters of two windows.

Strangely enough (and thank God!), Verena's bedroom is on the ground floor. On the gravel drive my footsteps sound loud. I take off my shoes and walk on the lawn. The entrance door is ajar. I walk through a dressing room with wall-to-wall closets and mirrors. Three more steps take me to another door and I am in Verena's bedroom. A wide bed. Two bedside tables with pink shades. Everything in this room is pink. The wallpaper, the chairs, the dressing table with its triple mirror, the carpet. Verena is without make-up. She wears a blue baby-doll pajama. Her hair falls to her shoulders. I just stand there and stare at her.

"Everything all right?"

We are whispering.

"That Fielding followed me. I lost him."

"Get undressed. There's the bathroom." She points to a second open door. In the blue-tiled bathroom I begin to undress.

"What happens if one of the servants wakes up? Or Evelyn?"

"No one will wake up. We'll lock the door. Hurry up!" Suddenly her breath comes quickly. She watches me undress and hang my tux over the back of a chair. When I am without my shirt she embraces me and kisses my chest quickly several times. Then she pulls off her pajama top and I see her beautiful large breasts. She clings to me. I smell her hair, her perfume, the soap she just used to wash with. I feel her breasts.

"Hurry up!"

"Yes."

"Hurry up! Quickly! I'm waiting for you."

When I return from the bathroom she is on her bed, completely naked, her arms spread wide. She smiles. I have never seen a more beautiful woman. I shall never see another woman as beautiful as she is. Her skin is still tanned by the sun of this past summer, her legs are long and shapely.

"Come," she whispers. Now I am as naked as she.

I sit on the side of the bed and caress her, her thighs, her breasts and her arms.

"You must be very gentle with me, darling," she whispers. "Can you be very gentle with a woman?"

"Yes."

"Really tender and gentle?"

"Really gentle."

"Come, darling, be gentle with me. I've been longing for it. We've both waited so long."

I place my face on her thighs. I believe that I have never been so tender, so loving. And I have never been so much in love. So much. Not ever. Never. The house is quiet, completely silent. A dog barks somewhere. And precisely the moment her legs open and her hands reach for my hair, I again have this premonition—this ridiculous feeling that I shall die soon. It passes quickly.

And then there is only Verena, only Verena, only Verena.

## [ 20 ]

I could forget my parents, Geraldine, everything. One thing never: This night. With Verena I know for the first time that a man and a woman can be as one, one soul, one thought, one human being.

With Verena I experience this night the reciprocity of love, our hands, legs and lips move in complete unison. The experience with Geraldine was a nightmare. This night with Verena is gentle and swaying, increases ever more, does not decline, does not stop, becomes stronger and stronger each time. We both were tight at the party. Now we are sober. And being sober we thrill to each other.

The hours pass. Two o'clock. Three o'clock. Sometimes I kneel in front of her and kiss her body, or we look at each other and tonight there is no sadness, resignation and disgust in her eyes: I only see hope, trust and confidence. We hold hands. Or she strokes my hair.

At one time, looking at me for a long time she suddenly turned her head to one side.

"What's the matter?"

"Why am I so old?"

"You are not old. You are young . . . you are wonderful."

"I'm twelve years older than you."

"You are not one day older than I!"

She looks at me. Her smile is tender.

"Come," her voice is soft and eager. "Come to me, Oliver. It is so wonderful. I love your body, your hair, your mouth, and your hands. I love all of you."

"I love you."

We melt into each other. She moans, quivering. I know this is the most beautiful night of my life.

I hear her say: "This is the most beautiful night of my life."

"Really?"

"I swear. On Evelyn's life."

"For me, too, Verena, for me, too."

"If one could undo the past . . . start all over again . . . a second life—"

"A second life?"

"I would like to be young once more. I long for that . . . as young as you are."

"You are . . . you will stay young. You will never be old."

"Oh, darling, let us be happy. Who knows how many more nights like tonight we might have?"

Now we are in the grip of a gigantic, overwhelming wave rolling toward the shore, majestic yet slow, rising gently . . . ever so gently.

Verena's lips have parted and I'm afraid she might cry out. She is quite still, quiet.

At the extreme moment she bites my shoulder, she has drawn blood, not much, but the imprint of her teeth is visible.

"Forgive me . . . I'm crazy . . . I've told you. Does it hurt very much?"

"Not at all. It's not bleeding any more."

"Oliver."

"Yes?"

"I—I just thought . . . I just thought of something terrible."

She sounds half asleep already.

It is four-thirty.

"Of what?"

"What is going to happen if I . . . if I fall in love with you?" She sighs.

She breathes deeply, stretches. Incoherent words. I can't understand everything.

"Portoferraio."

"What do you mean?"

"The sea . . . with you . . . the waves—"

"Verena!"

"The sails . . . the sunset—"

"What are you talking about?"

"Elba. He has a house there. Just once . . . alone . . . only the two of us . . . green waves——"

I caress her.

She sighs.

We are facing each other. I pull the covers over us. We cling to each other and go to sleep that way. Cheek to cheek, body to body, as close as two people can sleep.

"Crazy," she murmers sleepily. "Completely, utterly crazy."

And a little later. "A new life . . . a brand-new one . . . a second one . . . is that possible?"

## [ 21 ]

When I awake it is five-thirty. Through the slits of the shutters I see the gray light of the new day.

Verena's breath comes evenly and quietly. Carefully I detach myself from her arms so as not to wake her.

She sighs in her sleep: "To be young . . ."

I wash and dress except for my shoes. For a moment I stand by the bed. I would like to kiss her but I don't want to disturb her sleep.

Silently I open one of the shutters. It is almost light now. When I drop from the window I wait.

Nothing moves.

Running across the lawn I scale the iron fence, glide down

the other side, and run in stockinged feet for a hundred yards. Then I put on my shoes. I walk down the avenue to the garage. The attendant looks pale and bleary-eyed. Looking into my rear-view mirror I see I look like that too.

I have time to kill so I drive slowly.

How fast I drove the day I met Verena.

Only a few weeks have passed—and my entire life is changed.

Because of Verena.

I don't want to flunk school any more. I want to graduate next year and join my father's business. Then I will earn money. My father will see to it that I get more money than is customary. If he does not I'll threaten to go to the competition. Mansfeld's son leaves his father! That would make great copy. Then Verena can get a divorce.

She has jewelry, dresses and furs.

We'll find an apartment. And Evelyn starts public school next fall. That does not cost anything.

And then if I . . .

I almost landed in the ditch. I must watch out. I must not daydream.

Good Lord, am I tired! And now I have to go to school! The cold morning wind blows through my hair.

Soon winter will be here.

Will Verena call today?

Now we *have* to find a hotel. Now everything is different. Completely different.

I cannot be without her now.

Can she be without me?

I don't believe so.

Everything is changed. In the course of one single night.

I leave the Autobahn and see the same signs and houses and streets I saw with her that one certain Sunday afternoon.

The Angel of the Lord. Convalescent Home. A house. Woods.

Words like Elba, like Portoferraio.

I have never been to Elba. I don't know the Angel of the Lord. I will.

Verena will be with me.

Many things will happen.

Here, in Elba, and someplace else.

It will happen to both of us together. Always together.

The good.

The bad.

Everything.

## [ 22 ]

It is seven o'clock when I arrive at Friedheim. The young mechanic is just opening the garage and I drive in. My tux is wrinkled and I open my collar. Leaving the garage I run into the chief. He stares at me and does not seem to recognize me at first glance.

"Oliver," his flat voice held neither accusation nor excitement. "You didn't spend the night at the school."

"No, Doctor."

"Where were you?"

"In Frankfurt. Mr. Herterich doesn't know anything about it. I climbed over the balcony." I talk fast, walking alongside him. "He really doesn't know, Doctor."

"Miss Hildebrand is dead."

"What?"

"Two hours ago. I was there just now." He looks into the distance. "She had an attack. The landlord called the doctor. He said it was a heart attack and gave her an injection and called for an ambulance."

"Ambulance," I say.

"The doctor called me, too. When I arrived she was already dead. During her last minutes she scribbled something on the wall. The letters were large and crooked."

"What did she write?"

He tells me.

This morning, for the first time, the chief seems an old man.

"She was an orphan. That's why she loved all of you so much. The funeral is the day after tomorrow at three. Here in Friedheim. Will you come?"

"Definitely, Doctor. And I'm sure all the other children will be there, too." But there I'm wrong. Maybe twenty of the three hundred children came. Miss Hildebrand had been there so many years. She had helped or tried to help many children. All of the teachers and pedagogues were there. She had had no relatives. Noah and Wolfgang were there, and Rashid too. Hansi did not come.

[ 23 ]

He did not come even though Miss Hildebrand had left the building box to him in her will.

He does not play with it. He merely stuck the "mother's" head into the toilet. The toilet stands on his bedside table. That's where she has to stay. "For as long as I live," Hansi said. We collected money in school. A large beautiful wreath of fall flowers and gold letters on a black bow is lying on the new grave.

WE SHALL NEVER FORGET YOU

I leave the cemetery with Wolfgang and Noah. The chief walks alone, hands in his pockets, his hat pulled forward.

"Oliver . . ."

"Hm?"

"The chief told you what Miss Hildebrand scribbled on her wall?"

"Yes. She wrote: *Let me die. I don't want to live without my children.*"

We walk in silence until Wolfgang says: "Such a good human being. And such an end. It's very sad."

"One ought to cry for all human beings," declares Noah, "but that's impossible."

"And Miss Hildebrand?" I ask.

"One ought to cry for her," answered Noah. "But who will?"

## [ 24 ]

On the morning of the funeral our new French teacher arrived. Her name is Ginette Duval. She comes from Nîmes. She is about thirty-five years old and she would be pretty if she were not always so serious. Serious is the wrong word. Mademoiselle Duval seems tragic. She is simply but smartly dressed. She has a pale even face, beautiful brown eyes, lovely brown hair and she is wearing a pair of old shoes which must have been expensive at one time. She must be poor. Mademoiselle Duval never smiles. She is a very good teacher. She seems to have built an invisible wall between herself and all others. After dinner, Noah asked her why she is so unhappy. "At first she told me not to be insolent. But I suddenly had this feeling, and I was right. I told her that I was a Jew and that my family had perished. I have never done that before! But I had this feeling!"

"What kind of feeling?"

"That there may be something similar in her background. And there is."

"She is thirty-six years old. In 1942 she was eighteen. The Resistance shot five German soldiers in Nîmes. Following that the Germans shot a hundred French hostages. Among them were Mademoiselle Duval's father and brother. She had been very close to her brother. Her mother commited suicide a few years later. Mademoiselle Duval vowed then never to set foot on German soil, never to talk to a German, never to shake hands with a German. She has kept her vow. But now she is at her wits' end."

"Why?"

"She can't find a job teaching French in France. She is not strong enough to work in a factory. If she hadn't accepted Dr. Florian's offer she would have starved to death. Now she is very lonely. It is her choice. She took Miss Hildebrand's room in Friedheim. She doesn't talk to the teachers, not even at mealtimes. Too many people."

"Too many Germans," says Wolfgang.

"Yes, of course. She is scared."

"It depends on us and on what happens to her here," says Noah.

"If she should hear Südhaus spouting off she'll collapse," says Wolfgang.

"It's true, Südhaus constitutes a certain danger. But there aren't only Südhauses here in school. And there were not only Südhauses in Germany."

"Did you tell her that?"

"I told her that I for example am still alive because some people hid me who weren't like Südhaus. But they were German."

"And?"

"She smiled with tears in her eyes and shrugged her shoulders."

"You see. That's the way it will always be."

"Maybe, Wolfgang. Maybe not. One ought not to say *always*. One ought not to say *never*. She didn't want to come to Germany. But she is here. And she has the three of us. And Dr. Frey. There are a few others she will like. We have to make her realize. This country has changed."

"Has this country changed?" Wolfgang's voice is very loud.

"Yes!"

"You believe that?"

Noah's answer is hardly audible: "I *must* believe it. If I didn't there would be only one way out. To emigrate at once."

"Well, and?"

"I can't emigrate. I can't. My people in London require me to graduate here. My people are paying."

"And after your graduation?"

"I'm going to Israel."

"So the country has not changed," I say.

"We have to believe it," answers Noah. "Or talk ourselves into it. Think of the people who hid me and risked their lives doing it. Remember Carl von Ossietzky Dr. Frey told us about.

Think of Dr. Frey. And you, Wolfgang. There are many such people!"

"But they are little people. It makes no difference how they feel!" says Wolfgang.

"The day will come when they will be heard."

"You don't believe that yourself!"

"No," answers Noah. "But I would very much like to believe it."

# Chapter Five

[ 1 ]

"Darling—"

"Verena!"

"I'm so happy to hear your voice. When I woke up this morning and you had gone I was so terribly afraid—"

"Why?"

"That you could be dead. I . . . was half crazy with fear you could have had an accident on the Autobahn, you were dead, died somewhere in Friedheim." Someone did die in Friedheim, but I don't mention Miss Hildebrand's death to Verena.

It is five minutes past two. The sun is shining. A few hours ago Miss Hildebrand died. A few hours ago I left Verena. I just skipped three days in my story. Intentionally. I wanted to finish writing about everything else to have room for Verena and me. That's why I start a new chapter. It is cruel and heartless. A kind old lady dies. And I write: *to have room for Verena and me.* It is terrible but I am not even ashamed of the fact that I don't care about Miss Hildebrand's death the moment I hear Verena's voice. Don't care? I've forgotten it. Completely forgotten.

"It was wonderful, Oliver."

"Verena."

"When shall we meet again?"

"Whenever you say."

"Not the day after tomorrow. I have to take Evelyn to the dentist on Monday."

If she would have had time I wouldn't have gone to Miss Hildebrand's funeral.

"Tuesday, Oliver, at three?"

"Earlier!"

"At two then!"

"I won't have lunch. I'll get a sandwich. Where shall I meet you?"

"It is fantastic, Oliver, just fantastic. I have a girl friend. She and her husband are leaving for America tomorrow for three months. This morning she called me. They own a little weekend house . . . my friend asked me to look after it during the winter. She'll give me the keys."

"Where? Where is the house?"

"That's the most fantastic of all! In Griesheim. Near the Niederwald. You don't even have to drive to Frankfurt. My friend says it is very quiet there now. The owners of the other cabins don't go there now, not even for weekends."

"I can reach it in twenty minutes!"

"That's right! The address is 21 Brunnenpfad. No one knows us there. I've never been there. It's a bit rustic, from what I hear."

"Is there a bed?"

"Yes!"

"Then it's okay!"

"Darling. There is electricity and a boiler for hot water, a large electric stove for the cold weather! Isn't that a miracle?"

"I don't believe in miracles."

"Why—why then does God help us?"

"I told you. Because it is love."

"No! It isn't love. There is no love. Not for a woman like me. Why don't you say anything?"

"I'll never say it again. I'll wait for the day when you say it."

"And imagine. There is a radio and a record player too."

"Great. Then we can play 'Love Is Just a Word.' Bring the record."

"Don't talk like that!"

"Really, bring it. It's a nice record."

"Please don't torture me."

"I don't want to torture you. I love you. Tuesday at two?"

"Two-thirty. My husband is at a conference until five."

Until five. So I'll have to cut the afternoon classes. Latin. My last mark was A+.

"Oliver . . ."

"Yes?"

"I'm looking forward to Tuesday."

"I am, too."

And the day after tomorrow is Miss Hildebrand's funeral. But Verena has no time on that day. She has to take Evelyn to the dentist.

[ 2 ]

You remember that I said that Hansi and Leo are similar. If you have read this book you might perhaps think that this is no novel but at most a diary. There are not supposed to be doubles in a novel. But there are here. Hansi and Leo are blackmailing me. I can't help that. I can even say: It is not a double, it is a triple. In the near future not only two but three people will be blackmailing me. Something like that probably only happens in novels, rather than in real life. And just because of that, it seems to me I have lived a novel.

[ 3 ]

The cabin stands in the midst of an uncared-for garden. It looks dilapidated. The houses on either side are deserted. At the end of the lane the black Niederwald begins. The gate at Number 21 has no lock. The fence is crooked. I walk across rotting yellow grass past a bent watering can to the door of the cabin. A dirty, shaggy cat darts away. When I open the door I see three burning candles on a low tiled table. A few cheap prints (Van Gogh, Gauguin, Goya) on the walls, an old rocking chair, three low chairs, bottles on a chest, and an oversized couch. Everything here smells damp. But the bed looks recently made up and the covers pulled back. A board at the head of the couch holds cigarettes, an ashtray and a vase with fresh flowers.

A sound makes me turn around quickly.

Verena.

She is wearing black slacks, flat shoes and a red sweater. She must have stepped out of the tiny kitchen.

"Verena!"

"Psst!" She comes quickly to me, embraces and kisses me. The damp smell has disappeared, the dilapidated little cabin is now a palace.

Verena switches on a large electric heater.

"It will be warm in a second," she says. "Just finished cleaning up. My friend is terribly slovenly; I already cleaned yesterday."

Now my eyes are used to the soft warm light of the three candles and I see the record player, the radio and many books stacked on the floor, which is covered by a cheap carpet.

"How do you like it?" asks Verena.

"Wonderful."

"It's awful. But it's all we have."

"I think it's marvelous."

"It's the last thing on earth. But the bed is clean. And brand-new." Verena laughs.

"Did you try it?"

"Immediately." She leans on me and I stroke her hair.

I close the shutters. "We have to be careful. No one must know that someone is at home."

"At home!"

"This is our home, dearest." She takes my hand and holds it to her breast.

Since I've entered I've heard a low continuous ticking sound and ask Verena what it is.

"Wood-borers."

"What?"

"Wood-borers."

"Oh, well, I hope this place isn't going to fall down on us."

"That depends on us," she says and laughs again.

"You know we really are very lucky! Not just because of this cabin. My husband has to work a great deal. He is financing some high-rise buildings in Hanover. For weeks he'll be home late."

"You don't think it's a trap?"

"Not this time. He and Dr. Fielding are working together, you remember that old man—"

"Who would love to sleep with you."

"Yes. Fielding told me that they are working together."

"I have more good news! I forgot to tell you that there is no school on Thursday afternoons."

"And Saturday afternoon."

"And the entire Sunday," I say. "No, you must not always leave Evelyn."

"We won't be able to meet here every day." Suddenly she is nervous.

"What time is it?"

"A quarter to three."

"There is no time. You have to return to school."

"Don't worry about that. Latin. We have all the time in the world."

"No," she says. "We don't and you know it. In the kitchen is a present for you."

On the table in the tiny kitchen is a hammer, and, broken into five pieces, a small record. I fit the pieces together and read the title:

*Love Is Just a Word*
From the Original Soundtrack of
*AIMEZ VOUS BRAHMS?*

She destroyed her favorite record. Slowly I go back to the other room.

"Is it a good present?"

"The best! But—but now you have no favorite song."

"We will find a new one."

"I don't need one. I only need you."

"Say that again. Please."

"I only need you."

"In this shack? Always just for hours? Even though you know that I always have to return to him? Even though you know there is no future for us?"

"Would you have smashed the record if you didn't believe there is hope for us?"

[ 4 ]

We are lying on the couch. The coals of the electric stove are glowing. Music plays softly. The candles are burning down. Verena's head rests on my arm. We are smoking. One cigarette.

We are happy in "our house." For the first time we have a house, a home, Verena and I. Neither of us had ever had a home before. Now we have. It smells damp, winter is approaching, soon it will snow, no one knows what will be tomorrow. We are hiding behind closed shutters, we just listen to music and whisper so no one will hear us. We are very happy in this miserable shack.

Verena clings to me and I pull the cover up around our naked shoulders.

"Why did you break the record?"

She does not reply.

"Please hand me the ashtray."

"Verena!"

"You want to hear that I broke it because I love you!"

"No. Yes. Naturally! But it wouldn't be true."

"How do you know?"

"You would have said so. Why did you break it?"

"To please you. No that wasn't the reason. I broke it yesterday. I played it again and again while I was clearing up. Then I took the hammer."

"Why?"

So softly that I can hardly hear her she says: "I want . . . I would like . . . to change."

It is raining. I can hear the drops fall on the roof.

"Oliver . . ."

"Yes?"

"You asked me once where I came from."

"Yes. You got mad. You said it was none of my business."

"Do you want to know?"

"Yes. You broke the record. The time has come."

The rain.

The music.

Our home.

Verena talks.

Verena's great-grandfather, who founded the Upper Silesian Timber Company, was a stubborn, strong man who knew how to handle a saw and axe. When he died his son, a hard, disagreeable, calculating man unaware of the meaning of humanity, took over. It was he who tripled the worth of the enterprise. His death left as heir Carl-Heinz, a congenital weakling from whose hands the business, now the greatest in the country, would have quickly slipped had it not been for his shrewd and determined wife, Edith. Edith gave birth to his children: a girl, Verena, born in 1927, and a boy, Otto, born in 1930.

The father, hoping for a healthy, strong boy to maintain the business, made no effort to hide his animosity when Verena was born. He never showed her any love or affection. This atmosphere of indifference, in which the little girl grew up, increased when Otto was born. Soon it became evident that the boy was a sickly, stupid child and later a lazy student.

Verena grew up in a huge, palatial villa—the way I grew up, as alone as I was, as unhappy as I was. The business grew and grew. The family lived in the utmost luxury. Each child had a personal maid and a "Mademoiselle." Paris and Vienna were the sources of dresses and furs, and the Riviera became their home each spring.

Verena was a shy, quiet child to whom nobody paid any attention, while pedagogues, tutors and doctors tried to shape Otto into a man. No one loved Verena, not even her mother, whose marriage deteriorated as years went by. The father blamed her for giving him only a daughter and a miserable heir; he, who all his life was ruled by only one feeling—fear! He was afraid of everything and everybody. People, animals, every new day. He never realized how completely his son Otto resembled him.

[ 6 ]

With the advent of the Third Reich the company enjoyed its greatest prosperity. Hitler, preparing for a world war, needed coal, steel and lumber. Carl-Heinz Wilfried was so powerful that he was not pressured to join the Party.

When Hitler invaded Poland, Verena's father said "It's not going to come to a good end, you'll see." Thousands of Poles, Czechs, Yugoslavs and Frenchmen were forced to work in factories. Then America entered the war and the High Command spoke of orderly retreats, Verena's father grew increasingly worse. Bombing raids reduced him to panic. The summer of 1944 brought the landing of the Allied forces in Normandy and a Soviet offensive. "Town after town was taken by the Red Army until, on January 22, 1945, my father and mother did something they had never done before. They listened to the BBC. The next morning my father, his chauffeur and the car had disappeared," remembers Verena.

The next day saw a seemingly endless stream of half-starved, half-frozen refugees. "They are coming" was their cry.

Verena's mother did not intend to leave until the forced laborers killed their camp guards and set fire to Wilfried's home.

An old loyal foreman dragged Verena's mother and the children to safety. Accompanied by the rumbling of heavy weapons they sat in a horse-drawn wagon, driving west; one wagon among thousands.

Carl-Heinz Wilfried at that time was already on his way to Munich.

[ 7 ]

Verena's mother died in a barn outside Coburg. She had been feverish and had tried to hide it. During the day low-flying planes machine-gunned the endless column of refugees who tried to take cover in the ditches. The snow was red with blood. In village after village the natives locked their doors to the refugees and no doctor could be found for the now-delirious woman. The old foreman went looking for food. Verena wanted to help too and went to a farmhouse where a huge, red-faced man promised her bread. When she entered the house he tore off her clothes.

"He beat me until I could not defend myself any more. He raped me and then threw me out. He was the first man in my life. I was almost eighteen years old. When I returned to the barn my mother was dead."

[ 8 ]

They buried Edith Wilfried by heaping snow on her. There was enough snow for many dead, this January of 1945.

The foreman, by not using main roads, stealing food for the children and himself, brought them as far as Frankfurt-am-Main. In the large camp outside the town they lived until the spring of 1946.

[ 9 ]

Verena was now eighteen years old, a beautiful girl in rags. An American soldier, a guard at the camp, fell in love with her and not only promised food but kept his promise. He took care of

Verena, Otto and the old foreman, who died in 1946. "His name was Jack Collins and he came from Oklahoma," Verena tells me. He proved to be an inexperienced but gentle lover.

Verena had obtained employment at the PX. In 1949 it became possible for American soldiers to marry German girls. They were told that their chances looked good for getting their papers okayed by the middle of 1950. In the summer of 1950 Jack's unit was suddenly transferred to Korea. Another war had broken out.

Jack Collins was killed at Heartbreak Ridge on the thirteenth of November, 1950, in a battle with so-called Red Chinese volunteers. The War Department had only notified his parents, who wrote to Verena they were so sorry for her.

## [ 10 ]

Now Verena could be found almost any evening in the American clubs of Frankfurt. She flirted, she danced. Verena soon became known and high-ranking officers competed for her favors. She allowed herself to be wined and dined, accepted presents, kissed and—not too frequently—went to bed with them. It was at that time she promised herself never to fall in love again. Otto Wilfried became a black marketeer. The stupid, weak Otto made a fortune between 1950 and 1953. He rented a spacious apartment. His wild parties were notorious.

On April 12, 1953, he was arrested by the CID.

## [ 11 ]

The witness for the prosecution against him and his gang was a Robert Stevens. He spoke fluent German, French, Italian and Spanish. He was good-looking, well-groomed, a man of the world and he knew how to handle women. It was he who made Verena change her views about men and love once again. Mr. Stevens became her boy friend.

Mr. Stevens also spoke of marriage.

He bought her dresses and jewelry. At the trial documents pertaining to Otto Wilfried had mysteriously disappeared and Otto was found not guilty.

Mr. Stevens was an honest man. He said: "I'm married in the States. I'm getting a divorce. Naturally, it will take a while."

It took almost two years. Verena was not unhappy during this time. Mr. Stevens spoiled her and said he loved her. Mr. Stevens was also crazy about children. During the second year Verena became pregnant. Since, according to Mr. Stevens, the divorce was imminent Verena wanted to tell him. Four months passed and the divorce was not final.

Verena then told Mr. Stevens that she was expecting a child. She consoled the flabbergasted man and added: "It is too late to have it taken care of—but even if it takes ten years for you to obtain your divorce, I shall always love you and be happy with our child. Won't you?"

"Naturally, darling," said Mr. Stevens.

The next day he had left Frankfurt.

When after a week she had not heard from him, thinking him to be on an official business trip, she went to his office. There she was told that Mr. Stevens had been transferred and was not expected to return to Frankfurt. She left letters at the office to be mailed to him. The very pleasant gentleman there was abjectly sorry but he could not reveal Mr. or Mrs. Stevens' address in the U.S. because Verena would then know his real name.

"What do you mean? His name is Robert Stevens!"

"Please, Miss Wilfried, don't be naïve! No CID man can ever use his real name or he might not live very long. Surely you can understand that." Verena understood perfectly.

## [ 12 ]

Evelyn was born by Caesarian section. An infection developed and the doctors declared that only penicillin would save her life. Penicillin was only obtainable on the black market at exorbitant prices. When she was discharged from the hospital Verena was warned that another pregnancy might be fatal.

She was now without money. She had sold, one by one, all the gifts which Mr. Stevens had given her. Evelyn was taken care of in a day nursery to enable Verena to continue working. At night she took courses in shorthand and typing.

It was now 1956.

Through the Red Cross Carl-Heinz Wilfried succeeded in having Verena and Otto traced. He had received some compensation for his property in the East and had opened another lumber business in Passau.

Otto joined his father's firm.

Verena refused to see her father.

## [ 13 ]

It is four-forty-five.

Verena and I are lying on the wide couch. The candles have burned down. Only the glowing coals of the electric heater light the room.

"That was my life," she muses. "Now you know it the way I know yours."

It is warm in the room. Verena sits, her legs pulled close to her body, I caress her naked thighs.

"You said once that you had loved Evelyn's father. Do you still love him?"

"No. When I close my eyes I can't even remember how he looked."

"Were you a secretary for a long time?"

"You know, I had many different jobs. It was very difficult. My clothes were old and not modern. I had to move into a small apartment near the railroad. A hole in the wall."

She lies down again and we hold each other's hand. Finally, after a long pause, she says: "I've never walked the streets. Naturally, I met men. They took me out. Once they found out I had a child and where I lived they left in a hurry. Besides, men know intuitively when one fakes passion or love."

"And your husband? You don't love him and he doesn't notice?"

"Naturally, he knows. He told me it didn't matter. He loves me and that is sufficient. He told me he would never let me go. I don't know what he thinks." Her voice is louder now. "Maybe tomorrow he will throw me out. But tell me, Oliver: Can you understand that I never want to live in a dirty place by the railroad again, and not have enough to eat, and to have to drink champagne with any horrible man and have him touch me? Do you understand now that I never want to be poor again—never, never, never again?"

"I understand."

"You are marvelous!"

"I'm not marvelous. But you did break the record."

"I'm almost sorry I did."

"Don't say that."

"But if I am? We promised to be always truthful, didn't we?"

"I'm saving the pieces."

"Silly boy."

"I'll show them to you someday."

"Don't start that again, please! It was so wonderful. It has never been like that with anyone."

"Not even with Mr. Stevens?"

"Why do you ask?"

"Because he is Evelyn's father. I'm jealous."

"You don't have to be. I told you I don't even remember how he looked. And . . . and I can't remember how it was with him."

"But—"

She covers my hand with hers. "It is late. We must go. Oh, we have so little time, darling."

We kiss.

So little time!

# [ 14 ]

It is quite dark when we leave the little, crooked house. Verena locks the door and we walk to my car. Driving to the Autobahn I remember something: "Didn't you say your husband had obtained a business for your brother?"

"That's right. A year ago my father fired Otto for taking money from his business in Passau. Otto came to me, as usual. My husband helped him. My husband helps many people."

"That's very generous of him."

"He doesn't do it for the people."

"For whom, then?"

"For me."

"So that you will love him?"

"Yes."

"And will you?"

She shakes her head. At the gas station near the Autobahn I call a taxi for Verena.

"The day after tomorrow is Thursday. I have the afternoon off. Shall we meet at two-thirty?"

"Yes, Oliver, yes." She nods.

We look into the darkness and the rain and watch the cars sweep by on the wet road.

The taxi arrives.

"Don't let the taxi stop in front of your house, Verena."

"No."

"I love you."

"Good night."

"I love you."

"Stay here. I don't want the driver to see you."

She leaves alone.

The Quellenhof is empty when I arrive. The children are still at dinner. Going to my room, I meet Mr. Herterich.

"Thank God you came in time. Dr. Haberle called at four. I . . . I told him you had diarrhea and were in bed."

"Okay. If there is anything I could do for you?"

"No, thanks." He touches wood, his smile forlorn.

In my room I sit on my bed and something sticks into my ribs. I pull the broken record from my pocket and fit the five pieces together.

*Love Is Just a Word*
From the Original Soundtrack of
*AIMEZ-VOUS BRAHMS?*

I sit and stare at it. Rain beats on the window panes. When I hear the first children return I quickly put the pieces in an envelope and hide it in the drawer of my bedside table. I stretch out on the bed, and stare at the ceiling. She said she cannot remember his face. But he is the father of her child! And she said once she only loved two people: Evelyn and Evelyn's father. She said. . . .

## [ 15 ]

There are many storms and much rain during this month of November. Every Thursday afternoon and every Saturday afternoon I meet Verena in *our* house. Each time it looks more dilapidated and crooked. The garden has become a quagmire. And the wood-borers tick busily in the walls. The electric heater keeps the room where we make love comfortable. We bring little presents. A pipe. Perfume. A lighter. A lipstick. A book. Little presents that will not be noticed. Since paying off the loan I have to be careful with money. We drink tea. We don't need alcohol. Manfred Lord is still busy with the high-rise building in Hanover. He is also financing the construction of two hundred private houses outside Bremen.

After, for a moment our passion is spent, we talk about ourselves. Then we embrace again.

It is turning colder and foggy. The trees are bare now. Soon it will be December. The fog, the rain beating on the roof, the humming of the heater, our embraces, our talks—I have never known such sweet intimacy before. Nor, said Verena, had she. Before meeting her I always assumed that all people lie. I believe anything Verena tells me. I told her that. She replied: "But we agreed not to lie to each other."

When we cannot see each other we telephone—I still sit in Mrs. Liebetreu's garage and wait and write.

Geraldine is recovering. She is encased in plaster of Paris. My letter and flowers brought this reply:

> My dearest!
>
> Thank you for the flowers! I shall keep them all my life—even when they are withered. Before Christmas I shall be allowed to move to an apartment my mother rented for me. My father is coming from Cape Canaveral for the holidays. Perhaps my parents will become reconciled! I don't dare think of it. A reconciliation—and you! You'll have to visit me right after Christmas. Pray my spine will heal properly and I won't be crippled like poor little Hansi. I am very much in love. I told the doctors; they said it would help me get well quickly. Wouldn't that be wonderful?
>
> I embrace you and kiss you a thousand times.
>
> Yours,
>
> Geraldine.

I burned the letter immediately. What am I going to do after Christmas? Well, it's only the beginning of December.

I have developed a habit of postponing all decisions, and when I am with Verena I generally forget that there are any to be made.

[ 16 ]

The candles are lit. We are lying close to each other. Verena says abruptly:

"I can't stand Nietzsche, can you?"

"He makes me sick."

"Yes, but yesterday I found a poem that fits us." Naked and warm in my arms, she declaims:

"The crows cry and fly quickly to the town
Soon it will snow—happy he who still has a home."

"I didn't think he had it in him!"

"I didn't either."

"We have a home, don't we, Verena?"

"Yes, my love!"

The roof of the little house has sprung a few leaks. For some time now we have had to place bowls on the cheap carpet, because it drips from the ceiling.

"I don't mean this shack."

"I know what you mean."

"You are my home."

"And you are everything to me," she says.

Passion grips us again and drops of rain fall into the bowls on the carpet, the winter wind howls outside while the American forces' network plays the "Rhapsody in Blue."

[ 17 ]

On December 6th the chief sent for me. At first I was afraid it could have to do with Verena.

In his study he asked me to sit down and offered me a glass of wine, cigar or cigarettes. I accepted a glass of wine.

"Oliver, when you first came here I suggested that we talk once in a while. You remember?"

"Yes."

"Well, I'm sorry that our first talk does not touch on your problems but mine."

"I'm much relieved."

"Why?"

"Well, I'd rather discuss your problems!"

"Ah, yes." He smiles briefly. "I want to talk to you because you are the oldest here and you happen to be the only one I can talk to at the moment."

He asks me what I think of Friedrich Südhaus. It appears Südhaus had denounced Dr. Florian to his father, the Attorney-

General, for hiring Dr. Frey. It didn't matter that Dr. Frey was generally respected and loved by the children. Friedrich Südhaus had written to his father about the visit to Dachau. The TV documentaries, the books we read in class. According to the Attorney-General, Dr. Frey's methods of teaching history are detrimental to the German people, their honor and repute. Dr. Olaf Südhaus, a powerful man with friends in many government agencies, let it be known that we the pupils are being turned into Communists under the influence of an East German agent. As proof of Dr. Florian also being a Communist he cited the fact that Giuseppe, whose father is a Communist, had received a scholarship.

When the Attorney-General didn't make too much progress he wrote to about fifty parents. Since two-thirds of the pupils are foreigners, he only wrote to the German parents, of whom sixty-five per cent demanded the immediate dismissal of Dr. Frey.

It is quiet in the study. The chief is smoking his pipe. I'm sipping my glass of wine.

"Sixty-five per cent?" I finally ask.

"Does that surprise you? I expected more. You have to understand the parents' point of view. They don't want their children to come home on vacation saying: We saw Dachau. We saw the Third Reich! Parents want to be left in peace. They don't want their children to ask how something like that could happen!"

"How can I help?"

"For the moment I would like you to find out what the children think of this matter. If they share their fathers' opinions I see no hope. If they don't, I'll defend myself."

"Okay, chief," I say. "You'll have my report in two days."

## [ 18 ]

Since the beginning of December the tennis courts have become skating rinks used by many children each afternoon. Slacks, colorful sweaters, short pleated skirts over tights, with red, yellow or blue mufflers—a pretty picture against a background of black trees of the forest.

This is where I called a meeting at three o'clock.

I have brought voting paper and ballot boxes. I already have the votes of the few sick children who are not at the rink.

I have to talk loud to be heard. The children crowd around me. I had decided not to mention Friedrich Südhaus' name to ensure objective voting. So I say, "One of you has denounced Dr. Frey." Then I tell them what resulted. As soon as I have finished the unexpected happens: Friedrich Südhaus turns and runs. I hadn't thought that he would give himself away. The goddamn fool doesn't get very far. Wolfgang trips him and he hits the ice. Immediately Wolfgang pulls him up by his jacket and several boys are trying to get at Südhaus. He is shaking with fear, protesting his innocence. "Quiet!" I yell. I'm afraid a general melee is about to start. "This is not the way to do it!" I explain that we are going to take a vote. The children who write YES want Dr. Frey to remain, the ones who write NO do not. I open the ballot boxes and pass out the slips of paper. They vote quickly and soon the last child has dropped his piece of paper in a box. Rashid helps me count the votes.

## [ 19 ]

In twenty minutes we have counted: two hundred fifty-six YES votes. Another vote about the informer—to show the adults that we are not using their Nazi methods—results in two hundred fifty YES votes to send Südhaus to "prison." It is worse than the worst beating. It means that from this moment no child will look at him, listen to him, talk to him, or sit at the same table with him. Südhaus will be as alone as the man in the moon, solitary among several hundred children.

Wolfgang lets go of his arm and we watch Südhaus leave.

To show our parents that we are really serious we decide to call a strike. It was Giuseppe's suggestion not to attend school until we were assured that Dr. Frey would remain. Thomas, whose father is a NATO general, informed British journalists in Bonn of the happenings here. The next morning two hundred sixty-one children are absent from their classrooms.

The teachers assembled in Dr. Florian's study. On his door Noah and I had posted a note informing the director and teachers why we are on strike. We will not return to classes until we have assurances that Dr. Frey will remain at the school.

## [ 20 ]

The chief, naturally, has to avoid giving the impression that he is on our side. He uses the loudspeaker system to threaten us with force if we do not return to our classrooms. That proves impractical—it is twenty minutes' walk uphill—so we are not given lunch. We pool our money and shop for fruit, milk, and canned food in Friedheim.

At night the British journalists arrive at the A, listen to our story and take photographs. They have brought us a few cartons of cigarettes. Hansi sits on his bed, smoking one after another. "A strike like that is super," he says. "Ought to have that more often!"

"Yes," says Giuseppe, "but not the children, the adults."

## [ 21 ]

The first day of the strike the chief telephoned Südhaus' father, who still insisted on Dr. Frey's dismissal. Dr. Frey had been given leave and was staying in a hotel in Frankfurt.

On the second day a high official of the school administration in Frankfurt came (he was also photographed by the reporters) and declared that the school would be closed and we would all go to juvenile court if we continued the strike. He was completely ignored.

That afternoon the chief used the loudspeaker system again to tell us that the order of the Frankfurt school administration was canceled by a decree of the Ministry of Education. He again called upon us to return to classes. On the third day a chauffeur-driven Mercedes 300 arrives to pick up Friedrich Südhaus. He must have known in advance because his things were packed and he disappears quickly.

Since we had received no answer from Südhaus' father and his chums, Noah told Thomas to give the go-ahead to his two English reporters. On the fifth day of the strike pictures of the events in our school make the front page in three London newspapers. One day later these reports can be read in German newspapers, if not on the front page. The reporters who now come to the school are responsible for more reports on the sixth day. That night the chief informs us, using the loudspeaker system again, that Friedrich Südhaus and thirteen other students have left the school and Dr. Frey was staying on and teaching as before.

"I'm expecting you to be in your classrooms at eight tomorrow morning. Your strike is settled. I want to voice my disapproval of your strike. There will be an investigation. Meanwhile, I wish you all good night." "Good night!" They yell as one. In their robes and pajamas they are dancing and yelling, boxing each other. The first period next morning is history. Dr. Frey enters, limping as usual. "Sit down." We sit down. "We now come to the events where we were . . . hm . . . interrupted," says Dr. Frey. "Hitler's coming to power and the part played by the German heavy industry." His voice is faltering. He turns his back to us. A long pause. Finally, Dr. Frey says softly: "I thank you."

## [ 22 ]

The banker Manfred Lord laughs so hard he chokes and coughs. He takes a drink and smooths back his beautiful white hair. "That's a wild story," he says, "Isn't it, darling?"

"Yes, Manfred," answers Verena.

"One can't be grateful enough to you. Now other foreign countries will finally realize that things have changed here; a new generation is growing up immune to any kind of dictatorship," says the handsome Manfred Lord who also was a Party member—though he surely didn't do anything out of the ordinary. About twelve million party members didn't do anything out of the ordinary. How the entire horrifying thing happened not one of them can really explain today!

Or maybe, yes!

It was the SS.

Tonight is the fourteenth of December. Three hours after I had spent the afternoon in *our* house with his wife, he telephoned the school to invite me to an informal evening.

Now we are sitting in the conservatory in Manfred Lord's expensive villa. Tropical climbers in huge planters send forth tendrils across the glass roof from which baskets holding rare orchids are suspended. It is very comfortable in this well-appointed conservatory. He must have spent a fortune on the rare plants of which there are perhaps a dozen in the entire world. He loves and collects plants.

And old and rare books. He has a fantastic library. Must be worth a fortune too.

Verena and he are drinking whisky and ginger ale. I drink Tuborg beer from a silver mug. I have no intention of drinking too much again in Mr. Lord's presence. We are all wearing sweaters, Verena the red one that I told her I loved.

"You are splendid boys," says Manfred Lord, reaching for the bottle again. "And splendid girls. I really like that; I really do."

As often as he turns his back to us Verena and I exchange glances. We have been together a great deal in recent days. When we look at each other it seems as if we are embracing. When Manfred Lord left for a moment Verena stuffed some photographs in my pocket.

I look at Verena, her lips forming a kiss.

"But you know, Mr. Lord, the end was not that happy."

"What do you mean?"

"Nothing is said about it in the papers. But there is a sequel which is troubling Dr. Florian. He told me unless a miracle happens he has to close the school."

"I don't understand."

"One of the fathers who insisted Dr. Frey be dismissed and who consequently took his son out of the school is a Mr. Christiania."

"Christiania?" Manfred Lord frowns. "You don't mean Horst Christiania, of Christiania and Wolf in Hamburg?"

"Yes. He."

"But Horst is—" He interrupts himself. "What about him?"

When I tell him that he is the one who was financing the school when the chief bought the then-rented buildings, he whistles a little and says: "You don't have to explain any further, Oliver. I understand. Now he wants his money, right?"

"Yes, Mr. Lord." It seems incongruous how easily I talk to the man whose wife I sleep with, whose wife I love, how quickly one adjusts to such a situation. Lord laughs. "Not very nice, but I mean: Old Nazi. The son isn't. One has to understand other people's point of view. More than that. One has to try to think what one would do in their place. That's what I always say, isn't it, darling?" And he pats Verena's knee.

"How much is your chief supposed to come up with?"

"One hundred thousand."

"Hm."

Manfred Lord finishes his drink and rises. He walks between cacti and rare climbing plants, occasionally examining an orchid. Suddenly he turns to me—a good thing I had not been looking at Verena just then—and says: "Tell your Dr. Florian that he can have the hundred thousand from me. I shall talk to Christiania and if there is nothing doing there—we old guys are all a little rigid," he says, smiling disarmingly, oh so charmingly, "then I shall take over his obligations. Dr. Florian can stop worrying."

"But why should you want to do that?"

"I'm not taking any risks. The school is doing well. I shall even make money on the deal."

"My husband likes to be of help," says Verena. And I remember why he said he does.

He loves her. The poor man. It reminds me of a poem by Heine:

She was charming; he adored her.
But he lacked charm; she loved him not.

(We are again allowed to read Jewish authors.) Funny, this Manfred Lord is charming and still Verena does not love him.

"Ask Dr. Florian to be in my office tomorrow at four."

I thank him, feeling very happy for the chief, and after a little while I prepare to leave. He pats my shoulder. "Well, we wish you a very happy Christmas and a happy New Year. We'll both miss you very much, won't we, Verena?" (That without looking at her.)

"Yes, very much." (Without looking at me.)

"Oh, there is something else. Would you do me a favor?"

"Naturally."

"You know, your father loves books as much as I do. For about six months now I have been looking for a book I know he would like to have. He never asked me to trace it for him but I know he just didn't want to bother me. Now I would like to give it to him for Christmas. Would you take it to him for me?"

"With pleasure, Mr. Lord."

I swear to you, at that time I never had the slightest suspicion! Why shouldn't I take the book? They were both devilishly clever, my old man, that swine, and the so very honorable Mr. Lord!

[ 23 ]

There is a knock at the door in answer to his ring and now, in a plain black suit, but arrogant and smiling with eyes as cold as ever, in walks Leo. The same Leo who took my five thousand marks and stole love letters written by other men to Verena. Leo, the blackmailer.

Manfred Lord asks him to fetch the book. Manfred Lord's smile is wide.

"You are surprised to see him here?"

"Yes, well . . ."

"He asked to come. It is too lonesome for him in Friedheim. And we have many guests during the winter in Frankfurt. He is more useful here. My wife is glad to have him too. Aren't you, dearest?" All this is said without inflection, with insinuation, without looking.

"Yes," she says, and looks at me directly, smiling, "he is a big help, and a perfect servant."

The scoundrel brings the book and is dismissed.

It is an old book Lord hands me. Its cover is stained. It must have been lying in some basement for a long time.

"This is *The Dybbuk,* says Manfred Lord. "It is a famous dramatic Jewish legend of a bad spirit entering a human being." He opens the book to the title page. "The title here is *Between Two Worlds* and not *Dybbuk.*"

"But these are not Hebrew letters!"

"It is a translation into German. This first edition is a rare book valued and sought by connoisseurs. Well, if you would be so kind—"

In the hall I am getting into my duffle coat. Manfred Lord takes Verena's arm. I am hoping to have just one moment alone with Verena but Lord says:

"It is terribly foggy and slippery outside. On no account are you going outside, darling. I'll see Oliver to his car."

"Good night, Madame," I kiss her hand. Her fingers grip mine. "Thank you for a lovely evening."

I can't think of anything else.

Outside the wrought-iron lamps are lighting the drive to the gate.

"Ah," Manfred Lord sounds pleased. "Leo has already spread sand! He really is a gem. I can rely on him one hundred per cent. Always! He has been with me eight years! He would give his right arm for me!"

What does he know? What does he suspect? Did Leo—?

When we reach the car we shake hands.

"And remember me to your parents, Oliver. Good luck!"

I drive and raise my hand in answer to his wave. What else could I do! The fog is heavy this night and the road icy. I stop at a deserted parking place to look at the photographs Verena gave me. There are seven, some new, some old. Verena, a very young girl in short black pants, net stockings, tight-fitting jacket and top hat. She holds a cane in one hand and a long cigarette holder between her lips. One photo shows her nude. It must have been taken recently because she wears her hair the way it is now, and modern shoes. I wonder who took that picture?

Whoever it was, I hate him. I don't want anyone to know or see how beautiful Verena is! I burn the pictures and grind the ashes into the ground. At last I drive on. I would like to have kept the photos, especially the one that showed her nude. But I cannot risk it. A pity! I'm sure she thought to make me happy. No, I had to burn them.

Leo. . . .

## [ 24 ]

It is Thursday, the fifteenth of December, five o'clock. I have more time but Verena has to go home. At four o'clock the chief had an appointment with her husband. ("Thank you, Oliver. That was really good of you. And this Mr. Lord must be a great man! You don't know what it means to have someone help me right now! Well, you see, Dr. Florian, there are still a few decent people in this country.")

No, Verena must leave.

We spent four hours in *our* house. Now Verena is getting dressed. I love to watch her graceful movements.

She is so beautiful.

I am sitting on the bed smoking, already dressed. The candles have burned down again. Outside it is snowing. AFN sends continuous Christmas music.

"Why is Leo in Frankfurt?"

"To spy on me, naturally."

"Aren't you afraid?"

"Not since we are together." She fastens her stockings, steps into her skirt.

"Funny, before we were together I was always afraid."

"It would be wiser if you were still afraid."

"Why do you say that?" She fastens the zipper and reaches for the red sweater. "Did something happen?"

"No. But you yourself say that he watches you."

"I am terribly careful. I change taxis. I use different post offices. I am smarter than he." She smiles. "Chéri, this red sweater is not going to last for ever if you want me to wear it all the time."

"We'll buy a new one."

"Did you like my photos?"

I nod.

"What's wrong?"

"Who took the one of you in the nude?"

"Why?"

"Because I want to know!"

"Don't you like it? I took it. With a self-timer."

"Verena—"

"I lied. Enrico took it. Will you throw it away now?"

"I won't lie either. I burned it."

"Because you were jealous?"

"No, just as a precaution. Last night. I looked at them very carefully. And if I close my eyes now I can still see each of them. Especially one. The one of you in the nude. But we must be cautious, both of us. Leo is here. Remember that!"

"I'll remember."

"Verena—" I am standing in front of her now; she is looking at me.

"We really must be careful. If something should happen . . . if we should lose one another, I . . . I could not live any more." I turn off the radio. "Excuse me, I'm crazy."

"You're not crazy, darling. You are right. It's too bad. Those photos were supposed to be my Christmas present."

"I received it." I say and take a binder out of my brief case. "Now you'll get yours."

"What is it?"

"Our story. As far as I have got."

"Oh," she runs to me, still on stockinged feet, and takes it from my hand.

"You've written that much already?"

"It's all I've corrected and typed so far. It's going to be a thick book."

"It's also going to be a very great . . . affair, isn't it?"

"Were you going to say love?"

"No!"

"No?"

"No! No! No!" She touches my face gently. She opens the binder and reads the title page: *Love is just a word.* And on the next page *"For V—with love.* She kisses my cheek. "Oh, Oliver, I'm so excited!"

"The dedication has to be omitted, naturally, if the book is ever published," I say. "Unless you and Evelyn are with me by then."

She smiles and, not wanting to hurt my feelings, nods.

"You'll have to read it secretly. And hide it well. Here for instance."

"I know of a safer place. A vault. It is empty. I've had it a few years now. My husband does not know I have it. Oliver, I can't wait to read it!"

"Perhaps it is not good."

"It won't be bad. I know it."

"Don't be angry if you read something you don't like."

"I promise." She pats the bed. "So long, bed," she says and, walking around the room, "So long radio, so long candles, so long table, chair and lamp. You won't see us for a long time!"

"I'll be back the eighth of January."

"We won't return until the fifteenth. My husband is taking us to St. Moritz. He has made up his mind, so what can I do?"

"How can I reach you?"

"You can't. I'll have to phone you."

Since I am not going to live at home, she writes down the telephone number of the hotel where I shall be staying.

"Don't leave that paper lying around."

"No. My husband usually takes a nap in the afternoon while on holiday."

"Then we'll continue the way we've done up to now. I'll wait for your call between two and a quarter to four."

"All right, Oliver. But it could be that I'm not always able to call . . . for instance Christmas Eve or New Year's."

"I understand. But don't take the manuscript with you!"

"Of course not. I'll read it here tomorrow. All of it."

We turn off the electric heater, blow out the candles and lock up. It is snowing heavily now. We walk to my car. The streets are deserted. I can kiss her goodbye.

"Take care, little Oliver."

"I shall think of you all the time."

"And I want to give you as many kisses as there are snowflakes."

"I wish they would fall faster. Please, dear snowflakes, fall faster!"

## [ 25 ]

After eating a very substantial lunch on the twentieth, the pre-Christmas lunch, I run down to Friedheim to get my car. I run, because I ate too much. It tasted very good. Now I need some exercise. I think it is like that in all boarding schools. The food preceeding holidays is always excellent! In case the children are asked at home about the food they can supply the right answers. Or am I wrong? Is it love for one's fellow men and reverence for the high holidays of Christianity?

Next to the garage is a shoe store which sells very smart shoes indeed. As I am driving the car out of the garage I see Dr. Frey coming out of the store, two packages under his arm. When he recognizes me he flushes and pushes a woman following him back into the store. Ah well, I think, and step on the gas. Why shouldn't Dr. Frey have a liaison too! Bravo! More power to him! Back at the villa I select only clothes which are easy to pull off and on and pack my bag. Just a few changes of underwear (suits are in Echternach), a few books, shaving gear and *The Dybbuk*. Noah told me of the orthodox Jews of Eastern Europe. I am going to have a look at the book. It sounds interesting.

Three o'clock.

I have to hurry. Teddy Behnke wrote me to be ready to leave at four, in case of fog. I say goodbye to Noah and Wolfgang who are staying at the school, and Rashid and Hansi. The black Ali left yesterday in a Rolls-Royce. Rashid is sad but when he begins to talk about Persian politics and returning home, Hansi, who is strangely amiable, says, "Forget about politics, man! We'll have ourselves a great time. I have a little surprise for you, Rashid. A few girls are staying on, too. When it is dark we'll go to their villa. I'll show you something. Don't ask, you will see. It's my Christmas surprise. Maybe a few drapes have not been drawn."

"You are a dirty pig," I say.

"And still young too," says Hansi. "But, old man, take it easy!"

Giuseppe is standing by my car beaming. In his hand is a letter, crumpled and dirty, having been read many times.

"Froma my Mama, yes? She writea Prime Minister Fanfani give a Christmas amnesty. Gooda chance for Papa to be released. Then he come home to Germany. Happy Christmas for me, no, Oliver?"

"Yes, Giuseppe. I hope your father will be released."

We shake hands.

Driving down to Friedheim I pass Dr. Frey and Mademoiselle Duval, engrossed in each other. I notice Mademoiselle is not wearing her old shoes any more, but new, black fur-lined boots.

## [ 26 ]

Frankfurt airport. Customs. New officials. New faces. The old story. The Wanted List. Meaningful looks. The usual stupid fuss. Ordinary people go through Customs on arrival in Germany. I am not ordinary. I'm searched going and coming.

Thanks, Papa. Thanks!

"Your passport, please."

"Your name?"

Smile. Smile. Don't become impatient. If one has gone through it fifty times one can stand it for the fifty-first time too.

"Oliver Mansfeld. But I'm the son, not the father."

It does not make the slightest difference. It is the same cabin where, through the little window, I saw Verena kiss Enrico Sabbadini. Meanwhile Enrico has been discarded. Now *I* kiss Verena. Boy, oh boy, how time does fly. . . . While the customs official examines my shirts and shaving gear I think of Geraldine. I telephoned her this morning at the hospital to wish her a happy Christmas. She was so excited she could hardly talk. I could hardly talk because I didn't know what to say.

She gave me the address and telephone number of the apartment she is moving to. She told me to be sure to come and visit her after New Year. Then I shall have to tell her that we are through. I am sorry, really. But I must tell her.

## [ 27 ]

On the snow-covered runway I can see our Bonanza, the name *Mansfeld* printed in huge red letters, visible from the distance. Teddy Behnke is standing outside in a leather jacket and corduroy pants. He looks great. "I'm glad to see you again, Mr. Oliver!" The smile on his clean-cut, decent face is genuine. Now we are ready for take-off. Teddy is in communication with the control tower and I open the mahogany bar in the cabin. It is complete with ice in the cooler. My father is a well-bred man who intends to send my mother to a mental institution, who is a slave to my Aunt Lizzy and who cheated the Federal Republic of Germany out of 12.5 million marks. I fix myself a drink and wait for a chance to talk to Teddy. I cannot get any information from him about the situation in Luxembourg. He only says that the doctors are concerned for my mother. "Madame is becoming increasingly melancholy. She hardly talks." Bravo, Aunt Lizzy! My congratulations, Aunt Lizzy! Cheers! I empty my glass and fix myself another drink.

My mother. . . . It distresses me to think of her. I feel wretched all of a sudden. I have to find something to occupy my thoughts.

I open the yellowed pages of *The Dybbuk*.

> *First Act.*
>
> *Low, mystical singing from afar can be heard in complete darkness before the curtain rises.*
>
> *Why then does the soul plunge from the heights down to the lower abyss?*
> *There is rising in falling*
> *Fallen souls are striving upward.*
>
> *On the stage is an old wooden prayer house. Suspended from a beam, supported by two posts, is a brass chandelier. The Torah lectern is covered by a dark cloth. . . .*

I read, turning page after page. I drink the Scotch, and hear Teddy's voice from time to time. "Redhair seven . . . Redhair seven . . . this is Two–one–one–one–zero.

Just a moment!

I set my glass down.

Slowly, carefully my fingertips examine the entire page.

Something caught my attention turning page after page. A cursory examination at, for instance, Customs, would not have revealed anything. But if one smooths down a page one can feel two tiny almost unnoticeable irregularities. Now I discover a third. They are pin pricks. Something put a pin through an *e*, through an *o* and +.

I turn more pages.

I am not reading now, just feeling for more holes. On some pages I find more perforations, on some none. A perforated *z*, a perforated *b*. Two perforated *l*'s. I write down a few of the letters. Not all of them, there are too many perforations for that.

More and more perforations.

A . . . H . . . R . . . H . . . R . . .

I go through the entire book. More and more pinpricks.

My father and the honorable Manfred Lord. They are close friends. They thought of something pretty using *The Dybbuk*. Something very pretty for their dirty racket. K . . . L . . . I . . . T . . . R . . . E . . . E . . . R . . . W . . . P. . . .

# Chapter Six

[ 1 ]

Two cats. Three rabbits. A jackdaw. I am watching my mother, crouched on the floor of the little house in the park, feed the animals. It is five o'clock. Only a few paths have been cleared of the snow covering the park.

"I like this sanatorium best of all," says my mother. "There are so many animals here, especially in the summer. I don't ever want to leave here. The animals know me so well."

It has been this way for days now. At exactly five o'clock my mother feeds her animals. She does not have to stay in bed. The doctors said fresh air would be beneficial.

Mother refuses to see visitors. I am the exception.

"You didn't forget the peanuts, did you?" asks my mother.

No, I didn't. She asked me for them yesterday. I bought two pounds.

Since seeing my mother four months ago she seems to have aged twenty years. She has the appearance of a ghost. She cannot possibly weigh more than ninety pounds. Her hands are only skin and bone, her face is transparent, blue veins showing through the white skin. Her eyes are large and inflamed. On and off she turns her head as if to free herself of a rope round her neck. Her walk is unsteady; she often stumbles. The nurses say she hardly eats. She only demands coffee. Most of the time she lies on her bed, fully dressed, and stares at the ceiling. She has lost all conception of time, confuses hours, days, seasons, and it took quite a while before she recognized me.

I spoke to the doctor, who told me politely, but firmly, that mother was happy here and, keeping all disturbances of the outside world from her, she would remain so.

"You mean she is going to have to stay here for years?"

He nods.

"But you said she was much improved."

"She is. But, my dear Mr. Mansfeld, please consider that every time she was discharged and went home she suffered another setback. The family affairs . . ."

"I know them," I say sharply.

"Mr. Mansfeld, I do not deserve this tone of voice. We are doing everything possible to help your mother. I do not want to conceal the fact that repeated setbacks could prove dangerous."

"What do you mean?"

"You seem to underestimate the seriousness of her illness. Should a general breakdown occur we might have to transfer her to an appropriate institution. I believe this possibility can be eliminated if she is protected from all excitement and allowed to stay here."

"You mean until she dies?"

"I mean . . . Mr. Mansfeld, I cannot talk to you! You are so aggressive! You can see how happy your mother is with her animals!"

"Yes, I do indeed!"

"I'm sorry, my time is limited. Furthermore your father, with a rational point of view, shares my opinion. Good day!"

He just left me standing there.

Mother stands up. She says good night to each animal. Her smile is that of a small child. "When you are finished with your school, Oliver, we'll take all the animals and live a good life in our villa in Frankfurt. I am a rich woman! Just think of it,

Oliver! We'll have everything when you leave the school. The factories. Millions of marks. And this Lizzy will be jailed."

The factories? Millions of marks? Poor, poor Mama. She only has a private bank account. How much is deposited there? I don't know. She sends me money from time to time, to pay for the loan. But my lovely Aunty Lizzy, who rules my father, has her hands on the factories and the millions. Those two know what they are doing. Poor, poor Mama. The doctor was right!

"Mama, really. . . ."

"Of course! That's the law! I've talked about it a great deal with Dr. Walling."

"Who is he?"

"Dr. Walling is a lawyer. He had the room just next to mine when I came here. His room was much brighter and larger, and there was a balcony. He was dying and the nurses promised me I could have his room as soon as he died. Well, they told me for days that he was worse, and asked for the priest. Finally, the nurse told me he had died during the night and, as soon as the room was cleaned, I could have it." My mother is patting the deer.

I stand near her and put my arm around her to steady her and am shocked to feel—through the coat—an emaciated body.

"What can I say? Three hours later I hear the 'dead man' cough!"

"The dead man?"

"The supposedly dead man! Well, I really made a fuss! I asked them: 'How is it possible for the doctor to cough when he is dead? Do you think I'm crazy to believe such a thing?"

We are walking toward the hospital with its brightly lit windows.

"Oliver, what are they all singing?"

"Today is Christmas, Mama."

"Isn't it a little late for Christmas?"

"No, Mama. But you were going to tell me about Dr. Walling."

"Oh, yes. He came to my room the next day and insisted we change rooms right there and then. He is really charming. You'll have to meet him."

My mother cannot climb the steps in the park. Something is wrong with her legs. I lift Mother up to carry her. She is as light as a little girl and she giggles like a little girl.

Churchbells are beginning to chime.

"And, you know, Dr. Walling recovered completely! We older people have extraordinary vitality. Look at me, do I look one day over forty?"

"No, Mama."

"He is the smartest man you can imagine. You'll have to meet him because—"

She pauses.

"Because?"

"You won't laugh at me?"

"I promise!"

We have arrived at the house.

She whispers: "I'm going to get a divorce and marry Dr. Walling! Only if you like him, of course. He is very wealthy. . . . Where are the other peanuts?"

"Here."

She grabs the package and looks at it. For a moment she looks like a witch. Then her smile is angelic. "Good night, Oliver. Will you come again tomorrow?"

"Yes, tomorrow. Good night, Mama." I say and hear the bells chiming and the singing.

"I'll have to see Dr. Walling tonight. He is waiting for me." She kisses me hastily on the cheek and walks away quickly.

I see her doctor greet her in the hall before he comes to me.

"Ah, Mr. Mansfeld," his rosy fingers are smoothing down his beard and he seems in good humor now. "Doesn't your mother look well? Don't you have the feeling that she is happy here?"

I am standing in the snow stupified and answer: "Yes, sure. And anyway she has Dr. Walling, who . . ."

"Who?"

"The lawyer! She is going to him now. She seems to think a great deal of him."

"My poor young friend. . . . Now you can see clearly how right I was."

"I don't understand."

"Dr. Walling died the day after your mother came here. But naturally, she has never seen him."

[ 2 ]

"Monsieur Mansfeld?"

"Oui."

"Un moment, s'il vous plaît."

Then I hear Verena's voice: "Darling, Isn't it lovely that I can call you once more?"

I am lying on my bed in the hotel. The connection is poor, other voices can be heard. It is eight o'clock at night.

"Lovely. But how is it—"

"We are invited somewhere. My husband went ahead to pick up an English couple. They live a long way from here and don't know their way around. What are you doing?"

"I'm in the hotel."

"I can't understand one word! Hello . . . hello! Oliver, can you hear me?"

"Very clearly."

"What did you say? I was looking forward to—"

"I'm sorry, Verena. Hang up. There is no point to this."

"Perhaps you can hear what I'm saying. After you have seen your mother you should go out a little. But don't drink too much. And be good! Don't look at any girls. I am jealous too, you know."

"Yes, Verena."

"This connection is driving me mad! I think we have to give up."

"I think so too."

"What did you say? Oh, I could cry . . ."

"Don't cry."

"It's lucky for me Christmas is a happy holiday in foreign countries. It is solemn only in Germany. Here we have jazz and balloons and already a lot of drinks. I shall think of you all the time! Can you hear me? Hello. . . . hello . . . hello!"

I hang up.

It is lucky Christmas is a happy holiday in foreign countries.

[ 3 ]

I own two tuxedos. The older one is here in the hotel where everything is stored for me. I am putting on the tuxedo and go down to the bar. There, too, are intoxicated people and balloons and paper streamers and gay people. I order cognac. I do not feel well. The cognac does me good. Three glasses of it and I feel much better. Echternach is not a large town. I know on Christmas Eve Lizzy and my father are always out on the town. I do not have to search for long. They are at Ricardo's. This restaurant consists of many velvet-upholstered booths so it is relatively easy to watch someone without being seen. It is very crowded. I have to give the captain a large tip to sit at a table where I cannot be seen watching the two of them. A waiter comes and I order soupe de la maison.

"Your father is over there," says the waiter. "Would you like me to—"

"No. I do not wish my father to be informed of my presence here." The waiter also receives his tip.

"Very well, Monsieur."

I went to my father's beautiful house the evening of the twentieth. When I arrived I gave him the book from his friend Lord. *The Dybbuk*. "That gives me great pleasure! I shall have to give him a book, too. Will you take it for me when you return?"

I stayed half an hour. I couldn't get away sooner, though he was offended, as usual, when I told him that I wanted to stay at The Eden.

"You just do not love me. You have never loved me."

Since he always says that I did not answer. Then Aunt Lizzy arrived. She embraced me and kissed me on the mouth, not like an aunt! Apparently she cannot kiss any other way.

"Little Oliver! What am I saying? The grown-up Oliver! You look marvelous. I don't care if you do look at me with those furious eyes. I know you hate me!" (I do not answer again since she also says that every time.) "You detest me. I don't care! Why don't I? Because I love you, very much."

Apropos marvelous. She looks marvelous. Slim and yet curvaceous. Well-groomed. Sexy. Provocative. Her hair used to be black. Now it is dyed silver-gray. It has also been red and brown at times. I despise her. But honestly it must be a pleasure for any man to sleep with her. She does not seem to change. How old can she be? Forty? My mother is fifty-five. And looks eighty. Dear Aunt Lizzy could pass for thirty-five. Easily.

While I'm forcing myself to eat the soupe de la maison I am watching her. She is carefully made-up. Her dress, which must have cost a fortune, is high up to the neck and open in the back down to her—well! Jewelry on her arms, fingers, ears, neck and hair; jewelry everywhere. The eyes of many men look at her with that hungry look. How she laughs! How her beautiful eyes shine! And how she orders the waiters about.

I do not have to worry about little Daddy, either. He also is unchanged. Huge, fat, red-faced, loud. In great form. Drinks a bit too much. Apparently constantly. There are blue shadows under his eyes.

Rings.

You won't believe this—father sports rings on his long hairy fingers. Diamonds. Two rings on each hand. Lizzy is continually talking to him. Both of them have healthy appetites. Father drinks a lot. He eats crudely. (He always did!) A piece of meat falls off his plate.

Lizzy rebukes him. Loudly. In a high-pitched voice. I can hear every word she says. Everybody can. "Peasant," says Auntie to my father, "you can't even eat properly. I am ashamed of you! Use your napkin!" And since he does not take it, she ties it around his neck. In full view of everyone. I can actually feel how he enjoys this. He kisses her hand. There are many ways to make human beings happy!

[ 4 ]

After dinner they drive to a strip-tease club. Connoisseurs know where the Pigalle is located. I follow in a taxi.

It is almost midnight and almost everybody is drunk. The Pigalle is overcrowded. Naturally my old man had a reservation for the best table by the dance floor. Here I don't have to be afraid of him, to be seen by him. At the bar I drink cognac again. It tastes foul.

Father drinks champagne. Again and again he dances with the playmate of his youth, untiring, as if he were eighteen years old. Boogie. Rhumba. Cha-cha. Anybody would be out of breath. But not my father. Men are staring at Lizzy again. She looks obscene in her skin-tight black silk dress. My old man's face is lobster-red by now. Perspiration is dripping from his forehead but he continues. Lizzy dances around him, claps her hands and cries: "Olé!"

Next to me a fat woman says to her fat escort: "Look at that old guy go! He's not like you!"

"I have asthma."

"That's a vulgar whore he is with. But pretty, I have to admit."

"Probably some Mister Moneybags."

They are obviously not natives. If they were they would have known who the old guy and the vulgar whore are. In and around Echternach everybody knows. The couple, the center of all this admiration, return to the table. Lizzy is berating him. For the benefit of all who care to listen, or else Papa has no fun. Oh, my Papa.

"Another double, please."

"Right away, Monsieur."

Auntie dances with any gentlemen who asks. With every one

of them she dances as if she were his mistress. She was always like that. My father sits at the table, his eyes glazed and, drinking champagne, repeatedly raises his glass to her. Once, when the other couples leave the dance floor Aunt Lizzy and a young man dance a terrific rhumba; really, one has to be fair! Everybody applauds, especially my father. He kisses Lizzy's hands when she returns to the table. The young man comes to the table, too, drinks Father's champagne, but otherwise completely ignores him. My old man suddenly pales. On his way to the men's room he passes but does not see me.

At the table the young man kisses the inside of Lizzy's hands and then her neck. He writes something on a piece of paper. Telephone number and address, naturally. She takes the slip. Then they dance again. When Father returns the table is empty. I wonder if Mother is asleep? I wonder if in her dreams she and Dr. Walling are discussing how their wedding will be when my old man is dead and Aunt Lizzy is in jail?

"Cha-cha-cha!" the musicians cry merrily.

## [ 5 ]

The floor show starts at about one o'clock. Black-haired, brown-haired and blonde girls are undressing. Let themselves be undressed. Undress each other. A black-haired girl is being undressed by a blonde. The blonde is wearing a short, black raincoat. She is extremely affectionate to the black-haired girl. Kisses. Embraces. When the dark one is undressed the blonde throws off her raincoat and is naked too. They position themselves the way women do when loving each other. The lights go out. The floor show has excited most of the men. And women. But not Aunt Lizzy. She benefits from the next attraction. Three almost nude, very well-built youths are being chased around by a naked girl. She cracks a long whip, barely missing the young muscular bodies. Lizzy drinks one glass after the other. She is getting restless. Her lips move. Lizzy says something to my old man. He beckons the waiter. Suddenly he is in a hurry. Both of them are just waiting for the end of the number and they leave.

I think Lizzy is drunk too. As they are passing by I bend forward and say: "Happy Christmas!"

But they do not hear me. They do not see me. My old man is throwing money around. The waiters bow.

A vocalist has stepped in front of a microphone. After the first few notes I know what they are playing. I throw money on the bar and leave. Not quick enough, I hear the first words of the song: "Love is just a word . . ."

Out on the street I see my father's Mercedes drive off. Aunt Lizzy drives while my father is leaning against her shoulder. I have just one wish: to forget. To sleep. I take a taxi back to the hotel. I take four sleeping tablets and wake up at noon.

I visit Mother every day; never my father. I never hear from him. Daily Mother and I feed the animals. Sometimes we go to her room. (When Dr. Walling is busy.) I rarely talk with Verena. Apparently she does not get a chance to call me. I wait many days in vain and when she does call the line is mostly bad and I can hardly hear what she is saying. On New Year's Eve I take my sleeping pills early.

On the eighth, after dinner, I say goodbye to my father in his villa. He hands me an old book. An early edition of Niccolò Machiavelli's *Principe*.

"For my friend Lord. And my best regards!"

"Yes, Papa."

Lizzy is in the hall.

"Take care."

"You, too."

"You really hate me, don't you?"

"With all my heart."

"Then I'll tell you the truth. I hate you too, Oliver."

"Well," I say, "why didn't you say so before?"

Teddy is already at the wheel of the Mercedes to take me to

the airport. I ask him to stop at the sanatorium. My mother is watching the birds on the balcony. She does not realize I am saying goodbye.

"Look at that little robin! Will you bring some more peanuts tomorrow?"

"I'll ask Teddy to bring them, Mama."

"Why Teddy?"

"I'm going back to Germany."

"Oh yes, of course. But don't bother Teddy. I shall ask Dr. Walling."

The eighth is a beautiful day: clear and cold. The sun is shining as we are flying above the snow-covered country. I turn the pages of the Machiavelli and examine them. I make notes of all the letters which have been perforated:

A.S.H.G.F.D.R.B.N.M.C.X.E.E.I.O.U.

There are too many letters to finish on this flight. It does not matter. Mr. Lord will return in six days from St. Moritz. This time I want to know the entire message.

After landing I ask Teddy to take peanuts regularly to my mother at the sanatorium and give him money.

"I'll take care of it, Mr. Oliver. Was it very bad for you?"

"Bad?" I ask. "I had a fine time."

Teddy looks at me silently.

"What's the matter, Teddy?"

"Ah," he says, "isn't it a shitty world? I'm so sorry."

"Nonsense. So long, Teddy."

"Good luck, Mr. Oliver."

And he limps over to the office of the Air Weather Control and I go to Customs and let myself be searched again, as always.

Five o'clock.

Mother is feeding the animals.

What is Verena doing?

She will be back in six days.

Another six days. . . .

"I'd like a bottle of cognac," I say to the salesgirl in the airport delicatessen.

## [ 6 ]

Huge snowflakes are falling this afternoon in Frankfurt. If things progress the way they have, my mother will be in a mental institution inside a year. My father and Lizzy are the victors. It is happening faster than I thought.

I feel awful.

I do something I have never done before. I drive with my left hand while I open the bottle with my right and drink. The bottle hits my teeth and cognac runs down my chin. I stuff the bottle under the seat. I feel worse than before. That is when I decide to take a look at *our* house. I just want to see it. I do not have the key. Maybe I shall have another drink while I am looking at it. On this day I certainly am a sentimental fool. The window on the driver's side is open. A strange smell is getting stronger. I don't know what kind of smell it is but it is making me nauseated, frightened. Frightened?

I don't know why my hands feel clammy when I turn into the Brunnenpfad. Then I see what has happened. *Our* house is no more. Charred remains are lying in the snow. I see the burnt-out electric heater, parts of the couch, the shower—bent, blackened, broken. *Our* house burnt down! It is the charred wood which smells. I stop and get out.

I see no one. Only crows caw. I am standing in the snow, staring at the black ruin which was once a house and many many snowflakes settle on me and the wreckage.

"Sad, isn't it, very sad, Mr. Mansfeld?"

I turn around quickly.

Behind me stands Leo, the servant, sympathetically shaking his narrow head. He is dressed in a heavy winter coat, a muffler and a stiff, black hat.

## [ 7 ]

"And where do you come from? And how did you know where I was going?"

He just smiles.

"Such a pretty little house. Such a shame. It happened during the holidays. The newspapers said burglars ate all the food and drank all the liquor and then set the house on fire—by accident or intentionally, who knows? It is terrible, isn't it?"

"Terrible for whom?"

"For you, dear Mr. Mansfeld. And for Madame, if you don't mind me saying so."

"If you say just one more word—"

But he won't be interrupted.

"Madame's friend, the owner, is rich. It is not terrible for her. But for Madame and you—where will you meet from now on?"

I hit him with my right fist. Leo hits the snow. His nose is bleeding. He presses a handkerchief to his nose while he picks himself up and mumbles: "That's going to cost you another two thousand. I had only intended to ask for three. Now I demand five. Five thousand. The same as the first time."

"What for, you son of a bitch?"

He pulls five photographs from his pocket and hands them to me. One shows me entering the house. One shows Verena embracing me at the door. Two show us leaving the house together. The fifth shows us kissing in the garden.

"I have an excellent camera, Mr. Mansfeld. Aren't they clear?"

Photos, photos.

I tear them in little pieces and Leo smiles.

"What a child you are, Mr. Mansfeld. Have you never heard of negatives?"

He is cold and rubs his hands. "Let us get it over with. I need the money tomorrow."

"I don't have it."

"You can get another loan. A new Jaguar costs twenty-five thousand marks. Yours is almost new. I shall be waiting for you at six o'clock at the restaurant at the exit of the Autobahn."

"I have a receipt which says I already gave you five thousand marks!" "If you wish I shall bring you another tomorrow. You can show both of them to Mr. Lord. And if you wish I can show him the negatives at the same time. And you'll save five thousand marks. If you don't, I shall bring the negatives for you tomorrow. Have a pleasant evening. It is getting too cold for me here. Please excuse me."

He tips his hat and walks away slowly, carefully so as not to slip. I watch him until I can't see him any more. Snow falls on me and melts on my hair. I get in the car and have another go at the bottle. The wet burnt wood stinks. Did Leo set fire to the house?

My mother will help me once more. I hope she can. . . . Did Leo have the negatives duplicated? Perhaps. Probably. He will blackmail me. And then? What will he do then?

## [ 8 ]

"When I tell you what happened you'll crap in your pants," says Hansi. The usual yelling of little boys greeted me when I arrived at Quellenhof. Cars are parked in front of the house. The good parents are showing how good they are. They are driving poor Mr. Herterich half crazy with complaints, requests, troubles, needs. Did Fritz get a better bed? When will the new bathrooms be finished?

Hansi locks the door of the bathroom. "Give me a cigarette."

He gets one.

"You have a sense of humor, don't you? What I am going to tell you is worth a whole pack."

I give it to him. He tells me that Giuseppe's father really was released from prison under the amnesty and arrived, dressed in old clothes, at the school. He brought a new coat for Giuseppe and shoes and a sweater and a big package of goodies to eat. The two of them danced around with joy like two lunatics and then went out to eat.

Hansi begins to laugh, and splutters.

"What's so funny?"

"Well, then Giuseppe and Rashid told me that all Communists are criminals!"

"But his father is a Communist himself!"

"Just wait! His father *was* a Communist and—"

"Why *was?*"

"He is not a Communist any more! In jail he talked to other people. And with the prison priest. And he converted him. As soon as he got out of prison he had himself baptized in the Catholic faith. And Giuseppe is taking religious instruction."

"Where is Giuseppe now?"

"Ice skating," says Hansi.

"But he doesn't have skates!"

"Ali gave him a pair."

"Ali?"

"Well, he had two pair. Besides, now he is Giuseppe's brother. That follows, doesn't it? Ali is crazy about Giuseppe. He gives him chocolate, clothes, soap. Even a pair of ski pants. And they pray together. Well, wasn't that worth the pack of cigarettes?" asks Hansi.

## [ 9 ]

I went to Kopper and Co.

I took another five-thousand-mark loan. Now I have to pay six hundred thirty marks monthly. It is an enormous amount of money which I can only repay if my mother is able to help me even more than she previously did. I know now that it is useless to explain to her why I need the money. All I know is, provided there is sufficient money in her account, she will help me. Up to now I have paid four instalments of three hundred twenty-three marks. I only have a gold fountain pen, an expensive watch and a pair of binoculars which I can sell. That's all. I haven't received any money from my father in years. Mr. Lord pays for whatever I need. (And then squares it with my father.) I met Leo Galler and handed over the five thousand marks. He offered to give me another receipt. I spat on the floor and left.

Finally, at last, I realized that the receipts, which I had thought to be a certain security, are absolutely useless. If I had intended to show them to Manfred Lord I need not have given Leo one red cent. Mr. Galler would then—naturally—say what the money was for and, possibly, prove Verena's unfaithfulness. Mr. Galler knew that all the time. Only I did not.

## [ 10 ]

Thursday, January 12, 1961. I am on my way to Frankfurt, not to meet Verena—she will be back on the fourteenth—but to talk with Geraldine. I telephoned and spoke to Mrs. Bottner, the owner of the apartment. She was curt. Since Geraldine was not allowed to get up and Mrs. Reber was not there, I asked her to tell Geraldine to expect me on Thursday at three o'clock. It is a dark, stormy day. People walk braced against the wind. Watery snow falls and drivers seem to be nervous. A motorcycle nearly hit me crossing the bridge.

The house Geraldine lives in now is old. The apartment is on the third floor. I ring. A little lady opens and looks at me suspiciously.

"Excuse me, Geraldine told me her mother had rented the apartment for a while. I'm very grateful to you for looking after Geraldine while her mother is not here."

"What do you mean, she rented the apartment? She rented a room! This way, it's dark. The lamp does not work."

*"Mother rented an apartment for me. . . ."*

Typical of Geraldine. She always lied, always exaggerated.

Mrs. Bottner opens one of the doors.

"A visitor, Miss. Shall I bring the tea now?"

"Yes, please." Geraldine's bed is near the window. She is overly made up as usual, and wearing a black lace nightgown. She is sitting up against the pillow. By the bed is a table nicely set up for two people. Flowers. Colored napkins. Cheap china. A plate with cake. Cigarettes. The door closes behind me.

Geraldine smiles. Her face is pale, hollow-cheeked, but she looks better than I had expected.

"Hello," I say.

She smiles, but tears are trickling down her cheeks.

"Oliver," says Geraldine. And again in a whisper, "Oliver." She stretches out her arms to me.

Her lips open. I bend down and kiss her quickly. That is, I meant to kiss her quickly but she clings to me, her lips pressed to mine and it becomes a long kiss. Her eyes are closed. Her breath comes quickly. My eyes are open and through the window behind her I see a church, a cemetery, and a huge, gray hospital in a desolate park. It is the most dreadful kiss of my life. Geraldine's smile is radiant. "Oliver! I'm so happy! The doctors say it is a miracle! My spine healed perfectly and I'm not wearing the cast any more! Look!" She slips the black nightgown off her shoulders. Her breasts quiver. Her eyes have the crazed expression I know so well. "Caress them . . . kiss them."

"Mrs. Bottner will be back any moment."

"Just once, quickly. Please, please . . . You don't know how I waited for this."

I kiss her breasts. She sighs. I hear steps outside and just manage to drop onto a chair. Geraldine pulls up her blanket. The landlady appears with the tea, places it on the table, looks at me angrily and leaves.

"What's the matter with her?"

She saw the lipstick on your mouth." Geraldine laughs.

"Come, sit here with me. I just want you to hold my hand. Nothing else. I couldn't if I wanted to. Everything still hurts. . . . Come on!"

I sit on her bed. I pour the tea. I hold her hand. She looks at me incessantly. I look around the room, furnished in poor taste. A picture on the wall shows the Alps. Complete with deer.

"It's nice here."

"Don't be funny!"

"No, really . . ."

"It's awful! This room! That old woman! And the view! You think that's nice?"

Another sip of tea. But does that help? I have to talk to Geraldine. Now. At once. This minute. No, not right now.

In a few minutes.

I am such a miserable coward.

[ 11 ]

She strokes my hand; the blanket is sliding down. If only the nightgown doesn't. . . .

"Geraldine, didn't you say your mother had rented an apartment?"

"My mother!" Rarely have I seen so much bitterness in a face.

"What happened? Where is she?"

"In Berlin. With her husband. Since New Year's Day."

"But was she not supposed to stay with you?"

"Yes, she promised. But I was in the hospital then! Then she brought me here. An apartment? 'No money, dear child.' " Geraldine shrugs her shoulders. "She slept on the couch until her husband gave her a choice; either your brat or I. The telephone is in the hall and I heard them argue. But she went back to Berlin!"

"What about your father?"

"From the first moment on they argued. They screamed at each other all the time. They had completely forgotten about me."

"And?"

"Two days after Christmas Father took a plane back to the States."

"Why didn't he take an apartment and look after you?"

"He said Mother would leave me anyway and then I would be alone and would need a nurse. He said he didn't have that much money!"

"Is he lying?"

"They're all lying. Walter's parents too. Walter came to see me two days after Father left. I tell you, all parents lie! Walter found out what really happened. Walter's father found a younger, prettier woman. He knew his wife would never leave Germany because her parents are living here—somewhere in the South. So he figured that was a great chance. He went to Canada with this young woman and he was rid of his wife. And it worked!"

"What about Walter?"

"Well, he had his choice. His father knew he loved his mother. So there was no risk there. Now he is living in Augsburg with his mother and her parents. That's the way it's done! Great, isn't it?"

"Poor Walter!"

"And you? And I? And Hansi? I don't want to cry any tears but I tell you, when I am grown up I'll take revenge!"

"On whom? Your children?"

"Children? Do you think I want children, after all I've been through?"

She nestles against me and whispers: "Unless we stay together and you want one. Do you want one?"

"No."

"You know, I felt so sorry for Walter I kissed him. But it was only pity, I swear! Now are you angry?"

"No."

"I don't ever want to kiss another boy as long as we are together. I belong only to you, only you. I just have to wait a little longer." Her hand feels like ice stroking my back.

"When do you think you will be allowed to get up?"

"In three weeks. Four at the most! And then, Oliver! And then!"

And then.

## [ 12 ]

I don't know if there is such a thing as retaliation for the bad things one has done. Apropos bad things—what have I done? Quite a lot. All right. But on the other side. My father, my mother, Aunt Lizzy. Leo. The burnt-down little house. And now Geraldine. I think the scales are tilted too much to one side. Or not?

On the other side, it is to one's advantage to feel like this at the proper moment. One has less scruples. When I arrived here I had a lot. Now!

"Geraldine?"

She smiles.

It does not make sense.

One will always hurt another. Apparently life is like that. All right. We'll make it short. Who was ever indulgent toward me?

"I have to tell you something. I know this is not the most opportune moment, but I have waited too long already. What happened in the canyon was your wish. I told you I did not love you. I—"

She sits bolt upright in bed, teacup balanced on her knees, and says: "You love the other one."

"Yes. And that's why we must finish. When you return to the school there must be nothing between us. Nothing!"

Geraldine says very calmly: "Why? I know you don't love me. So I am not taking anything away from the other one! What do I want from you? Only what I need. Does *that* hurt her?"

"You don't only want that! You want all. I'm really sorry to bring this up now but . . ." (It is unnerving how calm she is.)

She smiles. "Because I am not quite well yet? Are you afraid I'm going to kill myself, jump out of the window or end up in a nuthouse? Don't be. I have survived Russia and Germany *and* my parents! I'm not even crying, you see? I'm not screaming."

"Really, Geraldine . . ."

"Wait, I have not finished. You have a new love. Fine! Bad luck for me. You don't want to make me happy any more."

"I can't, Geraldine."

"All right, all right. You can't make me happy. I can't make you happy."

"What do you mean?"

"It means I am going to do everything to make you unhappy, as soon as I get back to school."

"What does that mean?"

"I'm going to find the other one. How do I make you unhappy? By making your beloved unhappy. If she is a woman and married, I am going to destroy her marriage by telling her husband. If she is not married, I'll ruin her reputation. If she is a girl, I'll take care of her until she has to leave this part of the country. And you, too, dear Oliver. I'll make you miserable!"

"Geraldine, be reasonable! I told you from the beginning that I don't love you!"

"But you slept with me." The theory of retribution. "You know what you did with me! And now you tell me you'll never touch me again? You think that's perfectly all right? You think that is decent?"

"I'm not saying it is decent. But it seemed decent to me to talk to you honestly!"

She finishes her tea very slowly.

"Yes, Oliver, it was. Now I know. Now I have three weeks to plan how to find your true love."

"You'll never find her!"

Geraldine laughs!

"I'll have her within a month! And my revenge will be subtle. It will hurt her. If she loves you it will ruin her."

"She does not love me."

"Oh, really? Then it is the same situation as it was with us!"

"Yes," I lie.

"You are lying. I know all I need to know. You can leave now."

"Geraldine . . ."

"Don't you understand me? Shall I ask Mrs. Bottner to see you out?"

"All right, I am going. But—"

"I don't want to hear any more." She says something in Russian. But then she holds out her hand to me and smiles. "Give them all my regards. Especially Hansi."

"Why especially Hansi?"

"Well, he had the same problem with his spine, didn't he? I'll have to look after him particularly when I return."

What does she know? What does she suspect? What has the little devil told her, written her? Does she know anything at all?

"Geraldine, I beg you, don't do anything to—"

"I don't hear you any more."

"If you say you love me how can you destroy the woman who—"

"So it is a *woman!* Not a girl. One step further in the right direction."

I cannot be quite sane this afternoon.

My arms are extended and my fingers spread wide as I move toward her.

"Mrs. Bottner!" She screams loudly and falls back into her pillows. "Mrs. Bottner!"

Now my fingers are around her neck. "Mrs. Bott—"

The door opens.

The old lady.

I drop my hands immediately and turn around.

"Would you like to see this gentleman to the door, dear Mrs. Bottner? It is so dark in the hall."

"If you don't like it you can move out."

"Soon you'll be rid of me, dear Mrs. Bottner. Goodbye, Oliver. Give my regards to your girl friend too. We'll meet soon."

## [ 13 ]

On the street I stop for a moment. Not because I feel sorry for myself but because I feel sorry for Geraldine. What did she do to deserve this? Most dogs are better off than most people.

It is snowing heavily now. I take a drink from the bottle of cognac beneath the car seat. Another one. It makes me feel sick. It is fear which makes me feel I have to throw up. I think of Verena. Now Leo *and* Geraldine are against us. And if Hansi should get mad at me just once and say one single word to Geraldine— One word: Lord!

I take another drink.

What can I do? I have no money. I am in debt. Mother will be in a mental institution soon. I can't count on my father. The final examinations are not for another year. I can't take care of Verena and Evelyn. If Geraldine uncovers the truth, the very honorable Mr. Lord will push her back into the poverty she rose from. Whom can I trust, whom can I ask for advice? No one. I have two pieces of paper with the letters which my father and Mr. Lord had perforated in the books. To protect Verena (it is getting worse) I could blackmail her husband. I can't blackmail my father. And Mr. Lord? Just where are the books, he will ask. Go to the police and tell them this crazy story, dear friend. Just where is the book?

There are two of them.

*The Dybbuk* should still be in my father's library, provided it hasn't been burned yet. But the Machiavelli is still in my grip. Mr. Lord won't be back for another two days. Noah has a very good camera. I can photograph the pages so the perforations will be visible. Then, possibly, I could indicate to Mr. Lord that I possess the pages. This is Leo's method.

So I am no better than he. Who knows, maybe Leo really does long for a little restaurant? Where does it get one, finding an excuse for every meanness, forgiving everything? Can one, ought one, to forgive everything? Is love really just a word? On the other side: Is politics noble? The military? Business? My father's business? Aunt Lizzy's?

Hold it! That's not the way to start. One could go mad. There must be a gauge of ethics. Whatever lies above is good, whatever sinks below is bad. I have reached the Autobahn, snowflakes are driving toward me. At the Ober-Rosbach exit I see a woman waving. More than likely she needs a ride. Why not? This might be my last decent deed for the immediate future.

# [ 14 ]

"Excuse me, sir, are you by any chance going to Friedheim?"

"Yes."

"Would you be so kind as to take me there?"

She must have waited here a long time, she shivers with cold. Maybe fifty years old. Slim. Her face bespeaks only peace, nothing else. She is dressed in a black coat and black felt hat. Two fingers are missing from her right hand resting on the door of the car.

"Get in."

"Thank you so much. I missed my train in Frankfurt. And I must get back to the home. My children are waiting for me."

"By the way, my name is Oliver Mansfeld."

"I am Sister Claudia."

"Sister Claudia from the Philanthropic Society?"

"Yes," she says. "But how do you know?"

"When I passed your home once before I heard children call 'Sister Claudia, the rabbit is running away.' Isn't it strange the things people remember? Now I know where to drop you off. Tell me, Sister Claudia, who is the 'Angel of the Lord'?"

Her voice is calm and confident. "Our society was founded twenty-five years ago in Switzerland. We believe that a time of change has come. We believe in the teachings of the Redeemer but not the same way as the major religions." We have passed the little town and are driving along a snow-covered country road. Icicles are suspended from overhead telegraph wires. Sister Claudia is warming to her subject. "We want to be true Christians. We do not try to better the world for ourselves. If Christians were truly Christian there would be no war, neither communism nor capitalism, neither insurrection nor injustice. God's law is love for one's fellow men; do you understand, Mr. Mansfeld? The gospel mentions that again and again."

"But no one takes any notice of that."

"Exactly. But we do; our little flock. They are mostly poor people. We help them as much as we can, and I don't mean we just console them with words. We are fortunate to have rich patrons in America, England, Italy and France. You see, people do help one another."

"Very few, though."

"Up to now," she says and looks like a prophet. "Soon there will be many. Ten years ago we had no home where sick children could convalesce. Now we have thirteen in different countries. We have our paper, we can help unfortunate people. Not enough people. But the day will come."

"Yes."

"Very much troubled, aren't you? Can I help you?"

"I don't think so."

"Perhaps I could. Please come and see me. I'll show you the home and you tell me what troubles you."

A devotee. A fanatic. An association. Everything I don't like. And in spite of that I answer: "Yes, Sister Claudia, I'd like to come."

When we arrive at the home, she shakes my hand. I watch her walk toward the home, securely aware of her mission. I reach for the bottle under my seat and open it. Sister Claudia turns and waves. I wave back. Many little children come running from the home and hug Sister Claudia. I close the bottle and push it back under the seat, without having had a drink.

## [ 15 ]

"What did you say?"

"Burnt down. Completely burnt down."

"But—but how was that possible?" Verena's voice sounds choked.

"Allegedly burglars. Arson. We must not go there again."

"Why not?"

Again I decide not to tell her about Leo.

"A lot of investigators are around. We must not be seen there on any account!"

"Just—just to look at it once more? Now we have no place any more, no place in the world."

"Yes, we do. I found a little hotel." I give her the address. "Don't cry, darling. We just can't meet out there any more, you understand that, don't you?"

"Yes. But—we were so happy there, Oliver."

"We will be again."

"Where?"

"When do I see you?"

"Tonight. My husband invites you. He seems to be in a terrible hurry to see you again. It scares me."

It does not scare me. Mr. Lord needs my father's book.

"At seven-thirty, all right?"

"All right."

"Oh God, our little house!"

"Now we have the hotel."

"But it isn't our house. It will never be our house."

"It is better than nothing at all," I say.

## [ 16 ]

The evening is formal. Tuxedo, evening dress and Leo serves, wearing white gloves. He avoids looking at me. Manfred Lord is in high spirits: tanned, rested, optimistic. The Machiavelli pleased him.

"How nice of your father!"

Yes, isn't it, Mr. Lord. And when you're alone you'll be looking for the perforated letters and decode them. I don't know the code. But I photographed the pages, Mr. Lord. Only—will it help me against a man such as you? I am very depressed this evening.

Evelyn caught a cold in St. Moritz and has to stay in bed. I brought some marzipan for her, and Manfred Lord genially asked me to take the gift to her personally. Verena shows me the way to her room on the second floor. Her husband is preparing drinks meanwhile.

Evelyn won't accept the marzipan and refuses to look at me or speak with me because, according to her, I had not helped Verena and her. When we are outside her room I ask Verena if she had mentioned anything to Evelyn and she answered: "Yes, unfortunately I was so unhappy when I talked to you and the line was so bad. You remember?"

"Have you had enough of me, too? Shall we finish?"

In a second her arms are around me, she kisses me wildly. I try with all my strength to free myself.

"Don't! You are crazy! Your husband. . . ."

"When shall we meet in the hotel?"

"Tomorrow at three."

"I'll be there."

"Don't be disappointed in me. I know I am young, but I will do something! I don't know what as yet, but I will! Please stay with me, Verena, please!"

"I'll stay with you."

"You never stayed with a man before!"

"But with you, darling, with you. Tomorrow at three."

The hall leading to the stairs below is dim. Suddenly it is very bright. We pull apart quickly and see Manfred Lord standing there, a silver cocktail shaker in his hand. He says amiably: "If you please, the drinks are ready."

"We are coming," says Verena, walking down the wide stairs.

"I heard voices," says Mr. Lord. "It was dark so I switched on the light. . . . What's the matter, Oliver? You are so pale. Isn't he, Verena?"

Leo is passing by, a tray in his hand.

"Don't you think so too, Leo?"

"Excuse me, Sir?"

"That Mr. Mansfeld looks very pale?"

"Yes, rather pale, I would say."

You dirty s.o.b.!

"Well, back to the fireplace and have a good drink. The weather is terrible. I hope you won't catch a cold now, dear Oliver," says the very respectable Mr. Lord as he precedes us to the drawing room.

## [ 17 ]

The hotel, near the Ostpark, is a nice, clean-looking house. The desk clerk is polite. One does not even have to say one's name. The room on the third floor is furnished in red and has a huge mirror next to the bed. It is rather old-fashioned but still the nicest of all the one-bar hotels I had seen. And still everything goes wrong. I arrived first. Verena came by taxi, which stopped farther down the street. She is dressed simply, without any jewelry, a scarf on her hair and dark glasses.

The desk clerk smiles a lot, but he did that too when I was here before and had given him twenty marks. I get the key and as we walk up the stairs (there is no elevator) he calls out: "If you should need more towels just ring! The girl will bring them!"

That does it! I see Verena cringe and I know it will be a disaster. Verena stumbles, she says nothing until we reach the room. Then: "Horrible."

She does not notice the red carnations, the champagne, but walks to the window and looks out. Blocks of apartment houses, a small part of the frozen lake in the park, cheap shops.

"Awful," she says.

I switch on the light, draw the drapes and open the champagne. I take a glass to her and say: "At least take off your coat."

She is wearing the red sweater again. It cheers me up.

"What makes you so happy?"

"Your red sweater."

The champagne is bad. She does not mention it. I say so.

"Well, it really doesn't matter," she answers. "Thank you for the carnations." She inspects the bathroom, and shakes her head. When she returns she pours herself another glass, drinks it in one gulp, and then another.

"All right," she says. "Quickly. Come."

She pulls off her sweater, unzips her skirt and takes off her stockings. I am undressed and crawl into bed. The blanket feels stiff with cold. I hear a man in the next room cough and talk. A girl laughs loudly and incessantly. A lot of noises follow.

"Let's put out the light. Next time I'll bring a radio so we hear nothing but music." She takes off all her clothes, crawls in beside me and we kiss. I caress her but suddenly she is rigid.

I know: It is finished.

"Don't be angry, dear heart."

"No, No. I understand," I say. Daylight seeps through a few slits in the drapes. I hear running water somewhere, the man next door coughs again and the girl laughs.

"It really wouldn't be any good. We don't ever want to lie to each other. Here—here I would have to pretend. You know. . . ."

"You don't have to explain."

"I want to. . . . I must. Do you remember how angry you were in the beginning every time I said I was a whore?"

"Yes."

"I was just saying that for effect. I did not really mean it. I was merely flirting. In spite of everything I still had a very good opinion of myself. I just wanted to be contradicted, to have my good opinion confirmed."

Someone walks along the hall.

"Today, for the first time, I really do feel a whore. It is the truth. I have never felt like this! Not even with the most commonplace man during my worst time. And I really would like to. . . . But it won't work. Can you understand how I feel?"

"Yes."

"Oliver, let's get away from here. Quickly."

I switch on the light and we dress as fast as we can. (The man talks. The girl laughs. Water is flushed.)

"We'll never meet here again. I made a mistake."

"Let's go." I open the door and we run down the stairs as if we were being pursued. We walk, not looking at each other. Suddenly Verena stops, takes off her glasses and looks at me with her huge, black eyes as if she had never seen me before.

"Verena, what's the matter?"

Her smoky, hoarse voice says "Now I know."

"Know what?"

"Why it didn't work."

"Why didn't it?"

Strange people. Screaming children. Honking cars. And snow, snow, snow!

"Because I fell in love with you. I love you, Oliver."

## [ 18 ]

Along the way we find an old café. A bald little waiter in tails shuffles across to us. The windows are dirty, the electric lighting poor, and the tabletops ring-stained by many glasses. Two old men are playing chess, a third one watches. I order French cognac and the waiter promises to look for it in the cellar, since they never had any call for it before. Verena holds my hand tightly. We are still looking at each other.

"I love you, Oliver."

"And I love you. Only you. Always."

"I'm so glad we were in this terrible room. Or I wouldn't have realized. Not so quickly. Not so strongly. It is awful here, isn't it, but I feel fine!"

"Me too."

An amber-colored cat rubs along my leg. I stroke Verena's hand. The waiter brings a dusty bottle of Courvoisier. We invite him to have a drink to celebrate a special occasion.

"Now we have a new home," says Verena and takes a hearty drink. "It is crazy," she says. "You know something? All of a sudden I'm not afraid any more."

"Afraid?"

"Afraid of my husband. Of the future. The fact I'm so many years older than you."

"Everything will be all right."

"How? Tell me, how? I want to know, now that I know I love you."

"I can tell you. Finally. In Echternach I know a lawyer who told me that"—I mention the name of the largest of my father's competitors—"will employ me as soon as I have taken my final examinations. With glee! What a joke on my father! He would be the laughing stock of the business. They don't mind paying for the fun of it either. For a start we would have enough."

"Is that really true?"

"Word of honor!"

"I believe you. Even if it weren't true I would stay with you. But I know poverty. It kills all love."

"Don't be afraid. Right after the finals. Do you know that for the first time in my life I am studying? I want to pass my examinations!"

"I made a good student of you."

"You made a man of me."

"And you made a drinker of me."

"I didn't always drink so much. Only since . . ."

"Yes," says Verena, "I didn't either. Only since . . ."

"Since?"

"Since I was longing for you."

"How long have you been longing for me?"

"It started in St. Moritz."

I am terribly excited. In this dreary old café? I suddenly see our future together, our happy life.

"Just one more year, Verena! A little more than a year! Then I can work! We'll take a small apartment. You have furs, jewelry—"

"And you."

"And Evelyn. And my car. We will be the happiest people in Frankfurt."

"In all of Germany."

"In the whole world."
"No."
"No, what?"
"We must not say that or everything will go wrong. It always does if one says things like that."
"Can we at least think things like that?"
"How can one forbid thinking?"
"Verena—"
"Dearest?"
"Nothing."
"I know what you were going to say. Don't say it."
"I won't."
"Just think of it."
"Yes."
"I think of it too. The same thing."
"We'll have one more drink and then I'll drive you home. It is late."
"And you won't become impatient?"
"Never! But you . . ."
"I won't either."
"Soon it will be spring. My husband will go away on business again. You will come to me, as before, on our first night."
We drink.
The chess players argue.
Snow is still falling.
Why do I suddenly have this premonition of death again? Why? I am happy!
"What is it, my love?"
"Nothing."
"Yes, there is something. Your face suddenly looked so different—quite different."
"I thought of something."
"Of what?"
"Of how lovely it will be," I answer. (Why should I die?)
"You drink too much," says Verena.
"Only one more sip."
She smiles.

## [ 19 ]

We have a new match in school. Noah and Chichita. The chief called them and said: "Goldmund, you know how much I like you, but you must have taken leave of your senses! Chichita is only fifteen! And if I catch you just once—you are both going to get kicked out of school, you understand me?"

"First of all, Doctor, you would never catch us even if we did it and secondly I am very disappointed that you have such a poor opinion of me. I don't want to sleep with Chichita! At least, I am not in a hurry to do that."

"What do you want, then?" asked the chief.

"I am rather alone. And Chichita is too. I have always wanted to live with a human being I met very early and shape that person into my ideal."

"I see. Your creation."

"Yes."

"Pygmalion, eh?"

"Yes. Pygmalion. That is the reason I talk to her about Jaspers and Sartre, Oppenheimer, *Treason in the Twentieth Century,* collective guilt, Brecht, and so on."

"But she doesn't understand a word of that yet, Noah!"

"Well, I wouldn't say that. I gave her Camus to read. And Malraux. And Koestler. You are right. There are many things she does not understand as yet even though she insists she does. But a lot of things get into her head; she understands a lot—instinctively. She will never recognize it but at some time she will act as, for instance, Camus thought. Is that bad?"

"Do you really believe that?"

"I am very serious. I remember a sentence I read once and liked extraordinarily well. 'Later I went through many stupefying processes—but at fifteen I was clever and ingenious. One does not become more knowledgeable by merely growing older.' Excuse me, I meant nothing personal, naturally."

"I can take your silly jokes, you know that. So she is exactly what you were looking for?"

"Exactly."

"Wax in your hands."

"Yes, Doctor."

"Tell me: After you have formed little Chichita to your liking—then what are you going to do?"

"We shall go to Israel together."

"You will get married?"

"I didn't say that."

"You can't take her with you just like that."

"Why not? We want to live together. I think it will work out all right. But we do not want to have any children. We are agreed on that. You can see yourself what happens to children today!"

"Noah," said the chief. "To some degree I like your views. But irrespective—if you break your word, you're out!"

"Don't worry," Noah answered. "I want a human being, Doctor, a human being! Sleeping with Chichita is the last thing I'm concerned with."

Curious. When I was crazy about a girl I thought of nothing else but bed. Now Verena and I meet often in the little old café. We kiss. We pet. But *that*—no. Since two weeks ago. We talk. We have so much to talk about.

Noah is a smart boy.

## [ 20 ]

What has developed between Dr. Frey and Mlle. Duval seems to be common knowledge in the entire school. Everybody is talking about them. They are going for walks in the afternoon. At night they often go to the theater in Frankfurt or to the movies. Mademoiselle Duval has two new dresses and she visits the beauty parlor in Friedheim once a week. Sometimes she even laughs and Hansi says the two of them are secretly engaged. He should know.

He knows everything.

## [ 21 ]

Thursday I meet Verena again in the little café. Verena is changing. She is quieter, less nervous. Her face is changing too. It exudes serenity. And the sadness in her eyes is diminishing. She has good news. Next week her husband has to be away and I can spend another night with her. We are looking forward to it like youngsters, as lovers who have not yet embraced.

I have good news, too. For some time now I have been the best student in class. Actually it is not that great an accomplishment, at my age—but my teachers seem nevertheless nonplused.

Verena makes plans. Verena is realistic. She budgets the money I shall earn to see if we could manage on it. We are drinking a bit too much. In spite of our reminding and admonishing each other, when we meet we drink again! Because we are so sentimental, because of the limited time we have, because cognac brings us peace and warmth, confidence and mental calm.

"It is going to be a mild winter," says Verena. "Possibly I can move back to the Taunus as soon as March. And I thought of something else. My husband owns a house on Elba."

"I know."

"How do you know?"

"You talked about it that first night we spent together."

"I did? I must have been very drunk."

"You weren't drunk, just tired. I was, too. But I remember."

"You have never been to Elba?"

"No."

"We go there every year! The chauffeur takes the car to Florence ahead of us and we take the sleeping car. From there we go by car. Pisa. Livorno. Piombino."

"I have never been to Italy."

"At Piombino one can take the car on a ferry. It takes ninety minutes to arrive in Portoferraio. That is the capital of Elba. You could do that."

"If I still have my car next summer," I think. Then I realize what she had said: "You mean for me to go to Elba?"

"Yes! Evelyn has an Italian governess; she spends all her time on the beach. My husband travels a great deal. He is always away in Milan, Genoa or Rome. I am very often alone. It would be paradise."

"Is your house in Portoferraio?"

"It is on a bay called La Biodola, about ten kilometers outside Portoferraio. Look." Verena shows me photographs. A very blue sky and a darker blue sea, a sandy beach, palm trees and olive trees. A house, built almost completely of glass, perched on a cliff above the breakers. Stairs lead to the beach below.

"That is it, then," says Verena. "When my husband is on a trip you'll come to me. He is very busy. Even this house has a teletype. And the yacht has a two-way radio."

"You have a yacht?"

"A little one." She shows me the photo of a modern yacht, the name *Verena* on its bow. "There is a motorboat, too. I can go around the entire island, to see you anywhere."

"And he?"

"I told you, he is always working. Or he is completely exhausted and rests. Then he works again like crazy, with his secretary, with the teletype. Money, money. You know how it is with your father."

"Yes."

"Could you come to Elba? Or do you have to go home on your vacation?"

"I'll come. I'll come. But where shall I stay?"

"Wherever you wish. In Portoferraio. In Porto Azzuro. I can see you anywhere thanks to the motorboat. And if he is not there you come to me."

"And your chauffeur? The secretary? The governess?"

"They all live somewhere else."

She talks about Elba until I feel I have lived there for years.

"Can you speak Italian?"

"No."

"It doesn't matter. I'll teach you. As long as you come! I'll find a room for you. Then we don't have to be apart for months. After summer Evelyn will go to school. You'll take your final examinations. And we'll be together, for ever and ever." She raises her glass. "Let's drink to the wonderful time in Elba. Now we have a goal. We know that there is hope. We know we will be living together soon—without fear. We will not have to hide any longer. And Evelyn will be happy."

I refill our glasses.

"May all our wishes come true!"

I drink to all wishes which are Verena's. And one of my own. Not to have any trouble with Geraldine. Geraldine returns to school on this ninth of February. I did not take note of this day for nothing.

## [ 22 ]

The beginning is completely harmless.

She arrives by taxi. She does not appear to need the cane she carries. She waves and cries "Hello!"

It is a completely different Geraldine who arrives. Her lion-colored hair falls smoothly in a soft wave to her shoulders. Her eyelashes are not caked with mascara; there are no circles under her eyes.

Near the old chestnut tree she shakes many hands, accepts congratulations on her complete recovery. She kisses Hansi. Then it is my turn.

"I'm so glad to see you again!"

"Me too, Geraldine."

We shake hands. She does not give me one of those you-know-what-I-mean looks. I was prepared for anything but that.

I feel momentarily relieved. It is not as bad as I had expected. Geraldine is a nice girl. A decent girl.

The chief embraces the good girl and says how glad he is to have her back at the school and obviously glad she is not as made-up as she used to be, wearing all the cheap jewelry. She answers: "During the long weeks of my illness I thought about many things. I realized all the mistakes I had made. Now I shall try to remedy them. I hope I'll be successful."

The chief almost has tears in his eyes.

Dr. Haberle can hardly take his eyes off Geraldine. Funny, he never looked like that before. Lewd. Downright lewd! Wolfgang presents her a huge bouquet of yellow roses. "From all of us," he says. "We collected. Hansi bought them in Friedheim. It was his idea, too."

Hansi!

Flowers from a murderer. At least one who risked a murder in that canyon.

Hansi!

He beams and receives a kiss from Geraldine.

"You might have been crippled like me," says the scoundrel, who is morally responsible for Miss Hildebrand's death. With a gentle smile. In front of the children and the teachers he presses close to Geraldine. "That is why I thought of you all the time and wished that you, at least, would walk straight again." And he gets another kiss for that!

Everyone is touched.

Only Noah, next to me, says: "There is something wrong here!"

"What's wrong?"

He shrugs his shoulders.

In the afternoon I meet Geraldine. Can one blame people for taking revenge if one disappoints them, betrays them, leaves them? I suppose not. I believe, yes. But I just believe whatever I want to believe.

Ten minutes before classes resume under snow-laden trees in a Grimm's fairy-tale forest, Geraldine says:

## [ 23 ]

"You are a silly boy!"

"Why?"

"You should have seen yourself when I arrived. White with fear!"

"I'm not afraid."

"A blind man could have seen it! But you don't have to be afraid, Oliver." Her eyes are innocent. We are alone in the woods. Geraldine's voice is gentle. "When you came to see me I said a lot of stupid things. I lost my temper. I was nasty and mean—I was jealous. You ought to be able to understand that."

"Naturally."

"Don't look so unbelieving! I tell you, you don't have to be afraid. I regretted every word I said by the time you closed the door. Naturally, I won't spy on you or try to find out who the woman is. Why don't you say anything?"

"What should I say?"

"Then you don't believe me!"

"No."

And now she begins to cry and sobs: "Serves me right. I did behave like a blackmailer. . . . Oliver—please, Oliver, believe me!"

I leave her standing there and go.

That night at the Quellenhof I talk to Hansi.

"Listen, now that Geraldine is back again—"

"Can I help it that she recovered so quickly?"

"I don't mean that. She is jealous."

"You don't say!"

"Don't be funny! Aren't you my brother? Don't we get along well?" (To think I have to ask him that!)

"I can't complain."

"So if she tries to pump you about the woman—"

"Man, what do you take me for? A traitor? I'd rather have my tongue cut out than tell the luxury whore one word! Beside, she doesn't need you any more."

"Really?"

"You have that new boy in your class, the one who came Christmas, right?"

"Yes. Jens Larsen."

He is Norwegian, eighteen years old, blond with blue eyes, taller than I am and very good-looking.

"He is her hero. In three days, at the latest, she has—" Hansi tells me, as vulgarly as possible, what she will have done with Jens. "Three days, I tell you; not a minute longer. Bet? Pack of cigarettes?" It is true. During the following days Geraldine and Jens disappear for hours. The blond Norwegian looks as if someone had shown him paradise.

Hansi, that swine, reports what he has seen! What he overheard. In which house. Through which window. How often. At what times. It sounds very convincing.

"But this time it didn't even take seventy-two hours! So fork over the cigs, Oliver. I won."

Days pass. Jens seems to be in love.

"Writes poems," says Hansi, who knows all. "Gives them to her before they do it." And Hansi looks out of a window and assures me: "It will go for a long time." It does. Days. Weeks. Nothing happens. Hansi is nice. Geraldine friendly. Jens happy.

Fear is not fear any more. If it lasts too long one forgets and finally laughs about ever having been afraid.

Snow begins to melt. Soon Verena and Evelyn will come to Friedheim. Time passes. I have been afraid for nothing. What luck Jens came.

## [ 24 ]

The sun is already quite warm for February. Birds in great number are in the woods. I have seen snowdrops and crocuses and squirrels. Then I think of my mother's squirrels and feel awful every time. She is still in the same sanatorium. She sends money without asking what I need it for. I can pay off my loan.

Verena and I meet in the little café, I spend three nights in her house in Frankfurt when her husband is away on business and we can love each other. I feel safe again. I am not afraid of Verena's arrival in Friedheim because once more Geraldine talked to me.

"You are not mad at me?"

"Why should I be mad at you?"

"Because of Jens. After all the fuss I made about you. But, you know something happened."

"What happened?"

"It works with him, too. The same as it did with you."

"Since it clicked with me it will probably work with anybody else. With him it probably works even better."

"I didn't say that!"

"But it is true!"

"No—Yes! I don't want to lie. Yes, it does." She gives me a delicate kiss. "You were the first," she whispers, "I'll always be grateful to you—always—How could I have ever said those things to you?"

I swear, anybody would have believed her!

## [ 25 ]

The little Prince Rashid has grown very lonely since Ali found a fellow believer in Giuseppe. He is consumed with longing for his mother and his country. Added to this is the fact that Persia has another crisis. Universities are closed once more, a few thousand more people are in the already-overcrowded prisons.

And one morning Rashid has disappeared and cannot be found for five days. The police are notified. His picture appears in newspapers and on TV. On the twenty-fifth of February a police car from Frankfurt stops in front of the school and two detectives help the little prince from the car. Five minutes later I am summoned to the chief's office. It was Rashid's request I be there since he felt I was his only friend at the school. He looks disheveled and has obviously been crying. He composes himself sufficiently to tell us how he had saved fifty marks of his pocket money and taken a train to Frankfurt, where he bought some food and stowed away on a plane bound for Cairo. On arriving there he went to his uncle's apartment to get money to continue his flight to Persia. His uncle's housekeeper asked him to come into the house. Inside were two Egyptian policemen. His uncle was out of town. The German police had notified the police there since they surmised he would ask for assistance from his uncle. Lufthansa flew him back to Frankfurt where German police were waiting for him. Why did he want to get back to Persia? To help his country and to see his mother. When Rashid began to talk the chief had switched on a tape recorder. The microphone was hidden by a vase with flowers. Rashid could not see it. But I could. Now the chief switches it off and places his pipe in the ashtray.

"Rashid asked for permission to sleep in your room for a while, Oliver. It is all right with me and I'm sure Noah and Wolfgang won't mind."

"You know I have such terrible dreams," says Rashid.

"It won't be for long. Only a few days, until the dreams stop."

"It's okay, kid," I say. "Of course," I say.

"Thank you, Oliver," says the chief. "And now into the bathtub with you, Rashid!"

"And you, Oliver, return to your classroom." Which I do. I am halfway down the hall when I suddenly think of my brother Hansi.

## [ 26 ]

"But you don't mind, Hansi, do you?"

"But of course not. Why should I?"

"You understand why I had to fulfil Rashid's wishes, don't you?"

"I would despise you if you had not."

"Even though you are my brother and are not permitted to sleep in my room?"

"Because I am your brother! I have always known what a great guy you are!"

This conversation took place in the afternoon at the skating rink. I had to talk to Hansi as soon as possible because I knew I could not afford to anger him. He knows too much. He must never become my enemy.

Before dinner Noah and I put Rashid's bed in our room.

Many children bring chocolate, candy, and toys for the little prince. Hansi gives him his mouth organ. Hansi! Rashid is embarrassed by these demonstrations of friendship and sympathy. Rashid spreads his prayer mat facing east, and Noah, Wolfgang, and I are listening to his evening *sure*. During this, Hansi entered the room without being noticed. The little prince, having rolled up his prayer mat, crawls into bed, hugs me when I say good night to him and whispers: "I won't have a bad dream tonight!"

Then I hear Hansi's voice: "Giuseppe and Ali sent me. They wish you a good night."

"Thank you," says Rashid. "All of you are so nice to me."

"But Oliver mostly," says Hansi, who shakes my hand and smiles. "Bye," he says, and limps out.

It was the evening of the twenty-fifth of February.

## [ 27 ]

On the fourth of March I am invited to dinner again at Manfred Lord's. On the sixth, when we get our half-yearly report cards, we get three days off. I am going to see my mother in Echternach.

Manfred Lord is more charming than ever before. Leo as polite as never before. Verena is more beautiful than ever. After dinner—I am the only guest—we sit in front of the fireplace, smoking and drinking cognac.

Assad, the boxer, wags his stubby tail with pleasure when he sees me.

"Amazing how the dog is used to you," says Manfred Lord. "Isn't it, Verena?"

"Beg your pardon? Oh yes, amazing."

"You are so absent-minded, dearest. But you know, Oliver, usually Assad is very suspicious of strangers. But he likes you. And—after all, you are hardly a stranger any more. Right?"

"I hope not, Mr. Lord."

Luckily, the dog lies down and goes to sleep. Then it happens. Mr. Lord remembers something: "Oh, Oliver, it is a good thing I remember. The last time you went to Luxembourg you were good enough to take a gift to your father from me. Would you mind doing it once more?"

"I'll be happy to, Mr. Lord."

The book does not have to be fetched this time; it is already on the table. An early edition of Shakespeare's *Richard III.* While Lord is leafing through the book, explaining its value to me, Verena's foot under the table is pressing my shoe. During the last few days we have only spoken by phone but have not seen each other. Her husband has been away only once.

Manfred Lord is in an expansive mood. He kids me. Wants to know what is the matter with me. Was I not interested in girls? I never talked about even one girl in the school! And there are such pretty girls. . . .

"There are prettier ones. I do have to study a lot and—"

"Well, it can't be that bad!"

"I don't understand!"

Mr. Lord laughs. "What a rascal, Verena! He seems as innocent as a lamb and in reality—But don't be scared, I won't tell on you!"

"I don't know what there is to tell, Mr. Lord. Really, the girls at school aren't that pretty!"

"Well, my taste must be completely different from yours!"

Verena's shoe steps harder on mine. It means: Watch out!

"Just imagine, darling, all the things that can happen."

Manfred Lord cuts the end of his cigar with extreme care and lights it. He beams at Verena. "Could I fix you another drink?"

"No, thank you."

"I think I'll have another anyway. . . ."

"What happened, Manfred?"

Mr. Lord laughs again, warming the half-filled glass between his hands.

"Tell me, Oliver, do you know a Geraldine Reber?"

"Geraldine Reber? Yes—she is in my class."

"And you don't think she is pretty?"

"Pretty? No. Or maybe, yes. But not—— But how do *you* know Geraldine, Mr. Lord?"

He exhales a cloud of smoke.

"Just imagine, she came to see me. This morning. In my office."

"She was not in class. It was said she was sick."

"A little liar, eh? But a pretty little liar."

"Why a liar? Why—why did she come to see you?"

"Well, I must confess, nothing like this ever happened to me before. Imagine, darling, a young girl, perhaps eighteen years old. Right, Oliver?"

"Yes, eighteen."

"When my secretary told her she couldn't see me she just ran right through the two anterooms and stood before my desk: 'Mr. Lord?' 'Yes.' 'I have something to tell you. My name is Geraldine Reber. In my class at Dr. Florian's school is a certain Oliver Mansfeld. He is your wife's lover.' "

Manfred Lord laughs so loud he wakes Assad. He pats him until he calms down.

"How do you like that?" asks Mr. Lord.

"A lunatic?" asks Verena. Her shoe is not there any more.

"Is she crazy, Oliver?"

"I—I don't believe so."

"Was the dinner too rich?"

"Excuse me?"

"I thought you didn't feel too well."

"I am fine, thank you, Mr. Lord."

"In any case, have another cognac. And you too, darling."

He does not wait for our answers this time, but pours the drinks.

I see Verena's right hand shake. She steadies it with her left hand. I break out in a cold sweat. Cognac. Thank God.

"I'm sure she is crazy," says the host. "Maybe not crazy, but jealous. And because of you, Oliver."

Now I have recovered. There is only one thing to do now. Attack!

"That's right, Mr. Lord. She is jealous." I feel Verena's shoe again, encouraging me. "I went with Geraldine for a little while, then I stopped seeing her."

"Why?"

I shrug my shoulders.

"You had enough of her? That's the way we men are," says my host. "Beasts, inconsiderate beasts, who trample on your tenderest emotions, darling."

I drink some more cognac.

"The girl is still attached to you?" asks Verena, and I feel her foot.

"What do you mean still?" says Mr. Lord before I have a chance to answer. "Oliver is her true love!"

"Oh, God, no!" I say. (More cognac.)

"She told me so, Oliver! She told me a lot about both of you."

"Revenge," I say. "Plain and simple revenge. I'll see to her!"

"What did she tell you about us, Manfred?" Verena inquires.

Lord laughs again.

"I beg your pardon, but it really is too funny. These teenagers think of nothing but the lower halves of their bodies. For instance she told me how much you love each other."

"I shall complain to the Chief!"

"Don't do that, Oliver. The girl is dangerous!"

"But I can't take this lying down! And how did she know about your wife, Mr. Lord?"

"You said yourself: Revenge. A woman out for revenge will get the wildest ideas. The things a pretty little girl will think of . . ."

"What did she think of?" asks Verena.

"I couldn't remember all of it. There was too much. But wait! Yes, for instance. The two of you were supposed to have always met at the old watchtower last fall. You know which tower I mean, dearest?"

Now it is my turn: "That is a bare-faced lie! I'm going to see she is thrown out of school!" The shoe. The shoe.

"You were supposed to have met in town, too. Don't be so upset, Oliver! This sort of thing can happen if one gives a girl her walking papers."

"Mr. Lord, I wonder if it is necessary for me to vindicate myself . . ."

"Vindicate? Dearest friend, what nonsense is that? Haven't you noticed how much Verena and I like you? Would you really believe I would give credence to a jealous, silly little girl who tells me you are in love with my wife?" The honorable Manfred Lord can't help but laugh a great deal this evening. "But just the same. How clever of this Miss Geraldine. From all the people who own villas in Friedheim she had to pick us. Because my wife is so beautiful. Because it is known in Friedheim how much I love her. Because it could have been theoretically possible—theoretically, I say—possible for you to . . ."

"To what?"

"For you to have fallen in love with my wife. Do sit down, Oliver. We are not playing a melodrama! Why shouldn't you have fallen in love with Verena? Do you want to insult her?"

"What—what did you say to Geraldine, Mr. Lord?"

"Say to her? What do you take me for? I had her thrown out and told her not to bother me any more. After all, there are limits, aren't there? The little beast. It took two people to get her out of my office. She screamed she would bring me proof. Proof! Isn't that too comical. Verena, darling, don't trouble yourself! I shall ring for Leo to wipe up the cognac, he knows how to do that better than you. If it isn't done properly it leaves such ugly spots on the parquet flooring. Ah, there you are, Leo! Just look what happened! My wife dropped her glass."

# Chapter Seven

[ 1 ]

"My daughter is a genius," says Mrs. Durham. "She won first prize at a school play when she was only twelve years old. Then she acted on the legitimate stage. Just think, Oliver, at fourteen!"

Mrs. Durham is sixty-four years old; she told me herself. She is made-up and dressed up like a forty-year-old. Red lips, dyed black hair. A wildly colorful shirt, skin-tight slacks and sandals. Mrs. Durham told me her face had already been lifted three times. Soon it will have to be done for the fourth time.

The doctor in London will make her look new again in the fall because Mrs. Durham is going for a rest to Elba first, going all the way by car! She goes there every year. This is her twelfth trip.

She is a lonely woman and, like all lonely people, talks a great deal. She has been talking since she stopped her pretty Ford outside Florence where I waved and asked for a lift. It is very hot. I see hard, gray earth, stone pines, donkeys, little houses, buildings going to ruin and many men working with pneumatic drills and cranes on the highway. The sky is as blue as it was in the photos Verena showed me and I am in Italy for the first time on this fifteenth of June 1961. Mrs. Durham is a good driver. I was incredibly lucky. I only waited half an hour for a lift and she happens to be going to Elba, too. She said we should reach Piombino in three to four hours and be on the island she loves so much (where Verena is waiting for me) ninety minutes later. It feels strange to sit next to a driver when one has driven one's own car for a long time. I have no car any more. Kopper and Co. own my car. On display. They have not found a buyer for it yet.

"At fourteen? That's fantastic!"

"Isn't it? We were so proud of her! By the way, your English is fantastic too, Mr. Mansfeld. I really am very happy to have met you! It is so boring to travel alone. I like to have someone to talk to. Where was I?"

"Your daughter, Mrs. Durham. I'm sure she must be a great actress today. Would I know her name perhaps? Her stage name?"

"No. Because she is not an actress any more."

A tunnel, many snappy Fiats which are overtaking us, sounding their horns. Forests high on the sun-scorched hills.

"You know, Virginia was beautiful. There were a lot of eligible young men, millionaires who wanted to marry her."

Numerous advertisements lining the side of the road.

"Then she is married?"

"No, Mr. Mansfeld. Men weren't the right thing for Virginia. My daughter is director of our factories. I tell you, she is a genius. We'll have to leave the highway soon. The next town is Pisa. But first we'll eat at 'California.' "

[ 2 ]

Mrs. Durham talks and talks; does not wait for any answers while we drive along. It is hot. I have eaten too much, never having known Italian cuisine. Those antipasti! That spaghetti. Those Saltimbocca. The cheese. And such wine! I am drunk when we continue our trip. Mrs. Durham is not. She talks and talks and once in a while I say "Yes," once in a while "No."

She is happy! Someone is listening to her!

I am happy. Every kilometer a kilometer closer to Verena.

Stone pines.

Avenues lined with stone pines. The heat. The food.

If I weren't so sleepy I would understand what Mrs. Durham was saying.

But . . . I remember so many things. I remember what happened since the evening of the fourth of March when Mr. Manfred Lord talked about Geraldine. "Of course, I had her thrown out."

"You did the right thing," says Verena. (Leo had cleaned up the cognac she spilled.) "She could have been a blackmailer. You would never have been able to get rid of her."

"I don't believe that."

"Believe what?"

"That she was a blackmailer, dearest. She would have gone to you or Oliver. I can't be blackmailed. That is logical, isn't it, Oliver?" You could be blackmailed too, Superman, if you were shown those pages with perforated letters, I think, but I answer: "Completely logical, Mr. Lord."

"You see, Verena, Oliver shares my opinion. Really, perhaps you two did meet accidentally somewhere. Accidentally, I say. Perhaps this girl saw you. Or somebody else. One thing is certain, Miss Reber loves Oliver, right? And because Oliver is so sure of this being an act of revenge, I ask you both: Avoid being seen together when Verena goes back to the Taunus. We want to be seen *à trois!* We don't want to give this little miss an opportunity."

"What opportunity?"

"My God, darling, you don't know how bad people are, how quickly a nasty rumor can spread through the entire town! My business partners, our acquaintances. . . . Excuse me for saying so, Oliver, but I stand to lose a respected name. I would be the man people would laugh about. And I am too young for something like that."

With that he squashes his cigar in an ashtray. "I do not wish to be laughed about, Oliver. I would like you to settle the problem with this jealous girl. Well, enough of that! Let's have another drink."

[ 3 ]

"Mr. Mansfeld!"

I jumped up. Where am I? Whose car is this? My head hurts. What time? Which day?

Mrs. Elizabeth Durham smiles.

That damned wine!

"You fell asleep."

"Forgive me. It must be the heat. And the Chianti."

"Look!" Her slender hand points forward. I see the Ligurian Sea, perfectly calm and looking like blue glass. On a narrow beach people are sunning themselves, girls in tiny bikinis. Others are swimming. Colorful sails, colorful beach balls, swimsuits and hats.

The shore is lined with restaurants, little hotels and, most of all, bars. Apartment houses, bungalows and modern villas. We are already driving through Livorno. Bar. Bar. A night club, advertising strip-tease. . . . My father took Auntie to a strip-tease place like that some time ago in Echternach.

Two days later, after the dinner at Manfred Lord's, I went to Echternach. . . . I still see Hansi and Geraldine at the school.

It is quite clear to me that Hansi has informed Geraldine. He wanted revenge too. Revenge for Rashid. Revenge. Revenge. Everybody is taking revenge. But who would admit it? Would Hansi? Would Geraldine admit she had been to see Manfred Lord and was thrown out? Never. So there is no point in mentioning anything. Hansi and Geraldine are extremely nice to me and Rashid. Geraldine asked my forgiveness for being so happy with Jens.

She is a good actress. I have a feeling something didn't work out the way she had planned it. That does not mean she is going to give up. Did something go wrong? Did she really go to Manfred Lord? Did he really throw her out? Did they both work out a plan? Perhaps. One thing is certain: Geraldine and Hansi are still waiting to take their revenge. How much longer will they have to wait?

And then Echternach.

There were tears in Teddy Behnke's eyes when he came to pick me up in Frankfurt.

"It is better you find out now and from me, Mr. Oliver."

"What happened?"

"You'll have to be brave, Mr. Oliver."

"Ah, shit! What happened?"

"Your mother . . . she is—she is not in the sanatorium any more."

"Where, then?"

"Your father visited her a week ago. They had a big fight. The nurses told me they were both screaming at each other."

"Was there a reason?"

"A Dr. Walling seemed to be the reason. The nurses would not tell me who he is. Do you know him?"

I explain.

"Now I understand. Apparently your mother told your father that Dr. Walling would be looking after her interests. She demanded a divorce and all the money. The poor woman! The doctor declared he could not take the medical responsibility for your mother any longer."

In Echternach I am given the name of a mental institution outside town. Very beautiful country. Bars in all windows.

Overruling the objections of the doctor in charge, I insist on seeing my mother.

Her face seems even smaller. Her pupils are pinpoints. She does not recognize me.

"What do you want? Did my husband send you? Get out of here or I'll call Dr. Walling."

"Mother . . ."

"Get out!"

"Mother . . ."

"Don't you hear me?" Her voice breaks. She rings a bell furiously. Two attendants in white uniforms appear.

"Throw this blackguard out! There is poison in his pocket!"

"Please come," one of the attendants says quietly to me. "You can do nothing here."

I leave. In the corridor I meet the doctor and apologize for not taking his advice.

"Does my mother have everything she needs?"

"A Mr. Behnke brings peanuts for her regularly. She feeds the birds and it makes her happy. Whatever she needs she just has to tell us."

"Tell you?"

"Yes. We tell your father. He sends what she asks for."

"But mother has her own bank account!"

"Not any more."

"What do you mean?"

"I am afraid a person of your mother's state of mind is—excuse me—not able to take care of herself. Your father closed her account. Mr. Mansfeld, your mother is well looked after here. We do everything we can for her. Of course, we cannot perform miracles. I'm sure you understand."

"I understand, doctor. Good day."

## [ 4 ]

Dust. Dust.

Vineyards on the left. The sea on the right.

"We'll be there in an hour," said Mrs. Durham.

Alberghi. Pensione. Locande. Camere Private. Ristoranti. Trattorie. Bar. Bar. Bar. Coca-Cola.

It is so hot. So strange, everything. Soon I will be there. Verena said she would try and wait for the arrival of the six o'clock boat in Portoferraio. Verena.

How long since I've seen her, kissed her.

Mrs. Durham overtakes a black Jaguar with Dutch license plates. Pretty Jaguar. Larger than mine was. I have not had my little white Jaguar for quite some time now.

## [ 5 ]

When Kopper and Co. have found a buyer for my car I'll get some money too. I have paid seven instalments. Then mother's bank account was closed. So as not to lose my car I did something I shall be ashamed of for a long time. I asked my father for money. Since I would not tell him what I needed the money for he refused to give it to me. When I don't pay, a man from Kopper and Co. comes to Friedheim to collect my car from the garage. I lie to Verena that the car was never really mine but was just lent to me by my father. When we had an argument about mother he demanded it back.

"But how are you going to come to Italy?"

"By train."

"And on the island?"

"I guess by bus."

"You liked your car so much!"

"I hope nothing worse than that will ever happen to me. Besides it was never really mine, I just told you."

It is May when I lie to Verena, but I lied to her before in spite of our promise always to be truthful. I did not like to lie to her. Only the fear of losing her on the evening of the fourth of March when Manfred Lord told us about Geraldine's visit. I don't know how I got back to the school that evening. . . . The following day I was waiting for Verena's telephone call at Mrs. Liebetreu's garage. She has never called me on a Sunday before but she does on this one. She must be as afraid as I am; her voice is uncertain.

"What is going to happen now? What can we do?"

"Nothing," I say. Last night I could not sleep. I wracked my brains how to answer her.

"But if he knows anything—"

"But you saw, he does not believe it!"

"He put on an act. He is waiting. He is trying to trick us. You don't know him! If this girl should come once more—"

"She won't."

"But if she has proof? Maybe he already has proof?"

"Even then he will do nothing. He can't. I have proof, too!"

"You have what?"

"Don't be afraid, Verena. Your husband is clever, too clever."

"I don't understand."

"Where are you, Verena?"

"At a post office."

I think it is safe enough to talk and tell her about the books.

"I have photographed many pages. I have proof. I could even blackmail your husband if need be."

Blackmail.

Now I am just like Leo, like Hansi, like Geraldine.

"He gave me another book yesterday. My father will give me another, too. I shall photograph those pages too. The longer it takes the more proof we'll have. The most important thing is for you to remain calm. A few months more and we'll be in Elba. We'll be together then. The firm which is going to employ me has offered to give me an advance too." A lie. There was no such promise.

"Oh, Oliver, then I could leave him at the end of the year."

"Naturally. You and Evelyn will take an apartment. By the time you have your divorce I will have finished school and will be working."

Lies. Lies.

What will be at Christmas? At year's end?

An apartment? How will I pay for it?

A divorce? Verena will have to admit everything.

But it is a long time until December. It is March now. Who knows what can happen?

Lies. Lies. I'll have to continue lying.

"We'll have to be careful during the next three months. We must not meet at the tower any more."

"No."

"There is a little boy in school who is spying on me."

"I thought it was Geraldine!"

"No. Yes. No."

Now I tell her the truth, almost the whole truth. That I saw Geraldine and she vowed to revenge herself because I left her. That I hurt the little cripple, who wants to be my friend, by allowing Rashid to sleep in my room, that without a doubt Hansi and Geraldine got together.

"I understand."

Really? You understand everything? I don't.

Naturally Hansi told Geraldine all he knows. But how much can he know? He couldn't have followed me in Frankfurt. Only one man could have done that. Leo.

"Verena—"

"Yes?"

"You must be very careful. You must be suspicious of everybody, your friends, your employees, especially Leo."

"Why especially him?"

"I think your husband ordered him to spy on you. The little cripple can't know everything. Geraldine can't know everything."

"Leo can't either. We were very careful."

Not careful enough. Or I would still have my car. I wonder if Leo demands money from Mr. Lord for his information?

"Please be careful with Leo. Please!"

"I will. I'll do as you say. . . . Oliver, when shall we see each other again?"

"I'm leaving tomorrow and return Friday. If possible call me. I'll be waiting. When are you coming up here?"

"The fifteenth of March."

"That will make things easier."

"Easier!"

"We must not lose our heads now. I'm sure your husband will invite me again to get the book my father is sure to give me. You'll see how nice and friendly he will be."

Friday the tenth of March I return from Echternach and on the following day I'm invited by Mr. Lord. This time it is an old Bible my father brought to the hotel. I had telephoned him.

"I have a book from Mr. Lord for you. You'll have to come and get it yourself, though."

"Why?"

"I am not going to set foot in your house any more. Don't ask why. I just returned from the mental institution."

It only took him fifteen minutes to be at the hotel. He took Mr. Lord's book and gave me the Bible. He stayed three minutes. I looked at my watch.

After returning to school it took me half a night to photograph the pages containing perforated letters. Saturday night I went to the house on Miquel Drive in Frankfurt. Then I still had my Jaguar.

Sitting by the fire Mr. Lord says the nicest evenings are the ones one spends with only a few friends. Right? Yes, indeed! He admires the Bible. Then he leaves us alone for a few moments.

"When?" whispers Verena quickly. "Where? Quickly!"

"Call me tomorrow."

She pulls a small folded envelope from her dress.

"What is it?"

"You'll see."

The envelope contained many little, fine and short hairs.

They were curly.

[ 6 ]

This is Cecina. A charming little place.

"You are tired, Mr. Mansfeld? Shall I stop? We'll make the boat on time, don't worry! Perhaps you would like to stretch your legs a little?"

What am I? Who is this woman?

"You look pale. Don't you feel well?"

"I—I feel a little dizzy."

"I'll stop. I know this place like the back of my hand. There is a large square by the sea."

There it is. Huge. Desolate. The sun beats down on it and laundry hanging from the windows of the faded fronts of ugly, neglected houses. I walk up and down. Suddenly I am seized by overpowering fear. I believe that I have to die. Now. Here. On this huge empty square in Cecina. I stumble. I must get back to the car. I don't want to die. Not here. Not in this terrible sun-baked desolation! Mrs. Durham holds a flask out to me. I half-empty it.

"Scotch," says Mrs. Durham. "I always have some with me. Do you feel better?"

"Everything is all right again. Thank you. Thanks a million!"

"There is nothing like Scotch, I always say."

How much further to Piombino!

How much further to Portoferraio?

How much further to Verena?

## [ 7 ]

"Now we come to Sassetta, San Vincenzo, and then Piombino." My thoughts wander while Mrs. Durham is annoyed by a donkey pulling a cart which she cannot pass.

I must watch out for traps. I must watch out for three of us: Verena, Evelyn and me.

A trap: the Sunday after the party at Mr. Lord's I met Geraldine and Hansi in the woods where I had gone to be alone. They walk hand in hand. Geraldine beautiful and straight. Hansi crooked, crippled and ugly. They both are friendly in their greeting.

"We're going to church," says Geraldine.

"With Ali and Giuseppe," says Hansi. "We would have taken Rashid too—but with his religion—"

"You s.o.b." I say.

He smiles and his lips seem to disappear again.

"I really don't know what you mean."

"You understand perfectly."

"Not a word!" He squeezes Geraldine's arm and Geraldine's smile is friendly.

"By the way, Oliver, you can be as friendly with Rashid as you like. You can even become his brother!"

"I don't want to."

"That is up to you. Then you'll have none."

"What does that mean?"

"It means I am *not* your brother any longer. I have a sister now!"

"Geraldine?"

"Yes," she says smilingly. "Imagine!"

"Don't be sad," says the cripple. "But after her accident we became very close. She very nearly could have had the same spine I have!" He smiles an angelic smile, the miserable scoundrel, and Geraldine smiles too. I wonder if she had to show him her breasts and everything else before he told her about me. Or did he do it out of pique and without reward?

"Don't be angry with him for not wanting to be your brother any more," says Geraldine. "You have your hands full with Rashid."

Hansi does not take his eyes off me. He knows my thoughts. Can I, ought I to tell Geraldine that Hansi was the cause of her accident? What would be the result? Incalculable! Why didn't I report it when it happened? How would Hansi defend himself? ("He told me he wanted to be rid of the luxury whore!") And the dead Miss Hildebrand? And Verena. Verena. Verena.

"Let's go, Geraldine, we'll have to hurry," says Hansi. And to me: "Perhaps you'd go to the Quellenhof and console poor Rashid."

"What do you mean console?"

"He is lying on his bed crying."

## [ 8 ]

I went to the Quellenhof and spent an hour sitting on Rashid's bed until he stopped crying. He was crying because he was so lonesome.

Now nothing matters anymore. In a world where a potential

murderer like Hansi can become Geraldine's brother, in a world such as this one can say "Hansi is not my brother anymore, Rashid, do you want to be my brother?" His arms are around my neck in a second and in his excitement he talks German, Persian, and English, all at the same time.

I give him books, chocolate, and newspapers before I leave but he does not take any notice of them. He is lying on his bed, staring at the ceiling repeating "I have a brother . . . I have a brother."

[ 9 ]

". . . steel works, you know, Mr. Mansfeld? Two steel works. For generations in my deceased husband's family . . ." Who is this woman? What is she talking about?

"Where are they, Mrs. Durham?"

"About twelve miles outside Liverpool."

"I see." She talks, talks, I am dreaming. . . .

On the Sunday when Rashid becomes my brother I don't know what to do. I get in my car and drive to the "Angel of the Lord," to see Sister Claudia. Why? To this day I could not say why.

At the home I find a lot of children, and adults too. It surprises me. Sister Claudia is happy to see me.

"On Sunday Brother Martin speaks. Then there is a discussion. If you would like to listen. Later we could talk about your troubles."

"My troubles?"

"You must have worries. No one ever comes here who has no worries. I knew you would come, Mr. Mansfeld."

[ 10 ]

I see Italy, I think of Germany. I live the present, I think the past. I hear Mrs. Durham talking and I think of the events which took place during the past few months.

Castagneto, Carduzzi.

I remember Brother Martin talking about the impending end of the world in the flames of the atomic bomb, reciting the Revelation of St. John, and assuring the members of this strange "Philanthropic Society" that nothing would harm them. They carry God's mark imprinted on their foreheads.

Stabilimento Enologico Fabrica Liquori!

The sea shimmers golden in the rays of the slowly setting sun.

"The next town is San Vincenzo. We will catch the boat in plenty of time; we can even have a drink in the harbor, it is so romantic there."

An afternoon in July. Flowering bushes, huge red blooms everywhere, heat, blue sky.

And I think of the Sunday in March in the Taunus when the snow started to melt and I walked through the park of the convalescent home with Sister Claudia.

"May I . . . may I come again, Sister Claudia? Even if I don't become a member of your society?"

"You can always come. Anybody may come. The weather is improving. Would you like to sit in the park? Should someone come and talk with you? Do you have any questions?"

"Many. But no one here can answer them. You are all too good for my questions."

"You are always looking at my hand. I was in a car crash. Two fingers had to be amputated."

"I don't believe that."

"Then what do you believe?"

"That the Nazis . . . in the Third Reich . . ."

"No."

"Yes. Isn't it so?"

"Yes, it is, Mr. Mansfeld. I was interrogated by the Gestapo in Berlin. I was imprisoned for three years. But please don't mention it to anybody."

"I won't."

"I was very lucky to lose only two fingers. Just think of how much others lost."

"Sister Claudia, I have another request: May I bring someone else?"

"Naturally."

"A woman?"

"Yes. You are both welcome here, Mr. Mansfeld. Come soon, as often as you like. And don't be afraid. No one here will try to convert you. You will find peace here. That is what you are searching for, is it not?"

"Yes, Sister Claudia."

[ 11 ]

Cinzano. Cinzano. Cinzano.

Bends in the road. Huge trucks. Cacti. Peace.

Yes, that is what we are looking for, Verena and I. When Verena moves back to Friedheim I take her to the "Angel of the Lord." Sister Claudia shows us to a bench in the park. We sit there for hours. Verena and I. Flowers begin to bloom, later the scent of white and purple lilac permeates the air, spring comes quickly this year.

Peace.

Here we have it. No one is looking for us here. Not Hansi. Not Geraldine. Not Leo. We are always extremely careful, coming here. . . . We are there in March, April, May. Sometimes when we say goodbye to each other Sister Claudia makes the sign of the cross on our foreheads.

When we leave the "Angel of the Lord" we take different roads. I write a great deal during this time. Verena, who reads everything I write, says she does not know if it is good or bad. She thinks both our love and the book are good. But she is not sure. I am not either.

We still say good night to each other with our flashlights, she from her bedroom, I from the balcony.

Mrs. Durham breaks in suddenly.

"Hold on to a button. Make a wish!"

"Why? What is the matter?"

A bride and groom are crossing the street, she in white, he in black. Following them are relatives. Children. Very old people. The bride is carrying a bouquet of flowers. The bell of a small church chimes. In its entrance stands the priest. He is wearing a surplice over a black coat and peasant boots.

I hear an organ, weak and old. Somebody is not too sure of its keys. But it is very solemn, very solemn.

It was solemn in Friedheim, too, when Dr. Frey and Mlle. Duval married. At City Hall though, not in church. A lot of children came to watch. After the ceremony Mademoiselle turned around and called to the children: "Forgive me! Please, forgive me, all of you!"

"What should we forgive?" asks Rashid.

"I don't know," I answer. But I know. If all races would mix and all religions and all people! Their children and their children's children . . . how happy they would be.

Verena and I meet in the park and we count the days. Elba. Elba. A human being has to have hope, wish for something, long for something.

## [ 12 ]

Kisses and talks and holding hands are not enough. Verena says sometimes at night she feels as if she were on fire. Me too. I lie in bed listening to Rashid crying, and pray: "God, let time pass quickly. Let us be in Elba soon."

No, light signals and kisses are not enough. I always thought I could control myself. But my composure is wearing thin when Mr. Lord invites me and is so polite and charming. When Leo is serving. When little Evelyn looks at me with disgust and ignores me. And every time Verena looks past me and I look past her.

God, let it be June soon. Let me go to Elba. Let me be with Verena. Please God. Time passes. In May Kopper and Co. are taking my Jaguar away from me. But one more month and school closes for the summer. And then. . . . The thought of it excites us both and we behave carelessly and do it a few times during the following days in the forest. On green moss, beneath old trees which have new leaves. After the first time she said: "I feel as if you had just deflowered me."

She thinks it is because it has been such a long time since we embraced. We part quickly after it happened. It is not good for Verena or me. No, but it will be wonderful in Elba.

James Hilton, a young American, came to the school in April. Geraldine left Larsen and took James. A Greek came in May. She left the American and took the Greek. She is again what she always was: the luxury whore. She greets me but she does not talk to me. She takes walks with Hansi. The way one walks a little dog. Geraldine is the worst student in our class. All of the teachers take her illness into consideration and are lenient with her. In Latin she is doing very poorly and the polecat says:

"Unless you pull yourself together and improve, Reber, I find it simply impossible to give you a passing grade."

This remark will cost Dr. Haberle everything he worked so hard for in his life. The final test paper is being written. Right after the double period Geraldine is so insolent the polecat screams.

"Reber, you're coming back here at six o'clock and will be kept in! I am not going to put up with this!"

That night Rashid and the new pedagogue who is Miss Hildebrand's successor are playing in the library with the Szeno Test. The new pedagogue is young and pretty. Her name is Palmer. The older boys are paying court to her. . . . I don't suppose anybody will ever really know what happened. Rashid says Miss Palmer left him alone a few minutes to take care of a matter in the older girls' villa. It was about six-thirty. Rashid heard a girl scream for help. He was very scared but ran into the hall and up the stairs.

"Help! Let me go! Let me go . . . !"

A door flies open and a girl runs out. Geraldine. Her dress is torn from top to bottom, her stockings hanging down. And she screams:

"Help me! Get somebody! He is trying to rape me!"

Rashid said he didn't know what the word meant but he yelled for help too. Rashid saw a shadow glide from the room but could not recognize him. It was getting too dark. . . . When, in answer to the commotion, the chief and two teachers appear Geraldine is crying hysterically. She repeats again and again: "He was going to rape me!"

"Who?"

She does not say.

No, she does not say who.

[ 13 ]

We get those test papers back. Geraldine passed.

Dr. Haberle closes the period earlier. He says he has to talk to the chief. When he leaves, bent forward, his shoulders jerk. It looks as if he is crying. I never saw Dr. Haberle, the polecat, again.

In a school nothing stays a secret for any length of time. Mr. Herterich, who is taking too many sleeping tablets and is under a doctor's care, is only a shadow of his former self even though no one is taking any notice of him now. Maybe that is the worst. When no one takes any notice any more. He told me Dr. Haberle was fired because he raped Geraldine Reber.

"Nonsense!"

"He admitted it."

"I don't believe it. He is too cowardly to do that."

"He told Dr. Florian that he had been crazy about Geraldine for a year. And the afternoon she was kept in he lost his self-control."

"It's ridiculous. What did Geraldine say?"

"Nothing at first. Only when she heard that he admitted it did she say it was true."

"She says the polecat raped her?"

"Yes. Isn't it terrible? A man lives happily with his wife, has children, saves to buy a house. And this happens! I wouldn't like to teach the older girls! Would you? It is a devilish temptation."

"He has to go to court. He will never be able to teach again. His career is ruined. His marriage, too. His wife is getting a divorce."

"No!"

"She is selling the house and is taking her children to her parents. My God, the poor doctor!"

But Geraldine passed in Latin.

## [ 14 ]

Last day of school.

No one in our class flunked. Geraldine's face is expressionless when she receives her diploma from the chief. Where is the polecat? When is the house being sold? How long was Dr. Haberle married?

Yes, but he admitted it. . . .

The chief wishes us a happy vacation.

"Have a good time. Come back healthy and happy. The ones staying on here will have a good time too. We'll go swimming, go on hikes, and you can request what you want to eat."

He is a great guy. He has no one to whom he can go for advice.

Everywhere I go I hear "What are you going to do on your vacation?"

Many are proud and excited and tell the truth.

"My parents are coming to pick me up. We're going to Spain." Or to Egypt. Or to England. To Switzerland. To the Riviera. To the Black Forest.

And many are proud and sad and lie. "My father is taking me on a trip to India," says Santayana. We all know she is going to stay at the school and won't even see her father.

"I'm going to become engaged," says Clarissa. (Clarissa is seventeen. She is staying here too. Her parents are dead. She has a guardian.)

Many children tell lies, but no one contradicts them even though everybody knows they are lies. Children are sometimes more charitable than adults.

Hansi: "I talked to the chief. I'm staying here. When my old man comes the chief is going to throw him out!"

Geraldine: "I'm going to Cape Canaveral to see my father. I don't know if I'm coming back." She looks at me. "But I think I will."

Ali: "I have invited Giuseppe. We're going to Africa."

Thomas: "I have to go to Paris. Shit!"

Rashid: "I'll stay here this year. My uncle is coming to see me. But next year when everything in Persia. . . ."

Noah is the sensation: "I'm taking Chichita to Israel. Her father and the chief are agreeable. I still have relatives in Israel. We'll want to have a look at the country."

Chichita beams when he says that.

## [ 15 ]

Once more I'm invited to Manfred Lord's house. Naturally! I'm going back to Luxembourg to see my mother, right? And Mr. Lord has another old book for my father. He is so sorry that we won't be able to meet for two months. Verena sits between us, not looking at me.

"I have to thank you, Oliver, for being so fair and not seeing my wife without my being there too."

"Well, naturally!"

"Anyway, thank you! I have never heard from that girl again. We are all interested in not having any ugly rumors circulate, aren't we, dearest?"

"Naturally, Manfred."

"It is too bad you have to go to your mother's. I would have invited you to Elba! We have a little house there. I have to be away so many times. You could have kept my wife company. In Elba people don't lie and defame the way they do here."

"I would have liked to come, Mr. Lord, but I really have to see my mother."

"You are a good son. I have come to like you, Oliver. Haven't you, Verena?"

"Yes, he really is a nice guy."

"What is it, Leo?"

"Excuse me, I'm just bringing ice for the whisky, sir."

"Thank you, Leo. You saw Mr. Mansfeld's Jaguar, didn't you?"

"The white one, yes, sir. Did something happen? An accident?"

"No. His father took the car away from Mr. Mansfeld. I don't think that is nice of your father, Oliver!"

What is going on here? Why does Mr. Lord tell Leo?

"If I may say so, I too, think it is unnecessary harshness." You swine!

"I shall write your father, Oliver. You take the letter with you."

Is it possible that he and Leo together . . . ? No, it is impossible to believe. Is it?

In any case Mr. Lord actually does write to my father this evening to ask him to return the car. If he were to telephone him he would know right away that my old man didn't take the car. Did he telephone? Does he know already? No, those two never use the telephone. Or do they? I take the letter. On my way home I tear it up.

The next morning I meet Verena in the park of the "Angel of the Lord." I hand her the manuscript, the photographs I took of the pages of the old books, and the negatives. She is going to Frankfurt to deposit them in her bank vault. In two days she, Evelyn and her husband are leaving for Elba.

"And when are you coming?"

"On the thirteenth probably, at the latest on the fifteenth."

"I'm going to look for a room for you. Come soon."

"As soon as I can."

"If it is possible, take the boat at six o'clock. I shall try to wait for you in Portoferraio on those three days. If I am not there I'll leave a letter for you in the office of the steamship line."

She gives me money.

"Are you crazy?"

"It isn't much. I couldn't get hold of more so quickly. But I have more in Elba."

"But I'm not taking any money from you!"

"How are you going to come to me? On foot all the way from Luxembourg?"

"I—"

"Come on, take it."

"Thank you."

"The hard time of waiting passed quickly, didn't it? Now the happy times are coming. Then another short bad time. And everything will be good after that."

"Everything."

We say goodbye to Brother Martin and Sister Claudia. I tell them we won't see each other for a while.

"I shall think of you and pray for you."

"Please do," says Verena.

"You are not religious?"

"No."

"But you love one another, don't you?"

"Yes, Sister Claudia, we do."

"Then I will pray for you."

## [ 16 ]

Piombino!

We have arrived. The town is small and full of corners and angles, the suburbs ugly and spread out and smokestacks and other evidence of a steel and iron industry.

Mrs. Durham is forced to drive very slowly because people here walk on the roads. And how many people! The town is crammed full! An ants' nest!

Bar. Bar. Bar.

Chairs and tables on the streets. Men are drinking espresso or red wine thinned with water. Heated debates. Everybody is talking, gesticulating. Many movie houses. The advertisements are six times larger than in Germany! Colorful. Bosoms. Bosoms. Bosoms. Heroes. Heroes. Heroes. Beggars. Many beggars. They come to the car and extend their hands. Children in rags are begging, too. Mrs. Durham is generous.

We have reached the harbor. Not the large dirty harbor used by the industry but the smaller one used by the ships going to Elba. Here, near the water, it is cooler. A small house with terraces, a juke box and little tables and chairs.

"I have a few drinks here when I arrive," says Mrs. Durham. "I have a house on the island. In Bagno on the bay of Prochio. My caretaker always picks me up in Portoferraio and I don't have to drive any more." With peculiar pride she says: "I have never arrived in Elba without being drunk. Let's stay with whisky. All right?"

"Certainly, Mrs. Durham." (I hope she does not drink too much. My money. . . .)

"Two double Scotches, please."

"Due grandi Johnnie. Sì, Signora."

"Any brand of whisky is called Johnnie here, Mr. Mansfeld." She orders two more and wants to pay right away. I protest. She protests. We flip a five-hundred lire coin and she loses. She loses the third time, too. No one would know she has already had three double whiskies. The sea shimmers golden in the rays of a red sun and is very calm. Sea gulls circle. While we are drinking, more and more cars arrive. The car-ferry, when it arrives, is larger than I had expected. It docks and many cars drive off. Sailors are directing the unloading.

"Let's go," says Mrs. Durham. "It is time." We walk to the car and a sailor directs us to a place inside the ferry. We go up on deck. At exactly six o'clock the ship leaves the pier.

"How about another little Johnnie?" asks Mrs. Durham.

## [ 17 ]

The bar is large. Behind it are three bartenders, one of whom recognizes Mrs. Durham.

"Oh, Signora Durham! Glad to see you again. Two Johnnies, yes?"

"Sì, Roberto. Grazie."

"From now on as usual, Mrs. Durham?"

"As always."

The bartender laughs, showing beautiful white teeth.

"What does that mean, 'as always'?" I ask.

"It means he is going to bring us two new Johnnies every fifteen minutes."

"But that's impossible!"

"Why? The crossing only takes one and a half hours! Doesn't whisky agree with you?"

"That's not what I mean."

She looks at me, places her hand on mine and says:

"I understand. You don't have that much money. And you're too proud to let me invite you."

"Not too proud, but—"

"Listen, young man; I have more money than I can spend in my lifetime. What happens to it when I die?"

"Your daughter—"

Mrs. Durham takes a drink and turns her face into the wind.

"I lied to you, Mr. Mansfeld. Virginia does not work in our works. She married a poor composer and has lived in Canada these last ten years. She cursed me before she left. She never wants to see me again. She will never accept a penny from me because I forced her to work in the family business. I wanted her to find a husband who could carry on. Then she brought this composer. I refused even to shake his hand. Friends write that they are not doing well in Canada."

"Friends?"

"Friends, Mr. Mansfeld. Virginia does not write to me. She hates me. Maybe that is why I am traveling so much."

"Mrs. Durham—"

"The Scotch is really good, isn't it?"

## [ 18 ]

When I went to Echternach to visit my mother the doctor asked me not to see her because of her poor condition. So I did not see my mother. But I saw my father and Aunt Lizzy. They came to the hotel to pick up the book I brought from Manfred Lord. The conversation was as short as it was frigid.

From Echternach I took the train to Florence. The train was crowded. I could not sleep. In Florence I was groggy and left the train. I just could not stand it any longer. A taxi took me to the Autostrada del sole. I was in luck. Soon a Ford stopped and. . . .

"The fifteen minutes are up, Mrs. Durham."

I start. The handsome bartender has brought two more Johnnies.

"Grazie, Roberto. And one for you."

"Grazie, Signora, grazie!"

The sky is colorless now. I see the first stars. The water looks black. The wake is white. It has become quiet.

"Do you know where you are going to stay?"

"No."

"Here is my address and telephone number. You are always welcome. Do you play tennis?"

"Yes."

"Bridge?"

"Yes."

"Wonderful! I know a charming couple, an English major and his wife, who also have a house in Bagno. We could play a few games together. I have a tennis court and a private beach. But of course, you are never going to call, I know."

Mrs. Durham is high and she says so.

"Does it bother you?"

"Why should it? I'm high too!"

I have never been drunk like this. So elated. So merry. We

laugh and tell each other stories. The other passengers are looking at us suspiciously.

"They think you are my gigolo," says Mrs. Durham. "I would be happy if I had a gigolo as handsome as you. He could have everything from me."

She is silent for a moment. Then she says:

"You see those lights ahead? Portoferraio!"

## [ 19 ]

We have arrived.

I see little of Portoferraio. Blue, green, white and red lights. A street. Hotels. Bar. There are many people waiting on the pier but I do not see Verena.

"There is my caretaker!" The old lady waves. "I am a little drunk. Could you drive my car off?"

"I'll be glad to, Mrs. Durham. And many thanks for everything."

"Oh, nonsense. You won't call anyway."

"Yes I will."

"Never! Here are the keys."

A man in white shirt and trousers welcomes Mrs. Durham. He kisses her hand. He takes my suitcase out of the trunk of the car and sets it down on the cobblestone road. He looks at me with distrust. He gets behind the wheel of the car and Mrs. Durham winds down her window.

"Virginia—" she can hardly talk now. "My—my daughter. You know, Mr. Mansfeld, my Virginia is—I think I was wrong." The caretaker drives off and Mrs. Durham falls back into her seat. Cars continue to drive off the ferry. I sit on my suitcase near the embankment.

"My sweetheart!"

Verena!

She is dressed in tight-fitting yellow slacks, a colorful shirt and sandals. She kisses me.

"Darling," I say. "Darling, darling."

"You are drunk!"

"Yes, darling."

"Let's go. Home."

"Why—how do you mean, 'home'?"

"My husband is in Rome. Three days."

"But the servants—"

"I've sent them away. We'll be alone."

"Evelyn?"

"Is in Corsica. With the governess. They'll be back the evening after tomorrow."

"We'll be alone . . . until then?"

"Yes, Oliver! Come! The car is over there."

"Verena! I must tell you something."

"I know."

"What do you know?"

"What you are going to tell me."

"What?"

"That you love me."

"Yes. But how did you know?"

"Instinct. What did you drink?"

"Whisky."

"I love you too, dear heart. We'll go home. I have prepared dinner for you. We can still go for a swim. It is quite warm. And then . . ."

"I hope I'll sober up."

"I hope not too much. You are adorable when you have had something to drink. Come. Come quickly. Come very quickly, away from here."

# Chapter Eight

## [ 1 ]

Nude, completely nude she runs across the white sand of the beach toward me. Her arms wide open, laughing. Her breasts, her hair glisten in the light of the southern moon. There is the bay, the stone pines and olive trees, the sea. There is the sky and its stars, the surf, warm and gentle.

Everything I saw a long time ago in my mind, in front of my inner eyes. I am nude too. The sand is wet but warm. We meet. We embrace. And no one, not a single soul sees us; we are completely alone in the bay of La Biodola.

I kiss Verena's face, her neck, her breasts. Her skin tastes salty. We are coming out of the water. It is past nine o'clock. Waves lap at us. We fall into the sea. But we fall slowly and gently onto the warm wet sand. I lie on Verena. We still hold each other tight. The returning wave washes over us. Then the next one reaches us. The third. We let the salty water roll over us and feel the sand give way beneath us, and we sink deeper and deeper.

I sink into her while wave after wave rolls over us. We are silent and our lips do not part even once. Only the moon, the stars and the black trees on the cliffs around the bay are witness.

I am still not sober. Verena has had a drink, too, so as to be as one with me in that respect. Now we are and stay as one until the end, while wave after wave, in regular tender rhythm, never tiring, never ending, washes over us.

All this I feel I have seen before, dreamed of before.

[ 2 ]

It is a large bay, a long beach. Steep cliffs rise on its sides. The road to La Biodola is good but has many hairpin turns. I was glad Verena was driving. I probably would have driven over the cliff.

The road ends a little way before reaching the sea and becomes a gravel path which leads to Mr. Lord's garage. It is reached from the beach and is only a meter above the water, hewn out of the rock on which the house is built. An electrically operated gate opens onto seventy-seven steps leading to the entrance of the house. It is practically impossible for anyone to break in. The cliffs are steep and smooth and a deep canyon separates the house from the island. Assad, behind the gate, jumps up on me and nearly throws me off balance; he licks my face and hands.

The house is much larger than it seems from the outside. Everything is extremely modern: shapes, colors, furniture, pictures. And a fireplace. It stands in front of the wall-to-wall window and through its rear wall, made of glass, one can see the sea and stars and ships with their red and green lights.

Why do I find this fireplace in bad taste?

It is so romantic to see water through fire. I know why I don't like it. Because it belongs to Mr. Lord, like everything else here, because it does not belong to me, because it was not built with my money. Because I have no money—and Mr. Lord has so much.

In front of the fireplace is a thick white carpet on which Assad lies. The house seems unreal, seems to belong to the twenty-first century! The drapes are open and one sees the black of the night or lights far, far away.

Verena serves dinner in a dining area separated by a bamboo wall from the modern kitchen. A door hides an elevator which goes down to the winecellar below the garage, below sea level!

"It cost a great deal of money to build," says Verena. She looks at me. "Poor darling, I know what you are thinking."

"What?"

"How much money he has—and how little you have."

"Yes."

"But I love you. And I don't love him."

"Then let him have his millions and the house and the elevator!"

"Do you have anything on under the robe?"

"No."

"I'm not wearing anything under the sweater either."

I notice now that she has changed into little transparent panties and a red sweater. She is barefoot.

"Is that still—"

"No. You ruined the old one; this one is new. I bought two more, just to be on the safe side. Our love has just begun, hasn't it?"

I pull her to me but she breaks free.

"First you eat," she says. "And I'll have to have a couple of Scotches to catch up with you."

"Verena, are you quite sure that no one can see us here?"

"No one." She leads me to the table and I see a vase of red roses on it.

"You are crazy!"

"But I love you, too. Sit down and eat."

"I have not brought you any flowers!"

"You have given me enough flowers. Now it is my turn. Open your robe. No, close it. Quickly! Or I have cooked this nice dinner for nothing! Now you'll see that I am capable. You want a wife who is a good cook, don't you?"

"I only want you. I don't care if you can cook or not."

"Don't say that. A wife has to be a good cook so her husband won't leave her."

"I'll never leave you!"

"Anyway. It's better I cook well."

"Verena?"

"Yes?"

She stands by the electric range.

"Take off your sweater and your panties."

"Only if you take off your robe."

"Okay!"

Verena serves Riso Fegatini e Piselli in Brodo. It tastes delicious.

"Did you ever do that before with another man?"

"Do what?"

"Cooked for him and then dined together in the nude?"

"No. Everything I do with you I have never done before with any man."

"I haven't either with a woman. Please, draw the drapes!"

"Why? No one can see us here. The kitchen windows look out on the canyon."

"Shall we—shall we eat later?"

"No. You have to become sober, and I have to become drunk."

"I love you."

"You must eat more so you will be sober and I can enjoy you. Why did you drink so much?"

"It was excitement. Because I knew I was going to see you."

"Then I'll forgive you." We are sitting opposite each other, completely nude. We look at each other all the time and food falls off our forks.

"Verena—"

"Yes. I know."

"What do you know?"

"What you want to say. Don't say it. Me too, my love, me too. But later. Later."

Naked she goes to the electric range to serve the second course.

I follow her and caress her.

"Do you like me?"
"You are the most beautiful woman in the world."
"And in ten years?"
"You will always be the most beautiful woman in the world. For me."
"Now we'll have Pagari del Golfo. Don't touch me. I'll drop everything."
"You smell of Diorissimo again!"
"Let me go! I want you to let me go! Oliver! Now! See what you made me do? Everything is on the floor!"
"I'll eat off the floor, too. I love you. I love you."

[ 3 ]

We lock up Assad. Verena has another drink. We draw the drapes. Verena is tight now, too. She turns on the radio. Sentimental music, sad music. Radio Roma. We lie on the white carpet in front of the fireplace. We kiss. We caress. Whisky, soda and ice are close at hand. We drink. The flames in the transparent fireplace flicker and blaze.

Radio Roma apparently plays only for lovers.

Violins. Sentimental voices.

*Sull'eco de concerto . . .*

*Ovunque sei, se ascolterai . . .*

*Accanto a te mi troverai . . .*

Whenever you hear this concerto . . .
You will be with me . . .

"We shall never lose each other, Oliver."
"No."
"We shall always love each other."
"Yes."
She cries a little and my chest is wet with her tears.
"What is it?"
"It's nothing, really."
"Tell me!"

"This is a new song. *Il nostro concerto.*"

"Our concerto."

"Yes. And they're playing it today. They are playing it now . . ."

"You destroyed the record. 'Love Is Just a Word.' Now we have a new song."

"Yes, our song. Our concerto."

"Is that why you are crying?"

"No, not because of that. Kiss me. But don't ask . . ."

The flames in the fireplace are blazing. Far away a ship's whistle sounds. The beach is bathed in the green light of the moon.

"But I want to know. Why are you crying? Don't say you're crying because you are happy!"

"Because I'm afraid to be happy. I had a dream, last night. It was terrifying. I loved you in my dream. We were sitting here, by this fire, we were alone, we. . . . Everything was exactly the way it is now! I heard this song, too! They play it often!" She clings to me, her nails digging into my back.

"Verena!"

"When the song was over and the announcer came on, but it wasn't the announcer. . . . It was . . . it was—God."

"What did He say to you?"

*"dove serai mi troverai vicino a te . . ."*

Violins. Many violins.

"He said: 'This is Radio Roma. Signora Lord . . . Signora Lord . . . the man with whom you are now, the man with whom you are so happy . . . No, I can't go on."

"Tell me!"

" 'You are damned,' " God said. " 'You are damned. The life you have been leading is damned. You wanted riches. You married a man you did not love. You have been unfaithful to him from the beginning.' "

Violins. Only violins. The song is over.

" 'You will never be happy. Only for a little while will you be happy. You are guilty, Verena Lord. You want two things. You pit one against the other. You are destroying a young human being. You are evil.' "

"Stop it!"

" 'One day you will stand in front of Me, and I will judge you.' "

The music has stopped.

A man's voice: *"Qui Radio Roma. . . ."*

Verena screams. She presses her hands to her temples and stares at the white radio.

"Verena!"

"That's the voice! That is exactly how God's voice sounded!"

" *. . . abbiamo trasmesso 'Il nostro concerto' con Enso Ceragidi e la sua orchestra e il vocal Comet."*

"It's going to come to a bad end! It can't turn out well!"

Music begins again. This time a woman sings.

"Verena, please! Please, stop it. We are so happy!"

"Just because we are so happy. The voice said that, too. One can only live once. One cannot discard one's past as one can a dress. And my past was dirty—too dirty!"

"That's not true!"

"It is true. My present is dirty too! If I were put to the test some day, the voice said—"

The telephone begins to ring.

Verena stops. Both of us are staring at the telephone on a low table.

It rings again.

"You must answer it!"

"Who could that be?"

It rings a third time. I get up and turn down the radio.

"Come on! Answer it!"

She takes a few hesitant steps, lifts the receiver to her ear and returns to the white carpet.

Her voice is shaky, hoarse: "Pronto." A pause.

"Sì, Signorina, sì."

She places her hand over the mouthpiece and whispers: "My husband."

"What?"

"From Rome."

I move closer to her: "You must pull yourself together, Verena."

"Sì, Signorina, grazie. . . . Hello! Hello, Manfred?"

Now she is calm, terrifyingly calm. Terrifying because a moment ago she was terrifyingly hysterical.

I kiss her neck and I too can hear Manfred Lord's voice, the sonorous voice of this sonorous man.

"Darling, did I wake you?"

"No, why do you ask?"

I kiss Verena's shoulders.

"What are you doing?"

"I—I'm reading."

"I just got back to the hotel. I missed you terribly tonight. Did you miss me, too?"

"Excuse me?"

"The connection is not very good, is it?"

"No. What did you say?"

I kiss Verena's breast.

"I missed you terribly tonight! So I decided to call you the minute I got back to the hotel. The conference was long."

I kiss Verena's arms.

"Was it—was it very tiring, Manfred?"

"Do you have your radio on? I can hear it. I have one here in my room too. I just listened to 'Il nostro concerto.' Did you hear it too?"

"Yes."

I kiss Verena's hands, every finger, each fingertip. She caresses me.

"It is a lovely song, isn't it?"

"Yes, Manfred."

"How is Evelyn?"

"She insisted on going to Corsica. So I let her go with the signorina."

"Why didn't you go too?"

"Well, I just didn't feel like going. You know . . ."

I kiss Verena's body.

". . . . I'd rather rest. I feel so tired. I'm just lying on the beach all day. When will you come back?"

"Unfortunately I shall have to stay here another six days, darling."

"Six days?" Now Verena kisses my hand, my fingers.

"I'm so sorry. But the negotiations are taking a long time. I'll come as soon as I can. I'll call you again tomorrow about this time, if it is all right with you."

I kiss her thighs.

"I—I'm looking forward to it."

"Sleep well. Take care."

"You too. Take care."

She replaces the receiver and looks at me with her huge dark eyes. We don't speak. The fire is crackling. Verena suddenly jumps up and runs out of the room. I remain finishing my drink. I prepare two drinks, sit down in front of the fireplace and light a cigarette. They are playing *Arrivederci Roma.*

Two soft arms enfold me. Verena smells of soap and Diorissimo. Her breasts are pressed against my back. She kisses my neck.

"Forget what I said awhile ago."

"I have already forgotten it."

"It was nonsense. Everybody has dreams like that some time or other . . . and we love each other."

"Yes."

"Everything will turn out well, won't it?"

"All will be well."

"Do that again. Please, do that again. A little higher. Yes, there. Gentle, very gently."

"I do whatever you want—for as long as you want."

"You are wonderful. I love you . . . I truly love you . . . do you believe me?"

"Yes."

"The whisky! You fixed a Scotch for me!"

"Don't spill it."

"I won't. Yes, like that—do it like that!"

The fireplace. The flames. The water beyond it. On the shimmering sea in the distance another light, the light of a ship in the night, glides past.

[ 4 ]

When I awake the fire has burned down. The clock shows ten minutes past four. Verena, in her sleep, holds me tightly clasped in her arms. Before going to sleep we turned off the lights and opened the drapes and a window. In the east the sky is becoming light. I watch it changing color minute by minute. I see the sea changing from black to gray and then green. Then the sun rises. The sea is blinding me. Verena's breath is even and quiet. Higher and higher rises the sun; the cliffs catch its light, many red blossoms open on the bushes growing at the edge of the woods above the brown-and-yellow sun-scorched slopes. I am lying alongside Verena and dream how it will be living together, always. Perhaps one day we will own a house, too. Perhaps I will earn a lot of money.

At seven o'clock I gently free myself of her embrace and go to the kitchen to start breakfast. When the water for coffee boils I hear a noise. It sounds like sobbing. I turn around.

Verena, her eyes still red from sleep.

She is naked and, holding onto the door, stammers:

"Oliver—"

"Darling, what is it?"

"You were gone when I woke up. I—I got so scared. I thought you had left."

"You believe that?"

"Yes. . . . Hold me—hold me tight. Stay with me . . ."

"But I am with you! I'll never leave you!"

"Never?"

"Never ever!"

"Come to my room."

The water has boiled away, the kettle is broken. We heard it, but we didn't bother about it. We ate at nine o'clock. We were very hungry.

[ 5 ]

One can see Corsica. A black line on the horizon. Verena's motorboat is very comfortable. We are so far out to sea we cannot see our bay any more. We brought along wine, cold chicken and bread. The bottles of wine are suspended from the boat into the water. The sun is hot but there is a steady breeze. The water is very clear and in its depth one can see many fish and jellyfish of the most beautiful colors: gold, red, green, blue, yellow and silver. We are far away from people so we take off our swim suits and jump naked into the sea. We swim around the boat, embrace and sink down. Verena swallows a lot of water. I do too. We climb back into the boat and cling to each other. Fuse into each other. The boat rocks gently.

We pull up a bottle of wine. Naked, we sit in the little boat, eating chicken with our fingers and drink wine from the bottles.

And no one can see us.

The boat drifts. We are lying on an air mattress. We smoke a cigarette together.

"Do you believe that you will always love me?"

"Always, Verena."

"I rented a room for you in Casaccia, darling. It is a tiny village south of Portoferraio. You must live close to the water so I can pick you up with the boat at any time. The room is very cheap. I—I thought I would be able to give you some money here but my husband is very peculiar these last few weeks. I even have to balance my household budget. I have a little money, but not much."

"I have enough."

"I think you'll like Casaccia. And you will be safer there than in Portoferraio. He might see you there. He is there quite often. It would be too dangerous."

"Yes, Verena. You are right. And if you should not be able to come sometimes I can write our story. I brought a lot of paper and pencils."

She kisses me.

"Open another bottle, Oliver."

"But then we'll be high!"

"So what? The day is ours. We'll stay on the boat until tonight."

"Wonderful!"

"So open the bottle."

We drink the wine and I feel myself getting drunk. I must be drunk or I would not say:

"If you ever leave me I shall die."

"Nonsense."

"No, it is true."

"Give me the bottle. Thanks. And don't say things like that."

"Will you leave me some day?"

"Never!"

"Yes, you will."

"Oliver!"

"I'm not angry. I am just so afraid of it."

"Can the roots leave the tree?"

The boat rocks gently. Ships in the distance. Vapor trails of airplanes in the sky. The wine. The sun.

## [ 6 ]

We went along the north coast, through the bay of Prochio, past Bagno, where Mrs. Durham lives. We dressed as we approached the coast. We saw dark-green forests and, on steep cliffs, modern villas in luxuriant flowing gardens. We are sitting on the terrace of a bar in Marciana Marina, by the only road that seems to exist here.

We are drinking Chianti and watch the fishermen ready their boats for the nightly fishing trip. They laugh and joke. They are very poor and so happy. In Germany many people are very rich, but when do they laugh and when are they happy?

The sun is setting.

Suddenly we hear a song from the huge American juke box standing outside the bar. It is loud enough for the entire village to hear it.

*"Sull'eco del concerto. . . ."*

"Our concerto," says Verena.

We do not talk. We look at one another until the song has come to an end. The fishing boats are leaving. The hoisted sails look as red as blood in the light of the setting blood-red sun. I have never known a day like today.

"I have never known a day like today," says Verena at that moment.

Silence. Verena looks into the distance.

"What are you thinking of?" I ask.

"I thought, if I had to die now, at this moment, at this second, I would have died happier than any woman before me."

And the sails of the boats gliding silently out to sea are as red as blood.

[ 7 ]

Naturally, it could be my guilty conscience, but since my arrival in Elba the feeling of someone watching Verena and me oppresses me. I can't ever say: That is the one! You, what do you want from us? Get away from here or I'll knock your teeth out! No, it is not like that. Who, among the hundreds of people I meet and see every day, is it? What does he look like? I believe it is a man. But perhaps it is a woman? Or a man *and* a woman? However, it might just be my imagination. Guilty conscience. That's why I do not mention it to Verena. But this feeling, this feeling. . . .

Casaccia is a tiny village.

The family Mortula accepts me as one of their family. Grandfather Remo, eighty years old, often tells stories; he had worked for a while in Germany. His constant phrase is "*Dio ci aiuterà*—God will help us." The Mortula family is enormous. They all live in a white two-story house. Three, four people share a tiny room so as to have the large, tastelessly furnished rooms empty and ready for visitors. Not many tourists come to this out-of-the-way place and the ones that do move out soon because it is not smart enough. The gas station next to the house does not bring enough money to feed such a large family. Antonio, the owner, grumbles. Grandfather Remo says "*Dio ci aiuterà.*"

I learn Italian quickly. My Italian is probably atrocious but already I can understand a great deal. And I write my book. The table I write on stands by the window. I see the sea, the ships, coming and going and I know in a few hours I shall go to the beach and there will be Verena's boat, there will be Verena. And we will go out to sea and love each other, beneath the blue sky, far away from people.

Verena now has only hours she can spend with me because her husband has returned. She has to be with Evelyn, too. But not one day passes that I do not see her, that we do not love one another. Bottles of wine are always cooling in the water. We drink. I never drank very much. Now I do. I think it is not good, even though later, far out at sea, we are very very happy and Verena says: "One ought to be drunk all the time."

I don't know. . . . Thank God Evelyn is afraid of the boat and never wants to come along. Thank God, Manfred Lord is either very busy or asleep and resting at the house of glass. Thank God, Verena has had this boat for years and it is well known how crazy she is about it. It is not unusual to see her racing through the water. Close to the shore I lie on the floor of the boat so as not to be seen by acquaintances, but most of the time we go far out to sea where we cannot be seen. There we drink wine, jump into the water and make love after that, and I read to Verena what I have written. She says it is good.

Is it good? I don't know.

Whenever Verena has an afternoon free we drive to Marciana Marina and sit in the bar and listen to the juke box playing *"Il nostro concerto"* as often as we want. It is a trashy song. The melody is trashy. The vocalist sings trashy. Everything is trashy. But is *our* song. We hold hands, watching the fishing boats go out to sea in the red rays of a blood-red setting sun.

[ 8 ]

In the coolness of one afternoon we walked inland from Porto Azzurro. We came to an olive grove where we stay because Verena said she could not take another step without seducing me. So we embrace under an old olive tree. Afterward we drink Chianti. (Good intentions!) An olive lands on my back. I put it in my pocket.

"Milton," says Verena.

"Why Milton?"

"He did something like that, too."

"How do you know?"

"I'm not quite as uneducated as you think."

"I don't think—"

"Yes, you do. All my men have thought so. But I happen to know the story of Milton and the olive."

"Only I'm not yet seventy and blind and impotent."

"No, dearest. You are right there. You are a marvelous lover. There, now you've heard it. Become overconceited! Be unfaithful to me! Leave me!"

"I shall never become arrogant. I shall never be unfaithful to you. You are my true love—my only love, my only love. Without you there is nothing."

"Say that again."

"You are my only love. My true love. Without you there is nothing."

[ 9 ]

On any day when Verena cannot see me and I don't feel like writing I go to Portoferraio. To the narrow streets beyond the Piazza della Repubblica. I hang around. I sit at sidewalk cafés and drink espresso. I watch old men arguing as if they are going to come to blows at any moment. I look at small shops, ships arriving from Piombino, the yachts of the rich in the harbor, and the yacht of Mr. Lord, too. It is a very beautiful yacht.

There are two jewelers in the Piazza Cavour. One of them cheats, Grandfather Remo told me. But he has the more beautiful rings, necklaces and bracelets. My father's radio and TV factories are also much larger than those of most others. The one who cheats always has the better things. That is a fact one cannot change. One morning I see a gold bracelet, narrow strips of gold, one next to the other, connected by loops. I fall in love with this bracelet. Love at first sight! I have never given Verena an expensive present. Inside the shop a little man with oily hair, rubbing his hands, tells me the price for the bracelet is ten thousand lire. And only because gold is so inexpensive in Italy.

After bargaining with him for half an hour the price is down to eight thousand lire. Since that is all the money I have, I pay three thousand lire to have the bracelet set aside and promise to pick it up in a few days. Summer, heat, sea and the island have made me lose my reason. Will Verena ever be able to wear the bracelet? No matter. I want her to have it. Even if she has to hide it in her safety deposit box. I want her to have it. But where do I get the money to pay for it?

## [ 10 ]

Strangely enough I have found a way to solve that problem. On the Piazza della Repubblica, a very busy square, is a modern store for photographic materials. One day I see a man place a notice in his shop window. By now I have learned sufficient Italian to understand. The signor is looking for an assistant. Signor Fellanzoni, the owner, can explain his problem to me since I speak English and Signor Fellanzoni had been an American prisoner of war. (I realize how war can bring people closer together. Signor Fellanzoni and I can talk together! If Hitler had not started a world war Signor Fellanzoni would not have learned English in a POW camp. Do I have to be grateful to Hitler? There should be less bloody means to learn foreign languages free of charge.) I accept the offer of a job developing films at night. Since I don't know how to develop films Signor Fellanzoni promises to teach me.

"When can you start?"

"Tomorrow night."

I am spending the day with Verena. She is picking me up at ten o'clock. Her husband has gone to Genoa.

"At times you might not be finished until two or three o'clock."

"I don't mind, Signor Fellanzoni."

I do want to give Verena the bracelet!

## [ 11 ]

Now I work every evening. Sometimes it really is two or three o'clock before I finish. Signor Fellanzoni has an enormous amount of films to be developed. I take the last bus to Casaccia or, if I miss it, sleep in the store. Signor Fellanzoni has great trust in me and has given me the keys to the store. He is satisfied with my work and pays me each night. I have bargained with the jeweler in the Piazza Cavour again and the price is now seven thousand lire.

The fourteenth of August!

I remember the day because it is my mother's birthday and I had sent her flowers by wire. I could not see Verena all day; she and her husband are invited somewhere. So I arrived at the store at eight o'clock. For a change there is not much to be done. Signor Fellanzoni is just about to close the store when a car comes to a screaming halt. A Ford. English plates. An old lady alights from the car. Her skin is so sunburned it has the appearance of leather. She recognizes me immediately and comes running in the store.

"Mister Mansfeld!"

Mrs. Durham! What can I do!

[ 12 ]

The nice lady who is so lonesome. The nice lady I wish would go away.

"Mrs. Durham."

"You are not working here all the time, are you?"

"Only once in a while, to make some money."

She gives three rolls of film to Signor Fellanzoni to be developed. Then comes the question I have dreaded:

"You have never called me, Mr. Mansfeld!"

"I'm sorry but I have been very busy."

"Are you very busy tonight, too?"

"Yes, I am."

"Signor Fellanzoni" (in Italian now) "does he have very much to do?"

"Not very much, Signora."

"Could Signor Mansfeld come with me tonight? I have waited a long time for him to come and see me."

"Naturally, Signora. If Signor Mansfeld is an old friend of yours—"

"Signor Fellanzoni, several of the films are very urgent."

"But the Signora invited you! You can easily do the work tomorrow."

"That's very nice of you but—I'm not dressed to—"

"We'll go to your hotel and you can change. Where are you staying?" I tell her.

"I'm drunk, I'm sure you noticed. I'm always drunk here. My caretaker drives me, you don't have to be afraid, Mr. Mansfeld. You'll change, we'll have dinner together and my man will take you home. You can have a few drinks too. Don't be afraid; I'm not going to seduce you! Isn't this a shy young man, Signor Fellanzoni?"

"Yes, Signora, very shy indeed!"

## [ 13 ]

Mrs. Durham's house was built ten years ago atop a hill above the water of the bay. There are stone floors, partly inlaid with mosaic. It is very comfortably equipped but "No radio! No television. I only need newspapers, and only those once in a while. I want peace here."

Mrs. Durham drinks whisky. I drink wine.

Dinner is served by a dark-skinned girl from Elba. Mrs. Durham has already had six whiskies. It shows. On one wall hangs a portrait of a beautiful young woman. I don't have to ask; I know. It is Mrs. Durham's daughter Virginia. Every time Mrs. Durham looks at the picture I am afraid she is going to cry. But she does not cry. She just takes another sip of her drink.

Even here I have the feeling of being watched, followed, shadowed. It can only be my guilty conscience.

After dinner we play a game of écarté. I'm just thinking that in half an hour I might be able to leave when the caretaker calls Mrs. Durham to the telephone. Her cheeks are flushed when she returns.

"Quickly, come, come!"

"I beg your pardon?"

"Quick! Let's go!"

"Go where?"

"To Major Ingram."

"But Mrs. Durham—"

"No, no, no. You don't know what's happened in Germany! We must go to Major Ingram. It's only five minutes' walk. Quickly. Let's go. The Italian radio and television are broadcasting special reports! Perhaps there will be a third world war!"

"Mrs. Durham, please tell me what happened!"

"This Mr. Ulbricht ordered a wall to be built, yesterday, on a Sunday! It separates West Berlin from East Berlin. No one can get through. Families were separated. Man and wife, friend and friend. Major Ingram says Eurovision is showing a special report from Berlin."

## [ 14 ]

I have to help Mrs. Durham walk along the path to her friend's house. The moon is shining. Huge toads are sitting on the path and we have to be careful not to step on them. Donkeys are neighing in their straw huts.

"The Major was so excited he could hardly talk," says Mrs. Durham. "He was in the invasion, at Allied headquarters, and just now he said, 'Elizabeth,' he said, 'it damn well smells of war.' "

When we arrive at the Major's white house he opens the door for us. He looks like Winston Churchill's twin. Hefty. Wide-faced. Clever. A cigar and a glass of whisky in his hand. He kisses Mrs. Durham and shakes my hand.

"I didn't know Elizabeth had company. But you are German, Mr. Mansfeld, aren't you? Please come in. The broadcast is going to start in ten minutes. It must be of interest to you. Your country, right?"

"Surely, Major."

Mrs. Durham hiccoughs.

"My poor dear, you need a Scotch, right now!"

The Major walks ahead. We follow. On the television screen in the living room a black-haired singer sings a sentimental song. (Why does he remind me of Enrico Sabbadini?)

Major Ingram introduces us.

There are a few more people sitting before a fireplace.

Mrs. Ingram, for instance.

Verena, for instance.

Manfred Lord, for instance.

# Chapter Nine

[ 1 ]

There is naked horror in Verena's eyes.

What ought I to do? What can I do? I did not know they were invited to Major Ingram's. I did not know that Manfred Lord, as he smilingly tells me, and the Major are old friends.

Is it a mere accident?

"Oliver!" Arms stretched out, Manfred Lord comes toward me. "Well, what a surprise! I am so happy to see you! Verena, would you believe it?"

Before Verena could answer Mrs. Ingram says:

"Oh, you know each other?"

"Not just know each other! We are good, old friends! Since when are you on the island, Oliver?"

"I—"

Just then Mrs. Durham feels very ill.

"Excuse me, Mr. Lord. Just one moment."

I help Mrs. Durham to the bathroom. She comes out a little later.

"It must have been the ravioli. It couldn't have been the drinks. How do I look?"

"Fine."

"I put on a new face after I—"

"Mrs. Durham, I have a favor to ask."

"Yes?"

"I don't know if you can help me."

"I'll try."

"The couple, the people who are here at Major Ingram's, I know them. Would you . . . would you lie for me?"

"Lie? How?"

"Would you say that we have known each other for years, and that I arrived here only yesterday?"

"I don't understand."

"I'll explain later. Would you do that for me?" She looks at me, her eyes unsteady.

"Would you do something for me, too?" And when I don't answer: "Naturally, you won't. It would be asking too much. I think I understand. You can rely on me."

"Can I really?"

"Oh, sure. Too bad I'm not Mrs. Lord. But one can't have everything, right?"

We go back to the living room and Mrs. Durham says what an old friend of hers I am and how she met me at the boat yesterday. Her speech is a little slurred; she had had a lot to drink. But it works.

Does it?

In Verena's eyes is an expression of desperation, in Manfred Lord's eyes one of triumph.

"Where are you staying, Oliver?" asks Mr. Lord.

"In a small hotel near Portoferraio."

"Well, we can't have that! Starting tomorrow you are going to stay with us! I won't take no for an answer! My wife will like that, too, won't you, darling?"

She nods.

"In three days I have to be in Rome. I can't tell you how happy I am that you decided to come to Elba. You can keep my wife company. And people here are not as base as they are in Germany."

"That's right, Mr. Lord. That is why I thought I could visit you here without starting any rumors."

Mr. Lord has to laugh at that.

"This talk," he says. "Always this talk."

Eurovision is showing the wall, the closed-off Brandenburg Gate, East German tanks, barbed wire, everything. An Italian reporter narrates. We see pictures which shock us deeply. Germans ready to shoot at Germans. A young girl, just married. Now she stands crying in front of her parents' house. The doors to the house have been bricked up. In a third-floor window we can see the parents. The mother is crying. In an effort to console his wife the father puts an arm around his wife's shoulder, and he, too, has to reach for a handkerchief. They cannot even give their children, standing downstairs, their presents. Packages and flowers are lowered from the window to them.

We are all terribly stirred. A discussion begins. Mrs. Durham cries like the old lady in Berlin. Manfred Lord is even friendlier toward me than before.

[ 2 ]

The next day I leave the Mortula household and move into the house of glass on La Biodola. I leave my manuscript with Grandfather Remo and tell him that I will pick it up when I leave the island.

"Did something happen?"

"Yes."

"Something bad?"

"Yes."

"God will help."

Will He?

Now I spend days and nights in Mr. Lord's house, on his beach, by his side. When he goes on a trip he makes sure that the servants remain. Now Verena and I have to go far, far out to sea to make love; fortunately Evelyn still fears the boat.

When I met Evelyn alone she apologized for having been so naughty to me in Frankfurt. As small as she is she understood something of what is going on. She told me she would try to be patient, but how much longer would she have to wait?

"Until Christmas."

## [ 3 ]

The weather is still beautiful but occasional rainy days and stormy seas proclaim the coming fall. Soon we shall all have to go home.

I stopped working for Signor Fellanzoni when I had earned sufficient money to pay for the bracelet. Mr. Lord is very busy. He suggests trips to Marciana Marina. To Porto Azzurro. He mentions all the places Verena and I have visited and smiles sweetly without taking his eyes off me. So we take Verena's boat and go. It is a beautiful day but we feel very sad. But at last we can talk. I have thought whether or not to tell Verena my feeling of being watched. I had not mentioned it so as not to frighten her. Now I must. She stares at me.

"Someone is watching us?"

"Since I came to Elba. I am convinced of it. On behalf of your husband. I am also convinced that the meeting at the Ingrams was arranged. I'm convinced your husband knows everything, is informed of everything." Verena is very pale now. Her face seems even smaller, her eyes even larger.

"But—but if he knows everything why doesn't he say anything? Why did he invite you to his house? Why does he leave us alone?"

"I can't prove it, but I have a theory."

"Which is?"

"Your husband knows—how, I don't know—of those photographs of the perforated pages in your safe. He wants to have more proof against us to be able to say someday: Let's have those photographs! He does not have to agree to a divorce. Never. He can tell me never to come to his house again and send you on a trip around the world, or he can take me to court for adultery."

"No!"

"Oh yes. I have made inquiries. It does not occur very often. When it does the guilty party can be sent to prison. We won't have any choice: he gets the photographs and I get you."

"All that sounds too fantastic!"

"Really? Does it? Then I'll have to tell you another thing. I told you my father took my car. The truth is—"

I tell her the truth. It is the only thing to do considering the circumstances.

"You—you believe Leo acted on his behalf, too?"

"I am not sure. But he took photographs of us leaving the little house. Why couldn't your husband have said: Leo, go to Elba and carry on?"

"You really believe he instructed Leo to blackmail us?"

"Yes. The methods are similar. But even supposing Leo works for himself and shows the photographs to your husband—the result will be the same."

"I feel sick, Oliver."

"I do too, Verena. I do too."

## [ 4 ]

This afternoon we are once more on the terrace of the little bar in Marciana Marina, watching the fishermen, drinking wine and holding hands. It is as sad as it is ridiculous because just as I am giving Verena the bracelet she takes a gold wristwatch from the pocket of her blouse and says: "I have a present for you!"

Inscribed on the watch is:

*With Love—Verena*
*ELBA 1961*

Inscribed on the bracelet is:

*With Love—Oliver*
*ELBA 1961*

Verena is almost hysterical, laughing.

"What is so funny?"

She stops laughing and I see tears in her eyes.

"My dear—my dearest! I noticed you had no watch when you arrived here so I wanted to give you one but I told you my husband watches every penny I spend lately, so I took this bracelet to a jeweler in Portoferraio—"

"In the Piazza Repubblica?"

"Yes. He took it on consignment. I paid some money to have them set the watch aside. The jeweler said as soon as he could sell the bracelet I could have the watch. Now he has sold it!"

"To me! And you have your own bracelet back!"

"But you have a new watch. How did you get the money to buy the bracelet?"

I tell her.

"If you had not worked for Signor Fellanzoni you might not have met Mrs. Durham again. And ended up at the Ingrams."

"Possibly not at the Ingrams but with your husband nevertheless. I tell you he has a spy here. He plays a cat-and-mouse game with us. I'm positive we are being watched this very minute. There might even be a new photograph of us in existence!"

"I wish time would hurry up. I can't stand it much longer."

"Three months, Verena, only three more months!"

We give the watch and bracelet to Grandfather Remo for safekeeping.

"Gladly. God will help," he says.

[ 5 ]

Now we are invited to the Ingrams' and Mrs. Durham's for tea. To play tennis. Almost always Manfred Lord is there too.

"My old friend Ingram! I wonder when we shall meet again? Now everything is so uncertain. Will there be a war? Will there be peace? Let's be merry, friends!"

Merry!!

My last happy day on the island which I remember was the twenty-ninth of August. A strong northeast wind was blowing and the waves of the deep-green sea were as high as little houses. Verena still insisted on going swimming. The surf hampered us both but after we got away a little from the shore the water carried us way, way out. We did not have to swim; the waves and the high salt content of the water kept us afloat.

Far, far away is the shore.

Then we hold each other, going up and down with the waves. Our bodies are entwined, our lips pressed together.

When I am torn from Verena by a huge wave for a second I see the reflection of two shiny points on the shore. But I don't mention that to Verena. They must be the lenses of binoculars; someone watching us. I wonder who it might be?

On the first of September we leave Elba.

The weather is very bad. Many people aboard ship are seasick. I am sitting on deck with Evelyn. Manfred Lord is drinking whisky. Verena stands by the rail looking out to sea. Her hair is flying in the wind.

Three more months. Only three more months. Why do I feel again that I will have to die? I drink a whisky, too. But it does not help. The feeling is very, very strong today.

I am at my lowest point. Manfred Lord stands, glass in hand, smiling at me. I cannot stand this smile. My nerves are shot.

I have no more money. As Verena's lover I am ashamed of having to accept my return ticket from her husband. But Mrs. Durham is staying on the island. So Manfred Lord, Verena, Evelyn and her dog and I are going to Florence in a new Mercedes 300. We talk very little. It is raining. It is chilly.

In Florence we have two hours until the train leaves. Mr. Lord is handing the car documents and key to the chauffeur who is waiting for us at the garage near the railroad station. He is going to buy some jewelry for his wife on the Via Vittorio Emanuele.

He suggests I look around for a little while until the train leaves. He hands me my train ticket. We'd best meet on the train.

So I walk through Florence and look at many beautiful buildings and bridges and many, many people. I walk for a long time and have to use my last money for a taxi so as not to miss my train.

Evelyn has a compartment. I have one and Manfred Lord and his wife share one. After dinner Evelyn goes to bed. We drink Chianti, which Manfred Lord brought along. And another glass. And another.

The wine is strong and I have to be careful not to drink too much and talk.

"Good night, Madame. Good night, Mr. Lord."

"Sleep well, Oliver. Sweet dreams!"

He practically pushes Verena ahead of himself so she has no chance even to look at me. I go to my compartment. The conductor comes and asks for my passport. And hands me a sealed envelope.

"What is this?"

"I don't know. The lady in number fourteen asked me to give it to you."

When I am alone again I tear it open. Inside is a little record. On the label I read *Il Nostro Concerto.*

## [ 6 ]

School has started.

The old familiar faces, old friends, old enemies. The chief, the teachers, the pedagogues. All except Mr. Herterich. He now works at a gas station on the Autobahn. He is supposed to have said to Hansi:

"Here I earn three hundred marks more and I don't have to fret over you children."

It's a point of view.

Geraldine came back tanned and in good humor. She says all she did was lie on the beach at Cape Canaveral. She is friendly and I think our problem has been solved by time. I am a "smart fool," as Noah describes me. He is back, too. And Chichita. And Wolfgang.

Thomas did not come back. He wrote a very sad letter to us. His father insisted on his attending a boarding school at Fontainbleau, headquarters of NATO.

## [ 7 ]

Since Evelyn is attending school, too, Verena now has to live in Frankfurt.

Twice Verena and I pick her up from school. She is so small and looks very cute in her pretty dresses with her big bookbag. She is happy when we pick her up and we always get her ice cream.

Once we take a taxi to the old café where we used to meet. It is not there any more. A modern, new candy store is in its place, with pretty salesgirls and a fat manager.

Later, in the taxi, Verena says sadly: "Our café . . . our cognac . . . our waiter——"

## [ 8 ]

This is the worst time of my life!

I can only embrace Verena when her husband is away on a trip. I have no money. I have no car. Aunt Lizzy writes that my mother is very ill and will probably never leave the institution.

Whenever it is possible Verena comes to Friedheim for the afternoon. But it is not as it used to be. Fearfully and carefully we walk through the woods, remembering how lovely it was in Elba, in the green waves, in Marciana Marina, in Porto Azzurro.

Sometimes we go to the "Angel of the Lord." The leaves are changing color and are again golden, red, brown and yellow. The year has passed quickly as never before. Sister Claudia is happy to see us again. We sit on the bench in the park holding hands and the minutes fly by. We both know that Verena has to return to Frankfurt and that we can only telephone each other during the following days (whenever possible).

On a sunny, mild afternoon in October someone is coming through the park toward us. We think it might be Sister Claudia but then we recognize Geraldine.

I jump up.

She is very composed.

"Hello, Oliver," she says pleasantly. "Don't you want to introduce me to Mrs. Lord?"

I do it, stuttering.

Geraldine sits down on the bench. Her voice is matter-of-fact:

"You know that I stole your bracelet, Mrs. Lord. I know that you and Oliver are lovers. He left me because of you. I am very embarrassed but I still love him."

The wind rustles the trees, leaves fall from them, and Verena does not say one single word. I don't either. Only Geraldine continues:

"I have tried hard to forget my love. I cannot. There is only one thing left for me to do. I detest doing it because it is so mean."

"What do you intend to do?" asks Verena.

"Your husband is away on a trip, isn't he?"

"Yes."

"That is why you can be here. He is returning the day after tomorrow, isn't he?"

"How do you know?"

"That's my business. So the day after tomorrow I shall talk to him."

"About what?"

"Mrs. Lord, when school started again Oliver was surprised to see me so tanned. I told him then that I had been lying on the beach in Florida. I didn't even go to Cape Canaveral."

"You didn't—"

"Can't you understand me? My dear father wrote me before vacation time he had no time and I couldn't come to him. I couldn't go to Berlin either. My mother called me and said her second husband would divorce her if I came."

"Well?"

"I talked to Hansi. Hansi is so smart. He told me to see Leo. You know who that is, Mrs. Lord."

Verena is silent.

"Leo invited me on a trip to Elba."

"That is not true!"

"It's true all right. Do you want proof? Do you want to see photographs? From Marciana Marina? From Portoferraio? We took color photographs."

"What do you mean *we?*"

"Oh, I forgot to tell you. Leo introduced me to a young man. His name is Otto Wilfried."

"My—brother!"

"Yes, I believe he did say he was your brother, Mrs. Lord. A charming young man. We had a great time together!"

"You were both in Elba?"

"What's wrong with your hearing? Otto—excuse the familiarity, Mrs. Lord—your brother and I became very close friends. Otto happened to be on vacation too, at that time. He takes such marvelous photographs. Not like me. Leo lent us his expensive camera." Geraldine laughs. " 'Four eyes see more than two,' he said. And they did. They saw everything."

"At least now I know—"

"My brother, that blackguard! For money he'll do—"

"Please, Mrs. Lord! I love Otto."

"You? You'd love anybody! You would love Leo if he had not been smart enough to keep his hands off you. Where are the photographs?"

"Well, we had so many. We gave them to Leo for developing."

"That's right up his alley, isn't it?"

"What is?"

"Taking photographs."

"Why? Other people take photographs, too."

"Get out of here!"

"I'm going. I'm going, dearest. You'll probably ask yourself why I came here since Mr. Lord is going to see the photographs in two days anyway. Well, I just wanted to meet you, Mrs. Lord—meet the woman Oliver preferred to me. Your taste is not very good, Oliver."

## [ 9 ]

"I see only one possibility," says Sister Claudia.

"Which is?"

"You are going to get married?"

"Yes."

"Then you'll have to tell Mr. Lord. As quickly as possible. You'll have to talk to Mr. Lord before this—what is her name?"

"Geraldine."

"Before she does. You'll have to tell him the truth. Only then do I see a chance of his giving up his wife and avoiding a scandal."

"I suppose you know, Mrs. Lord, that in the event of a divorce you, as the guilty party, will not receive even one penny?"

"I know that."

"Then tell him the truth. As quickly as possible. You will just have to be sure of one thing."

"Of what?"

"Of whether or not you love each other sufficiently," says Sister Claudia. "That is the one prerequisite. If either of you is not quite certain the whole affair is going to come to a sad end."

"We are certain," says Verena.

"We are very certain," I say.

"Then talk to Mr. Lord," says Sister Claudia.

## [ 10 ]

"Mr. Lord—"

"Manfred—"

The banker waves his hand gently.

"Now, now, my dear children," he says.

He returned two hours ago; we have been waiting for him in his villa in Frankfurt. Once again we are sitting before the fireplace where a crackling fire is burning. (It is cold early this year.) Mr. Lord smiles as he fixes a stiff drink for himself since we refused his offer of one.

"We are not your dear children," I say. "I came here because we have something to tell you. And because we want to tell you before you hear it from someone else."

Mr. Lord takes a sip and says calmly: "But I already know."

"What do you know?"

"Everything there is to know, dear child."

"Since when?"

Manfred Lord deliberates ironically, smoothing down his white hair. "Almost from the beginning," he replies pleasantly and takes another drink.

"You're sure, you wouldn't like a drink, Oliver?"

"Yes. Quite sure. You're bluffing!"

"I?" Manfred Lord's smile grows tired. He walks to a window. "Would you please come here, Oliver, and take a look at something?" I go to him and look out into the autumnal park surrounding the house. On the leaf-strewn gravel drive stands my white Jaguar.

"Yes?"

"Now you can have your car back. Here are the keys and papers." He holds them out to me and I take them automatically. Lord is walking up and down the room.

"You see, Oliver—"

"Mr. Lord—"

"Now *I* talk! You are in *my* house. We are not getting anywhere interrupting each other. A man such as I has to be cautious, you understand? He cannot be sufficiently cautious."

"That I believe!"

"I don't care what you believe. In any case it is wrong. For instance, you believe what your friend Geraldine told you, namely that Leo would give me the photographs from Elba today. He gave them to me as soon as he had developed them. Why should he have waited? Really, you don't seem to be very intelligent! By the way, I am not favorably impressed by Geraldine either. She really believes I had not seen the photographs as yet. It was taking too long. She wanted to hurry things up; at least that's what she told Leo when she telephoned him."

"Telephoned him? When?"

"The day before yesterday. Honestly, Oliver, you can't be that simple."

Verena gets up and tries to leave the room. Her husband shoves her and she falls into a chair.

"You are staying here. You are going to listen to it all. I have been silent long enough." He says all that calmly, very calmly, not at all angrily. And before continuing he fixes two drinks:

"Perhaps you'll need them," he says. "Well now, it is not a pretty story I have to report. But which true story is pretty? I know all my wife's lovers. Darling, didn't you understand me, you're to sit down! I have read all the letters she received and neglected to destroy. I know all telephone conversations."

"Leo, this scoundrel—"

"Don't say scoundrel, Oliver. Leo is a servant devoted to his master. He showed me the letters before he showed them to you. I heard the tape recordings before you did. He blackmailed you according to my orders. Regretfully. Most regretfully. He has a good heart. But I had to be certain. As always. The money you gave him after you took a loan on your car he gave to me. When you couldn't pay, your car was taken away from you. That's the way it was, wasn't it, Oliver?"

I say nothing.

"Now that I knew enough I bought back your car from Kopper and Company. After all, I could not keep your money."

Suddenly Verena picks up her glass and half-empties it.

"You see how you need that drink, dearest," says Manfred Lord. I take a gulp too. My hand shakes and I spill a little of the whisky.

"I instructed Leo to blackmail you because I know how much young people love their cars. Your willingness to be blackmailed and to give up your car showed me exactly just how much you were attached to Verena." He bows. "You must love her very much."

"I do."

"That I can understand. She is deserving of love."

"Mr. Lord, I'm sorry to have deceived you and abused your hospitality. But since we are now being truthful I must tell you, too, that Verena has decided to leave you and marry me."

"But my dear Oliver, why are you shouting like that? I already know all that!"

[ 11 ]

"You—you know that?"

"My poor dear, did I frighten you? I didn't mean to do that! Now you'll have to remain calm. Look at me. I am calm too. And for me it is probably more difficult than for you, because—"

"How do you know?" I ask.

"My dear young friend, you seem to have no manners after all or you wouldn't continually interrupt me. But surely you have other qualities. Where was I? Oh yes. . . . Your friend Leo has been watching you, on my orders, for almost a year now. I know of your meetings in the little house, I know the café, and I know that you didn't only spend a few days but a few weeks in Elba. I know that you stayed in my house when you arrived there, that you spent entire days with Verena on the boat out at sea, in Marciana Marina and in Porto Azzurro. I know what took place on the boat, what was said there. Would you like to listen to one of the tapes?"

"Tapes?"

"There are very small, excellent pickups available. Your dear brother, Verena, called my attention to them. He is very handy with things like that. These miniature devices switch on and off automatically. Such a wonder of technology. Otto built one into the boat, dearest. The photographs he took are excellent too."

"The bastard! The bastard! The bastard!"

"But such an intelligent bastard! In contrast, excuse me, to you for instance, Oliver. That is also why I would not let Geraldine go to Elba alone. She impressed me as being stupid too. But with Otto's guidance she only had to carry out his orders. . . . No, no, I'm really quite satisfied with her too. Very satisfied."

It is beginning to rain. Drops fall on the autumnal trees, the fading lawn, the gravel drive, my white car. Manfred Lord is still walking to and fro in the library.

"As I said before, a man in my position cannot be cautious enough. Each one of your lovers was a potential enemy of my business and could have been troublesome. Each one had his own file. Not to brand him as an adulterer, I mean, not only for that, though I would have used the threat, but to keep him in line as far as business was concerned." Lord laughs, "Signor Sabbadini was the only exception! My friend! My partner! And he was the one you threw out! You ruined a few big business deals for me by doing that. You know that, sweet? But I'm not angry at you for that."

"Go on," I say. "Keep talking."

"Now you are curious, eh? Well, I gave you those books to give your father. And your father gave you the old books to give to me. You photographed a great many of those pages."

"How would you know that?"

"Geraldine told me."

"She couldn't know that!"

"Do you know a little crippled boy called Hansi? Well, he was the one who watched you photographing the pages and told Geraldine. And Geraldine, loving you the way she does, told me."

"So what?"

"Don't say 'So what,' young friend. A man who is once accused of adultery can never marry the woman whose husband he deceived, not even after her divorce. You didn't know that, did you? I can see you need another drink."

## [ 12 ]

It is now so quiet in the library one can hear the rain fall outside. I fix myself a drink. Mr. Lord smiles. He is leaning against a tapestry. Verena is staring at both of us. I know it is my turn to say something. I must say something.

I ask: "What about it?"

"It's going to protect my reputation and help you to attain your happiness."

"Our happiness!" Verena's laugh is sarcastic.

"Don't laugh, darling. You have no conception of how much I love you. I know you have never loved me."

"Manfred—"

"I was merely a last resort for you, security and a home, never a lover. Or you wouldn't have deceived me from the start. So, one cannot force love. It was my misfortune . . ."

Either he is a great actor or he is really suffering now.

"I loved you more than any other woman I met. I gave you everything I could."

"You can have it all back!"

"I don't want it. You can keep it. I'll agree to a divorce. Can Oliver take care of you?"

"Starting Christmas, I can," I say, and think: I am lying. But I will get my father's competitor to give me an advance!

"You must believe me when I tell you that I am really not angry. There is no cure for love. But you must understand that I had to protect myself. After all, Oliver, be honest. You would have used those photographs against me if I didn't agree to a divorce, right?"

"Naturally."

"You see. And that's why I want them. All eighty-seven of them."

"How do you know that there are eighty-seven?"

"You were careless and had the photos developed by Mr.

Eder in Friedheim. His business is not doing well at all. I gave him a little loan and. . . . Do I have to continue?"

"No."

"Well, then. The photographs and the negatives. You see, we both use the same methods. There is only one difference. You give me the photos and negatives and I keep the ones Leo and Otto took. And if one day—I don't really believe it will come to that, you are an honorable man, you're just taking my wife from me—if one day I should find out that you still possess photocopies, I will find a lawyer who will use the tapes and photographs I posess to destroy you and your marriage. You know me, Verena. Am I serious? Would I do that?"

Verena nods.

"You see, Oliver. A smart woman. By the way, where are the photographs?"

"In a safe place."

"I did not think they were not. When will I get them?"

"Half of them when you institute divorce proceedings. The other half when the divorce is final."

"I'll agree to that. When shall we get a separation? It is already the end of October."

"Sue for divorce right away. That way the divorce will probably become final in January."

"Excellent, Oliver, excellent. Perhaps we can still celebrate the New Year together? No, no, I see you would rather be alone."

He looks through the window. "And just now that you have your car back. A car is really very useful in the cold season, isn't it? 'The crows cry and fly quickly toward town. Soon it will snow, happy he who still has . . .' "

"How do you know?"

"Otto. He took the liberty and taped a few of your meetings in the little house. He only had to fasten the microphone to the outside of the house. It really is a very sensitive little piece of engineering, Oliver."

## [ 13 ]

Perhaps someone else would have shown more character and not accepted the Jaguar. I accepted it. All things considered I would have felt an idiot to refuse it. After all, I had been blackmailed.

The weather is terrible. Two days after the discussion with Mr. Lord, Geraldine suddenly leaves the school for another one. When she says goodbye to me she gives me the long green bead necklace with a smile I shall never forget and says:

"To remember me by. Save it. I'm not saying it will bring you good luck. You have enough luck. I used unfair methods to gain your love. That's probably why I lost out."

"Geraldine, look—"

But she waves deprecatingly:

"It really is *passé* as far as I am concerned. I heard you and Mr. Lord came to an understanding."

"How did you hear that? From whom?"

"From my new sweet love."

"And who is he?"

"Otto, naturally."

"How does he know that?"

"From Leo. Mr. Lord is going to get a divorce. I had no idea that you, too, had photographs which could have hurt him."

"You are lying! Hansi told you!"

"So I'm lying. Why shouldn't I? I have always lied. You are going to give the photographs to Mr. Lord and then you'll marry Verena. Be happy. I hope the stork will bring you many sweet little babies."

We are talking inside the school. A horn sounds outside.

"I have to go, my dear. And forgive me, if you can. After all, in a way I have contributed to your bliss, haven't I?"

She nods her head—once again she is the old luxury whore with enormously teased hair, mascara-caked eyelashes, and overlipsticked mouth. She swings her hips, leaving the school building on very high heels.

[ 14 ]

My mother is getting worse.

This I hear from the doctor in charge of the institution. He writes she is completely apathetic and only says my name from time to time. I should come to see her at Christmas. I shall do that. According to the doctor it might be her last Christmas.

Rashid, with the chief's permission, continues to sleep in my room. Hansi does not speak to me any more. When I enter a room where he is he leaves at once.

My car enables me to do more and the lie I told Verena has become truth. My father's competitor, when I approached them, agreed to give me a substantial advance. It is at my disposal from New Year's. It means Verena and Evelyn are taken care of and secure until I start work.

On the twenty-eighth of November Mr. Lord takes his wife to a lawyer to start divorce proceedings. On the twenty-ninth I am invited to Mr. Lord's again. Verena had taken half of the photographs and negatives from the safety-deposit box and we give them to him. He examines them carefully, using a magnifying glass.

"One has to be a good loser. I was probably not the right man for Verena. That reminds me, I almost forgot! Say good night to Evelyn, Oliver. She is waiting for you. You will have to get used to certain parental duties."

Evelyn is in bed and holds out her arms to me: "Uncle Mansfeld!"

Very softly she says: "Mommy told me we'll be divorced after New Year?"

I nod.

"Thank you, Uncle Mansfeld. We can hardly stand it any

more. I promise I will always be a good student and step-daughter."

"I'll promise, too, that I'll always be a good student and step-father."

That makes her laugh.

"I have brought some marzipan for you. Will you accept it?"

"Oh yes!"

Then she gives me a kiss.

On the eighteenth of December we start Christmas vacation. Mr. Lord has to go to Vienna on the fifteenth. He telephones me at the school.

"We don't have to put on an act any more. I know how many nights you spent in my house when I was not there. Should you want to talk with Verena before you leave for Luxembourg—be my guest."

"Mr. Lord, I—"

"Don't be afraid. I sent the servants away, even Leo. You will be alone with Verena and Evelyn."

"I don't know."

"Then I'll tell Verena you are coming on the fifteenth. I'll say goodbye now, Oliver. All the best for you and your family. Goodbye."

On the fifteenth (it is raining, there is an icy wind) I go to Miguel Drive and the three of us, Evelyn, Verena and I, are having dinner together. Evelyn is helping her mother serve. Suddenly she says:

"You know, Daddy is quite a guy, isn't he? To let us go like that! I didn't think he would do that!"

"My precious, next year at long last the three of us will be together!"

[ 15 ]

Then Evelyn is asleep and Verena and I are sitting before the fireplace. The logs are crackling.

"The other half of the photographs are still in the deposit box," I say, "and the manuscript too. Our story. Would you take out the manuscript too? I have written the last part and I want to add it to the manuscript and then send the book to a publishing house. Why do you hesitate?"

"Well, actually, Manfred has been very decent to us. Even Evelyn says that."

"Well, I guess—under duress. Yes, you're right, it was decent of him."

"And if the book is accepted by the publisher Manfred will probably go to trial because of his shady business with your father."

"I thought of that, too. What I wrote is more or less a diary. Right?"

"Exactly."

"The editor who reads it is pledged to silence."

"But if the book is going to be published?"

"I couldn't care if my father's and Aunt Lizzy's real names were used, if people found out what kind of scum they really are."

"But then Manfred would—"

"Wait. What I wrote is true. The names have to be changed so that nobody will recognize the real identity of the people involved. That is why I cannot dedicate the book to you."

"But I'll know it was written for me."

"Only for you, Verena."

"Yes."

"Shall we—do you want to—can we go to bed now?"

"Yes, my love. I want you very much."

"When we are married we'll never be apart again, will we?"

"Never."

"You go with me on all my trips."

"We'll always sleep in the same room together."

"We'll always share the same bed."

"Did you think it would turn out so well?"

"I hoped it would. But I was afraid it would not."

"Me. too."

"Coward, take a coward's hand."

## [ 16 ]

Naturally there is a Christmas party at the school. The children who are going home are happy. The ones staying here, sad. Hansi is the exception. He is happy he does not have to see his shit-parents.

Giuseppe laughs and sings and dances. Ali has flight tickets to Rome for him and his father. "From Rome it is only three hours to Naples," says Giuseppe. He is going to spend Christmas with Mamma, Papa and all his relatives.

Rashid is trying hard to remain calm.

"When are you coming back, Oliver?"

"On the seventh, in the afternoon."

"May I meet you at the airport?"

"Sure, kid."

"I'll be there. May Allah keep you safe wherever you go."

"You, too, Rashid. Don't be sad. Perhaps you'll soon be able to go home too."

"Do you think so?"

"I'm sure!"

And the little prince smiles.

Before leaving I type the remainder of the manuscript and write the foreword to the editor.

I also make up an imaginary short farewell scene.

Verena takes me to the airport.

Here we mail the manuscript in the airport post office. We have to wait a long time. Because of the holidays there is much activity. I sent the manuscript to the best publisher in Frankfurt. If they should not accept it, I can always try another. Verena and I hold hands as we place the package on the counter.

Teddy Behnke and the Bonanza are already waiting for me when I arrive at the customs and have to say goodbye to Verena.

"Give my regards to Evelyn. To your husband too. And whenever you are able, call me at the hotel in the afternoons."

"Yes, my love."

"Why are you crying?"

"Because I'm happy."

"That's not true!"

"Yes, it is!"

"No. But soon you will be. Now things are going to move fast. Look, I wrote such a thick book—and only one chapter is missing, and that will be finished too."

"Yes," she says while people in a hurry bump into us and voices through the loudspeaker continually announce the arrival or departure of planes. "That will be finished too."

"Mr. Mansfeld, please come to the customs and passport barrier! Mr. Mansfeld, please."

We kiss.

"Are you afraid?" I ask.

"Yes."

"Of what?"

"Mr. Mansfeld . . . Mr. Oliver Mansfeld, please come to the customs and passport barrier!"

"What are you afraid of?"

"I'm so happy with you. And always when one is happy something terrible happens."

"Nonsense. The divorce is final in January. Then I'll quickly write the last chapter."

"The last chapter . . ."

# Epilogue

[ 1 ]

On the ninth of January 1962, about two o'clock, three hundred children who had assembled in front of Dr. Florian's boarding school saw a huge shadow appear out of the raging snowstorm which had been going on for many hours. It was an Army helicopter which hovered a long time above the school until the pilot could spot the white sheet with the painted blood-red cross. The helicopter landed quickly now on the red cross, the draft of its blades forcing snow into the children's faces.

The pilot and co-pilot jumped out.

They opened a door and helped an older man, who seemed extremely clumsy and awkward, from the helicopter. This man wore a heavy, old-fashioned coat, a warm muffler and a large hat. Dr. Florian left the building to meet him.

"My name is Albert Lazarus."

"Dr. Florian. We were expecting you, Mr. Lazarus."

"Expecting me?"

"The detectives here used a short-wave transmitter because all telephone lines are down."

"I just came back from Vienna this morning and talked to Police Inspector Wilms of the Frankfurt Homicide Department. You see, I'm an old, sick man who is not going to live much longer"—hastily Lazarus stuffed into his mouth three different-colored pills, of which many seemed to be lying loose in his pocket—"but I am the one who read Oliver Mansfeld's manuscript and I asked Inspector Wilms to allow me to bring it myself, in spite of the danger and strain to me, so as to be present when the case is solved, which surely won't take long now."

One of the pilots handed Lazarus an old, much-used suitcase from the helicopter.

"Thank you," said the editor. And to Dr. Florian: "The manuscript is safely in here. Is Inspector Hardenberg here?"

"He is questioning witnesses in the A. Excuse me, the A is—"

"A hotel, I know. I do believe I know everything there is to know about the A, your school, you and your children. And certain adults. How can I get to the Hotel Ambassador?"

"We have a sleigh at your disposal. The roads are all snowbound."

"It is good it is such a large sleigh," said Lazarus. "We also brought a coffin. We can take that along at the same time."

The pilot and co-pilot lifted the coffin from the helicopter. Many, many snowflakes fell on the dully shining coffin.

"Is the body at the A?"

"Yes. The police doctor has examined it there."

"Then we can leave," says Lazarus.

## [ 2 ]

Inspector Hardenberg sat on the green table of the poolroom in the Ambassador, smoking a short pipe. He was still slim. The years since working on the "Mansfeld case" seemed to have passed him without trace. He was still white-haired and slim. Nor had his character changed. He still loved children and was pleasant, patient and sympathetic when he talked with them.

"Believe me, I have known Oliver much much longer than you," he said to Rashid. The little prince was sitting in a chair near the pool table. "I know he was your friend; you loved him too. When I saw him for the first time he was only a little older than you. Rashid, will you help me?"

The prince nodded, tears trickling from his eyes. He did not wipe them away.

"Who—who murdered Oliver?" he asked, sobbing.

"How do you know it was murder?"

"It must have been, Sir. I met Oliver at the airport."

"Tell me again exactly when you met him."

"The day before yesterday. Sunday. At half-past three. He came in his father's plane. I promised I would meet him. But I already told you all that!"

"Tell me again. Take your time. Be calm. Oliver won't come back to life again. But if you help me, Rashid, we will surely find the people who are responsible for his death."

"Yes, Sir," said the little prince. "I promise I'll do everything I can to help. Oliver was my brother. That's a game we play at school."

"Yes, I know it. Where I went to school we played it too," said Hardenberg. He rolled a white ball across the green cloth of the table. It hit a red one.

"Now that Oliver is dead I'm all alone," said the prince. "I am very unhappy about it because I'm afraid I will never be able to go home."

"Don't be despondent, Rashid. Things do change."

"Yes, Sir."

The inspector rolled a second ball across the table. He said: "Most people are alone, Rashid. Oliver was too, when I saw him the first time."

"I think children are poor wretches," said the prince.

"I'm afraid you are right. Tell me. You met him at the airport in Frankfurt."

"Yes, sir. He told me he was happy that I met him there."

"What else?"

"That his mother was very ill. And he asked me to see about having his car brought from the airport garage."

"Why didn't he get it himself?"

"He said he had to make a telephone call and he didn't have much time."

"Did he seem happy?"

"Yes, sir."

"Did he tell you whom he was going to telephone?"

"No, sir."

The door opened and Marcus, a young, eager officer, entered. In his hand were three photographs which were still wet. The inspector nodded to Rashid.

"Excuse me a moment."

"Surely, sir."

Marcus spoke quietly to Hardenberg: "These are the fingerprints we found in the bloodstained car. They are Oliver Mansfeld's. These are from the little boy there. We took his prints and they match. But they are not recent and not bloody." He lifted up the third photograph. "And these are fingerprints we have not been able to identify. I have checked with Federal Detection in Wiesbaden. They are not registered there. The prints are much older than the little boy's prints."

"Probably prints of people Oliver had in his car at some time."

"Probably."

"How much longer is Dr. Peter going to be?"

"Inspector, you know how difficult it is with hanged people."

"Yes, I know. Did Mr. Lazarus arrive?"

"Yes, he did. He says he feels ill. He asked to see you as soon as convenient."

"Then will you stay here with the little boy while I talk to Mr. Lazarus?"

"Yes, Inspector."

Hardenberg patted Rashid's head as he walked to the door. "I'll be just a few minutes," he said. "I'll be back."

Hardenberg winked at Marcus, who then sat next to Rashid and patted his shoulder: "Can you shoot pool?"

"Yes, sir."

"You want to play a game?"

"No, sir. I'd rather not."

"Why not?"

"Because they murdered my brother," answered the prince. "I'm very sad. Please don't talk to me. Or I shall cry and my father always says it is inconsiderate to cry in front of strangers."

Marcus stared at the little boy. He gave a ball an ineffectual push. Then it was silent in the large room. Outside snow was falling, blocking streets and paths, causing branches of old trees to break beneath its load. It seemed as if air itself consisted of snow. Soon even the oldest people would not be able to remember a snowfall such as this.

[ 3 ]

Mr. Lazarus introduced himself to Inspector Hardenberg in the luxurious foyer of the Hotel Ambassador. He sneezed twice. "This trip will probably kill me. I am a very sick man, any kind of overexertion can be the end of me."

"Then why did you come?"

"Because I wanted to bring you the manuscript."

"One of my men could have done that."

Lazarus, a piece of uneaten cake still before him, wiped his mouth and replied with dignity: "I was the first man to read the manuscript. I had to bring it to you. After reading it you are not a stranger to me. And in spite of my illness I am—perhaps you could understand that—curious of other lives. I think that curiosity of life is nowhere as strong as in those who know they have to leave this world very soon. That is why I ask you to let me be your assistant."

"Impossible."

"I am giving you the most important evidence. This manuscript. Could I not then be your assistant for one or two days?"

"And why?"

"Because I would like to know the last chapter, Inspector."

"The last chapter?"

"The last chapter of the transcript I gave you. It is missing. Read the manuscript. It will help you. And from now on you will introduce me as your assistant, won't you?"

"Well, as far as it is possible for me—"

[ 4 ]

Inspector Hardenberg returned to the poolroom and dismissed Marcus. He placed the manuscript on the table and sat down once more on its green cloth.

"Now, you left Oliver to see about his car. Where was he when you returned?"

"In the bar. The Blue Bar it is called, I believe."

"Did he drink?"

"Oliver had had a cognac and made his telephone call. He had just replaced the receiver when I came. The telephone was on the bar. There were many people there."

"The bartender said he thought Oliver had telephoned a woman. Would you know who it could have been?"

"Yes, sir."

"Who? What is her name?"

"Excuse me, I'd rather not say. Oliver was my friend. And this lady— No, I'm sorry, I'd rather not say."

Hardenberg patted the manuscript: "Your friend wrote a novel. I'm going to read it tonight. Then I shall know who the lady was. You won't tell me?"

"Never. I would feel like a traitor."

Hardenberg looked at the little boy with the silky eyelashes and black, enormous eyes and sighed: "All right. Of course you have to protect your friend."

"I'm glad you understand that."

"What happened after you had gotten the car?"

"We went to Friedheim to the school."

"Was Oliver in a hurry?"

"A great hurry. He dropped me off at the Quellenhof—

that's where I live—and said he had to go somewhere else."

"Where?"

"He did not say."

"Was he happy or sad?"

"Very happy and exited."

"You know that we found Oliver's car about two kilometers from the school, half-buried in snow?"

"I heard about it."

Hardenberg rolled another white ball across the table. Rashid rolled it back. They did it a few more times while they talked.

"The car was drenched in blood."

Rashid swallowed hard. "Oliver was full of blood, too, wasn't he? Somebody beat him up terribly before hanging him."

"So you really believe he was murdered."

"I am convinced of it."

"But Oliver had only friends here and not a single enemy!"

Rashid lowered his head and did not reply.

"If you believe he was murdered do you believe, too, that the woman whose name you won't mention had some connection with it?"

"Please, don't ask me any questions which I cannot answer."

"Then you believe it is so."

"I did not say that!"

"But you thought it!"

The little prince looked up. Then he nodded.

"And although you believe that, you won't tell me who the woman is?"

"No."

"I'll know who she is when I read the manuscript."

"Yes, sir, but at least I won't have betrayed Oliver." Rashid opened and closed his hands. "Can I—may I—is it possible to see Oliver once more?"

"I'm afraid not."

"Why not?"

"The doctor. . . . Your friend—does not look the way he did."

"I understand." He was silent for a while. Then he said: "I have a request, sir." Rashid pulled two envelopes from his pocket. "Lately, Oliver sometimes said that he had a feeling he would die soon."

"He did?"

"Yes. He did not feel threatened. He was not ill. He just said that he sometimes had this feeling. And he said if the feeling became reality I should see to it that these two envelopes would be buried with him."

"What is in them?"

"I don't know, sir. The envelopes are sealed. But I sleep in his room and when you called for me I brought them with me."

Hardenberg got up and put an arm around his shoulder.

"Thank you. Will you be able to get back to the school by yourself in this snowstorm or should one of my men go with you?"

"I'll get back by myself, sir."

"Thank you for talking with me."

"You're welcome. It's just so sad that Oliver is dead, isn't it?"

"Yes," said Hardenberg, "very sad." He watched the boy walk to the door, turn and bow to him and then break into tears. When he started to cry he ran quickly from the room.

Hardenberg lit his pipe and opened the envelopes. From one of them fell the broken pieces of a record, from the other an unbroken record. The title of the complete record said:

*Il Nostro Concerto*
*Umberto Bindi con Enzo Ceraglio e La Sua*
*Orchestra e il vocal comet*

Only after fitting the broken pieces together could the inspector read its title:

*Love is Just a Word*
*From the Original Soundtrack of*
*Aimez-vous Brahms?*

## [ 5 ]

The police doctor, Friedrich Peter, was short and fat. During his career he had examined so many bodies he could not even approximate their number. For the examination of Oliver Mansfeld he had been assigned a small room in the basement of the hotel.

Oliver Mansfeld was lying nude on a table. Hardenberg entered the room.

"Was it murder?"

"No. It was suicide."

"But the wounds—"

"I know, Inspector. Cases like this one we like least of all. But I tell you the boy committed suicide."

"How did you come to this conclusion?"

"There are many textbooks about genuine and simulated suicide. In this case, the person who beat the boy—all injuries were made by a blunt, heavy instrument—did not even take the trouble to make it appear a suicide."

The doctor bent over the body. "You see these strangulation marks here on his neck?"

"Yes."

"And now have a look at the injuries. Here. Here. And here. I have made several microscopic tests. The blood from the car is the blood of the dead boy. There is a sure method to find out when and how blood was lost. We found blood in the tower, on the steps of the tower and in the car. The fight could not have taken place in the little car."

"Could the wounds have been self-inflicted?"

"Impossible. I am convinced that the boy was attacked and beaten in the tower. Then he dragged himself to his car. Death occurred, as I already told you, in the early evening of Sunday. It was not snowing at that time. Your men have found blood underneath the snow."

"That's right. Why did he go to the car?"

"I have no idea. To escape. To hide. Who knows? When it began to snow he went back to the tower."

"How do you know that?"

"His clothes and shoes were full of snow when we found him. Even the soles of his shoes were caked with snow. And I also found blood on the soles. But that is not the critical point. You see, this blue ring around the neck was caused by the rope and occurred without a doubt two hours later than the injuries. And those injuries—there is no doubt whatsoever about that—were inflicted while he was still alive. But they were not so severe as to prevent him from going to his car and back to the tower."

"It is possible someone smeared the blood on the car. The boy needn't have gotten into the car."

"He did. The blood we found was blood which had dripped and was not smeared on the car. Now," said Dr. Peter, "we differentiate between typical and atypical hangings. Suicides hang themselves—"

"Typically."

"It's just the other way around. They hang themselves atypically."

"What does that mean?"

"If I were to hang you, Inspector, the knot of the rope would be right on the nape of your neck so you would break your neck quickly and properly. And if I beat you I would do it in such a way there would be no blood on the rope."

"Was there blood on the rope?"

"Yes. The boy's blood. There was blood on the beam, too. I believe there had been a fight between the boy and another person during which the boy suffered several injuries. They were not so severe as to make it impossible for him to hang himself. An examination of his stomach proved that the young man had not been drugged, or drunk or incapacitated by sedatives. In my opinion it was not murder made to look like suicide. I mean: it is impossible that injuries were inflicted after death. That is proved by the microscopic examination of the tissue."

"Then he was beaten, dragged himself to his car, stayed there a while . . ."

"Right."

". . . dragged himself back to the tower and hanged himself. Why?"

"That," said Dr. Peter, "is your problem, Inspector. I have requested Professor Mokry of the University of Frankfurt be flown here to confirm my findings. He should be here soon. Believe me, it wasn't murder. What is that?"

"Two envelopes. Nothing special. Would you do me a favor?"

"I'll be glad to."

"If you and Professor Mokry are of the same opinion I shall release the body. When you place the body in the coffin would you put in these two envelopes, too, please?"

"If you wish," said Dr. Peter.

Hardenberg looked at the corpse.

"I knew him when he was just a little boy. If it was suicide, why did he do it?"

"That is another question," said Dr. Peter.

Hardenberg left the basement.

In the foyer of the hotel he met the stout editor.

"I expect you are going to your room now to read the manuscript."

"I intended doing just that."

"I think that by tomorrow night you will have solved the case. Tell me, Inspector, did you find much in the boy's pockets?"

"Not very much."

"Did you find an olive among other things?"

"What makes you think that?"

"When you have read the manuscript you will understand my question. Then he did have an olive in his pocket?"

"Yes, an old, dried olive."

"Where is it?"

"In my room."

Very quietly Albert Lazarus said: "If you should not need the olive any more could I have it?"

"What do you want it for?"

"Just because," answered the fat, awkward man, blushing. "Just because."

[ 6 ]

On the tenth of January 1962, about two o'clock, two men made their way through the more than knee-deep snow near Friedheim. The roads above the school had not been cleared and were not passable for sleighs. The only possibility for Inspector Hardenberg and Mr. Lazarus to reach their destination was an extremely difficult march on foot.

They had been lent boots by the hotel. Again and again the awkward Lazarus slipped. His face was lobster-red and perspiration dripped off him, though it was bitterly cold and continued to snow heavily. Hardenberg was perspiring, too. Every step in this enormous sea of snow meant an immense strain, and the Inspector thought grimly that the people they were going to see might not even be at home. The snow had interrupted telephone service and it had not been possible to reach them.

"I—I have to rest for a moment. This is too much for my heart," said Lazarus.

"The last chapter," said Hardenberg slowly.

They were both resting, staring at the falling snow. Suddenly they jumped when, with the noise of an exploding bomb, a hundred meters away an ancient tree broke off near its root. It fell forward and, caught in the branches of other trees, remained standing at an angle.

When the tree broke Lazarus had jumped up and cried out. He sat down once more next to the Inspector. He was embarrassed. "Excuse me, Inspector, I—I—I'm terribly nervous."

"I am too, but my reactions are slower."

"How could that happen?"

"I can't exactly explain it, but once, in Russia, during the war, something like this happened. We examined the tree and found that a beaver had been gnawing at its root."

"A beaver?"

"Yes. He must have been gnawing at it for months. The beaver probably would not have been able to do it alone. But then came the snow, the weight of the snow. It was too much for the tree. What's the matter?"

Lazarus wiped his face with a handerchief. "Nothing," he said. "I just thought how like each other trees and human beings are."

"Yes," said Hardenberg, "only it is not a beaver which tortures a human being, which gnaws him, drains him and readies him for the downfall."

[ 7 ]

A servant in a striped waistcoat opened the door of the villa. His face was pale and its expression haughty.

"Good day, gentlemen."

Hardenberg identified himself and his companion and asked to see Mr. and Mrs. Lord.

"May I ask the nature of your—"

"You may not," said Hardenberg, taking a step forward while Leo took a step back. "I wish to speak to Mr. and Mrs. Lord. What I have to say to them is no concern of yours."

"Excuse me, please."

Just then Manfred Lord entered the hall. He was dressed in a gray suit, white shirt and black tie. He stopped directly before the Rubens which showed a voluptuous blonde woman washing her feet. The Inspector thought of what he had read this past night while Manfred Lord, smiling, asked, "What is it, Leo?"

"The gentlemen are from the Homicide Department, sir."

"Homicide Department?"

"Yes, sir."

Manfred Lord came closer, offered his hand to Hardenberg, who introduced himself and his assistant.

"Welcome gentlemen," said Manfred Lord. He looked imposing. Hardenberg noticed an occasional nervous twitch in his right eyelid. He thought: The man is afraid.

"What is it all about?"

"The death of the student Oliver Mansfeld. Perhaps you have already heard."

"Yes. My gardener's wife told us yesterday. She had gone to the village."

"I'm sure you will understand that I have a few questions to ask."

"Naturally, I understand that, Inspector. What I can't understand is why you should want to ask me those questions."

"You and your wife."

"And why?"

"I should like to explain that later, Mr. Lord. Was your wife very surprised when she heard of Oliver Mansfeld's death?"

"I don't understand."

"If you don't understand, I should like to talk to your wife first."

Manfred Lord paled.

"My wife tried to commit suicide."

Lazarus jumped excitedly and gasped. "What?"

Lord looked at him haughtily.

"When did your wife try to commit suicide?" asked Hardenberg.

"Yesterday. She slashed her wrist." Lord's lips formed an ironic smile. "Leo and I stopped the bleeding and put on a first bandage. The doctor from Friedheim came to her this morning."

"And?"

Lord smiled again: "There is no danger, if that's what you mean."

"Could she answer a few questions?"

"I'm sure she could. The question is whether she will."

"We'll see."

"If you wish. Leo—"

"Yes, Sir?"

"Take these two gentlemen to my wife's room."

Lord was once again before the Rubens: "If you need me, I'll be in the library. No doubt you know how much I like books?"

"Excuse me?"

"Especially old books."

"What do you—"

"Inspector, I'm sure you have read this fantastic story Oliver Mansfeld wrote. You are clever, aren't you? And your colleague, too. It is probably just a crazy notion for me to imagine that he is not a detective at all but an editor of a publishing house."

[ 8 ]

Verena Lord looked as if she had died. Motionless, she rested on her bed in the large, expensively furnished bedroom. Her skin was waxen, her lips bloodless, her eyes closed. Her voice without strength, she whispered.

"You have read the manuscript?"

"Yes," said Lazarus.

"Then you know everything." A thick bandage covered her right wrist.

"Not everything," said Hardenberg. "That's why we are here. It is my duty to inform you that you do not have to answer my questions. You can refuse to answer."

"Ask."

"Is what Oliver Mansfeld wrote in his manuscript true?"

"Only partly."

Lazarus, who had recovered somewhat, picked up a little bottle of perfume from the bedside table and replaced it. Softly he said "Diorissimo."

"Yes," said Verena, "*that* is true."

"What is true?" asked Hardenberg.

"Everything Oliver wrote about us. My husband knows that, too."

"And the other things?"

"What, for instance?"

"The photographed pages with the perforated letters, which are in your safety-deposit box."

"There are no photographs in my safety-deposit box."

"Did you take them out?"

"They were never there."

"Mrs. Lord, why are you lying?"

"I—I'm not lying."

"Did you love Oliver Mansfeld?"

"No."

"But he wrote that you did."

"He believed it. He wrote what he believed and what he wished for. For instance the story concerning those pages of the books. He would have liked to have the means to blackmail my husband."

"But he did not have them?"

"No."

"He invented the entire story?"

"Yes. You can open my safety-deposit box. You can search the house. The villa in Frankfurt. You can search wherever you want. You will find nothing which would incriminate my husband."

"Because you destroyed it."

"That's what you say."

"Mrs. Lord," asked Lazarus. "Why did you try to kill yourself?"

"I have tried to take my life. I am prone to hysteria and depressions. I opened my wrist in a fit of mental aberration."

With mild irony the Inspector said: "With not too much determination."

"What do you mean by that?"

Verena opened her eyes and looked at Hardenberg with contempt.

"What would you know?"

"Nothing. But I would like to know something else."

"You would never understand."

"Perhaps I would."

"Never! Nor would you, Mr. Lazarus!"

The Inspector rose, stepped to a window and looked out into the whirling snow. His back turned to Verena he asked: "When did you see Oliver Mansfeld the last time, Madame?"

"Just before—before he left on his Christmas vacation."

"That is not true." The Inspector was bluffing. "I have a witness who says Oliver Mansfeld talked to you on the telephone and made a date. In his manuscript he mentions also that he intended to meet you on this day after returning from Luxembourg in the tower near the school."

"It is a novel, isn't it? Since when do the police investigate a death on the basis of novels?"

"It is no novel," said Lazarus.

"But?"

"A factual report."

"Ridiculous!"

"Then why, Madame, are you crying if it is so ridiculous?"

"I am not crying," said Verena, wiping tears from her face with her uninjured hand. She was shaking uncontrollably now and Lazarus became alarmed, calling: "Inspector!"

Hardenberg turned around slowly.

"Inspector, look—"

"Hysteria," said the Inspector, intentionally ruthless. "Madame just told us she is prone to hysteria. Don't worry, Mr. Lazarus." He approached the bed and lifted up the face of the crying woman. "You are a liar and a traitor."

"How dare you? I shall—" Verena did not finish the sentence. The door opened.

Manfred Lord entered.

"I'm not interrupting, I hope," he asked, smiling.

"You are," said the Inspector.

"I'm terribly sorry, Inspector, excuse me. But you have no search warrant, not even an official request to question us."

"I can get both inside half an hour."

"Yes, but you neglected to do it! You are questioning a weakened, nervous woman in the most—as I suspect—don't cry, dearest—inconsiderate manner. I have friends in the Frankfurt police headquarters. I would be careful if I were you. Be quiet, sweetheart. Calm down."

"Mr. Lord, a human being died."

"Yes, Mr. Hardenberg. My wife's lover. Oliver Mansfeld. How regrettable."

"You find it regrettable?"

"But, Inspector, he was so young. Don't you have a heart?"

Verena moaned and turned her head to one side.

Lazarus stuffed another pill in his mouth.

Lord walked up and down, smiling.

"I think I can answer any questions you might have. My wife is still too upset about Oliver's death. Aren't you, dearest?"

Verena began to cry again. She covered her face with both hands. She cried silently, without sobbing. All strength seemed to have left her.

"Go on," said Hardenberg.

Lord sat in an Empire chair, crossed his legs and pressed his fingertips together.

"You want to hear the whole truth?"

"Naturally!"

"As you wish. You know in my business one usually profits more that way anyway."

And Manfred Lord talked.

What he said was partly the truth. He only concealed or lied about those incidents which would have incriminated him. But had he told the whole truth this is what he would have said:

## [ 9 ]

The eve of New Year's was very quiet.

After dinner Verena and Lord sat before the fireplace and had a drink. In a while he said: "Now we are going to talk like two sensible people, my precious."

"What do you mean by that?"

"The divorce will be final in January. Then you are going to leave me."

"Evelyn and I."

"Evelyn and you, naturally. Forgive me for forgetting the child. And where are you going?"

"To Oliver. He is going to take an apartment for us and with the advance his father's competitors have given him—"

"No."

"What do you mean, 'No'?"

"He is not going to take an apartment for you. He did not receive an advance."

"But he said—"

"He lied."

"He didn't lie! I know the people promised him an advance!"

"They reconsidered."

"How do you know that?"

"I own thirty per cent of their shares. I have—"

"Prevented Oliver receiving his advance?"

"Not only that my dear, I have also seen to it that these people will never employ him. If you leave me you have nothing. Not a penny. You will have to live in poverty. Naturally, Oliver will be with you. How long does love last if you're poor, darling?"

Verena was silent.

"I am a man who has many connections. It will present no problem to me to make sure no one will employ Oliver. You, then, will be a divorced woman with an illegitimate child and an out-of-work husband. A young man. A good-looking man. A man who probably better than I can— But I'm getting off the subject."

"He will find work," said Verena.

"Naturally. He can surface roads or put roofs on houses, once he has learned how. Meanwhile you will sell your jewelry and furs. Unfortunately he will not earn very much money, darling, because he knows nothing which is well paid. The worth you women attribute to us men differs from the worth other men attribute to us."

"You are a bastard!"

"You know, precious, actually you come from quite a respectable family. In a respectable family one does not say certain things."

"Bastard!"

"Well. It seems I thought of you too highly. Many people—among them Oliver's father—were of the opinion you are a whore, a born whore. Be quiet. You are. I have nothing against whores, otherwise I would never have married you."

"You are so mean—you are so mean."

"Perhaps I've had a little too much to drink. You, too, by the way. *In vino veritas,* right? Oh, I forgot; you don't know Latin. It means 'in wine is truth.' Cheers, my darling!"

"I am leaving you tomorrow morning!"

"Naturally, you can't leave before then. You are too drunk to do that. Where are you going to go? The apartment has not been rented for you yet!"

"I'm going to a hotel."

"And who is going to pay for that? And where is Evelyn going to live? And what will you live on?"

"Oliver—"

"Oliver doesn't have a penny. I have found a means of telling his father that he is your lover. Even his father is not going to give him a penny. He is a friend of mine, he is very obligated to me. On the contrary, if Oliver should talk to him during his vacation his father will—"

"You lousy bastard!"

"Now, now, darling. You have mixed with better people for quite a time. I had really thought you had given up certain peculiarities."

"My family is at least as good as yours!"

"I don't doubt that. Your brother Otto has given me a shining example of that."

Now they were both drunk. Slightly staggering, Lord took a Venetian mirror from the wall.

"What are you doing?"

"Would you—would you do me a favor and look in the mirror?" He held the mirror to her. "You are beautiful. You are very beautiful. But have you noticed that the first few wrinkles around your eyes have appeared? I have dozens myself. My hair is white. I am much older than you and not a lover like Oliver any more. But I love you. I surround you with riches and luxury. I shall continue to do it as long as I live. When I die you will receive a fantastic sum from the insurance company. You will live in the most beautiful houses. You will be able to afford anything. Will you ever have all that with Oliver? He is so much younger than you. I don't mind your wrinkles. Neither does he. Not yet. Will he mind them in ten years' time? I won't, my sweetheart, I won't. But will he?"

Verena looked in the mirror. She was drunk but not drunk enough not to see those tiny wrinkles around her eyes. She looked at them closely and thoroughly.

"Manfred," Verena said. "I'm afraid."

"Of what?"

"Just afraid," she answered, still looking in the mirror.

"They are just tiny wrinkles, but in ten years— And he is such a handsome boy! Maybe one day he'll fall in love with your daughter."

"Be quiet! Be quiet this moment!"

"Surely."

"And take away this mirror!"

"At once. But that won't make the wrinkles disappear," said Lord. He hung the mirror and returned to his wife, who was holding her head with both hands. Lord said: "I am willing to forget everything—adultery, betrayal, everything. I'm willing to keep you and Evelyn here. I shall even adopt Evelyn, if you wish. Greedy as you are, I'm sure you do."

"Lousy—"

"Shut your mouth! I pulled you from the gutter. I can put you back there. So far I've always thought you were a sensible woman. Aren't you? Yes? Well, there you are. As soon as Oliver returns from Luxembourg you will tell him it is all finished."

"Never! Never! Never!"

"When a woman cries *never* three times it always means she has already decided to do what is demanded of her. You, too, have just decided, haven't you, darling? You have just realized how completely senseless and hopeless what you two planned to do is, didn't you?"

"You are a devil!"

"Yes. But a rich one and a clever one. You surely don't intend to marry a stupid and poor devil?"

"He is no devil!"

"Excuse me. You are not going to marry a stupid and poor angel, are you?"

She took a heavy glass ashtray and threw it at him. It hit Lord on his right temple, which began to bleed furiously. He pulled out a handkerchief.

"I see you are sensible, darling," he said.

Below, in Friedheim, bells of a church began to chime.

"I wish you a blessed New Year, sweetheart," said Manfred Lord, pressing his handkerchief, which quickly became soaked with blood, to his temple. "Tomorrow is a holiday. But the day after tomorrow we are going to the bank to take the other half of the photographs from your safety-deposit box."

[ 10 ]

On the second of January 1962 they went to Frankfurt.

Verena took the photographs from her safety-deposit box and handed them to her husband.

"Where are the negatives?"

"Here."

In the car, on their way back to the Taunus, Verena suddenly began to laugh.

"What is so funny?"

"You are sitting in the trap, my dear."

"Excuse me?"

"Oliver wrote our story and submitted it to a publishing house. He also mentioned the perforated pages, the films and photographs."

"In an other hour they are not going to exist any more, my precious. That leaves only the story. What, after all, is a mere story?"

*"The police—"*

"The police need proof. The only proof which exists I possess. I liked Oliver. But naturally, that is all over and done with now. And as soon as he returns you will tell him that."

"I can't—I can't!"

"Sure you can. You have a hardy nature."

"Manfred, I beg of you! I really can't! I—I simply wouldn't know what to say."

"In cases like this it is best to write a letter," said Manfred Lord.

[ 11 ]

Verena Lord wrote a letter to Oliver Mansfeld. She remembered their stay in Elba, mentioned, for sentimental reasons, the bar in the Marciana Marina, she recalled Porto Azzurro, the green waves of the sea where she had embraced Oliver, and she also didn't forget to tell him he was the only love of her life. Never would she be able to forget him; he should try to forgive her, begged Verena Lord.

"You are my soul," she wrote. "You are my breath." She had started the letter with "Oliver, my beloved Oliver!"

Although these and other signs of her affection were contained in the letter, Verena Lord could not but plainly point out to her beloved Oliver that, due to compelling reasons, she had to terminate her relationship with him. She made it very clear indeed. She had to think of her child, she wrote. She was afraid of poverty and afraid of the differences in their ages. Someone older than Oliver Mansfeld would have admired this honesty —especially since honesty in women is extraordinary.

Verena showed further proof of her strength of character. She had decided to meet Oliver in the old tower after his return and to give him the letter personally.

When Oliver called Verena in her villa in Friedheim from the airport in Frankfurt she bravely agreed to meet her lover in an hour.

The sky was black when Oliver began his drive, and heavy snow was expected to fall soon.

Oliver dropped the little prince at the school and went on to the tower. About a hundred meters away from it he parked his car in the thicket. In the tower he found Verena waiting for him. He embraced and kissed her and immediately noticed a strange coldness in her.

"What is it?"

"Nothing!" said Verena.

"Yes, there is something. You are different. Quite different."

"Am I?"

"Yes, you are. And where is Assad? And Evelyn?"

"They are at home."

"Did something happen?"

"Yes."

Oliver's eyes narrowed.

"What? Everything was settled before I left."

"Now it is not," answered Verena. "I have written a letter to you."

"A letter?"

"Yes."

"Why?"

"We are through."

"Verena!"

"Read the letter, then you will understand everything."

"What should I understand? We were agreed, completely agreed—"

"Everything has changed, Oliver, everything." Verena Lord began to cry. Tears were running down her face. "I—I'm sorry. I'm very unhappy."

"Verena—Verena! But we love each other!"

"It is not enough, darling. Read the letter. I—I can't go on. I'm leaving. We will never see each other again."

"You are mad!"

"No, my poor little Oliver, I'm quite sane."

"But you simply can't—"

"I must. I have a child. I need security."

"But I can give that to you, you and your child!"

"You cannot. Let me go. I don't want to be with you when you read the letter."

"Why not?"

"It is the most difficult letter I ever wrote!"

"Stay here."

"No!"

"You are a coward!"

"Yes," cried Verena, running down the steps of the spiral staircase. "Yes, that's what I am, a coward, a coward, a coward!"

Oliver remained motionless. In a while he sat down on an old box next to which was a long rope and opened the letter. It had grown darker meanwhile but through the windows of the room the country was plainly visible.

Oliver did not see it.

He sat on the old box, the letter he had just read in his hand. He was so completely absorbed he did not hear Manfred Lord's approaching steps. Lord had been hidden for two hours in a corner of the room. He had heard the anguished talk between his wife and Oliver. He had waited patiently. Now he did not wait any longer. He approached the sitting boy from the back, grabbed him by the shoulder and pulled him up.

"What—what?"

After having said these two words, Oliver received the first blow in the face. The second followed. Oliver fell against the wall. Lord followed him. He beat the boy indiscriminately with his heavy cane. Oliver began to bleed. Lord continued to beat him. Oliver did not defend himself. Lord kicked his legs, his body with his heavy boots. He did not speak a word. His face was distorted with hatred.

After a few minutes Oliver collapsed. Blood from his wounds dripped on the dirty floor. He moaned.

## [ 12 ]

"I had hoped that you would defend yourself, Oliver," said Lord. "I had been looking forward to a man-to-man fight. I would have liked it better had you fought back."

Oliver was lying on the floor, his legs pulled up against his chest. Next to him was Verena's letter.

"I am more than twice as old as you. I'm sure you could beat me. Why don't you beat me up?"

Oliver did not answer. The pools of blood around him grew larger.

"You thought you were very clever, didn't you? Well, I was smarter. A woman is a woman. Verena reacted the way all women react. You don't want to believe that. You can't believe that because you are still a childish idealist."

He kicked the motionless boy. "A woman needs security. You can't offer that to Verena. She is used to luxury. You can't offer her that. She is a whore. One ought not to be angry with her for that." Another kick. "I have humiliated and lowered myself before you, Oliver. No more! Now I have your negatives and photographs. It really was very clever of me to humiliate myself and to permit you to be my wife's lover. Now she has chosen: Security and me."

Manfred Lord left. He felt very satisfied with himself. He had considered every possibility. He had, he thought, neglected nothing. Only one thing: to pick up Verena's letter.

## [ 13 ]

That, then, is what actually had happened.

"I'll admit to having behaved in a barbaric manner," said Manfred Lord, "but I think that other men will understand my way of handling the situation, considering how much I had put up with and for how long."

"It is a matter of taste," answered Hardenberg. "I'm not as much interested in that as in another matter."

"Yes?"

"In this book Oliver mentions photographs of pages from books which apparently contained coded messages. He wrote that you gave him these books every time he went to Echternach and that his father also gave him books when he returned."

"That is a vicious lie!"

"Madame?"

Verena looked at her husband, then at a photograph of Evelyn standing on her bedside table, then past Hardenberg at the whirling snow and answered in an extremely indifferent tone of voice: "I have never heard of anything like that before."

Lord smiled.

Verena began to cry again. Lord patted her consolingly.

"Nerves," he said. "Just nerves, gentlemen."

"Naturally," said Hardenberg. "By the way, did you know that the Walter Mansfeld file has been reopened and the statute of limitations is not applicable?"

"I have heard of it."

"If Mr. Mansfeld should come to Germany he will be arrested immediately."

"Mr. Mansfeld will probably not come to Germany then," answered Lord, patting his wife. "Really, darling, you must calm down."

Verena stopped crying.

Inspector Hardenberg said that there would be a charge of

infliction of bodily harm, voluntarily admitted, and further examination of the case. Lord remarked that he would remain calm and with this in view named three of his lawyers.

When Hardenberg and Lazarus left the house they met a little girl in the hall.

"You are Evelyn, aren't you?" asked Lazarus.

"Yes, sir."

"Do you know who we are?"

"I think so. You are from the police, aren't you?"

"What makes you think that?"

"Because of Uncle Mansfeld."

"What is the matter with Uncle Mansfeld?"

"But you know that."

"Did you like him?"

The little girl answered very quietly: "Yes, I'm very, very unhappy he is dead." They were the only words of sorrow for Oliver Mansfeld in this house.

## [ 14 ]

In the course of the morning Inspector Hardenberg's assistant Marcus questioned Leo, and the gardener and his wife. They stated that Manfred Lord had left his villa in the afternoon of the seventh of January for a while but had returned at least one hour before the snow began to fall—about a half-hour after his wife had returned.

Marcus took fingerprints from Leo, Manfred and Verena Lord and Evelyn. A few hours later he reported to his chief. "In the car we found the prints of Mrs. Lord and the child. We could not find any belonging to Mr. Lord."

"And the other prints?"

"Several other people. For instance employees of Kopper and Co. They are being checked now. I am not expecting any new developments."

"And what do you believe, Marcus?"

"The boy hanged himself. Professor Mokry agrees completely with Dr. Peter. Oliver was beaten up, went to his car to go somewhere and completely went to pieces. He went back and hanged himself."

"What about the paper we found in the tower?"

"Near here is a convalescent home which belongs to a religious sect. I sent a man over there who talked to a Sister Claudia. She remembered Oliver Mansfeld and Verena Lord coming there frequently. The boy often accepted the *Herald,* which was distributed there. We ascertained that one of these papers had been in the glove compartment of the Jaguar when Kopper and Co. took possession. The boy must have taken the paper out when he crawled into his car and taken it with him to the tower."

"But why?"

"The actions of desperate people are not rational and logical. Perhaps it was a kind of support, of consolation—how would I know?"

Inspector Hardenberg took the paper which had been found in the tower room and looked at it thoughtfully. On the first page a headline said:

FAITH, LOVE, HOPE, THESE THREE.
BUT THE GREATEST OF THESE IS LOVE

"I think you are probably right," said Hardenberg.

"We have word that trains will run on schedule by tomorrow. Shall we place the body in the coffin?"

"Yes," said Hardenberg, suddenly very tired, "close the coffin. But do not seal it. Customs regulations."

The Inspector was interrupted by an assistant who informed him of a call from Inspector Wilms at police headquarters in Frankfurt. A Geraldine Reber insisted on speaking to Inspector Hardenberg personally. When she did speak to him it was not about Oliver Mansfeld's death but about a Dr. Haberle.

"Dr. Haberle?"

"You don't know him. He was a teacher at the school. He was dismissed because I said he had raped me. He is out of work. His wife and children are still living in Friedheim. Their house is not sold yet. There is still time to make amends."

"I don't understand."

"I lied. Dr. Haberle did not try to rape me. I—I—I half undressed before him. I kissed him. I drove him crazy. We were alone. I was kept in after classes. I was a very bad student. I thought if I—"

"I understand. Make an official statement."

"Do you think Dr. Haberle will be rehabilitated?"

"Yes, I do."

"And—and Oliver is dead?"

"Yes."

"I loved him very much."

"That won't help him now."

"No, No, naturally. I—I just thought—"

"What did you think, Miss Reber?"

"I could make some amends if I went to the police and told the truth about this. Perhaps it is childish, probably it is idiotic."

"Miss Reber," said Inspector Hardenberg, "I thank you. You are a decent human being."

"No," said the voice through the receiver. "I am bad. But I—"

"But?"

"I loved Oliver. Do you understand? I loved him!"

"Yes, yes," said Hardenberg.

"Is it possible to see him?"

"I'm afraid not."

"Did he take his own life?"

"Yes."

"Because—because of this woman?"

"I think so," said Hardenberg. He then spoke with Inspector Wilms and gave him a few instructions. When he turned he saw Lazarus leaning against a wall, his eyes closed.

"Hey!"

The editor opened his eyes: "What is it?"

"What's the matter with you?"

"I feel sick."

"Me, too," said Hardenberg. "Let's go. You too, Marcus. Let's have a drink."

## [ 15 ]

During the night of the eleventh of January 1962 the snow stopped. As promised, the trains were operating on schedule by the next morning and the coffin containing Oliver's body was placed aboard one. Dr. Peter and Professor Mokry entered a first-class compartment. Hardenberg and Lazarus stood on the empty platform.

Shortly before the train was due to leave Rashid came. With him was a lady who wore a veil. It was Verena Lord.

She had aged visibly.

"We came to say goodbye, gentlemen," said the little prince.

"What are you going to do now?" the Inspector asked Verena. She shrugged her shoulders and averted her head.

"We don't know yet," answered the little prince. "But Mrs. Lord said she is going to be my sister from now on. Then it isn't so bad, Sir."

Verena looked at the train.

"Is he in there?"

"Yes."

"Do you despise me?"

"No," said Lazarus.

"And you?"

"I don't despise you," answered Inspector Hardenberg. "Considering the circumstances you could hardly have acted differently. It would have called for a great deal of courage."

Rashid bowed low to the two men and said: "May Allah be with you always. May He make up for my brother Oliver's death."

"May He return you to Persia," said Hardenberg, climbing aboard the train. He stroked the boy's hair. *"Bona causa trium-*

*phat*. You know what that means, don't you? 'The good will triumph.' "

"I know, Sir, but I don't believe it."

The train began to pull away.

Hardenberg had opened a window in his compartment. He and Lazarus waved to the little boy and the veiled woman, who remained on the snow-covered platform. They waved back.

"And He judged me," said Verena softly.

"Excuse me?" asked Rashid.

"I once had a dream. Last summer in Elba. I was judged there."

[ 16 ]

The train jogged along through a snow-covered fairy-tale forest.

Lazarus asked: "Will the good triumph, Inspector?"

"In the case of the unfortunate Latin teacher it will."

"And nothing else?"

Hardenberg shook his head.

"Walter Mansfeld will stay in Luxembourg."

"And the dirty business he and Lord carried on? The perforated pages? The crooked deals?"

"Can you prove anything? Do we possess a photograph of just one page? Nothing! And Mrs. Lord will not say anything against her husband now."

Lazarus' face was that of an unhappy child.

"Then the manuscript isn't any good either."

"No. God help you if you publish it! You would be involved in *some* libel suit! Lord is a powerful and influential man who has friends everywhere."

"I know it, Inspector. You still have the manuscript. I want you to keep it. It is safer with you. I'm an old, sick man. I don't want to have anything to do with it."

"*Bona causa triumphat,* eh?" Hardenberg said bitterly. "Thanks for the present." Lazarus did not answer. He stuffed two colored pills into his mouth and looked through the window at the snow.

That same evening Lazarus sat in a rocking chair in the library in his apartment in Frankfurt. He was in robe and slippers and his right hand was clenched into a fist. He was staring into space.

He sat motionless and thought that he, who never had any wishes, now wished for something: A love like the one he had read about. Even if it were to end as this one. Even if it were to make him unhappy. Suddenly he realized he had never known love.

What is love?

An unknown land, mused Lazarus. There are so many kinds of love, but few make for happiness. Yet that may not be all love's purpose.

[ 17 ]

At that time a customs officer conscientiously examined the coffin and corpse of Oliver. Finding the broken pieces of one record and another Italian record on Oliver's chest he consulted a colleague. "It's better we remove them," he said. "Just to be on the safe side."

The records were removed and sent to the police station in the airport building. Inspector Hardenberg cursed when he was informed of it the next morning and had the records sent on. Teddy Behnke broke with his rule of long standing and drank while piloting the plane to Echternach. The coffin was behind him in the luxuriously appointed cabin of the plane.

At that time Lazarus sat in his rocking chair, nervously opening his clenched fist.

Oliver's mother, in the mental institution in Luxembourg, received an injection because she was extremely restless.

At that time Dr. Florian got drunk in his room and thought how much he would have loved to have had a child of his own.

At that time Grandfather Remo Mortula, confronted with a financial crisis in his family, said: "Dio ci aiuterà."

At that time Geraldine Reber slept with Otto Wilfried in a casual hotel. He thought of a lost factory and she thought of a lost love.

At that time the crippled Hansi slowly strangled a fox which was caught in a trap in the forest just above the Quellenhof. His eyes were glittering.

At that time Soviet scientists completed preparations prior to starting a giant rocket to Venus.

At that time Noah, writing in bed, explained the symbolism of the novel *The Plague* to his friend Chichita from Brazil.

At that time Sister Claudia in her room of the convalescent home said: "Our father, who art in heaven . . ."

At that time three hundred fifty-four children died in China of starvation.

At that time Walter Mansfeld and his friend Lizzy were waiting for the arrival of the Bonanza. They were drinking, assuring each other of the need of a few drinks after the tragedy.

At that time Wolfgang Hartung was reading a book by Ernst Schnabel which denounced the horrors of the time during the Nazi regime, titled *Power Without Morality*.

At that time the song "Il Nostro Concerto" blared from the music box in Marciana Marina.

At that time Inspector Hardenberg sat in his apartment before a stove. Oliver Mansfeld's manuscript was on his knees. He had opened the binder and threw a few pages at a time on the fire. The first page of the story was in his hand. He hesitated for a moment, reading the title.

LOVE IS JUST A WORD

Hardenberg threw that page too.

It burned quickly.

At that time the editor, Lazarus, had just fallen asleep in his rocking chair. The clenched right fist opened. Something fell on the floor. It was a little dried olive.